MISSING LIES

A gripping detective mystery full of twists and turns

CHRIS COLLETT

JOFFE BOOKS

Revised edition 2018 by Joffe Books, London.

First published by Severn House in 2014 as "Dead of Night."

www.joffebooks.com

This book is a work of fiction. Names, characters, businesses, organizations, places and events are either the product of the author's imagination or are used fictitiously. Any resemblance to actual persons, living or dead, events or locales is entirely coincidental. The spelling is British English.

ISBN-13: 978-1-78931-049-8

To my agent, Juliet Burton, for all the years of wise counsel.

Chapter One

Something is very wrong. She's lying on her side on something cold and damp. Has she fallen over? Although she doesn't remember having a drink, her head hurts and her brain is hangover muzzy — the kind of headache you get from sleeping in too long in the morning. She's on a mattress, she decides, but not her bed at home. It's not springy enough and it smells like the outdoors. Her hip and shoulder ache and her arms seem stuck where they are. When she tries to free them they refuse to move, tingling in that heavy pins-and-needles way they do when the circulation's been cut off. Goosebumps crawl over her bare flesh and her mouth is so parched that her lips feel tight. She tries to wet them with her tongue, but it won't push through and her breath whistles lightly through her partly blocked nose. Around her she can make out indistinct shapes in the semi-darkness, but the images tumbling through her head make it hard to ascertain if she is awake or only dreaming, the thoughts so fleeting she can't grasp them for long enough to draw any meaning from them. From time to time, she hears the ebb and flow of sirens, sometimes quite nearby. A memory tickles at her mind, invoking thrill and anticipation. It had been an adventure at first, something that would make Mum and Dad sit up and take notice. But this wasn't how it was meant to end.

A light snaps on. Blinking back the glare, she fixates on the naked bulb dangling on its cord. Only then does she notice the face floating above hers, covered by one of those flu masks, the eyes roaming over her exposed body. Then they look directly into hers and she feels a click of recognition. Surely he can see she's in trouble? Summoning all her effort she tries to alert him, but her groan is thin and weak, and to her horror his eyes crinkle into a smile. He knows! A hand looms towards her, the outstretched fingers sheathed in a surgical glove. Suddenly and brutally her remaining airway is blocked. As her vision turns red and starbursts of light explode behind her eyes, a tune plays round and round in her head — so familiar but just beyond reach — until after a slow succession of agonising heartbeats, the darkness spreads in and subsumes her.

* * *

The tension in the lobby of Symphony Hall was palpable, and DCI Tom Mariner could feel it in the prickle of perspiration on his back. He wondered fleetingly if this was how the performers felt, moments before they took to the stage. Holding around 2,000 people, the venue had been open for more than twenty-five years now, and the tradition of world-class orchestral conductors was evident all around them on the walls — covered with black-and-white images of intense concentration. Mariner had never quite understood the purpose of conductors. At the few classical concerts he'd been to it was obvious to him that the musicians knew pretty much what they were doing, while the man (it was usually a man) on the podium stood up front and took the glory. Much as Assistant Chief Constable Dawson was doing at this very moment, choreographing the media, with Mariner's immediate boss, Superintendent Davina Sharp, at his elbow for support.

Not that Dawson was entirely to blame. This was a delicate situation and he, like all of them, had been forced into the role, which right now meant keeping the press occupied while they all waited for the signal. Not for the first time, Mariner was struck by the comic potential of Sharp, close to six feet tall in her heels, towering over the ACC, who had puffed himself up to his squat and balding five-and-a-half feet. Still, he'd been doing a sterling job of talking about bugger all for the last ten minutes, and you had to admire the man's ability for that. It was one of the reasons Mariner was never likely to rise above his newly appointed rank of DCI (Acting). Bullshit wasn't his forte. But tonight, even the ACC was less than his usual composed self, and as he wittered on, Mariner could see him casting anxiously around the multilevel glass and granite atrium for any indication that the action might start soon, looking second by second, more rattled than Rattle.

Mariner had his own reasons for wanting proceedings to get under way. Since he'd yet to master the art of being in two places at once, this was just the latest example of the frequent race against time the last few weeks of his life had become. He needed to get this over with and be gone. To control his growing impatience, he slipped along a side corridor away from the ACC's circus and put in a call to his home, five miles away in Kingsmead. As the phone rang and rang, Mariner felt his pulse quicken, until at last the line clicked and a sleepy voice said, 'Hello?'

Jesus. He breathed out again. Why did she do this, and why did he fall for it every time? He pictured her sprawled on his sofa in front of the new flat-screen TV, bag of Doritos on her lap. 'Hi, Mercy. It's me. How's everything?' he asked.

'Hey, Tom.' She made it sound as if he'd rung for a spontaneous social chat. 'Everything's fine here.' Although born and raised a Brummie as far as Mariner was aware, she had inherited that West Indian lilt to her voice that perfectly characterised her relaxed approach to everything.

'What are you up to?' he asked.

'Oh, you know, had our dinner and watchin' a bit of TV.'

'And Jamie's OK?'

'He's doin' fine.' Mariner didn't like to ask exactly what that meant. He was afraid he might not like the answer. But presumably it indicated that Jamie was safe, which was the most important thing and it was hardly as if he was in a position to quibble over the finer details. 'Are you all right to stay on a little longer?' he asked.

'Oh, you know me. I'm good. You take as long as you need.'

'Thanks, I'll get back as soon as I can.' He ended the call and tried to ignore the guilt gnawing at him.

Considering what a big part of his life Mercy had become, Mariner knew ridiculously little about her own personal arrangements — only that, to his great relief, she seemed to have almost limitless time and inclination to mind Jamie. Mariner, through necessity, exploited this quite ruthlessly, while at the same time hating the unfamiliar feeling of obligation. To ease his conscience he paid her what he felt confident was a generous remuneration, and so far the arrangement seemed to suit them both. Everyone a winner — except possibly Jamie. No complaints from him for obvious reasons, but spending his hours cooped up in front of the TV with only a middle-aged woman for company was far from ideal for the thirty-eight-year-old, autistic or not.

Mariner was unsettled, too, by a recent, vague intimation that Mercy might be considering moving back to Grenada to be closer to her extended family. It seemed improbable, but then he didn't even know her exact age — only that she was divorced, or possibly widowed, and that, for the moment at least, she seemed to find Mariner's house, with its brand-new entertainment system (replacing the one that had been stolen) and well-stocked fridge, preferable to her own. How had it come to this? Through Mariner's own stupidity, mainly, and now he was stuck with the situation, like it or not. But it wasn't a problem he was going to solve tonight, so having successfully parried his anxiety, he forced his attention back to the task at hand, slipping easily back into professional mode.

At Granville Lane the response from Detective Constable Charlie Glover was instant and alert, the verbal equivalent of standing to attention. Mariner could picture Glover in his customary sports jacket and tie, the latter firmly knotted and his hair neatly combed.

'Ready when you are, boss,' he said, his flat Midlands accent always stronger at times like this. 'We've got five lines manned and standing by.'

'Same here,' said Mariner. 'We're on the starting blocks, waiting for the signal.'

Mariner half expected Charlie to offer up some biblical quote about patience and virtue, but for once he held back. 'Do you think it's going to help, all this?' he asked instead.

It was a question and a half. Mariner had been involved in only a handful of reconstructions in his whole career and popular belief had it that whenever one came, it signalled a sticking point; the time in an investigation when all the initial leads had been exhausted and even the press were beginning to lose interest. Tonight he was ambivalent about the strategy, coming as it did only two weeks after Grace Clifton, the eighteen-year-old daughter of Councillor and Mrs Clifton, apparently vanished off the face of the earth, somewhere between leaving her job as a steward at Symphony Hall and meeting her friends for a late-night drink across the city in Hurst Street. It was a distance of about a mile, over territory alive with activity — theatre- and concert-goers on their way home and youngsters out in the bars and clubs of the city — but as yet not a single witness had come forward.

That Grace was missing was an indisputable fact, but any certainty ended there. The nature of her disappearance, and the appropriate police response to it, were open to wider interpretation. There was no doubt that Councillor Bob Clifton enjoyed the kind of money and power that would make him a target for potential kidnappers and Grace was an attractive young woman. But it was also too early to rule out the more mundane explanations: that Grace herself had chosen to disappear, or that someone closer to home knew where she was. While there was undoubtedly some value in using a reconstruction to turn up the heat on whoever lay behind the disappearance, be it Grace herself or persons unknown, Mariner and his team were well aware that it was also a political exercise, undertaken to 'reassure' Grace's father that her disappearance was being taken seriously. As the current Council Leader, Clifton would have substantial influence over police budgets for the next twelve months, at a time when 'public spending' had become a dirty phrase. And this was a man with an established record of criticism of the police.

In terms of generating leads, the enterprise was far from ideal for a number of reasons. In reality, the audience for the City of Birmingham Symphony Orchestra was unlikely to be made up of the same crowd who had been in attendance two weeks ago, and the proportion of people repeating their experience on Broad Street would also be low. Back in the day, Saturday night meant clubbing in the city, but for many young people now it was a luxury. Unable to afford the inflated prices every week, they confined their outings to special occasions. The weather wasn't helping either. This evening was dry with a clear, starry sky, but the Saturday when Grace had vanished had been wet, the steady drizzle punctuated with heavier downpours. In other words, the kind of night when people kept their heads down, intent on getting from one place to another as quickly as they could, without noticing much of what was going on around them.

Was this enactment going to be of any help at all? 'It won't do any harm,' said Mariner diplomatically to Charlie.

'Well, good luck with it anyway,' Glover replied, before ringing off.

Finally Mariner contacted DS Vicky Jesson. The line was poor, the interference symptomatic of Jesson's location out on the street in the Arcadian area of the city, where she'd be surrounded on all sides by people enjoying a night out. 'Sounds lively there,' he said.

'Saturday night in Brum, what do you expect?' came Jesson's cheerful response. Mariner envied her equanimity. No hint from her that she felt pulled in different directions. On the team for a matter of weeks only, as an outcome of the extensive service reorganisation, Vicky was quickly establishing herself as a reliable successor to DC Millie Khatoon. A single mum to her three kids, she had assured Mariner at interview that her domestic arrangements — not that he'd been allowed to enquire about those — would not be an issue. So far she'd been true to her word, though Mariner couldn't help wondering how she'd managed to square things at this time on a Saturday night.

'I'll keep in touch,' Mariner said. He ended the call with a feeling not entirely new to him — that there was something missing . . . at least, not something, but someone. DS Tony Knox, normally his right-hand man, had been recently seconded to Operation Athena, tasked with clamping down on the circulation of illegal firearms in the city. The initiative had begun a year ago, in direct response to a series of gang-related shootings that had culminated in the ambush of two police officers, one of whom had been shot dead. Over time, personnel had been drafted in from every operational district to work on the city-wide initiative, and Mariner and Sharp between them had managed to convince Knox that it would be a good career-building opportunity. But there were few days when Mariner didn't slightly, selfishly regret that strategy.

Pocketing his phone, Mariner heard a slight stir out on the main concourse and crept along the corridor to see Gary Moore, Symphony Hall's stage manager waddling towards the box office, walkie-talkie in hand. A big man in his forties, Mariner scrutinised Moore's shiny, round face for any hint of a salacious thrill. Though he didn't know it, Moore was one of the people Mariner's team were keeping a special eye on, having been amongst the last to see Grace Clifton before she left Symphony Hall on the night she was alleged to have disappeared. But Moore's face was neutral enough as, at that moment, he saw Mariner and changed his course, bypassing the press and the ACC, and headed towards the side door of the locker room. 'It's finished,' he said. 'They're just taking the curtain calls, so any time now the audience will be starting to leave.'

As if in response, on the far side of the atrium a door swung open and a middle-aged couple hurried out, whispering and pulling on coats before they scurried off towards the exit to catch the last train, or to beat an expiring car park ticket.

Chapter Two

Mariner opened the door immediately behind him, marked 'Staff Only,' and he and Moore went in. As they did, Mariner caught the full-on reflection of Pippa Talbot as she frowned with studied concentration into the mirror, adjusting her clothing and inspecting her hair and make-up one last time. Younger by far than anyone else in the room, it was on her narrow shoulders that the real responsibility rested tonight. For her this was a kind of performance; a benefit show for her best friend, complete with a media audience all waiting outside to see if it would be the hoped-for triumph. But it wasn't the kind of show that even the most confident of performers would choose to be part of, and Mariner could see the girl's ill-concealed nervousness in the way that she checked and re-checked her lipstick, pouting at her reflection.

Under a jacket similar to the one Grace had been wearing, she wore the uniform of the theatre staff: black skirt and waistcoat, and a grey blouse, with a name badge pinned above the breast pocket — except that it didn't bear Pippa's name. That had been touch and go. Taking her friend's name, as well as her identity, had clearly felt that bit too uncomfortable, like stepping over a line.

They'd had enough trouble persuading the theatre to produce a duplicate badge. Apparently that in itself contravened normal procedure. Mariner had been forced to point out, with great restraint, that there was little that was 'normal' about any of this. In the end the FLO had managed to smooth the way. 'It's just the kind of detail that can make all the difference,' she'd said encouragingly. And when Symphony Hall capitulated, Pippa had followed suit, showing the kind of mature attitude that in a few short days they had come to expect from her.

So this was it.

'All ready, Pippa?' Mariner asked gently, suppressing his own ripple of anticipation.

The eighteen-year-old pulled her face into something resembling a smile and nodded her head. The FLO squeezed her arm in a gesture of solidarity, then Pippa was on her own, smoothing down her skirt before standing up straight, shoulders back. Mariner pushed open the door and they emerged into the glare of TV lighting. But for once there was no clamorous surge of reporters. In its place was an unnerving, respectful silence, broken only by the whispering ricochet of camera shutters, whose operators maintained their distance. It gave Mariner the creeps. Beyond the journalists the hum of conversation grew louder, as the swell of punters began spilling out from the auditorium. Some turned and others stopped to look at what the fuss was in this corner of the atrium. 'Right,' Mariner prompted. 'Let's go.' And Pippa stepped out into the mêlée, like a royal princess leading her bizarre entourage.

In other circumstances, a reconstruction would have commanded universal attention, but Broad Street was as Broad Street is on a Saturday night: the youth of the city and beyond out on the lash. Many of the pedestrians were too well oiled to even give them a second glance — which was why, if this worked, it would be a miracle. From those who did notice the spectacle, Mariner overheard a gamut of reactions.

'What's going on?'

'Is it someone famous?'

'Must be that girl.'

That girl. Already her name was beginning to fade from public consciousness and it was hard not to take it personally. There had been doubts and mixed messages about Grace from the get-go. She was a bubbly, friendly girl, yet strong-willed and assertive, who knew her own mind. And therein lay the element of doubt. Councillor Bob Clifton was a man with a notoriously volatile nature and quick temper. He would have said he did not suffer fools. The alternate perspective presented a man intolerant of any views opposing his own, whose negotiation tactics consisted of bullying fellow council members into submission. He had been a controversial appointment as leader but was well supported as a tough politician who would make the hard decisions at a time of austerity, when bankruptcy for the city presented a real and conceivable threat.

Significantly, he struck Mariner as the kind of domineering father Grace might have wanted to escape. Or it could be that Councillor Clifton knew rather more about what had happened to his daughter than he was admitting. Both had to be considered along with other more traditional lines of enquiry. But if they were to pursue either of these lines they needed to be founded on something more substantial than Mariner's feeling that Clifton was a ruthless bastard. He, along with most of the extended family, were alibied for the time when Grace vanished by her older sister's engagement celebration, at the Masonic Lodge on the Hagley Road. It wouldn't have been easy for Grace's father or brother to slip away from the party unnoticed, but nor was it impossible. If nothing else, the reconstruction might provide some badly needed traction in a case that felt as though it could potentially slide away from them.

In theory the wide media coverage, including the sight of a similar-looking girl walking the same route, should provide enough of a context to trigger a memory, however vague, of something or someone witnessed that night on the streets. But that was on the understanding that Grace had been taken. Equally, Mariner saw it as another step towards ruling out that particular possibility.

Outside Symphony Hall, Pippa led the procession along the pre-arranged route, turning left across the Plaza between the war memorial and the iconic library with its purple-lit curlicued exterior. They continued across the wide footbridge and through the undercover complex of Paradise Forum, one of the places in the city where the homeless were beginning to re-appear and find refuge. Turning into Victoria Square they passed the back of the Town Hall, which was even now disgorging its own concert-goers. Two ends of the social spectrum within the space of a few short metres.

From here the route was, in part, guesswork. Grace would have had a number of alternatives open to her. It was impossible to cover them all, so Mariner had chosen the one that was the most direct: down the relatively quiet Hill Street, past the drop-off for New Street station, across the four-lane ringway and into the top of Hurst Street, to the Arcadian, Chinatown and the gay quarter. The walk-through took less than half an hour, at the end of which Mariner read the usual prepared statement to the press, requesting information from the public. He deftly fielded the inevitable questions that, at the moment, he had no answers for, then an astute hack observed: 'Up until now, you've been asking Grace herself to get in touch. Does this reconstruction signal that things have changed?'

Mariner hesitated, torn between telling the truth — that this enactment was mostly a sop to Councillor Clifton — and being professionally discreet. From the corner of his eye he saw the ACC's shoulders stiffen in anticipation. 'It just means that we are keeping all options and lines of enquiry open,' Mariner said.

Superintendent Sharp stepped forward. 'Thank you for your time and co-operation this evening,' she cut in, and suddenly the press attention was on her, allowing Mariner to slink away to the sidelines.

Jesson stood a little way off and Mariner went to join her for a moment. 'Tactfully done,' she said. Diminutive alongside Mariner, she shared Superintendent Sharp's liking for trouser suits, but where Sharp's hung loosely on her willowy frame, Jesson's was snug around her full figure. Tonight her dark brown hair was tucked up into a French pleat and she wore plain gold stud earrings.

Ideally Mariner would have liked to stick around, but after a brief conversation with Jesson that reassured him she had things under control, it felt acceptable for him to leave. In the background he heard Sharp reiterating the need for anyone with information, however insignificant it may seem, to come forward. The footage would be shown tonight and tomorrow across the news channels, and during the week on *CrimeTime*. The uniformed police presence in the area tonight would remain high, with regular officers and PCSOs continuing to distribute leaflets bearing Grace's photo and talking with anyone and everyone they met out on the street in the hope that they might just encounter that one individual who, maybe without even knowing it, might be able to help.

Mariner was glad to get back to the seclusion of his car. Exiting the city centre the traffic was light, predominantly black cabs and minicabs heading in both directions. Idling at the traffic lights along the new Selly Oak bypass, he made a quick hands-free call to the taxi firm he regularly used for Mercy's lift home. As the adrenalin rush of the last few hours began to flatten into a blanket of fatigue, his gaze was drawn towards the face of Old Joe, the Chamberlain tower clock, which seemed to be suspended in mid-air over the old part of the university. For a second or two he tuned out of his surroundings but was shocked back to the here and now by an apparition bearing down on him from out of the night sky. Black and menacing, powerful floodlights beamed out from its underbelly as it headed straight for him. Mariner didn't believe in UFOs but in that moment, he was seized by a fear of the unknown and the incomprehensible . . . until the pulsating roar of the twin T55 turboshaft engines filled the car and he saw the two sets of rotor blades chopping through the sodium-pale sky.

Chinook helicopters had become an increasingly common sight over the south of the city in the last couple of years, bringing in wounded personnel from Afghanistan. At the start of the war each casualty had merited a national news item, but now the steady flow of wounded soldiers went virtually unnoticed by all but those directly involved. The traffic lights switched to green and Mariner moved off, tracking the aircraft's grim progress towards the three illuminated drums of the Queen Elizabeth hospital, where it would be met by another team of professionals whose work would last well into the night.

* * *

Dee Henderson gazed down at the patient lying motionless in the bed before her, the rhythmic pips and bleeps and the hiss of the ventilator beating out their musical tattoo. She knew that he was a young man, though it wasn't immediately obvious beneath all the tubes, dressings and wiring. There had been little change in Private Lomax's condition since he'd been admitted two weeks ago to the critical care ward, but to Dee's trained and experienced eye, the subtle indications that he might regain consciousness quite soon were there to see.

'Hey, you — time you knocked off.' Ellen Kingsley pushed open the door, tapping an imaginary wristwatch. 'We wouldn't want anyone getting the impression that you're dedicated to the job or something.' Of a similar age to Dee and a consultant, Ellen far outranked Dee in medical terms, but they couldn't afford to stand on ceremony here.

Dee returned the smile. 'Yeah, couldn't have that, could we? I thought I heard the chopper a minute ago. Do you want me to go down?'

'You've got good ears,' said Ellen.

Too heavy for the hospital's Air Ambulance helipad, the Chinooks were forced to land on playing fields to the rear of the hospital, which meant having a team of medics on hand to assist with the transfer across to the main building.

Ellen shook her head. 'No, you're fine. They've got enough hands down there tonight, and this one's straight in for emergency surgery, so we won't be needed for a few hours yet. You get yourself off home. Is Paddy picking you up?'

'He hasn't texted me yet to say that he is.' Dee sighed. 'Should have stuck at it, shouldn't I?' She was end-of-the-week tired and finishing the late shift was one of the few times when she really wished she had persisted with learning to drive. It wasn't that she hadn't tried, but after taking her test six times and failing each time on an entirely different transgression, she'd decided that it was never going to happen. 'Might be useful tonight though,' she went on. 'Charlie Flint, you know, the comedian? He's coming to the Town Hall next month. I want to book tickets for Paddy's birthday. I can see if the box office is still open and save on the booking fee.' She dipped her head towards the unshaven figure snoring lightly in the plastic chair beside Private Lomax's bed. 'That's what I call dedication,' she said to Ellen. 'How on earth can he sleep, chin folded over on his chest like that?'

'Anywhere will do when you're that knackered,' Ellen said, with a wry smile. 'I remember it from when I was a junior. Gets to be a way of life.' The memory made her smile, as she walked around to the other side of Lomax's bed and placed her hand lightly on the snoring man's shoulder. He opened his eyes, instantly alert. 'Come on,' Ellen said to him. 'Nothing's going to happen here in the next few hours. Why don't you go home and get some rest?'

'You can walk me out,' Dee said to him. She turned back to Dr Kingsley. 'I'm for my comfy bed then. I'll see you tomorrow.'

* * *

Mariner drew into the service road at the back of his remote canal-side cottage to find it in darkness but for the glow of the TV screen from a ground-floor window. Letting himself in, he called out a greeting before switching on the living-room light. Mercy roused herself, blinking, from where she'd clearly dozed off on the sofa, and Jamie, at the other end of the room stood up, his attention still riveted to his iPad on the table. A dark stain was spreading down the front of his trousers, from crotch to knee.

'Jamie!' Mariner reprimanded him wearily.

Jamie shifted his weight from one foot to the other, refusing to look up. He knew this wasn't good.

'Oh dear,' said Mercy, struggling to her feet. 'That must have only just happened. Shall I get him cleaned up?'

A car horn tooted outside. 'No, it's fine,' said Mariner. 'I'll see to him, your taxi's here.' He took some banknotes out of his wallet. 'This is what I owe you for this week, and I'll let you know about next week, if that's OK?'

'Sounds good to me,' said Mercy, putting on her coat. 'I'll see you soon, Jamie. You have a nice weekend.'

'You too,' said Mariner. He saw her out to the waiting car.

'I think my Carlton might be coming over tomorrow,' she said.

'That will be nice,' said Mariner. The only person Mercy ever talked about was Carlton, a male of indeterminate age, who seemed to drift in and out of her life depending on his need for money and Mercy's laundry services. For a while, Mariner hadn't been clear on whether Carlton was a son, partner or other, but recently Mercy had taken to referring to him as a 'boy' — as in, 'he's a good boy' — so Mariner had to conclude that it was the first of these. In his experience a mother who routinely described her son thus generally did so out of misplaced loyalty and a need to convince herself of the fact. Mariner was beginning to draw his own conclusions about Carlton. It didn't help that a couple of weeks ago he'd been late home after interviewing a remand prisoner out at Long Lartin. When he'd explained his delay, Mercy's face had lit up with recognition. 'Ah yes, I know that place,' she'd said. 'My Carlton told me about it.' As Mariner closed the door on her he heard the distant sound of emergency sirens.

Chapter Three

Dominique lay in bed with Animal pressed up underneath her chin, comforted by the feel of his soft towelling body and his smell that was mostly like Mum's perfume. This was her worst time of the week, but she couldn't tell Mum that. On the ceiling she could see the shadows made by the night light: grey squares and oblongs that looked to her like another tiny city, where there might be little people going about their lives too. Outside the flat she could hear muffled voices and sometimes the banging of a door nearby and she didn't know if the shouting was on a TV or if it was the man and lady who lived next door having a row.

It still felt funny to Dominique, being in this little box up in the sky with other people all around them in their little boxes too, like the little green boxes that her school shoes came in, stacked up, one on top of the other, in the shoe shop. In London they'd had their own proper house squashed in between other houses, in a crooked line stretching along the street and up the hill. Not that it was really their house, Papa said. They had to pay money to borrow it off the landlord. Here in Birmingham, Mum said they borrowed this flat off the council, so they paid money to them. And now that they didn't have Dad's car mechanic wages coming in, Mum went to work in the day while Dominique was at school, and on Fridays and Saturdays she had to go to work at night, while Dominique was in bed, so that they could pay all the bills and buy the food.

Dominique didn't tell Mum, but she liked the landlord's house better. They'd had friends in the street and because Papa lived with them, he could stay at home with Dominique while Mum went out to work. Mum wouldn't have agreed; she said they were *better off on their own*. One day they had just packed up their things and left. They went to stay with Auntie in London at first, but Auntie's family was big and her house was too full, so after a few days, just Mum and Dominique had caught the coach to Birmingham *to make a fresh start.* It had sounded lovely and sunshiny with a big blue sky, but it hadn't been much like that yet. It had been cold and grey and wet, and they didn't know anyone yet, so sometimes it was lonely.

Dominique tried hard to be brave when she was in the flat on her own. Mum said there was nothing to be scared of. The door was locked on the latch, so no one could get in, but if she needed to, Dominique would be able to get out. Mum didn't say why Dominique might want to leave the flat at night, and she couldn't ever imagine wanting to. The noises in the street far below were scary: men shouting and big dogs barking. It was much safer in here. Every Friday and Saturday night Dominique thought she would never go to sleep but she always did, and by the morning, like magic, Mum would be back, sleeping in her own bed, as if she'd never been gone. Dominique's favourite thing in the world was creeping into Mum's room on Saturday and Sunday mornings, trying hard not to wake her up, and getting into the nice warm bed beside her to snuggle up — just her and Mum and Animal. Thinking about that made her feel much better.

* * *

Millie Khatoon's head lolled forward, jolting her awake as she sat in the armchair of the spare bedroom. She had never felt so tired in her life. After years of all-night ops and twelve-hour shifts she had a growing sense that this tiny armful would be the thing to finally finish her off. Nothing had prepared her for the sheer relentlessness of motherhood and she was exhausted. On the fringes of her consciousness, she became aware of a distant, undulating scream, its volume gradually increasing. It was joined by the jarring clash of another. Standing up, she went to the window, carefully cradling her infant son to keep him latched onto her breast. Not that Haroon was likely to let go. *Born hungry*, the midwife had said, like father like son. Millie craned her neck to see to the end of the street, and just about glimpsed the tell-tale flicker of blue as two, maybe even three, emergency vehicles flashed past and hurtled out of sight. She felt a sharp but unmistakable twinge of longing, imagining the adrenalin-fuelled banter going on inside those cars.

Much as she loved her baby, Millie was astounded to find just how much missed the whole camaraderie of CID, especially those sudden bursts of activity when they were on a shout. Without the sense of belonging that came with being part of a unit, both relied and reliant upon, she felt cast adrift. So far motherhood was proving to be a largely solitary experience. She had Suli, of course, but he was out at work all day and ever since they had moved to this neighbourhood, and up until a few weeks before Haroon was born, Millie had worked too. As a detective constable, hers had never been the most sociable of hours, and admitting to being a police officer rarely paved the way to instant friendship, so the only people she knew on more than just nodding terms were the immediate next-door neighbours, a retired couple on one side and a family with three teenaged kids on the other. It was a long time since she'd needed to establish a new social circle and she'd forgotten how hard it could be. She hadn't been naive enough to expect to fall into one straight away, of course, but neither had she envisaged it being this slow. She missed her colleagues. Tony Knox had been to visit a couple of times, but the boss had remained strangely distant and Millie didn't really understand why.

In the last week, however, things had taken a slight turn for the better — at least they might do soon, if she could only ignore two small facts: firstly, that she and Louise seemed to have little in common, and secondly that they'd allowed themselves to be manoeuvred into their tentative friendship. With hindsight it was glaringly obvious that the whole encounter had been choreographed by the bossy midwife, which didn't seem like a satisfactory foundation for a lasting bond. Granted, she and Louise did have one piece of common ground, as outsiders; Millie as a policewoman and Louise, well . . . for lots of reasons that were becoming increasingly apparent.

Millie had been sitting alone in the waiting room at the health centre when Louise had come in and, ignoring the rows of empty seats, had chosen to take the one right next to her. Millie's instant and uncharitable thought was that this might be 'nutter on the bus' syndrome, as Louise was rather eccentrically dressed in what looked like an oversized farmer's smock over pantaloons in shades of dark pink and purple. For a few minutes the two women had sat silently side by side, until Millie, sensing a growing awkwardness, had ventured the first words. Even those had got them off to a rocky start. 'He's a smiley little chap,' she said of the woman's baby, dressed all in blue.

'Actually she's a girl. Abigail.'

'Oh, I'm so sorry.' Millie pulled her face into what she hoped was a comic grimace. 'I'm a bit new to all this. I'm Millie,' she indicated the pushchair, 'and this is Haroon. He was born four weeks ago, so now I'm a stay-at-home mum.'

The woman managed a smile. 'Louise,' she said, simply.

Millie would probably have left it there, except that Shona, the health visitor, chose that moment to bustle in and must have noticed the last brief seconds of eye contact. 'Great,' she beamed. 'You two are starting to get to know each other. How about a nice cup of tea when you're done here? You only live down the road there, Mrs Khatoon. And company is just what our Abigail needs, don't you, darlin'?'

Millie glanced at Louise for signs that she too felt that she was being handled, but the expression on the woman's face was more like relief. 'That would be lovely,' Louise said, smiling properly for the first time and leaving Millie with little choice in the matter.

'You'd be doing me a favour,' she conceded graciously. 'I'll start to go mad if I have to spend much more time with only Haroon for conversation.'

When it was Haroon's turn to be weighed in the health visitor's office, Shona pressed home her point. 'Don't let her off the hook,' she said in a stage whisper. 'It will do Louise good to get out and about a bit. She's a quiet one and I think she's already feeling a bit of the baby blues. Abigail had a suspected heart murmur when she was born, so they've had a lot to cope with.'

An hour later, Millie was welcoming Louise and Abigail into her home and filling the kettle to make tea.

'I love your house, it's so cosy.'

'Untidy, you mean,' said Millie, cheerfully, at the same time wishing she'd had the foresight to at least tidy up a bit before she'd set out that morning.

'No! It's welcoming. And homely,' Louise said, casting rather a dubious eye over the pile of un-ironed washing and yet-to-be sorted junk mail. That had been ten days ago and since then Louise had been back to Millie's house on two further occasions, though the invitation had not yet been reciprocated.

The excitement past, Millie looked out over the darkened rooftops towards the slight incline of rolling treetops that marked out where Louise lived. About half a mile away, Louise's house was significantly bigger than most of the properties around here and on a small private estate of about a dozen houses, set back behind wrought-iron railings and wide gates. When she'd found this out, Millie had got Suli to drive them past on the way back from his mum's. It was like a different neighbourhood altogether and made Millie wonder why Louise would want to slum it round at hers. Millie hoped that baby Abigail was sleeping through. Though not quite sure why, Millie instinctively knew that a crying baby in the middle of the night would be unlikely to improve her new friend's quality of life.

Chapter Four

After a couple of hours of restless sleep, Mariner was woken by the thudding against Jamie's bedroom door that signalled he was awake. Twenty past six was not bad going. Automatically reaching for his phone, Mariner checked for messages, but he had none. If there had been a breakthrough someone would have called him and he hadn't really been expecting one anyway, but even so, he felt slightly let down. *Thud, thud, thud.* Mariner pushed off the duvet and got out of bed.

Twenty minutes later he and Jamie were pounding along the canal towpath, coming to the end of a two-mile run and breathing easily. It was a crisp, clear morning, the sun beginning to break through the trees and sparkle off the water. On his first morning at what was the former lock-keeper's cottage, Jamie had been like a caged animal, pacing the rooms and literally bouncing off the walls. Only too aware of the stretch of deep water that was the Worcester and Birmingham canal six feet from his back door, Mariner had deliberately taken him out through the front and into the park beyond. He'd intended on a brisk walk, but Jamie had set off at a run, forcing Mariner to keep up with him. Now, having gradually acclimatised him, their routine most mornings was to run a couple of circuits of the playing fields and, if the weather was OK, to extend it along the canal as far as the Wast Hills tunnel, with a longer walk at the weekend. For years Mariner had detested running, considering it an assault on the body's natural functioning. He had always been lean, but what with the running and their occasional weekend swim, he was developing the kind of stamina and muscle definition that would impress any woman. Just a shame the only woman likely to be impressed was a hundred miles away.

It had been a bolt from the blue for Mariner to learn just a few months ago that he was still the guardian for his late ex-partner Anna's disabled brother. He'd wondered since if the shock of it had skewed his judgement. It had been an impulsive decision to uproot Jamie from the residential facility in Wales where he'd been living, and even now Mariner couldn't completely rationalise why he'd done it, except that on his brief visit to the Towyn community, there were aspects of the place that had made him uneasy: Jamie's dishevelled appearance, the neglected buildings and the casual attitude of the staff to name but a few. He'd kept a watchful eye on the headlines since to see if his misgivings about the place would be justified, but so far they hadn't been. At the time it had seemed like the only way of keeping Jamie safe was to have the severely autistic man come to live with him and Mariner had acted immediately, bringing Jamie back to Birmingham there and then.

Within twenty-four hours the foolishness of that decision had become glaringly apparent and now Mariner lived daily with the consequences. In the early days of Mariner's relationship with Anna, Jamie had moved residential accommodation more than once, seemingly with ease. But that was before local authority cutbacks, and Mariner had been ill-prepared for how much the picture had changed. A couple of abortive phone calls to the relevant council department and more hours surfing the internet looking at private organisations, had brought reality crashing in. His current care arrangements, stretched between the local authority day centre and Mercy, were as precarious as a spider's web that could be snapped in an instant by any additional strain, and the tension between fulfilling his responsibility and earning his salary was thrown daily into sharp relief. But despite all that, deep down, Mariner's gut still told him that this had been the right thing to do.

The other advantage of starting each day with a run, Mariner found, was that Jamie was much more co-operative with going in the shower and the laborious prompt-and-reward routine of getting him dressed afterwards. The prize at the end was to watch a recording of whatever was his current favourite TV show, at the moment the aptly named *Pointless.*

Opening the fridge door for breakfast, Mariner knew that it would be in a sorry state. Sunday morning also meant the supermarket shop. One of Jamie's least favourite activities, it had to be undertaken when things were relatively quiet. It was amazing how quickly Mariner was beginning to fall into Jamie's strict routines. Anna, Jamie's sister, had hated the repetitiveness but Mariner was finding he didn't mind it that much at all. He told himself that somehow it was a natural compensation for the unpredictable nature of his day job. Anna would have thought differently. *It's because you're probably autistic too*, she'd have said.

'*Very-well-done-if-you-got-any-of-those-at-home*,' Jamie chorused, in unison with the presenter as the programme came to an end for the umpteenth time.

Mariner passed him his breakfast toast (thin smear of honey, no butter). 'Thank you,' he prompted.

''K you,' Jamie echoed back meaninglessly, eyes still fixed on the TV as he bit into the toast.

* * *

When Dominique woke up she forgot again where she was at first. Then she remembered, she was in the flat and it was Sunday morning. Excitement bubbled up as she jumped out of bed. They might go out today — to the pictures or to the shops. Mum had said she would buy Dominique a new winter coat soon, like Somia's, with fur round the hood. Taking Animal with her, she tiptoed with exaggerated care along the hall with its cold vinyl floor, to Mum's room. But Mum's bed was empty, the duvet smooth and flat like it was when Mum made the bed. Dominique ran through to the kitchen and then the lounge, hopeful that perhaps Mum had fallen asleep on the sofa, like she had before when she got home late. But she wasn't there either. Dominique checked once more in all the rooms, but she knew by now that Mum wasn't here; the flat felt cold and empty, and out in the hall she saw that Mum's shoes weren't in their usual place on the mat. It was strange. It couldn't be helped that Mum had to go out after tea, but she always made sure she was there again when Dominique woke up — at least, nearly always. Perhaps another man had got cross with Mum's friend, Ricky. That time Mum hadn't got home until after Dominique had got up and was watching TV, and she had come in a taxi. 'It's all right,' Dominique said to Animal, snuggling him up under her chin. 'Mum will be home soon.'

Chapter Five

'Are you even looking, Tony?'

'Course I am, love.' Walking back down the aisle to where Jean stood, between a shelf of toilet brushes and another of toothbrush holders and soap dishes, Knox slipped his phone back into his pocket, but not before he'd noted, with some disappointment, the absence of any new messages that might legitimately present him with an escape route. A year ago Knox had never even heard of 'Athena.' He knew all about the events that had led up to it of course, as did the whole country. But he hadn't realised at the time how significant it would become for him. The operation itself had begun slowly and quietly, with a recognition from the outset that its execution would be a long game. The initial stages had involved the gradual introduction of a small team of undercover officers to strategic positions in the arms supply chain. Over the following months those men had worked hard to forge relationships and build the kind of trust that would allow them to infiltrate the gangs for whom guns were the natural currency of everyday life. Now, almost a year on, the operation was beginning to bear fruit in the form of regular, reliable intelligence and that was when Knox had signed up.

Athena was not, as Knox would be the first to admit, as exciting as he had hoped. The day-to-day work was largely logistical: recording conversations, monitoring vehicles and mobile phones. The data had to be meticulously collated to provide evidence strong enough for the level of convictions sought, and Knox, alongside other officers, had been seconded in for that purpose. Now the net was beginning to close, and as it did, the levels of expectation were beginning to rise. The last place he wanted to be was here. He and Jean weren't married or anything — yet. But if things ever progressed that far . . . he wondered idly how frequently *Sunday mornings in Ikea* had been cited on divorce papers in recent years.

'Well, what do you think?' Jean was holding up what looked to Knox like two virtually identical shower curtains. They were both white. They both had bits of green and blue on them.

'Great,' he said, hoping that his firm endorsement would mean they could get this over with. A young Chinese couple, the woman heavily pregnant, was trying to squeeze past them, and a toddler a few feet away had started to grizzle. Knox felt like doing the same.

'But which one do you think most closely matches the tiles?' Jean persisted, over the noise.

Knox didn't understand the question. The tiles in Jean's bathroom, as far as he could remember, were blue. The shower curtains each had blue on them. 'Well surely they both—' he started to say.

'We'll take this one,' Jean cut in, exasperated. 'If it doesn't look right we can bring it back later and swap it for the other.'

'Actually, I've got plans this afternoon, love,' Knox said, impulsively.

'What plans?'

'I said I'd go and sit with Jamie for the boss. He wants to go and see Millie and the baby.'

'I thought you said he was avoiding her.'

'Yeah, but he can't do that for ever, can he?'

While Jean was in the checkout queue Knox took out his phone again and selected Millie's contact number. *Fancy a visitor this p.m.?* he put in the text. *I'll sit with Jamie so that boss can come over.*

* * *

Mariner was standing in a queue almost identical to the one Tony Knox had joined, but in his local Sainsbury's, where he was mentally urging the checkout girl to speed things up a bit. So far Jamie had done well, but Mariner could tell from the increased tic level that he was approaching his limits. Then, just as it was their turn to start loading the conveyor belt, his phone chimed. He grabbed it, thinking it must be news from the investigation, and was surprised to see a text from Tony Knox.

Since his secondment, Knox had become an expert at text-speak and it took Mariner some seconds to decipher the code: *Got some free time this afternoon so can mind Jamie. Time 2 visit Millie. C u @ 1.*

Hm, Mariner could think of better things to do with a couple of free hours, but now he'd have to face up to the visit. He wondered what had brought on this sudden, altruistic gesture. Tony was always brilliant at helping out when asked, but volunteering his services was a departure. In a flash of inspiration, Mariner texted back: *Jean going to Ikea?*

* * *

Millie was making the most of a few free minutes to put her feet up. Suli had gone round to his brother's to help with putting up a fence. Haroon was fed, changed and down for his midday nap, with the baby monitor plugged in. She had just put in her second load of washing and, out of the blue, Tom Mariner texted to ask if he could stop by at about two. By her calculation that meant she should have at least an hour to read a couple more chapters of her book, if her concentration was up to it. When the doorbell rang she felt a flush of irritation. Who on earth would come calling unannounced at this time on a Sunday? Louise would not have been at the top of her list of likely candidates, but opening the door, there she was with Abigail in her pushchair.

'Hello. Is everything all right?' Millie asked, partly from professional habit.

Louise seemed equally surprised by the question. 'Yes. It's just that Greg's had to go in to work today, so I thought I'd pop round. I hope you don't mind. I wondered if we might go to the park or something.'

Millie glanced over Louise's shoulder at the angry grey clouds sweeping across the sky. 'Perhaps later,' she said. 'It's nice to see you anyway,' she added, making an effort. 'I'm expecting my boss to stop by soon, but that's OK. You can meet him too.'

'Oh.' Louise looked panic-stricken. 'I wouldn't want to intrude.'

'It's fine,' said Millie. 'I expect he's coming to talk me into going back to work. And if he doesn't, you can prompt him.'

Between them, the two women manoeuvred Abigail's pushchair into the house, and Louise lifted the baby seat from its chassis and took a sleeping Abigail into the lounge.

'You're keen to get back then?' said Louise, as she and Millie sat nursing coffee mugs at either end of the sofa. She looked genuinely worried at the prospect of losing her new-found friend.

'Oh, it won't be for ages yet,' said Millie. 'And not at all if Suli gets his way.'

'He's against it?'

'So he says. We've already had heated words about it and tend to avoid the subject now. I'm sure he's not even speaking for himself. He's just going along with what the parents want. They're all of the generation that clings to traditional ideas of what a wife and mother should be. I can see it all over my mum and dad's faces — the relief that I've got these silly thoughts about having a career out of my head and will be satisfied now with taking care of my family. I bet you're not subjected to that kind of pressure. I've never even asked you. What did you do before Abigail?'

'Oh, I haven't really worked since I got married,' said Louise. 'It didn't seem like a good idea for us to be together twenty-four hours a day.'

'You met at work?'

'Yes, I was a secretary at Greg's company.' She smiled at the memory. 'As soon as I saw him I was smitten and he says it was the same for him, though it took him a few months to ask me out. It was quite a big staff back then and he was popular with all the girls. Anyway, we started dating and one thing led to another and here we are. Even if I hadn't been at Pincott's I don't think I'd be working. Greg prefers it that way. It means I can attend to the house, and now of course I've got Abigail to look after. Greg likes things tidy and he works so hard I like to have dinner ready for him when he gets home. And he earns a good wage, so financially there's no need for me to be out working too.'

Wow, thought Millie. *And I thought my family was traditional.* 'What does Greg do?' she asked.

'He's a gun-runner. At least, that's what he tells everyone.' Louise managed the kind of weak smile that indicated this was a vintage joke. 'Actually, he's a salesman, but he is a very good one. It's a family business and he's a partner and all that, but the company just happens to make guns.'

'What kind of guns?' Millie was intrigued.

'Oh, you know, sports pistols, hunting rifles, that kind of thing. It could be for anything really. A lot of Greg's time is spent travelling to sales conventions and entertaining clients. It means he's away a lot, or out in the evenings. It sounds glamorous, I know, but it's stressful too; they rely on Greg to bring in any new business. Often he doesn't make it home until the early hours.'

'You must spend quite a bit of time on your own then.' It was beginning to become clear to Millie why Louise was looking for the company, if that's all there was to it.

'I knew it would be like this when we got married, and most of the time I don't really mind, especially now I've got Abigail.' As if recognising her name, the little girl opened her eyes and not much liking what she saw, she screwed up her face and began to whimper. 'She's probably hungry. Do you mind if I . . .?'

'Of course not.' Millie stood up and collected their used mugs with the intention of stepping momentarily into the kitchen to allow her friend some privacy, but as she did so, Louise slipped off her cardigan, and Millie caught sight of a deep purple mark on her arm, the size of a small plum. It looked to Millie's trained scrutiny like a grab mark and she found it hard to tear her eyes away. Her gaze met Louise's for an instant.

'It's an insect bite,' Louise said, brushing it with her fingers as if to make it go away. 'I seem to react so badly to things these days, ever since I got pregnant.'

But it wasn't the time of year for insect bites and Millie couldn't help wondering if it too had something to do with Louise preferring to spend time at her house.

* * *

After making herself a jam sandwich for breakfast, Dominique washed her face and cleaned her teeth like always and put on her weekend clothes. The dirty washing bag in the bathroom was getting full and there was no clean school uniform in her cupboard. They were still saving up for a washing machine, so Sunday was sometimes launderette day. Dominique did wonder if she should try to go there on her own, but she didn't much like the lady who worked there. So retrieving what she'd worn to school on Friday, she spread the things out flat on her bed instead, so that Mum wouldn't have to worry about the washing when she got home. She might be really tired like before.

Going over to the window Dominique rested her arms on the ledge and looked out over the grey of the city. Mum had told her she worked near all those big, tall buildings in the middle; the thin one like a cigarette, with funny bumpy bits on top, and the shiny turquoise one. Suddenly Dominique thought that she could go and look for Mum, but she'd only been to the hotel once and though she knew it was in the city and a bus ride away, she couldn't really remember how to get there. Instead, maybe if she tried hard enough, she could think a message to Mum to tell her to come home.

* * *

'I appreciate this,' said Mariner, letting Tony Knox into his house.

'No problem, boss,' said Knox. 'Millie was asking after you, so I thought it was about time.' He shot Mariner a meaningful look.

'Yeah, you're right,' Mariner admitted. 'It's overdue. But you know what it's like, what with Jamie and a major case going on.'

'If she was off sick you'd have been to see her by now,' said Knox. That was unfair — true, but unfair. 'So how's it going?' Knox went on. 'I saw the reconstruction.'

'Possibly one big, fat overreaction,' said Mariner. 'We still haven't entirely eliminated the family, so all we need now is a few false leads thrown into the mix.'

'So what do you think is going on?'

'Really?' said Mariner. 'I don't know. It's so hard to get a handle on Grace Clifton. Everyone we speak to seems to have a slightly different take.'

'She's a steward at Symphony, right?' said Knox.

'Temporarily,' said Mariner. 'She passed her A levels back in the summer and is "on a gap year" while she considers her options.'

'Gap years,' Knox snorted. 'Where the hell did they come from? Some of us never had the luxury.' Knox wore his Liverpool working-class origins like a badge of honour.

'I'm fairly sure that *considering her options* was a euphemistic way of her mum and dad saying *while we persuade her to do the sensible thing*,' said Mariner recalling that first difficult visit to the big, detached house. He'd heard the effort in her parents' voices as they tried not to compare Grace unfavourably with their other two children. The youngest child of three, one studying medicine and the other practising law, Grace was what her parents had described as 'the creative' one in the family, the one with the 'bubbly personality.' *She's a sweetie; everyone loves her.* The subtext here appeared to be that Grace's siblings were bright enough to have got into the local grammar schools and good universities, whereas Grace was not. 'They openly admit to having had problems with Grace in the past,' Mariner went on, 'which include her having absconded from her expensive, fee-paying school, forcing her to finish her education at the local sixth-form college. But according to them, she's put all that behind her and has applied to Ealing University to be a drama teacher.'

'Sounds reasonable,' said Knox.

'They made it sound like the last resort of the desperate,' said Mariner. 'But apparently after some discussion, Grace came to see the sense of having a back-up plan.'

'Or giving in to what they wanted,' said Knox.

'Yes, her friends are more emphatic about Grace's ambitions. According to them, she's determined to be an actress, not a drama teacher. The picture from them is all about "Grace the rebel," slapping on make-up on the way to school and smoking a couple of fags on the walk from the bus stop. Interestingly,' Mariner added, 'they also refer to "Grace the flirt."'

'Do you think she might have come on to the wrong person that night on her walk across the city?'

'Or she has executed the ultimate rebellion,' Mariner said. 'Her friends were open about Grace's sense of the theatrical. She's not averse to making things up when it suits her. She'd dropped some hints about meeting an older man, but they weren't inclined to take it seriously and certainly we haven't found anything to suggest a meeting with anyone. The last text she sent just said: *Leaving now. See you soon, unless I get a better offer!!!* They took it as a joke.'

'No boyfriend?' asked Knox.

'Not as such.' Mariner was warming to the discussion. It was reminding him why he missed his sergeant. 'She's got a wide-ranging group of friends, both from the private school and the state sixth form, and among them are several boys who are friends. But they've all given accounts of their whereabouts on the night that Grace disappeared.'

'And the family?'

'Growing frustration with what they obviously perceive to be our endless circular questioning. We started with them, of course, but there are some wrinkles to iron out. We can't pin them down for the whole of the evening in question, and what doesn't help is the brother's testimony that Grace and her dad had a spat that afternoon.'

'About what?' Knox asked.

Reluctant to admit to it at first, when pressed, Councillor Clifton had finally conceded that it was true, but insignificant. 'Grace wanted to lend a friend some money,' Mariner told Knox. 'He was opposed to it on the principle that young people should learn to manage their own finances. But he wouldn't say, or didn't know, which friend this was. I'm inclined to think it was more likely that Grace was trying to tap her old man for extra funds.'

'And how's the new team shaping up?' asked Knox. He seemed happy to prolong the conversation and Mariner wondered if for him too it was like slipping back into a comfortable routine.

'We're OK,' he said. 'Though I'm probably more hands on than they want and quietly driving them all mad.'

'Business as usual then,' Knox observed. 'Has Charlie tried to convert you yet?'

'Not that I've noticed. I'm hoping it's because he recognises a lost cause. How's Athena going?'

'I could tell you, but then I'd have to kill you,' said Knox. 'Actually it is starting to warm up a bit now,' he admitted. 'You know how it is. Patterns start to emerge. The same names cropping up in the same places — snippets of conversation that are giving us some context for past events. We've got a couple of so-called legit organisations under close surveillance too. Looks as if there might be a kind of laundering operation going on; weapons coming in on authentic customs licenses that aren't all they appear to be.'

It was vague, but Mariner was well aware that he couldn't say more. Knox's enthusiasm stung a little. Reading between the lines, he seemed to be enjoying himself.

'Anyway,' Knox said, suddenly. 'If you don't get a move on, your time will be up. It might start to look as if you're stalling.'

* * *

Mariner drove over to Millie's house with mixed feelings. Had he truly been putting off seeing her? It had been a hectic few weeks, that was all, what with work and taking care of Jamie. But Millie was a close member of his team, and the observation Tony Knox had made had hit home. It was true, and Mariner had no obvious defence, except for a slight apprehension about meeting little Haroon, which would have sounded laughable had he voiced it out loud. It wasn't that Mariner was *afraid* of babies, he was just completely lacking in experience and therefore didn't have much idea of how to respond to them. Even going into Mamas & Papas to buy a gift had brought him out in a cold sweat. Twice, in quite different circumstances, the opportunity of fatherhood had been tantalisingly close, before being snatched away again, but on the rare occasions when he gave it any thought, it was with an acceptance that it was something that would probably never happen for him now. It didn't feel like a great loss, though he'd never discussed it with Suzy and had no idea how she felt about children.

Most of all today he hoped he wouldn't be required to engage too actively with the baby, and it was something of a relief that Haroon was not in evidence when Millie came to the door. After they'd exchanged greetings she went into the kitchen. 'Go on through,' she said. 'Are you still on the black-no-sugar?' Confirming that he was, Mariner went into the living room just in time to see a woman he'd never met before exposing her bare breast to him, the nipple standing out vivid and pink, as she removed her baby from where it had been suckling. The first hit of embarrassment was entirely spontaneous.

'Shit, I'm sorry,' he blustered, trying to look anywhere but directly at her. It was closely followed by a second hit of shame in recognition of his pathetically gauche reaction. *Grow up, you tosser.*

'It's fine,' the woman lied, flushing deeply and hastily covering herself with a voluminous smock. 'We were just going.'

'Don't leave because of me,' said Mariner, taking a seat at the far end of the room and feigning a sudden interest in the garden.

'No, really. We have to be getting back anyway.' The baby seemed less sure and was straining to get a closer look at Mariner as her mother hurried from the room with a cursory, 'Nice to meet you.'

Mariner heard voices in the hallway followed by the closing of the front door before Millie came in, bringing his coffee and looking bemused.

'Where's Suli?' asked Mariner, his complexion restored by now to its original colour. *A whiter shade of pale*, Suzy called it.

'Out doing a job with his brother,' said Millie. 'What did you do to frighten off Louise?'

'Poor timing,' he said, taking the mug from her. 'I think I caught a bit more of her than she would have liked. And I handled it with my usual finesse.'

'That bad, eh? No wonder she ran.'

'She looks like an interesting friend.'

'Hm. I'm not sure if we're quite friends yet,' said Millie, taking the place vacated by Louise. 'I certainly don't feel as if I know her very well. Part of me thinks we've been drawn together out of desperation. It's probably not a nice thing to say, but she seems a bit needy.'

'Same-sex couple?' speculated Mariner.

'What's that supposed to mean?'

'Well, you know . . . that's a pretty savage haircut. And the clothes . . .'

'Not that you're making assumptions or anything. Actually, it crossed my mind at first too,' Millie admitted. 'But she's married to a guy named Greg. He works in the gun trade, I've just found out.'

'Legally?'

Millie gave him a look. 'I haven't met him yet but I'm beginning to have a few thoughts about him that might explain Louise's personal style.'

'How do you mean?'

'She seems in awe of him. And he prefers her not to work, likes his dinner on the table, house kept tidy instead.'

'Welcome back to the 1950s,' said Mariner.

'That's what I thought,' said Millie. 'Abigail, their baby, had a few health problems at the start too, so I think Louise's self-esteem is at rock bottom, hence the weird, baggy clothes. And I saw an unusual mark on her arm just now. It concerned me.'

'Did you challenge her?'

'I didn't really get the chance. She got in first with an explanation, but it wasn't a very convincing one, so I don't plan to let it go.'

The baby monitor crackled, followed by a tiny, human wail and Millie disappeared to fetch Haroon. Moments later, she returned cradling the tiny sleep-suited infant in her arms. Already she looked so natural as a mother that Mariner struggled to reconcile this image of her with the case-hardened copper he knew. Mariner eyed Haroon. 'He is a very handsome baby,' he said, truthfully.

'Want to take him?' Holding Haroon out towards Mariner, Millie broke into a grin. 'Only joking. I just like to see the sheer terror on your face.'

'Oh, I'm happy to drop him on his head any time you like,' countered Mariner, slightly uneasily. 'It won't be me social services come after.'

'At least come and sit over here next to me,' said Millie. 'He needs to get a good look at you; get to know his Uncle Tom.'

'Thanks. That makes me sound as old as I feel.'

'Or as old as the woman you feel, ho ho? Speaking of which, how *is* Suzy?'

The question threw Mariner off balance. 'She's fine,' he said, suddenly fascinated by the inside of his coffee mug, 'as far as I know.'

'An interesting answer.' Millie raised an eyebrow, and when Mariner didn't immediately respond. 'You've let it drift, haven't you?'

'Strange as it may seem, having Jamie in residence hasn't exactly helped the relationship along, and now we're in the middle of a major investigation. What do you expect?'

'And before Grace Clifton disappeared?'

Mariner sighed. 'We Skyped a few times.'

'Oh, come on!' Millie was exasperated. 'You're talking to the original bored housewife here. If you can't do any better, I'm going to start describing in great detail the contents of Haroon's nappies for the last week. You'd be astonished at the variation in colour and consistency . . .'

'So this is what I'm competing with?'

'Sorry, but that's my life. I like Suzy. I mean, I know I've only met her once, but I liked her. She seemed fun.'

'She was. *Is,*' he corrected himself.

'Another one bites the dust,' observed Millie now.

'Not necessarily,' said Mariner defensively. 'Anyway, it hasn't always been my fault.'

'No. That was tactless. Sorry.'

Mariner was rescued from further interrogation by Millie's landline ringing out from the hall. 'Your turn,' she said, and in one smooth movement she deposited Haroon in Mariner's arms and went to answer it. Holding him rigidly, Mariner looked down at the baby's tiny features and his soft layer of dark hair. Haroon frowned back up at him with dark eyes, pursed his lips and expelled a bubble.

'There,' said Millie returning and retrieving her son. 'That wasn't so bad, was it? You didn't break him.' She looked up and caught Mariner watching her. 'Just think, he might have been yours,' she said cheekily.

'Lucky for him that he's not,' Mariner shot back. 'Anyway, when are you coming back to work?'

'Oh, smoothly done,' said Millie. 'Negotiations about my return to work are ongoing. I do miss it, though. God, sometimes I even catch myself hankering after Tony's crappy jokes.'

'You *are* in a bad way,' said Mariner. 'Only one cure.'

'I don't know.' Millie was rueful. 'I'm honestly in two minds. I like the idea of coming back but our job isn't exactly conducive to a quiet family life. We're going to have to see how you turn out, aren't we?' She gazed down at the baby and for the first time Mariner had the sense that he would have to manage without his DC for some time to come. And with Knox out of the picture too, it was beginning to look as if Mariner's newly formed team might turn into something more permanent.

'Anyway, I hear you've got a good new DS.' Millie looked up again. 'Tony told me,' she added, anticipating his next question. 'She's settling in all right?'

'Yes. She's efficient and reliable, though not as good as you, of course,' Mariner added, quickly.

'Naturally,' Millie agreed.

'It's odd, though,' Mariner continued. 'I keep getting this feeling that I've met her before. When I first picked up her application the name struck me as familiar, though I'm pretty sure we've never worked together.'

'Maybe you've just seen her name somewhere,' said Millie.

'That wouldn't surprise me, given the volume of stuff that crosses my desk these days. But when she walked into CID on the day she started and we met face to face, I still felt as if I knew her.'

'Did she give any indication of feeling the same way?'

'No. I'm probably showing my age, you know, that feeling that you already know complete strangers?'

'That'll be it,' said Millie. 'How's it going with Grace Clifton? Is there any news from the reconstruction?'

Mariner grimaced. 'You know how to kick a man when he's down. Bugger all, in other words.' He cast a guilty glance towards the baby. 'Sorry.'

Millie laughed. 'Don't worry, I don't think his understanding's that advanced.'

'If there has been anything significant, no one's told me yet,' said Mariner.

'You think she's run away?'

'Her mates say she's a rebel. What better two fingers up to your parents than this?'

'You'd know,' said Millie.

'Yes, I would,' said Mariner, though it hadn't really occurred to him until then. 'But I did have the decency to let my mother know I was safe. Eventually.'

Suliman, Millie's husband, returned just as Mariner was leaving. 'I hope you haven't been trying to talk her into anything,' he said, and Mariner couldn't quite tell if he was joking or not.

* * *

When Mariner got out of his car, back at the house, he heard an unfamiliar sound: Jamie laughing. Not just the faint chuckle of satisfaction he allowed himself when they went swimming, or when a new packet of Hula Hoops came his way, but a real belly laugh.

He opened the door to find Jamie apparently snowboarding in the middle of the living room, in between bouts of jumping and flapping his hands with glee. Knox had brought across a Wii.

'Our Siobhan's kids like it, so I thought Jamie might,' said Knox. 'How's Millie?'

'She's good,' said Mariner. 'But you'd know that better than me. She said you've been over a few times.'

'Yeah, well I seem to find myself over that side of the city quite often, so I just pop in, you know?'

Mariner didn't really. It had never been his habit to 'pop in' on anyone. But his colleagues had always been more sociable than him. What rubs off from the kind of family life Mariner himself had never experienced, he supposed.

Chapter Six

Dominique woke on Monday morning feeling the warmth of her mum's arms around her, and with the sound of Mum's voice whispering soothingly in her ear and she nestled back into the pillows. But they felt cold and hard and when she opened her eyes Mum wasn't there. For the first time Dominique felt frightened and burning tears began to form behind her eyes. She remembered waking up in the night to the noise of banging and shouting in one of the other flats along the landing. It reminded her of when they lived at home with Dad. She had never seen Mum and Dad fighting, but she'd heard it a lot and she knew it was one of the reasons they had come to Birmingham. Most of the shouting happened when Dominique was in bed and they thought she couldn't hear. It had got worse and worse, until Mum said they had to go, and they went to Auntie's. Suddenly Dominique wondered if that was where Mum had gone now. But Auntie hadn't really wanted them there the last time, so somehow Dominique didn't think she'd be very welcome. Thinking about London gave her a sudden longing for her dad.

The food monster in her tummy started to growl. Today was Monday but Dominique wasn't sure if she wanted to go to school. What if Mum came home while she was there? But when they'd first come to Birmingham, before Dominique had made friends at school, she'd wanted to stay at home and mum had told her about the *trooncy* lady. She was seriously scary, mum said, like Miss Trunchbull in the *Matilda* film. Dominique didn't want her to come to the flat, so she had to go to school. Besides, it would be nice to see Somia and Evie. It had been lonely having no one to talk to. It felt funny at first, setting off all on her own again, but as she got closer to school she started to see some faces that she knew and that made her feel much better.

'Mummy let you walk on your own today?' asked Asha's mum.

'Just from the corner,' said Dominique, looking back and giving a little wave, as if her mum might still be waiting and watching there.

Finding Somia in the playground, Dominique felt a surge of joy, and scampered over to see her friend, and for a little while she almost forgot about Mum. She hadn't got any money for toast, but Somia shared hers (although they both left the crusts) and Dominique knew she was on free dinners so would get something for lunch. It made her think about sausages and cheese flan and pizza, and her tummy rumbled again.

* * *

For obvious reasons, Mariner had never truly understood what life was like for his colleagues who were also mothers, and who often rushed into work at the last minute breathless and harassed. Since Jamie had moved in, he'd developed a genuine sympathy for anyone who had to get their kids ready for school. The deadline for Jamie was the community centre bus that turned up every weekday morning, at eight twenty sharp, on its circuitous route to pick up the attendees. It had taken weeks to perfect a routine that worked, and it could be thrown off course if the slightest aspect was not to Jamie's liking. But this morning all went about as smoothly as it ever would. They'd had their run and Jamie was dressed, fed and waiting when the bus pulled into the service road.

'Hi there, Jamie! How are you doing?' The escort today was Declan, who was unfailingly cheerful, and swung energetically down from the doors to help Jamie on board. As Mariner watched Jamie lope along the aisle to take his favourite seat, the half-dozen or so other passengers, all without exception white-haired, gazed blankly out at him, reminding Mariner once again of the inappropriateness of this arrangement. One elderly woman had her forehead pressed against the window, the personification of a 'windy-licker,' an expression which Declan had once explained was still in common usage in parts of Ireland. The driver then executed what had become a well-practised three-point turn in the tight space available, and Mariner watched the bus disappear again out onto the main road. He walked back into the house to get his coat, thankful nonetheless that Jamie was taken care of for a few hours.

A day spent on tenterhooks had brought little reward. One of the first in CID, Mariner walked through a virtually empty bullpen and along to his new office, one of the so-called perks of his temporary promotion. Superintendent Sharp had moved up a whole floor, vacating the space for him, and Mariner still wasn't used to it. Down a short corridor off CID, he felt it distanced him from the rest of the squad and he often found himself roaming around the main office instead, perching on desks and staying engaged with what was happening on the ground, all the while ignoring the ever-growing pile of paper in his in-tray. But this morning he sat down at his own computer and went straight to Grace Clifton's policy log on HOLMES, to check what, if any, new information had been entered since Saturday night's reconstruction.

He didn't get very far. As the screen was coming to life, Vicky Jesson knocked lightly on his always-open door and came in. As she often did, she'd brought him an unsolicited mug of coffee — black, no sugar — which she placed down in front of him. 'I thought you might like an update,' she said.

'Thanks,' said Mariner. 'Should I be excited?'

'I wouldn't get your hopes up.' Just as she was pulling up a spare chair, Charlie Glover appeared, dapper as always, and clutching his Birmingham City mug. The man did himself no favours.

'When did you knock off on Saturday?' Mariner was asking Jesson.

'I think it was about half eleven in the end,' Jesson said. 'I left a couple of uniforms. But by that time of night people are either off their faces or desperate to get home. There didn't seem much point in hanging around.'

'I was about the same,' said Glover. He remained standing, leaning back against a filing cabinet. 'We had a handful of calls at most while I was here. None of which sounded especially promising.'

By now the log had come up on Mariner's screen and, taking a slug of coffee, he scanned what was there. 'One of the uniforms out on Broad Street by Symphony was approached by a couple of people who thought they might have seen something,' he said.

'It's vague,' said Jesson, reading from her corresponding printout. 'They thought they saw a man and woman arguing outside a bar, but the female doesn't fit Grace's description.'

'And three of the calls logged are from people who thought they might have seen a "dark-coloured" van in the area, on the night Grace went missing,' Mariner read. 'Great. Given how common they are, it would be more surprising if they hadn't seen one.'

'And no one seems to have got a make or a licence plate number,' said Jesson. 'Without those, it's hopeless.

"Might have been one of those transit vans" seems to be the extent of the observations.'

'In other words, naff all,' said Charlie. His lexicon of expletives had changed somewhat since he and his missus had been born again. Mariner wondered if anyone else had noticed that.

'Well, I don't think any of us is that surprised that so little new information has come to light,' Mariner said. 'If anything, it's vindication of what we're all thinking. But it doesn't move things any further forward, either.'

'Well, if she has run away, I for one am starting to get increasingly annoyed by a little cow who's too selfish to consider that her parents might be going out of their minds with worry, and who can't be bothered to at least contact them, directly or indirectly, to let them know she's OK,' said Jesson, with feeling.

'Where are we up to with friends and family?' asked Mariner.

'We've pretty much exhausted all avenues,' she said. 'The friends were all together waiting for Grace, which has been verified by bar staff. Close family have sound alibis through this family gathering.'

'Let's make sure they can account for their movements throughout the evening,' said Mariner. 'Hour by hour, if necessary. The Hagley Road isn't that far away, and at a big get-together like that it can be easy enough to slip away for a short time. Other than that, it's either that Grace herself has initiated this — in which case I agree, selfish little cow — or we're looking at someone outside of that circle, someone we don't yet know about or a complete stranger, which is the least likely scenario statistically.' He was voicing what they were all thinking. 'We've gone over all the social networking stuff?' he checked.

'Max has, with his usual diligence,' said Glover. 'We're following up on a couple of students from her old school who aren't local, but pretty much everyone else is accounted for. No mystery emails. We haven't got her phone, of course.'

'It goes straight to voicemail when we call it?'

'Every time. Her family keep trying too, and they've promised to let us know if they get anything different.'

'Do you get the impression that anyone is holding back?' Mariner asked. He had his own thoughts on that but he was interested to hear what Jesson and Glover had to say.

Jesson chipped in first. 'I don't,' she said. 'If there's anyone I'd have reservations about, it's her dad. They crossed swords frequently, according to more or less everyone else. I did wonder . . .' She paused.

'Yes?'

'Even if his alibi checks out, would he have had the means to arrange something?'

'How do you mean?' said Glover.

'Well, we're looking at a wealthy and powerful man, who's operated in the business world for years. I can't help thinking that at some time he might have come into contact with the kinds of individuals who could make something like this happen. And he's certainly got the resources.'

There was a knock on the door and one of the civilian admin staff came in to deposit Mariner's post, which he acknowledged with a nod of thanks. 'You don't sound as if you really believe it,' he was saying to Jesson. 'And we have to come back to the motive. Would a father really take such drastic action with his daughter, just because she's a bit rebellious? Grace may have caused them some embarrassment by choosing a different career path from her brother and sister, but I'm not sure that it's cause for such an extreme reaction.'

'He might be tempted when she turns up alive and well,' said Glover wryly.

The clerk remained, hovering indecisively in the doorway.

'Was there something else?' Mariner asked him.

'There's this,' he said holding up a bulky package. 'It's addressed to *DCI* Sharp, but as she's not a DCI any more, I didn't know . . .'

'Is she in yet?' Mariner asked.

'She's not in her office.'

'OK. Leave it here and I'll pass it on if necessary.'

The clerk deposited the parcel on his desk. 'It came by courier this morning from Friar Street,' he said. 'It got wrongly delivered to one of their dog handlers, PC Dave Sharp, in the middle of last week, but he's been off sick. It wasn't until he came back and saw *DCI* on the address that he realised it was meant for us here. It's happened before with odd pieces of correspondence and luckily he spotted the mistake before . . .' He tailed off. 'Sorry, you probably didn't need to know all that.'

'Thanks,' said Mariner. The bulky eighteen-inch square padded envelope looked as if it had arrived via a war zone. Along its deep creases, the bubble wrap was bursting through the outer shell, like a series of polythene hernias. Mariner absently picked it up and began prying open the seal. 'So, in the meantime,' he said, wrapping things up with Glover and Jesson, 'we keep on pushing against doors, hoping that either Grace has a sudden crisis of conscience and gets in touch, or we learn something new and important that gives us a clue about where she is.'

Jesson dipped her head towards the parcel. 'Let us know if you want us to sing "Happy Birthday,"' she said.

But Mariner didn't respond. His attention had been snagged by what was inside and he was opening his desk drawer to take out a pair of latex gloves. 'Go and get some sterile paper and forensic bags, Charlie,' he said.

As Glover disappeared, Jesson moved forward to see. 'What is it?'

The air in the room had thickened and Mariner was suddenly hypersensitive to the hairs on the back of his neck. Gloved-up, he reached inside the envelope to retrieve a small object which he placed carefully on the desk. It was a plastic badge bearing the Town Hall/Symphony Hall logo. Alongside it was the name *Grace Clifton.*

Chapter Seven

Returning to Mariner's office, Charlie was the last to snap on his protective gloves. By which time Mariner had spread out the brown paper he'd brought and placed the package on top. Now he slid out a pile of clothing, pressed and perfectly folded. One by one he picked up the items and laid them out on the table: a black skirt and waistcoat, bra, panties and tights. A separate, bulkier plastic bag at the bottom of the pile contained a pair of highly polished black shoes with a two-inch heel.

'It fits the description of what she was wearing,' Jesson said. 'And it's the right size: eight to ten, size four shoes.' She reached over to check the labels in the underwear. 'This is Hollister,' she said. 'And we've got H&M, and New Look. Those are a young person's shops. I can check with her mum to make sure.' She inhaled deeply. 'Smell that?' she said. 'Detergent. It's all been freshly washed. Nice fabric conditioner too. Sainsbury's Summer Meadow, unless I'm very much mistaken.'

'Really?' Mariner was impressed. Her look told him he was being ridiculous. 'So why go to the trouble?' he said.

Charlie landed on the obvious. 'To get rid of any forensic evidence,' he said.

'It's still a risk though,' said Jesson. 'If you're worried about forensic traces, why send them at all?'

'There's no blouse,' Mariner observed.

'Perhaps it didn't wash too well,' said Glover, grimly.

As they absorbed individually what the contents of the package signified, Mariner picked up the items and dropped each into an evidence bag that Jesson held open. For him this was their first solid indicator that Grace Clifton might not have engineered her own disappearance. He wondered if the other two were thinking along the same lines.

'What if Grace herself has sent them?' offered Jesson, tentatively.

'Why would she do that?'

'Well, say she has just run away, either on her own or with someone. She'd hardly want to wear her work uniform, would she? So maybe she has other clothes to change into and she's sent these, I don't know, in a misguided attempt to let people know that she's safe.'

'Or perhaps a symbolic thing. Letting go of her old life?' said Glover.

'If that's the case, why send them to us?' said Mariner. 'Why not to her parents?'

'Because it would freak them out?' said Jesson.

'All the more reason to do it,' Charlie speculated. 'Everyone says she has a wicked sense of humour.'

'But that would be plain cruel,' said Mariner. 'And why be so cryptic? Simpler to write a note, stick a stamp on an envelope and drop it into a post box, surely?'

'It might give away her location,' Jesson pointed out.

'Not necessarily.'

'What if it's a cry for help?' said Glover suddenly.

'What do you mean?'

'Say Grace has run away, with someone we haven't yet identified, someone unknown to any of her friends or family. Someone she met. Perhaps at first it was exciting, dangerous even, and it seemed like an adventure. Now she could be getting cold feet. But whoever she's with has some kind of control over her, and this is her way of trying to let us know.'

Jesson was shaking her head. 'It overcomplicates things,' she said. 'And we've found no online activity linking her with persons unknown.'

'She doesn't have to have met them online,' Charlie pointed out. 'Some people still do that thing called face-to-face contact.'

But they were straying into the realm of speculation. Mariner picked up the envelope again. 'Looks as if Dave Sharp's dog had a good chew on this.'

'It must have been posted to Friar Street,' said Jesson. 'That postage label looks like your usual Post Office printed one, so we should be able to find out where it was sent from.' The Friar Street address was in neat block capitals written in black marker pen.

As Mariner tipped up the package he saw something else, stuck to the inside. 'Hold on,' he said. It was a slim plastic bag, like a re-sealable sandwich bag, which contained something that at first glance looked like a black hair net, but when Mariner broke the seal and peered inside he realised he was looking at short clippings of human hair — and body hair at that.

'Is that what I think it is?' said Glover with distaste.

'Looks like it,' said Mariner.

'So it's one of *those*,' said Jesson.

'Or made to look like one of those,' said Mariner. 'I think we can safely assume that this will match Grace's DNA, and that her parents will recognise the clothing.' He checked the envelope again. 'But no communication from whoever sent it.'

'Why bother then?' Glover wondered aloud.

'To let us know that someone's got her,' said Mariner.

* * *

Given the lack of any headway over the weekend from the reconstruction, it was a despondent team that gathered in CID for the first briefing of the day. The arrival of the parcel injected some fresh enthusiasm, the subsequent discussion following much the same pattern as the one that had already taken place in Mariner's office, though the focus was more on the laundering of the clothes.

'Whatever it might mean,' Mariner said, 'we share with the media that we have received some clothing. But details of what else the package contained, we keep to ourselves for now. Is that understood?'

It appeared to be. Individuals were tasked with following up existing lines of enquiry. Meanwhile Mariner went to speak to Superintendent Sharp. He explained the parcel and its contents. 'I think it's a clear indication that we're looking at something more than a straight MisPer,' he said. 'I'd like to start directing the enquiry through an incident room.'

'I agree,' said Sharp. 'Let me know as and when you need additional resources.'

'Have we made a big mistake with this?' Mariner said.

'No,' said Sharp. 'We've been suitably cautious.'

* * *

Grace's mother and father were asked to come in to positively identify the clothing. Whilst Mariner welcomed the opportunity for further close scrutiny of the couple, he was acutely aware of their potential distress in the face of so little contextual information. On the surface they were composed; Mrs Clifton was stylishly dressed, her olive skin dark against a lemon-coloured suit. She was of Middle Eastern origin, Mariner seemed to remember. Dwarfed beside her husband's powerful physical presence, she seemed nonetheless calm and contained.

With Vicky Jesson in attendance, Mariner took them to the forensic suite where the clothes, visible through the transparent panes of the evidence bags, had been laid out on the table. The shoes remained in the plastic bag they'd arrived in. 'I have to ask you not to touch anything, please,' Mariner said. 'Just confirm for us, if you can, that they belong to Grace.' He could tell immediately from the quiver of her lip that Grace's mother recognised them. She nodded wordlessly.

'You're certain about all the clothes?' Mariner asked, gently.

'Yes,' Mrs Clifton replied, her voice barely a whisper. She cleared her throat. 'And those are definitely Gracie's shoes. I keep telling her they're ridiculous to wear for work, when she's on her feet all night, but she swears that they're comfortable. She'll suffer for that when she's older.'

'I really hope she does,' added Councillor Clifton, and Mariner saw that suddenly the possibilities were becoming real to him too. Until now he had been brash, and confident to the point of bombastic, but seeing these items spread out, Mariner could see he'd taken a body blow. It took several seconds for his wife to grasp the implication of what he'd said, and when she finally did, she glanced up briefly, pain distorting her attractive features. 'No. Do you think this means . . .?'

Jesson touched her arm in a sympathetic gesture. 'We're still trying to figure it out ourselves,' she said.

For several minutes Mrs Clifton continued to stare at the clothing. 'There's something wrong here,' she said suddenly. 'I'm sure those are Gracie's shoes, but she never keeps them this clean. None of the kids have ever polished their shoes. I always end up doing it for them, when they get really scuffed.' She caught Mariner's eye. 'I don't understand. Why would she have cleaned her shoes?'

'I'm sorry, that's something else we don't yet know,' Mariner had to admit. 'I realise this is an odd question, Mrs Clifton,' he went on, 'but is it possible to tell if the clothes smell like your usual detergent or fabric conditioner?' He opened up one of the bags and she dipped her head over it, sniffing at the clothes.

'It's a pleasant smell,' she said. 'I don't think it's the one I use, but it's hard to say.' Finally, unable to resist, she put her hand on the bag containing Grace's shoes, as if that would somehow bring her closer to her daughter.

* * *

'You smell,' said Ethan Fisher, holding his nose in exaggerated fashion and wafting his free hand in front of his face. The other boys in his little gang laughed and did the same. 'She stinks!' cried Sajid Latif and the others joined in the chant: 'She stinks, she stinks!' Dominique couldn't help it then. A big pain came up inside her and she wanted to shout, 'I want my mum!' But instead she covered her ears and ran, as far away from them as she could get, onto the grass and behind the low bushes. There she sat down where nobody else would be able to see that she was crying. When the whistle blew and they all filed back into school, one of the dinner ladies stopped her. 'Are you all right, darlin'? Have you been crying?'

'I fell over,' said Dominique, touching her knee for effect. 'But I'm all right now.'

At the end of the day, when it was time to go home, Dominique scanned the crowd of waiting parents, desperately hoping to pick out Mum's cloud of dark, curly hair, and a sign that things would be back to normal again. But as she stood straining to see, one by one the other kids dispersed with their mums, disappearing off down the road and calling out goodbye as they went. Some of them were going to do what Dominique liked best, and stop off at the newsagents for sweets. The others would climb into their mums' cars and be driven home. Bit by bit, the mob at the gate started to thin, conversations between the grown-ups dwindled and parents and children drifted away. The last stragglers ran out of the cloakrooms, racing to catch up and being chastised for being slow.

A group of year two boys who'd started to kick around an empty water bottle while they waited for play dates to be arranged, went tumbling noisily off down the street. Dominique followed them out and looked each way down the road to see if Mum was coming, hurrying and breathless and sorry she was late. She didn't want to go back to the flat alone, and perhaps if she waited for long enough, this time Mum *would* come. All day long she had thought about telling a teacher. But then she would also have to tell her secret. And she couldn't do that.

Dominique stood watching the cars go past, mostly mums driving with kids in the back. Black, shiny cars, silver cars, big people carriers, and a workman in his white van. She hugged her coat tightly round her. The sun had gone down behind the big, grey clouds and the wind was clattering the dead leaves around on the pavement. Miss McBride said that autumn was coming early this year because it had been such a nice warm summer. Dominique spied a loose thread on the sleeve of her coat and was concentrating hard on pulling it free, so that the man's voice behind her made her jump.

'Hello, bab, are you all right?'

Dominique looked round to see the building supervisor, Mr Warren, with his bunch of keys, swinging shut one of the steel gates. He was bigger than Dad and quite old, and the skin on his face was red with lots of tiny holes and tiny wiggly lines in it. The gate squealed like a creature in pain.

'Yes, thank you,' Dominique replied, good manners having been drummed into her at an early age. 'I'm waiting for my mum. She's just coming.' Dominique glanced off down the road. It wasn't quite a lie. She was sure that Mum would come in the end — it was just that she couldn't see her yet.

'Righty ho.' Mr Warren smiled, showing his brown teeth, then, pulling the gates together with a clang, he snapped shut the big padlock and clomped away again. On the far side of the playground Dominique saw the teachers beginning to come out to their cars and drive out through the other entrance. She turned away hoping that they wouldn't see she was still there. Mr Rhys got cross about kids whose mums didn't collect them on time. Picking up her school-bag she started out along the main road, carefully stepping on the paving slabs. She'd see if she could get all the way home without standing on a crack.

* * *

Mariner was starting to feel the now-familiar claustrophobia as the walls of Superintendent Sharp's new second-floor office began to close in on him. He, Sharp and the ACC were sitting around Sharp's desk, discussing the significance of Grace Clifton's clothing. As soon as he had learned about this latest development, Dawson had insisted on a personal briefing, and his frustration that they could determine so little from it was patently evident. As always his timing was bloody awful, arriving just as Mariner was about to leave for the afternoon, and now Mariner's only point of focus was the second hand on his watch as it bumped the minute hand inexorably towards the point of no return. He'd heard barely anything of the last five minutes of discussion — mostly the ACC offering procedural advice that added nothing to what Mariner and his team had already put in place. Instead Mariner's mental energy was consumed by calculating the time it was going to take him to drive from Granville Lane out to his Kingsmead home at this time on a Monday afternoon, and anticipating in graphic detail the potential delays along the way. Even with a clear run, any second now he would go past the limit at which it was achievable. And here it was.

At that precise moment Superintendent Sharp's voice cut into his consciousness. 'You need to go, Tom,' she said, throwing him a lifeline.

'Yes, I do,' said Mariner, getting to his feet. 'Sorry.'

The ACC's accusing gaze swept his way. 'Oh. Of course, that's fine, Tom.' Mariner thought he saw a tell-tale flush of annoyance fleetingly cross Dawson's face. It was a look he knew well, but usually from the other side — the gut-deep disbelief that anything else could be more important than — in this case — locating a missing and vulnerable young woman. Even though the meeting had been approaching its natural conclusion, the guilt cut through Mariner as he hurriedly shook hands and left the room, hearing the door bang loudly behind him in the deserted corridor. Now he was free, he bounded down the stairs with the lightness of a kid who's been let out early from school. Seven and a half minutes to make the three-mile suburban journey on the cusp of rush hour. Where was a Tardis when you needed one?

He pulled into the service road, at the end of which was his house . . . and his heart sank as the parked-up bus came into view, *Joseph Chamberlain Centre* emblazoned along the side. He would incur a fine for this. It wasn't the money that mattered, but Mariner hated the thought that he was letting people down. Coming to an untidy halt he saw that it was Declan once again who waited in the open doorway, finishing a sly cigarette and watching over Jamie as he paced around in what passed for Mariner's front garden. His was a strange job, Mariner had often thought. A couple of hours in the early morning, a few more in late afternoon and the rest of Declan's day was his own. He was a relatively young man. Not for the first time, Mariner wondered what on earth the man did with the rest of his time.

'Have a great evening, guys,' he said, brightly, swinging back into the bus. 'I'll see you in the morning.'

* * *

The walk home seemed longer than ever, and though she was tired when she rounded the corner of her street, Dominique couldn't help running the last hundred metres or so to their block. The main door was propped open with a brick as always and she climbed up the cold, concrete stairs to the fourth floor. Reaching in through the aluminium letterbox she groped around for the rough-edged string, its key dangling on the end. 'Shouldn't really do this,' her mum had told her, when they'd fixed it there. But she said that Dominique had to have a way of getting in if she needed to. And Dominique couldn't see that anyone else would ever want to get into their flat. Mum had tried hard to make it nice and Dominique had thought it was cosy until she'd gone for tea at Somia's house. With its thick carpets, squashy leather sofas and a special room for eating their tea, it had been like going into a palace.

She was glad to be home, and pushing open the door she felt a rush of hope that Mum would be there. But the flat was even colder and emptier than it had been before. Dominique was hungry again, but the yogurts had all gone and the bread in the cupboard had furry spots on it and smelled funny. She switched on the telly for company and the electric fire and, when it got dark, the lamp in the corner. But a bit later, while she was watching a cartoon, the TV screen suddenly went black and the light went off. The meter had run out. Dominique knew that when this happened Mum had to put more tokens in the slot, but now that it was dark she was too frightened to move off the sofa. After a while, when her eyes got used to it and she could see the shapes of things, she felt braver and she went out to the cupboard in the hall where the meter was. She knew she had to put a token in, but when she found the jar where Mum kept them, it was empty, and Dominique didn't know where to get more from.

Chapter Eight

On Tuesday morning, Mariner had been at his desk just a short time, and was fixated on his computer screen, when something large plopped onto the desk before him. 'Someone must really like you,' observed the post clerk. Except that today's parcel was in much better condition than yesterday's offering. It was identical to the one that had contained Grace Clifton's clothes, but this time it was directly addressed to Mariner and the franking mark suggested it had come through the regular external post.

'Shit,' he said, staring at it for a stunned moment, then he phoned through to Vicky Jesson and Charlie Glover. Minutes later, the three of them were experiencing an unpleasant case of déjà vu.

'Not much doubt about it then,' said Mariner, sweeping his gaze over evidence bags containing, this time, jeans, underwear and well-worn but highly polished ballet flats, black, with a decorative row of steel stars. To one side, he'd placed an identical plastic bag containing hair, along with another plastic identity badge. Today there was no distinctive logo to help them out and the name, in block capitals, simply read *ROSA*.

Mariner picked it up. 'Not one of Symphony Hall's,' he said. 'This one is cheaper and more generic.'

'And less formal,' Glover pointed out. 'Grace's has her full name on it.'

'So who the hell is Rosa, and what, if anything, does she have to do with Grace Clifton?' said Mariner, more to himself than to anyone else. 'Any of her friends go by that name?'

'None that have been mentioned to us,' said Jesson.

'Can you see a date on that postmark?' Mariner said, getting in close. The others did the same, so that all he could hear for several seconds was the sound of their collective breathing.

'Looks like the fourteenth to me,' said Charlie. 'Yesterday.'

'So this one has definitely come straight here.'

'And it's got your name on it,' added Vicky. 'Whoever sent this must know that you're in charge of the investigation.'

'From the reconstruction perhaps,' said Charlie. 'It's been aired a few times now, and they'll have seen the Q&A afterwards with your name scrolling along the bottom.'

In the newly created incident room, the development was shared with other officers working the case.

'Our first task is to check through missing persons for the last week or so and see if anyone with this name has been reported,' Mariner said to Charlie. 'Start locally and work your way incrementally out to a wider radius. There could be all kinds of reasons why this girl or woman hasn't come to our attention.' Mariner couldn't help but think back to the case of Ricky Skeet a few years ago, one of the many hidden victims in this over-populated city. 'If that doesn't work then we'll need to harness our friends in the media. We can also get the hair DNA tested, though that will only help if Rosa is already on our database, and it will be a good couple of days before we get an outcome.'

'What about Grace?' Charlie asked.

'We keep pursuing the current lines of enquiry. And we start to cautiously explore the possibility that these two women are somehow linked.'

'Do we now believe that Grace Clifton may have been taken?' Vicky Jesson asked.

'I think we have to accept that as an increasingly strong possibility,' said Mariner. 'Either she's really yanking our chain, or both these women have been taken by person or persons unknown.'

* * *

It was such a beautiful, sunny afternoon that Millie decided to take Haroon for a walk. On impulse she arranged her route so that she could call on Louise. It was about time she saw inside her new friend's house and this might be the only way to make it happen. As she entered the cul-de-sac she felt as if she were walking into a different world. The noise of the city seemed to melt away behind the mature trees, and the shrubs and expansive lawns gave an illusion of rural charm. Louise's house was a large though far-from-ostentatious brick build, detached and with mullioned windows that rendered it dark and mysterious. Millie stepped into the porch and rapped the brass knocker three times. She was preparing her 'surprise!' face for Louise, and was therefore completely wrong-footed when the door was answered by a man, who could only be Greg. Millie was immediately on her guard, which made two of them apparently — although a less observant eye than Millie's might have failed to notice the split-second delay before he turned on the dazzlingly handsome smile. Of average height, he was dark-haired with film-star good looks and confidence radiating from him. Millie's first thought was what a mismatch he was for Louise. She could imagine him being very successful at his sales job.

'Hello, I'm Millie,' she said, though he'd probably worked it out already. 'I live a couple of streets away. I met Louise through the baby clinic.'

'Yes, of course,' Greg greeted her as if they were old friends, the Red Riding Hood's granny smile shifting up a few kilowatts. 'Come in, come in,' he urged. 'Lou's just upstairs changing Abigail.' Opening the door wide he helped Millie manoeuvre the pushchair over the threshold, peering in at the sleeping baby. 'And this must be Haroon,' he said, his voice low, so as not to wake him. The buggy parked, he took Millie through to a lounge decorated in pale, neutral tones and spotlessly clean and tidy, with not even a hint that there was a child in the house.

'Is there anything I can get you?' Greg asked solicitously. 'A cup of tea or a cold drink? Lou's like a fish in human form at the moment. The breastfeeding, I suppose.' He was trying too hard . . .

'I'm fine, thank you,' said Millie.

'We've just got back from the hospital, where Abi passed her last check with flying colours.'

'That's great news!' said Millie, genuinely. It had surprised her when Greg had come to the door, and even more that he would welcome her so readily into his house. But then she had to remind herself of how clever domestic abusers could be. It was how they managed to get away with it for so long. She decided to test Greg out. 'Actually,' she said. 'I'm glad to meet you too. Suli, my husband, and I were wondering if you and Louise would like to come over for dinner, perhaps next Saturday, or the week after?' It was an impulsive invitation and Millie anticipated prior engagements, or at the very least babysitting difficulties, but Greg didn't hesitate.

'That's so kind of you,' he beamed. 'And it would be great. I've been worried about Lou. She will have already told you how poorly Abigail was when she was born and, for some reason, Lou seems to blame herself for it. Her confidence has taken a real knock — not that it was particularly secure in the first place.' He lowered his voice. 'The doctor has alluded to post-natal depression. I'm glad for Abigail's sake that Lou's met you and coming to yours for dinner would be lovely.'

'If babysitting's an issue, just bring Abigail along,' said Millie.

'Oh, I'm sure we can find someone. Louise's mum would love to, I know, but she lives just that bit too far away,' he added. 'Apart from her, I'm all Lou's got. This Saturday would be fine. It might help to restore us to normal.'

Taking in the obsessively tidy room, Millie wondered exactly what counted as 'normal' in his book.

Just then Louise came down the stairs, looking surprised and slightly anxious to see the two of them together, almost as if they might be conspiring against her — which perhaps, in a way, they had been.

'I thought you and Abigail might like a stroll to the park in the sunshine,' Millie said. She glanced over at Greg. 'But if you've got other plans . . .'

'That would be nice,' said Louise, checking for Greg's approval.

'Oh, don't mind me,' he said. 'I've got to get straight back to work. No rest for the wicked, eh?'

'I'll get Abigail's coat.'

'It's a great idea,' Greg beamed. He reached out for the baby. 'Come here, you, and let your mummy get ready. Daddy's little—'

'No! Don't say it!' Louise snapped, startling both the babies and making Abigail's face crumple. 'She's not Daddy's little anything. She's a little girl!'

Catching Millie's eye, Greg smiled indulgently. 'It's all right, darling. I was going to say "angel." I know what she is, and I've no doubt she'll be a feminist through and through, just like her mum.'

The park was just a short walk from Louise's home and the day was breezy but mild for the time of year, so after a circuit of the park that had lulled Abigail back to sleep, the two women found a bench to sit on in the sunshine. The wind blew Millie's hair across her face and she pushed it away in irritation. 'God, I must get this cut soon. It's driving me mad.' Louise's dark hair was cropped short, elfin-style. 'Maybe I'll go for your look. Is that a post-baby haircut?'

'Oh no, I've always worn it like this,' Louise said, touching the nape of her neck self-consciously. 'Well, at least since I was quite small. Mum cut it the first time. She said it was more practical. If I let it grow it would be really thick and curly. It did used to be pretty wild, and my brother used to take great delight in pulling it.' She turned as an ice-cream van tinkled into the nearby car park and children began appearing from all over the playground. 'Goodness, I didn't think it was *that* warm.'

'That will be our two in a few years,' said Millie.

'I suppose so.' Louise was watching Haroon. 'I wish I'd had a boy,' she said suddenly.

It wasn't the first time she'd said this, but where Millie had previously ignored the comment, this time she said, 'I'm sure you don't mean that. You've got a beautiful daughter.'

'I know, but Greg really buys into all the pink, girly princess stuff and I hate it. It feels so wrong. Do you know what I mean?'

Millie wasn't sure that she did, but she was beginning to learn that her new friend was far from straightforward. 'Just wait 'til they're in their teens,' she said. 'You and Abigail will have fabulous mum-and-daughter time together, while Haroon won't want to be seen with me.'

One of the silences that sometimes elapsed between them took root.

'Your boss seems like a nice man,' said Louise, suddenly.

'He's all right,' said Millie. 'For a copper.'

Louise giggled. 'I'm not sure that he was ready to be confronted with my bare boob though. I felt like saying "I've shown you mine now you show me yours."'

'You should have,' Millie said, pleased by this sudden playfulness. 'It would have really freaked him out.' Impulsively, she added, 'And his is worth seeing, I can vouch for that.'

Louise's mouth dropped open. 'How do you know?'

Ordinarily, it was a confidence Millie wouldn't have dreamed of sharing, but she hoped that doing so might help to gain more of Louise's trust. 'Oh, we had a bit of a thing, a few years back,' she said, casually.

'You minx,' said Louise.

'Not really. It was way before I met Suli, and it didn't last. It wasn't a very good idea when we were trying to work together.' Millie gazed out over the park. 'A bit like you and Greg, I suppose, except that we decided not to pursue the affair. You didn't seem surprised,' she said.

'About what?'

'That my boss is a police officer. That *I'm* a police officer.'

'No.' Louise avoided her gaze.

'A lot of people are thrown by that.'

'Actually, I already knew,' Louise admitted. 'Shona told me. Only in passing,' she added quickly. 'Not because she thought I needed to know or anything. Perhaps she thought I would understand you were sensible and dependable. But I was glad to find out. It made me come to sit next to you at the health centre.'

'Why?' Millie turned to face her, sensing that they were on the cusp of something here.

'Because at the time I thought I might want to ask for your help, but now . . .'

'Help how?' Millie prompted gently.

'I'm not sure.' She looked away. 'It feels as if I'm being disloyal.' Reaching out, Louise took hold of the handle of Abigail's stroller and despite the soundly sleeping baby, began pushing it back and forth in quite an agitated fashion. 'Look, I shouldn't have started this. Can we just forget—?'

'Does Greg hit you?' Millie blurted out.

'No!' Louise's face registered such pure shock that Millie almost believed her. Louise sighed. 'I am worried about him, though. He's being secretive, furtive even. I mean, he's always worked late, as I told you, but it seems to be happening a lot lately, and he's very vague about where he's been. If I ask him any questions, or even just try to show an interest, he gets irritable and evasive, and says he's "in important meetings." I happened to ask one of the other partners about one of these so-called meetings and it was obvious that he knew nothing about it. And Greg's definitely drinking more. Last time I put out the recycling I was horrified by the number of wine bottles there were. I'm hardly drinking at all while I'm breastfeeding, so Greg must have polished off the rest, and that's in addition to anything he might have while he's out entertaining clients. The last couple of times he's come home late there's been this . . . smell too.'

'What kind of smell?'

'He's been smoking again. He promised to give up when I got pregnant and I thought he had. He thinks I don't know, but his clothes reek of it. And that's the other odd thing, I'm fairly certain some of his clothes have gone missing.'

'Such as?' Millie was intrigued now.

'A couple of pairs of jeans, shirts, sweaters — that kind of thing. I asked him about them and he said that they've been clearing some of the empty offices, so he had to take in some old things that he didn't mind getting dirty, but that was a couple of weeks ago, and he hasn't brought them home again yet. I know Greg puts on this confident front, but he does worry and I know there's something going on that's stressing him. I'm scared he's got involved in something that he shouldn't have.'

'Like what?'

'I don't know. But he works in the gun trade.' Louise gave her a meaningful look.

'And how long has Greg been like this?'

'I don't know exactly. Maybe from about the time when Abigail was born, or just before.'

'It could just be the responsibility of becoming a father for the first time,' said Millie. 'Some men take it very seriously and perhaps mixing with the people he does, in his line of work, makes him anxious about how he can keep you and Abigail safe. Her being poorly won't have helped, either. One of the guys I work with, Charlie Glover, he told me once that when his kids were born he had a terrible time worrying about how he could protect them, knowing what he does about the worst that can happen in the world. I feel the same about Haroon sometimes.'

Louise turned to Millie. 'There's something else too. You'll think I'm being paranoid. I know Greg does.'

'Try me,' said Millie.

'I think we're being watched. Me and Abigail.'

'What makes you think that?' Millie asked.

She glanced quickly around, as if seeking out proof. 'I don't know. That's it. Most of the time it's just a feeling. I look all around and there's no one there. But sometimes there's a van. It's either parked nearby or driving past . . . I'm sure it's the same one.'

In Millie's experience the phrase 'I'm sure' often meant just the opposite, but at the same time it was clear that Louise was experiencing some kind of issue. 'What sort of van?' she asked.

'I don't know.'

'Colour?'

'Blue, I think, or maybe green? Do you think I'm going mad?' she asked now.

'Of course not,' said Millie, forcing some conviction into her voice.

'Is there anything you can do?'

'How do you mean?' Millie was taken aback by the question.

'Well . . . you know. You're a police officer. Could you ask someone to look into it?'

It was patently clear that Louise had not the faintest idea about how the police operated, but what she needed above all, right now, was reassurance. 'Well, I'm a bit limited, being on leave, but I might be able to talk to someone,' said Millie. 'What's the name of Greg's company?'

'Pincott and Easton. It's a family business. It belongs to Greg's uncle. You will be discreet, won't you? If Greg ever found out . . . he'd go medieval if he knew I'd told you all this.'

'I'll do what I can,' said Millie. The sun had come out and was warm on her back. 'Now, they might be too little for it, but we're not. Fancy an ice cream?'

* * *

The only approximations to the name 'Rosa' that emerged from Grace Clifton's friends and family were an elderly great aunt, Rose, and a classmate, Rosie, whose tall, well-padded frame ruled her out of ownership of the second parcel of clothes the moment Vicky Jesson set eyes on her. Nor could Mr or Mrs Clifton identify any further contenders among Grace's social circle.

Charlie Glover spent the day trawling missing persons data online for Birmingham, the West Midlands and beyond, and checking in with relevant voluntary organisations. Again, the Rose and two Rosemarys he turned up were possible but unlikely, having disappeared over the last few months and in one case, two years ago, from outside the city. Mariner's next strategy was to get an alert broadcast through the news media to make it known that, in connection with the Grace Clifton case, police were trying to trace a woman known only as Rosa, who may have information relating to Grace's disappearance. She was being urged to get in touch due to concerns for her safety. The press officer came back to say that the appeal would be put out via local radio and TV news, so until then, where Rosa was concerned, they were largely back to the waiting game.

Chapter Nine

They don't show this on the glossy telly ads, thought Sam McBride as she discreetly wiped a snail-trail of snot from her sleeve and turned her attention back to the child before her. She regarded Dominique Batista with interest. Thanks to a number of high-profile child deaths, all through her PGCE training, and in induction and CPD, the imperative of picking up any initial signs of neglect — which may in turn indicate a more serious safeguarding issue — had been drummed into Sam and her colleagues. What hadn't been dwelt on was how hard this could be. To begin with Sam had felt fairly confident. It wasn't that she was inexperienced in this area. Much of the school's catchment comprised what the policymakers these days helpfully labelled 'troubled families' — a euphemistic way of describing the families deemed to be entirely responsible for society's ills, as if they bore some biological characteristic that set them apart from the rest of the population. All of which was to miss the point that actually these were simply 'families *in* trouble,' exposed to circumstances that were, in the main, beyond their control. Give any one of those Eton-educated slime-buckets a month in the shit-hole that was the Fen Bridge estate and they'd be troubled enough to want to deaden the sharp edges with drugs and alcohol too — and probably not before they'd taken it out on the wife, girlfriend or kids, either.

But Sam had been badly stung last year when a casual expression of concern had almost led to the Spicer twins being taken into care, after what looked like cigarette burns turned out to be impetigo. 'Try to step back and see the wider picture,' Gordon had said at the time, and that was what she'd tried to follow ever since. And now a concern seemed to be popping up in one of the places she would have least expected it.

This afternoon while listening to Dominique Batista read, Sam became aware of several things all at once. Usually so beautifully turned out, today Dominique looked, to put it mildly, unkempt. Her clothes were creased and her school sweatshirt had what looked like an inch-and-a-half dried jam stain running down the front of it. Her beautiful, black, curly hair, normally tightly tied back, was escaping in whole chunks from its badly fastened elastic band and, close up, there was a stale smell about the little girl. But most of all Dominique seemed tense and uncharacteristically quiet. Already identified as a child with a cheeky sense of humour, today Sam's little quips about the story they were reading fell on stony ground. 'Is everything all right, Dominique?' she asked tentatively. 'How's Mummy?' But the little girl had just nodded her head, without looking up, and said, 'Fine.'

Of all the parents in her class, Dominique's mum was one of the friendliest, and she and Sam had quickly built up a good working relationship. Perhaps it was that she was not much older than Sam, or that Sam had a natural sympathy towards her as a single parent (an inevitable disadvantage as far as the head was concerned), but she was obviously keen for her daughter to do well in school. The term was just a few weeks old, but she'd already been in a couple of times to ask how she should be helping

Dominique at home in the evenings, and she seemed like a bright woman. Sam knew vaguely that she and Dominique had only moved to the area recently, having come up from London, but she knew nothing of the circumstances. By origin Ms Batista had indicated that she was Portuguese.

Sam was only too aware that at the slightest whiff of something amiss the head would haul in social services. Dominique and her mum were very close. It only took half a minute watching them having a giggle in the playground at going home time. If Sam betrayed her to 'the social,' how would Dominique or her mum ever trust her again? And she didn't know for sure that anything was amiss. All she'd got here was a kid who was a bit scruffy and uncharacteristically quiet. At what point did that spill over into being a safeguarding issue? Dominique's mum was on her own, so today her daughter's demeanour could mean anything. Ms Batista might be working longer hours, or she could be ill. Maybe the washing machine had broken down. Did they even own a washing machine? The best thing would be to catch Ms Batista at the end of the day for a chat. But then, when three thirty came, Archie Lewis's mum was there complaining that her son had gone home without his designer baseball cap yesterday, and by the time they had found it (safely tucked away in Archie's drawer, of course) and Sam got outside, Mr Warren was there, pulling the gates shut on an empty playground.

It wasn't until later that evening, when Sam was at home and sitting on the sofa in front of the six o'clock news that she recognised what a mistake she had made. One of the featured items about that missing young woman triggered a ripple of unease. As always on a Tuesday, Sam had brought home the children's news books to annotate, ahead of writing up their assessments, and now she sorted through the pile until she found Dominique's. In the first week of term it was customary to ask the children to write about themselves — their homes, families and friends — as a way of helping them to settle into their new class and to find out a little bit about them. There it was on the first page of Dominique's news book in her big, crooked handwriting: *My name is Dominique Batista and I am eight years old. My mummy is called* Rosa. Sam was reaching for her phone just as it started to ring. Sharon, her teaching assistant, had also been watching the news.

* * *

Millie had got home from the park, fed Haroon and then the two of them had promptly fallen asleep on the sofa, so that when Suli came home she hadn't even started on dinner. 'Sorry,' she said. 'We went to the park with Louise this afternoon and I don't seem to have the energy to do more than one thing each day at the moment.'

Suli didn't seem to mind a bit. His easy-going nature was what she loved about him. 'Want to get a takeaway?' he suggested.

'That sounds great.'

'Did you have a good time at the park?' Suli asked Millie later, as they unpacked the cartons of food on the kitchen table.

'Yes. I hope you don't mind — I've asked Louise and her husband for dinner at the weekend.'

'Not at all, it will be nice to meet them,' said Suli. 'They sound an interesting couple.'

'Oh, they're that all right,' Millie told him. 'I can't work them out at all. Greg referred to Louise as a feminist. But what kind of feminist gives up work when she gets married to look after her husband and his house?'

* * *

It had taken all of Mariner's skill and ingenuity to convince Jamie that a game of *Angry Birds* would be preferable to endless repeats of *Pointless* this evening, but he just about managed to get access to the TV as the regional news started. The appeal went out exactly as planned, with the contact number for Granville Lane displayed at the end, but he wasn't holding out much hope. That Rosa's clothes had already arrived through the post was an indication for Mariner that, if she had been the victim of some kind of crime, it had probably already happened, and at least a couple of days ago — during which time any concerned family, friends or work colleagues would surely have come forward. If they hadn't so far, what would persuade them do so now, even if they did get to hear the appeal?

As occasionally happened, Jamie was whacked out and finding it hard to keep his eyes open, so that when Mariner's mobile went, they were going through the nightly prompt-and-reward waiting game that was Jamie's bedtime routine. Mariner had found little to incentivise Jamie apart from the iPad and the TV, so, as payback for brushing his teeth (with help), using the toilet (with verbal encouragement) and putting on his pyjamas (with help) he got to have his iPad in bed for twenty minutes (timed with a clockwork egg-timer) before the light went out. They were at the pyjama stage when the call came, and Mariner thought it might be Superintendent Sharp. What he didn't expect was the duty sergeant from Granville Lane: 'The head teacher from St Martin's primary school has been in touch,' he said. 'They've got an eight-year-old child whose mum, they think, might be missing. Her name is Rosa.'

'What does that mean, "might be missing"?' Mariner asked. 'That's it, Jamie, keep going, one arm in . . .' Jamie was making listless and unsuccessful attempts to get his hand through a non-existent arm hole.

'The class teacher noticed something unusual about the little girl's behaviour and appearance, but she wasn't sure what was going on, so she didn't ask the right questions. But if it's your Rosa, she's a single mum so this child is at home on her own, possibly without any support network. It would explain why she hasn't been reported missing.' The duty sergeant cleared his throat. Everyone, it seemed, was conversant with Mariner's current circumstances. 'Are you able to follow it up, or shall I contact Superintendent Sharp?'

'No, it's fine. I can take care of this,' Mariner lied. 'Where are we up to?'

'The head's got hold of the child's address from their records — it's a flat in Milton Tower on the Fen Bridge, and her name is Dominique Batista. I've suggested that he and the teacher who alerted him meet you there as soon as possible.'

The sergeant gave Mariner the precise address and, after hunting around for the suitable means to do so, he wrote it down. 'Have social services been contacted?' he asked.

'Yeah, but they can't get anyone out there for a couple of hours at least, so I guess it will be a question of bringing the child here in the meantime.'

'That sounds about right,' said Mariner. 'Open up the family interview suite and get some heating on in there, will you? And see if Vicky Jesson is available to come in too. It might help to have her there. It'll be frightening enough for the kid without me wading in with my size tens. Tell the head teacher I'll be there in about fifteen minutes,' he said, his fingers crossed. Jamie had finally succeeded with the T-shirt. 'Well done, mate,' Mariner said.

'Just doing my job,' said the sergeant at the other end of the line.

All the while he was talking Mariner had been mentally reviewing his options, something that had started to become an automatic, reflexive response. He didn't like to call on Tony Knox again so soon after Sunday, so this time he rang Katarina. Since she'd moved into her own flat he saw her only intermittently these days, but she got on well with Jamie and had always assured him he could call on her if he needed to. But her landline rang on unanswered and her mobile went straight to voicemail, which wasn't encouraging. Mariner didn't like asking Mercy to come out this late in the evening, but in the end he was left with no other option. 'Jamie's eaten, and he's all ready for bed, so he shouldn't be any trouble,' Mariner told her. 'Get a taxi, and I'll pay for it when you get here.'

As always, Mercy was offended by the extravagance of a taxi. 'Let me find out what Carlton is up to. I'm sure he will be able to drop me off.'

There were two reasons why Mariner wasn't keen on that idea. For one thing he didn't know how long it would take to locate the elusive Carlton and secure the lift, but also he wasn't (for reasons he couldn't even admit to himself) thrilled at the idea of Carlton knowing where he lived. Secluded as it was, his house had been the target of burglars and drug users in the past, and Carlton was probably well aware of all the property had to offer, including its state-of-the-art entertainment system. 'Look, if this is going to be difficult . . .' he started to say, thinking that maybe this time he would have to let it go and ask Jesson to deal with it. But Mercy hadn't heard him and eventually came back on the line. 'It's fine,' she said. 'Carlton's pickin' me up. I missed the last episode of *Casualty*, so I can catch up on that.'

Mariner went upstairs to change into more suitable work clothes, and as he came back down again he heard the approach of a souped-up engine, revving loudly against a thumping bass beat. He opened his front door to see Mercy climbing out of a tank of a four-by-four — complete with tinted windows and bull bar — that had pulled across the end of the service road. As soon as Mercy had stepped down the driver executed a rapid turn and accelerated away, with the faintest squeal of tyres on tarmac.

Mercy waddled breathlessly to where Mariner stood, waiting with his coat on and car keys in hand. 'See? I told you he's a good boy,' she said, even though Mariner had never questioned that fact out loud. Given that Carlton didn't seem to have a proper job, Mariner was tempted to ask how it was that he could afford such an extravagant car, but now wasn't the time. Minutes later, he was in his own vehicle, hurtling towards the Fen Bridge estate, wondering instead, at the back of his mind, where Carlton might be on his way to or from in such a hurry at this time on a Tuesday evening — maybe it was his embroidery class.

Milton Tower was one of three angular blocks sprouting out of the dingy grey spread of social housing that was the Fen Bridge estate. Bordered by a fringe of scrubby green grass and a collection of undernourished saplings, it was rendered no more attractive by the harsh glare of sodium lighting. Mariner had decided long ago that the council planner who'd come up with the name had a sense of the ironic. Paradise had been irretrievably lost in this neighbourhood, somewhere down the back of life's sofa. Parking his car in the only bay that didn't seem to excessively sparkle with broken glass, he double-checked that the doors were locked before entering the bare, concrete lobby. In the last couple of years, efforts had been made to render the flats more appealing. A jacket of insulation and double glazing had been added around the outside, while the lobby, decorated in an overly bright salmon pink, smelled primarily of fresh paint. A couple to one side seemed to be surreptitiously waiting for the lift, but on closer observation, Mariner noticed the considerable age difference between them. That, along with the man's good quality wool overcoat, seemed to indicate that these were not locals. He went over, already anticipating the negotiations for how the situation should be handled. 'Hello,' he said. 'You're the teachers from St Martin's?'

The man, as tall and lean as Mariner and with a fulsome head of grey hair swept back from his forehead, stood straighter, bridling a little. 'I'm the head, Gordon Rhys,' he corrected Mariner, keeping his hands planted firmly in his pockets. 'And this is my Year Three teacher, Sam McBride.'

'DCI Tom Mariner.' Mariner held up his warrant card for them to see. He couldn't help noticing the proprietorial 'my' and raised an eyebrow at McBride as they shook hands. Blonde and petite with a shapely figure under her parka, Mariner could imagine that the young teacher had to work hard to be taken seriously.

'I feel terrible,' she said. 'I knew there was something not quite right with Dominique, but I just never guessed that this was what it could be.'

'We don't know what it is yet.' Rhys was impatient. 'The mother could be anywhere. Might be on the Costa del Sol for all we know.' He was distracted, keeping an anxious eye on his surroundings, and Mariner realised he was nervous about being here.

'With respect, Gordon, I don't think that's very likely,' Sam said. 'Ms Batista isn't like that.'

'How would we know, Sam? We know hardly anything about her.'

'I know enough to understand that she's a committed parent,' Sam said, firmly.

'Have you any idea where she works?' Mariner asked, partly to diffuse what he sensed was a growing tension.

Sam frowned. 'I don't think I've ever really known, although for some reason I got the impression that it's somewhere in the city centre. On the odd occasions I've tried to talk to Dominique about her mum's work, she's completely clammed up. The contact number we have on file is a personal mobile number, but that's nothing unusual.'

'You've tried calling it?'

'Yes, about half a dozen times,' said McBride. 'It just goes straight to voicemail.'

'It's probably because the job is cash-in-hand and she's claiming benefits as well,' said Rhys. 'It happens, you know,' he added, as if that were proof enough.

‘Actually, I don’t think that has anything to do with it,’ McBride said, flushing deeply. ‘When we’ve had school trips Ms Batista has always paid her contribution, and she’s never asked for—’

Rhys cut her off by ostentatiously checking his watch. ‘Now that you’re here, Inspector, do you actually still need me? We’ve contacted social services, and Sam here is the one who knows Dominique. This has taken me away from a meeting that’s been in the diary for some months—’

‘That’s fine,’ Mariner cut in, annoyed by the man’s skewed priorities. ‘I’m sure we can take it from here.’ He sought confirmation from Sam McBride.

‘All right with me,’ she said.

‘Good, well, I’ll leave you to it. Best of luck,’ said Rhys, with obvious relief, and hurried towards the main door. As an afterthought he turned back from the doorway. ‘You’ll keep me informed, Sam?’

‘Of course.’

‘He’s a charmer,’ said Mariner, when Rhys had gone.

‘Sorry about that,’ said Sam. ‘Gordon’s all right really, but he does seem to have a particular downer on single parents, and it makes me a bit defensive. My mum raised me as a single parent and it hasn’t done me any harm.’

‘Nor me,’ said Mariner.

‘Oh.’ She looked at him anew.

‘I know I look old enough to have grown up in black and white, but we weren’t all Kellogg’s Corn Flakes families back then.’ She waited for further elaboration. ‘You haven’t a clue what I’m talking about, have you?’

‘Not really,’ she smiled sweetly up at him and Mariner could imagine any child warming to her instantly.

‘Right,’ he said. ‘Let’s crack on, shall we? I don’t think social services are going to show up any time soon, so if we do find that Dominique’s at home alone we’ll need to take her to Granville Lane police station to wait for them there. How does that sound?’

'Good,' said Sam. 'I only hope she doesn't panic when she sees me at this time of night.'

'I can't imagine she will,' said Mariner. 'OK, let's get this done. What's the flat number?'

Neither of them was inclined to trust the lifts, so Sam led the way up the concrete stairwell to a flat on the fourth floor, their footsteps echoing as they climbed.

'It'll be better if you make the first approach,' Mariner said to Sam as they climbed the stairs. 'Are you OK to do that?'

They emerged halfway along a narrow landing that had two equally spaced doors on either side. The lighting was dim, and up here the smell of urine had not been entirely successfully glossed over. Flat forty-one was at the end. The small, rectangular reinforced glass window in the top half of the door reminded Mariner of the observation panel in the custody cell doors back at Granville Lane. No light shone behind it. He knocked hard on the wood and they waited, but there was no response. Squatting down, Sam lifted the letterbox flap and peered in, before calling: 'Dominique, are you in there? It's Miss McBride. I've just come to see if you're all right.'

'Can you see anything?' Mariner asked.

McBride straightened up again. 'No, it's pitch dark. Maybe I've got this completely wrong and she isn't there. Oh, God — what if I've got you out here for nothing?'

'It's fine,' said Mariner. 'Better that than she really is in trouble and we fail to act. Why don't you try again?'

McBride crouched by the letterbox, pushed up the flap and called again. This time, as she did so, she stopped short. 'Oh, there's something here.' Bit by bit she pulled through the rough string with its key tied to the end.

'Christ,' said Mariner. 'I hope no one else knows about this.'

'Do we use it?' said McBride.

'It saves me having to demonstrate my manliness by breaking down the door,' Mariner said. 'You go first and I'll follow, just in case she's in there.'

Opening the door they entered the darkened flat, which felt as frigid as the landing outside. McBride flicked the light switch but nothing happened.

'The meter's run out,' said Mariner. He took a torch from his inside coat pocket and switched it on, directing it down at the floor to light the way.

'Dominique?' Sam called, softly. They progressed carefully along a short hallway, and McBride pushed open the first door they came to on the left. The torch beam bounced around an empty bedroom. A second door, on the right, swung open to reveal a small bathroom, but as she pushed open the door at the head of the passageway, Mariner saw instantly from McBride's body language that they had found the little girl.

'Hi, Dominique,' Sam said brightly. 'It's Miss McBride. We were a bit worried about you, so I just came to see if you were all right. I've brought my friend, Tom.' As Mariner came into the room, his eyes adjusting to the darkness and keeping the torch beam directed away from Dominique, he was in time to see McBride slowly advancing on the little girl, who seemed to be frozen to the spot sitting at the end of a sofa. But as McBride cautiously sat down beside her, Dominique flung herself into her teacher's arms and McBride hugged her close. 'It's all right, sweetie, you're safe now,' she soothed, a crack in her voice. After a moment she said, 'We came to see Mummy too. Is she here?'

And Mariner could just make out the little girl's whispered reply. 'I don't know where she's gone.'

Chapter Ten

Leaving Sam to help Dominique gather some belongings and clothes together, Mariner went back out onto the landing and phoned in to the duty sergeant to say that they were on their way back to Granville Lane, and to get that message conveyed to social services. He learned in return that Vicky Jesson had arrived and was waiting for them.

As he paced the landing he became aware of voices, possibly a TV coming from the flat next door, and took the opportunity to ring the doorbell. The thirty-something man who answered, clad in jeans and T-shirt and with a scrubby beard, didn't really know much about the family who lived next to him and had done for the last six months. 'There's a kid, isn't there?' he said. 'The missus said she's seen the woman going out weekends and we hear her come back in the middle of the night. It's the same time, regular as clockwork, but I've never seen a babysitter. The kid must get left there on its own. I thought about reporting it to social services, but you don't like to interfere, do you?' Mariner left his card with the undertaking that he might be back to talk to him again.

When they were ready, securing the flat behind them, they went down to Mariner's car. Tempting as it was to start questioning the little girl on the drive back to Granville Lane, the last thing they needed was for her to clam up on them, so they drove almost in silence, Mariner aware of Sam McBride murmuring comfortingly to her small charge about what would be happening next. In the rear-view mirror he could see Dominique pressed up close to her teacher, a towelling soft toy tucked up under her chin as she sucked on her thumb. Back at Granville Lane, Vicky Jesson met them and took Sam and Dominique into the PPU family room where there were comfortable chairs, books and toys. While they got settled Mariner made a quick call to Mercy to establish that all was well at home. As he got back to the family suite, Jesson emerged, keeping her distance for the moment, as Mariner had. 'I expect she's hungry,' Jesson said, and they went together to get juice, crisps, chocolate and fruit from the canteen. 'How does she seem?' Jesson asked as they loaded up a tray.

'Not bad, considering,' said Mariner. 'I was glad her teacher was there though. I'm not sure that she would have come with a complete stranger.'

'That's reassuring,' said Jesson. 'And her mum is definitely missing?'

'Oh, yes. I think we've found our Rosa. And we haven't asked her yet, but if those clothes were posted when we think they were, sometime on Saturday, it means Dominique has been at home alone at least since then, if not longer.'

Without disturbing them, Jesson took the tray into the room, leaving it close to where Dominique and Sam were beginning to explore the toys, then she retreated to the observation room next door, where Mariner waited and watched. Once she'd overcome her initial shyness, Dominique tucked in to the food.

'God, she must be ravenous, poor little mite,' said Jesson. 'Do you want me to go in and talk to her?'

'It would be helpful if we could at least confirm absolutely that Dominique's mum is the same Rosa whose clothes we've been sent,' Mariner said. 'What do you think?'

'We could try the shoes,' said Jesson. 'They're fairly distinctive and in my experience most little girls are interested in shoes, so hopefully she'll recognise them.'

'After that it's just about getting as much background information as we possibly can about Rosa: her job, her friends, her routines,' said Mariner. 'According to the neighbour she goes out in the evenings and leaves Dominique on her own. It might be why Dominique is reluctant to talk about her mum's job. But if we're to find Rosa, the sooner we can establish where she works, the better. Are you OK to have a go?'

'If I get the chance before social services get here, yes,' said Jesson.

But as they went out into the corridor, the door at the far end opened and a young man, who could only be the duty social worker, appeared with the desk sergeant. There followed a delicate negotiation process at the end of which Jesson was allowed ten minutes with Dominique, on the understanding that she wouldn't ask the little girl anything that would make her more distressed. It was the best they could hope for, but Jesson would be up against it.

Bringing her maternal experience to it, Vicky Jesson's interview technique was flawless. Mariner remained behind the one-way glass of the observation room, taking notes, with the social worker also watching. The air was loaded with expectation, all the adults focused on one little girl and desperately trying not to make it look that way. Mariner was impressed at how quickly Jesson established a rapport with her.

'We don't think that Mummy just decided not to come home,' she said. 'We think something might have stopped her. She might be poorly, or she might have hurt herself, so we want to try and find her to make sure she's all right. But we need you to help us. Is that OK?'

Dominique nodded.

'Does Mummy go to work?' asked Jesson.

Dominique briefly glanced up to make eye contact with Jesson, acknowledging the question, but she offered no definitive response.

'What kind of work does she do?' Jesson asked, disregarding this.

Dominique returned to her picture. 'It's a secret,' she said, in a barely audible whisper.

'I see,' said Jesson, neutrally. 'Why is that?'

The little girl lifted her shoulders.

'Is that what Mummy says?'

Another nod of the head.

'Mummy wears a special badge with her name on it when she goes to work, doesn't she? Why does she need to do that?'

'So the people know what she's called.'

'Which people are they?'

Dominique shrugged again, unable or unwilling to say.

'Perhaps you could draw me a picture of Mummy,' Jesson suggested lightly. 'And then you could tell me all about what she's doing.'

'That's a good idea,' Sam McBride smiled encouragingly. 'You're really good at drawing. We've got some of Dominique's pictures on the wall in the classroom,' she told Jesson, but mainly for Dominique's benefit.

It did the trick and they waited patiently while she drew the picture. Nearly ten minutes had passed. While she was engaged in drawing Mariner slipped into the room and placed the shoes down on the floor beside Vicky Jesson. Although Dominique glanced up momentarily, he didn't distract her from her task. When she had finished, shortly after Mariner had returned to the observation booth, Dominique sat back so that Jesson could see what she had drawn.

'That's brilliant,' said Jesson. 'I love Mummy's hair. It's like yours, isn't it? Lovely and dark and curly. What's that she's holding in her hand?'

Dominique murmured something in response.

'A brush?' hazarded Jesson. 'Is Mummy a hairdresser?'

A flicker of a smile crossed Dominique's lips. Mariner couldn't see the picture, but there was a hint that Vicky was teasing her. Dominique shook her head and said something.

'Oh, a sweeping brush,' said Jesson. 'I see. She's sweeping the floor. Is Mummy cleaning up? She's a cleaner?'

And finally Dominique smiled broadly and nodded her head, as if all along this had just been a simple guessing game.

'And is that where Mummy went on Saturday?'

'No, that's her other job,' said Dominique, as if Jesson was being a bit slow.

'So what does Mummy do at the weekend?'

The little girl's head was down again as she added more detail to her drawing. 'That's a secret,' she said, without looking up.

And that was as far as they got. Despite Jesson's careful questioning, either Dominique didn't know exactly where her mum worked, or she was determined to hold on to that particular nugget. Mariner was inclined to think it was the former. Jesson tried to get at the question obliquely, asking how Mummy got to work but all they found out was 'on the bus' which without a number, could have been to anywhere in the city. And when Dominique yawned, twice in close succession, the social worker said that was enough.

Jesson brought the bag containing Rosa's shoes out of the room with her untouched. 'She's a bright little cookie,' she said of Dominique. 'I think it wouldn't be beyond her to work out why we've got her mummy's shoes and it's not fair to put her through that. I think we can be pretty certain they belong to Rosa Batista.'

Mariner couldn't fault Jesson's judgement on either count.

'Is there anything more I can do?' asked Sam. She looked shattered.

'You've already helped a great deal,' said Mariner. 'If it wasn't for your vigilance we'd still have no idea who Rosa is.' He gave a wry smile. 'Don't want to join the police, do you?'

'No, thanks, I'm quite happy being a teacher,' she assured him. 'Do you think something's happened to Ms Batista? You're linking her to that girl, Grace, who's gone missing, aren't you?'

'There are some common factors,' said Mariner, deliberately playing it down.

'Oh, God.'

'How did everything seem with Dominique and her mum, before this week?' Mariner asked.

'I've been thinking about that,' said McBride. 'There was something. A sort of incident, a few weeks back.'

'What kind of incident?'

'Well, more something I noticed. When Ms Batista came to collect Dominique she had some quite nasty bruising around her eye and to the side of her face. I wanted to ask her how it happened, but I chickened out a bit. I just asked generally if everything was OK, and she said she'd had an accident at work. It was obvious that she didn't want to talk about it.'

'What about Dominique's father?'

'We've never seen him. Ms Batista has always described herself as a single mum, though I understand they moved up here from London a few months ago for what she said was a new start, so I assumed that might have meant leaving him behind.'

'What about partners since she's been here?'

'None that Dominique has ever talked about, or who I've seen. As far as I'm aware it's always been her mum who collects her from school.'

'Does Rosa have any friends, other mums that she talks to in the playground?' Jesson asked.

But Sam shook her head. 'I've never really seen her with anyone, but I can ask around at school tomorrow.'

'That would be great,' said Mariner. 'I'll get someone to run you home.'

* * *

Much later, when the social worker had left to take Dominique to a temporary foster family, Jesson and Mariner walked out of the building together.

'I could have handled this, you know,' Jesson said.

'I do,' said Mariner. 'But I wanted to be here myself. As I'm sure you know, my domestic circumstances at the moment are a little restrictive, so I feel it's important to . . .' Mariner floundered, unable to identify exactly why he'd felt this compulsion to be here.

'Prove your commitment?' Jesson added for him. Knowing she'd nailed it, she smiled. 'Without meaning to sound chippy or anything,' she added. 'Now you know what it's like to be a woman.'

'It's a fair cop,' said Mariner. 'You came here from Steelhouse Lane, didn't you? Where were you before that?'

'Bromfield mostly.'

So, north of the city and not a patch that Mariner had ever worked. They walked in silence for a few minutes, until Vicky said, 'My partner was Brian Riddell.'

Ah. Now Mariner felt clumsy and insensitive. 'Of course. God, I'm sorry. I felt sure that we had met . . . your name and face were so familiar to me, yet . . .'

'Yes, well, I was all over the papers for a while. And perhaps you came to the memorial service?'

'I did.'

'There were a lot of people there—'

'And most of us in uniform. You could hardly be expected to remember us all. I'm very sorry about Brian. From what I understand he was a good officer.'

'Thank you.'

She seemed perfectly controlled and Mariner tried to remember exactly when it was that Sergeant Brian Riddell and his partner had responded to what they thought was a routine 999 call in the Aston area of the city, only to be greeted by a hail of bullets. According to the stories, Riddell had acted fast, throwing himself in front of the young PC as a shield and had effectively saved the man's life at the cost of his own. It had been a heroic last gesture. By the time back-up had arrived at the scene the gunman was long gone, though traces of his presence remained in the derelict building from which the fatal shots were fired. The incident had shaken officers the length and breadth of the country and out of this was born Operation Athena, its aim to track, monitor and ultimately curtail the illegal importation of guns into the country. At the same time, they were also working to locate the murder weapon, a Mach 10, commonly known as the 'spray and pray.' How long ago was it now — eighteen months? It explained a lot about how contained and pragmatic Jesson seemed.

* * *

Rosa Batista was having one of those terrifying dreams in which she was completely powerless and unable to move. She had a sensation of being stranded somewhere dark, cold and alien to her. She knew she would wake up from it soon. These nightmares came to her on a regular basis, though not so much since they had moved away from London. All the same, as part of the dream, she couldn't help being fearful for Dominique, hoping she had given her daughter enough skills to be able to look after herself. Dominique was a sensible child but she was still only eight years old. Even though rationally Rosa knew that she would wake up from this soon, she had no idea what was happening to her — or why. Was it something she did? Was it her fault? She couldn't begin to comprehend it. She only knew that she wanted to wake now.

* * *

It was late when Mariner got home and he thought his tired eyes must be playing tricks when — as he was locking his car — he saw a shadowy figure emerge from round the back of his house, setting off at a brisk walk towards the edge of the park. Tall and wearing some kind of tracksuit with a hood, it was impossible to identify the individual, though Mariner was fairly sure it was a male. As he watched, the figure seemed to increase its speed, keeping close to the trees and finally disappearing out of sight. It may just have been a man walking back from a night out along the tow path, but even that would have been pretty unusual behaviour.

'Was there someone else here?' Mariner asked Mercy when he'd let himself in.

She looked suddenly awkward, the first time Mariner had witnessed her in any kind of discomfort. 'Whatever makes you think that?' she said struggling to meet his eye. 'Just me and Jamie here, same as always. Isn't that right, Jamie?'

'I've never asked you,' said Mariner, 'what it is it that Carlton does. His job, I mean.'

She chuckled, relaxing again. 'Oh, this and that. He's a clever boy. He can turn his hand to lots of things. I try not ask too many questions, you know?'

Mariner could quite imagine. He couldn't stop himself, as they were talking, from scanning the room, just to check that everything was intact. He hoped that Mercy didn't notice. He phoned for a taxi, and when Mercy had gone, made a mental note to look Carlton up on CRIMINT to see if he was known; an urge that up until now he'd resisted. He felt bad about it, as if he were somehow betraying Mercy's trust, but he told himself it was as much for her protection as his. And whatever his personal reservations might be, his first responsibility was to Jamie.

Chapter Eleven

Charlie Glover and a couple of uniforms were assigned first thing on Wednesday morning to search Rosa Batista's flat.

'What are we looking for exactly?' one of the officers asked Glover once he'd briefed them.

'Anything that tells us more about Rosa, basically. Where she works, details of friends, family, that kind of thing,' said Glover.

In daylight, especially on such a dreary day as this, the flat looked barren and unwelcoming and after a couple of days with no heating the air was frigid. The furnishings were minimal, and apart from the beds, seemed to have been chosen for function rather than aesthetics and Glover quickly realised that this search wouldn't take them very long. In fact, he probably could have managed alone.

The living room contained what looked like a second-hand sofa, the brown upholstery faded and sagging, a TV on a stand and a small coffee table, on which an ashtray had been pushed to one side to make way for a child's drawings. Dominique had been busy in her mum's absence. Against one wall was a small sideboard that looked of post-war vintage and a couple of photo frames on top displayed a picture of Dominique in her school uniform and another informal shot of her in an affectionate hug with a man, presumably her dad. Sam McBride had estimated Rosa's age to be about twenty-five, but this man looked older. It was here that Glover concentrated his efforts, leaving the other rooms to the uniforms. A drawer in the cupboard was evidently where Rosa Batista kept her paperwork and Glover quickly found a passport and medical cards, confirming Rosa's age as twenty-six, and a P60 from a couple of years ago that had her National Insurance number on it.

A couple of letters from a council housing department pertained to an address in south London and there was a handful of other, more personal correspondence, including a couple of postcards from Istanbul, both addressed to Dominique and signed 'Papa.' But though the P60 provided details that could be traced, there was nothing here that gave any clue as to Rosa's extended family or, more importantly, her current place of work. At the bottom of the drawer were the odd bits and pieces that accumulate in any household: paperclips, what looked like broken bits of things and a number of insignia of the kind given in exchange for charity donations — a daffodil, a poppy and crossed rifles.

The others turned up nothing of significance in either of the bedrooms, but Glover had a quick look around both, just to make sure. Whilst the double bed in the main bedroom was turned back and seemed to show signs of having a recent occupant, the single bed in what was clearly Dominique's room was neatly made. Glover thought it probably meant, rather touchingly, that the little girl had slept in her mum's bed for comfort, like his own three often had when he was on nights, snuggling up with Helen. It had been brave of Dominique to stay here on her own for two nights, which made Charlie Glover wonder what kind of life she'd had up until now that would give her the resilience to cope with it.

There were few clothes in Rosa Batista's wardrobe, most of them casual — jeans and T-shirts, along with a couple of summer dresses — and Glover couldn't help but compare it with Helen's collection that sometimes seemed to take over the whole bedroom. It was one of the things they occasionally disagreed about. Most effort of all had been made in the little girl's bedroom, where duvet and curtains matched, a chest of drawers held lovingly washed and pressed outfits in co-ordinating colours, and the bookshelf groaned with picture books above a row of cuddly toys sitting on the bed. It was obvious where Rosa Batista's wages ended up and the sight of this room made Glover feel cold inside. Rosa Batista would not have abandoned her precious daughter. Something bad had happened to her.

In the small kitchen was the evidence of Dominique's recent efforts to prepare food. A knife rested on an open tub of cheap margarine and there were breadcrumbs and smears of jam on the counter top. But aside from a few tins and packets in the cupboards, there was no other food in the flat. A mouldy loaf had been consigned to the bin, which, half full, was beginning to smell, despite the cold. A biscuit tin in a high cupboard contained a large amount of cash and several pre-payment tokens for the electricity meter. It had been placed too far out of reach for the little girl. Charlie counted out the bank notes: two hundred and fifty pounds — a large sum to have been left lying around the house like that.

* * *

Mariner was making the most of a few spare minutes at his computer by looking up Carlton Brown on CRIMINT. To his slight disappointment, Carlton wasn't listed as someone already known to West Midlands Police, but then the boy didn't necessarily share the same surname as his mother. He'd have to find a way of getting that information from Mercy without arousing her suspicion. Tony Knox would have known how to do it.

There were still plenty of times when Mariner missed his sergeant, both personally and professionally, and although the new team was starting to gel, there were still odd moments when he could sense the tension between Jesson and Glover. So far the only reason he could see for this might be Jesson's frustration that Glover didn't seem to share her sense of urgency. She had been keen to search Rosa Batista's flat, Mariner could tell, but instead he'd asked Glover to do it. Charlie Glover had a reputation within Granville Lane for being a bit dull, lacking initiative and therefore never likely to rise above the rank of detective constable and Mariner knew that at the moment he was struggling to try and fill Tony Knox's rather more inspired shoes. A committed family man and newly converted to a brand of evangelical Christianity, Charlie had also become more circumspect, rarely sharing in what could sometimes spill over into lewd office banter. But he was also reliable, a workhorse who would keep labouring away methodically at accumulating the required evidence.

There was a knock on the door and seeing Superintendent Sharp, Mariner quickly closed the CRIMINT page.

'How's it going?' Sharp asked, leaning on the door frame and folding her arms.

'You know we've identified Rosa — that we found her daughter?' Mariner said.

'I saw on the incident log,' said Sharp. 'She'd been at home alone since Saturday?'

'Looks like it, poor kid. We didn't get much from her, but I think it was everything we could.'

'Well, I've agreed to a press briefing at eleven,' Sharp told him. 'So perhaps before that you could bring me up to speed.'

'We're just waiting for Charlie Glover to get back from his search of the Batistas' flat.'

'OK, let me know when he's here and I'll meet you in the incident room.'

* * *

Sharp joined them as Mariner was asking the newly returned Glover about photographs of Rosa.

Charlie shook his head. 'This was all.' He produced the snaps of Dominique with the man presumed to be her father.

'That's a pain,' said Mariner.

'How about the teacher, Sam McBride?' said Jesson. 'We could get her to help us put together an e-fit.'

'Looks as if we'll need to,' said Mariner. 'Are you OK to organise that?' She noted it down on her pad.

'Now that we've got hold of Rosa's social security details, it should be straightforward enough to trace her employer,' Glover went on. 'I've phoned it through and the DWP are going to get back to us as soon as they can.'

'Let's not hold our breath,' said Sharp. 'They're not known for their speed and efficiency.'

'And if there is no record?' queried Jesson.

'Then we have to wonder if Rosa's extra weekend job is somehow illicit,' Mariner said. 'She's in her mid-twenties. At the weekend she works nights, probably in the city centre and hasn't told her young daughter exactly what it is she does, because "it's a secret." There are obvious conclusions to be drawn from that.'

'We recovered two hundred and fifty in cash that was stashed in a tin in the kitchen,' added Charlie. 'And it might explain why none of her work mates has come forward.'

Now they were all wondering the same thing. 'But how many toms do we know who wear name badges?' said Jesson, quashing the idea.

'I've rung the foster carer,' she went on. 'If she gets the chance she's going to ask Dominique again about her mum's job.'

It was a big ask and the foster carer had been understandably reluctant to subject Dominique to anything that would make the little girl more anxious about her mother. *I'll see what I can do*, was the most that she would promise.

'We found an address in Acton,' said Glover, moving along. 'So I've contacted the Met and they're going to send someone out to talk to the extended family and check things out there.'

'Thanks, Charlie, that's good work,' said Mariner, noticing Jesson's brief nod of approval.

'So what do you think?' she asked Mariner.

'That there are too many similarities between the disappearance of Rosa Batista and Grace Clifton to discount as simply coincidence,' he said. 'I mean, they're obviously linked now by whatever has happened to them, but there must also be something they have in common that has made them both subject to . . . well . . . whatever it is that's going on here. A priority is to try and establish Rosa's last known movements.'

'That's going to be difficult until we've found out where she went to work on Saturday evening, or indeed if she even turned up there,' Jesson pointed out.

'We've got a press conference shortly,' said Sharp. 'Now that we have Rosa's name, hopefully someone will come forward and will be able to fill in some of the gaps for us.'

'Meanwhile,' said Mariner, 'we continue to work on finding out what, if any, common ground there is between these two women.'

'You think we're talking abduction?' said Glover.

'That would make the most sense,' said Mariner. 'And by someone who's been kind enough to send us their clothes, washed and neatly pressed, the shoes polished. Someone who has taken a good deal of care over them.'

'It's ritualistic,' said Jesson. 'Or what another woman might do.'

'Possibly.'

'And quite clever, when you think about it,' said Sharp. 'If these women have been the victims of someone who has harmed them, sending the clothes to us means not having to dispose of them and run the risk of them being discovered somewhere that could incriminate them. And washing them first eliminates the risk of DNA evidence.'

'Clever but risky,' said Mariner. 'Depends how thorough they've been about covering their tracks in sending them. We need to follow up on that franking mark and find out for sure.'

'Mister Toad strikes again,' said Jesson, with a wry smile. 'Looks like we're up against a washerwoman.'

'A washerwoman who likes to keep some mementoes for her– or himself,' Mariner reminded them. 'Grace Clifton's work shirt was missing and we haven't got a top for Rosa Batista. We might be looking at a trophy collector. Unless there's some substance on those garments that didn't come out in the washing of them, which could also mean that he or she has some forensic awareness.'

'But even after the reconstruction, no new witnesses have come forward,' Jesson pointed out. 'If we are looking at two cases of abduction, whoever has taken these women was able to do it without drawing attention — and has possibly done it twice.'

'In the city late at night,' said Glover. 'How about taxi drivers?'

'There's nothing to suggest that either woman is in the habit of taking taxis,' Jesson countered. 'I think it would be an extravagance for both of them — they're essentially on their way home from work, remember, and neither of them is especially well off. Also Grace had a firm commitment to meeting her friends. She sent that text, just as she was leaving Symphony Hall, to say that she was on her way. If that was genuinely from her and she then changed her plans, she surely would have let her friends know.'

'It's also probable that these women are of the same physical "type", isn't it?' said Sharp. 'Grace's mother is Iranian, we think Rosa is Portuguese in origin. She would also have had dark hair, olive skin, surely?'

'Could they have been mistaken for Muslim women?' Jesson wondered.

'And if they were?'

'I'm just thinking that Grace was a bit of a rebel. The clothes of hers that have come to us are a miniskirt and high heels.'

'Rosa's wardrobe was mostly strappy tops and dresses that would leave a lot of flesh exposed,' said Charlie. 'It might be someone who has a thing about Muslim women dressing more modestly.'

'Let's just resist jumping to any premature conclusions,' said Mariner.

'What about mobile phones?' Sharp asked.

'Neither found and when the numbers are called, they both go straight to voicemail,' Mariner told her, 'which would indicate that they've been switched off, run down or possibly even destroyed.'

'Do we think this is someone they know?' asked Sharp.

'It's possible. We'll continue working our way through friends and acquaintances. There's nothing yet to suggest that Grace has ever crossed paths with Rosa, but that's something else we have to determine. We have to accept that there's some kind of link between them — some distant acquaintance, or simply someone they have both come into contact with, maybe even in the vicinity of where they disappeared. Could be something as casual as buying coffee from the same Starbucks. Something we *do* know: they've both been described as outgoing. It's possible someone may have read too much into that warmth.'

'Then it could be someone asking for their help,' suggested Charlie.

'That's true. They would need to be plausible and unthreatening, which again I suppose might point to a female. We're told that both women are friendly but no one has said anything to suggest that either of them is naive or stupid.'

It was just coming up to eleven o'clock and Sharp got to her feet. 'Right, Tom, we need to go and talk to the press.' Mariner got up to follow her.

'You might want to ditch those,' said Jesson.

Looking down to where she was pointing Mariner saw that he'd still got the fob of Jamie's PECS picture communication cards dangling from his belt.

'Yes,' said Sharp. 'We wouldn't want our friends in the media to think we're finding it that hard to talk to one another.'

'Vicky Jesson seems to have settled in well,' said Sharp as she and Mariner descended the stairs to what was used as the main press briefing room.

Mariner nodded in agreement. 'She did a great job with Dominique last night.' He turned to look at the superintendent. 'I wish I'd known who she was though. I felt a right tit when she told me she was Brian Riddell's partner.'

'Ah, so you found out,' said Sharp. 'Sorry, but it was the way she wanted it. A new start, with no fuss. I think it's one of the reasons she chose to come here.'

'One of the reasons?'

Sharp shook her head in disbelief. 'You really don't have a clue, do you?' she said, enigmatically.

As agreed, the focus of the press conference was the continuing appeal for anyone else who may know Rosa Batista, especially her employers, to come forward. Details of her known working pattern were shared accordingly. Press co-operation was crucial in keeping communication channels open, increasing the chances that anyone with new information would come forward and encouraging women who may be around the city centre at night to take extra care. Sharp admitted that concerns for the safety of the two missing women were growing and she ended the short interview by looking directly into the camera. 'We now have two young women who have disappeared in unexplained circumstances in or around the city centre and we would urge members of the public, especially women, to be vigilant.'

Chapter Twelve

On Wednesday morning, after Suli had gone to work and Haroon was fed, changed and sleeping, Millie logged on to her computer to do a little research. She began on the NHS website with a search for 'heart murmurs.' She'd heard the phrase before, of course, but didn't know exactly what it meant. Once she began reading, the reasons for Louise's excessive anxiety became only too apparent. If this had happened to Haroon, Millie would have been beside herself. Even though Louise's baby had turned out to be fine, she could see how the stress would be enough to put a strain on the strongest of marriages.

Next, Millie looked up 'Pincott and Easton gunmakers.' At first glance it was far from the modest little company that Louise had implied. The website was a slick multimedia platform that proclaimed the outfit as a world leader in the production of sports and hunting rifles and pistols. The buying options, offering a choice of currencies (headed up by US dollars), indicated a worldwide market, especially the United States where hunting and shooting were firmly embedded in the Constitution.

Looking into the background of the company confirmed what Louise had already told her — that it had begun as a family concern and had a rich history dating back to the early nineteenth century. One of the first of its kind, Pincott and Easton had been established when gun-making was just one of the hundreds of manufacturing businesses in Birmingham. Started by Greg's great-great-grandfather, it was now his uncle who was the chief executive. Most similar companies had long since gone under, but Pincott and Easton had survived and seemed to be thriving, mainly thanks to its ability to adapt to the changing market. A whole page was given over to the 2012 London Olympics, Pincott and Easton having supplied hardware for some of the shooting events. The firm had naturally diminished somewhat from its heyday, when hunting and shooting were a way of life, but the main premises in the city's old gun quarter had been retained. There remained a small, specialist manufacturing operation, with an emphasis very much on custom-made quality and craftsmanship rather than mass production, along with an import/export sideline.

There was nothing as vulgar as pricing quoted on the site, which in Millie's experience meant that the figures were high enough to deter potential customers, but it was clear nonetheless that this was a lucrative business. Weekend breaks staying on the family's country estate were also advertised for particular times of the year (presumably coinciding with the hunting season, but as a city girl this was all new territory for Millie), allowing customers the opportunity to properly test out Pincott and Easton's merchandise. The emphasis was very much on an individualised service and prospective clients were encouraged to contact Greg directly to discuss their requirements, making him easily approachable for anyone. There was nothing, on the other hand, to indicate that it was anything but above board. If Greg was up to something illicit then Millie would have to look elsewhere.

Before leaving the page Millie looked up the other company personnel. It was a small team and predominantly male, though there were also photographs of the chief executive's PA and another female administrator, both of whom were young and attractive. She considered what Louise had told her about Greg's behaviour: staying out late, being secretive, smelling different . . . it could all be explained by the age-old routine — that Greg was having an affair with a colleague. She could see how hard that would be for Louise to stomach, especially at this time in her life.

* * *

On Wednesday evening, Mariner was home for once in good time to meet the day-centre transport, and found a message waiting for him on his answer machine. It was from Simon at Manor Park, a specialist residential facility for adults with ASD, to say that they had a space that weekend for Jamie to come and stay for a couple of days. 'Bring him over first thing tomorrow and he can stay until Monday evening,' said Simon.

Before Anna had uprooted Jamie to Herefordshire, he had lived very happily at Manor Park for a while. By virtue of this, it was one of the first facilities Mariner had contacted when the responsibility for Jamie had landed on him. In high demand, it was full, of course, but after some negotiation, he'd managed to secure Jamie the occasional day or two back there on the understanding that if and when a more permanent place arose, it would be offered to him. The term 'respite' had become unfashionable, with its negative connotations of relief from some kind of burden, but for Mariner, it was the perfect description. It meant three days in which he could be confident that Jamie was safe, but enjoying himself too. 'You're going on your holidays,' he told Jamie. 'Won't that be nice?'

'Nice,' Jamie agreed, as if he fully understood.

Driving into the grounds on Thursday morning Mariner was struck anew with the contrast between Manor Park and Towyn. In a rural area and similarly based around a former manor house, at Manor Park the complex was dominated by the new and modern wings that had sprouted up on either side of the original building: light, airy and well maintained. There were always staff about, making it impossible to walk into the establishment at will, and everyone they encountered had a smile and a greeting — first for Jamie and then for Mariner. The facility was also a prestigious practitioner training facility, so many of the employees were young and enthusiastic about their work, and despite the challenging needs of many of the residents, the atmosphere was invariably relaxed. All of this meant that the competition to get in to Manor Park was fierce, which was why Jamie belonged to a privileged minority who could afford to pay the hefty fees.

'Swimming today,' said Dan, who came to meet them, instantly putting a smile on Jamie's face. One of his favourite activities, but a rare treat, it was something Mariner tended to shy away from — in his experience, visits to the pool were simply too fraught. Public swimming baths and Jamie's general lack of inhibition didn't go well together.

Jamie happily settled, Mariner's return journey was long and drawn out, thanks to a succession of slow-moving farm vehicles along with the normal morning congestion into the city, but he took it all serenely. As a result, he was in the incident room catching up on overnight developments when a call came through from Detective Chief Inspector Spratt at Lea Green police station.

'We have a Paddy Henderson here,' said Spratt in his deep, Welsh baritone. 'His partner, Dee Henderson, didn't come home last night after her two-'til-ten shift at the QE. Given what you've got going on over there I thought you might want to come and talk to him.'

'Christ on a bike,' said Mariner to no one in particular, covering the receiver with his hand. 'We might have another one. Someone's gone into Lea Green to report a missing woman.' He looked over at Jesson. 'Grab your coat, Vicky, you've pulled.'

Jesson looked up from her computer screen. 'Actually, do you mind if I don't, sir?'

Mariner met her gaze and saw her colour rise a little. He'd never known her to refuse a request before. He could make an educated guess as to the reason and decided to let it drop.

Glover had noticed too. 'What do you think all that was about?' he speculated mildly, as he and Mariner drove out towards the north of the city.

'You know whose partner Vicky was?' asked Mariner.

'Ah, right,' said Glover. 'Is Lea Green where Riddell was based?'

'I'm not sure,' said Mariner. 'But it was somewhere up in the north. If it's not where he was at the time he died, he probably worked out of it at some point.'

'I keep forgetting about all that,' said Glover. 'She copes with it so well, doesn't she?'

'Yes.' Mariner didn't like to admit that he hadn't managed to work it out for himself. 'I suppose she's had no choice but to get on with it in some respects, for the sake of the kids.'

'And how are you doing?' Glover asked.

It took Mariner a moment to grasp what Glover meant. 'Oh, I'm fine,' he said, when he did. The question caught him off guard. Although there was rarely a day when Anna didn't pass through his mind, those visits were, he realised, becoming more transient and less painful.

'Well, if ever you feel the need for further support, you know the Lord—'

'Yes, thanks, Charlie. I'll be sure to let Him know,' Mariner said. He should have seen that one coming. It was going too far to describe Charlie as a 'bible-basher', but at the same time he rarely missed an opportunity to remind his colleagues of the Lord's presence in any hour of need. In this situation Mariner was tempted to ask Charlie what the Lord's reasoning might be in taking two young women from their families and putting their loved ones through hell, but he knew from experience that the answer would be entirely unsatisfactory, so he let it be. But he did also wonder if Charlie had made a similar offer to Vicky, and if this had given rise to the apparent tension between them.

* * *

Lea Green was one of the few remaining Victorian city police stations, brick-built with the original arched windows and Gothic-style entrance. The reception area had, for obvious security reasons, been modernised, but the history of the place was ingrained in the atmosphere and the smell. The interview rooms were of the formal questioning variety, with high, frosted windows and the harsh strip-lighting gave Paddy Henderson a washed-out pallor. Small and muscular, his shaven head masked male-pattern baldness and a livid scar about two inches long ran along the left underside of his jaw.

'I thought she must have stayed over at the hospital, like,' said Henderson, of his partner. He spoke quickly, with a hint of an East Midlands accent: Derby or Nottingham, Mariner thought. 'When she's working late shifts, she sometimes doesn't want to trail all the way back over here. So if I can't get over to pick her up, she stays in the nurses' home overnight, like. But she always texts me to let me know that's what she's doing. When I called her mobile this morning to find out if she wanted picking up tonight, her phone went straight to voicemail. I rang the ward where she works and they said she left at the usual time last night to come home.'

'And she's a nurse?' Mariner checked.

'Yes, on the critical care ward.'

'So when did you last see her?'

'Yesterday morning before I went to work. She was going out soon after. She doesn't drive, you see. I mean, she tried learning, like, but she never passed her test, so she's on public transport. She gets the train into town and walks through the city centre to get the bus from there. I don't like her doing it at night but . . .' He shrugged. 'I try to get over and pick her up when I can, but what with work and the kids, I can't always get away. And she's careful, like. She'd only take the main streets that are brightly lit, and where there are folk about.' Reaching into his trouser pocket Henderson got out a packet of cigarettes and a lighter.

'I'm sorry,' said Glover. 'You can't . . .'

'Oh, right.' His face fell.

'Do you want to step outside for a bit?' Mariner suggested.

'Nah, you're all right.' But the pack remained in his hand, and he turned it over and over in his fingers as they talked.

'So after leaving work, Dee would be in the city centre at what, about half past ten?' said Glover.

'Yeah, if she managed to get the train all right.'

'How long have you been married?' Mariner asked.

'Oh, we're not married — not yet.' Henderson allowed himself a sardonic smile. 'Had to wait for the divorces to come through first of all and then what with the little 'un coming along . . . But we've been together five years now, and Dee decided to take my name.'

'Mr Henderson, there are some questions I need to ask you that will probably feel intrusive, but I need to ask them nonetheless,' Mariner said. 'How are things between you and Dee?'

'We're good,' said Henderson quickly. 'Ups and downs like everyone else and the kids keep us on our toes, but we're OK.' The cigarette pack swivelled at speed and he looked from Mariner to Glover and back again. 'We have a nice life together.'

'And where were you last night?' asked Mariner.

'At home with the kids. We've got three. I mean the older two are Dee's kids, and then we've got our little princess, Tia.'

'Would the older children be able to back you up on that?'

'Up until about half nine, when the oldest went to bed.'

'And after that, what did you do?' Mariner asked.

Breaking eye contact, Henderson shifted in his seat. 'I spent a couple of hours on the computer going through the books for the business, then I went to bed myself at about midnight.'

'What kind of business are you in?'

'I'm a plumber, self-employed.'

So the white patches under his fingernails were probably builders' caulk, thought Mariner. 'Is it doing well?' he asked.

'Not too bad, as it happens. I work with a couple of regular building contractors, like, as well as doing a few domestics.'

'Do you have a photograph of Dee?' Mariner asked.

Henderson took out his wallet, and from it a creased snapshot of a woman with three young children. 'It was taken a couple of years ago, like,' said Henderson. 'The kids are older now: eleven, nine and four.' Dee Henderson had short brown hair and a wide, toothy smile.

'How would you describe her?' Mariner asked.

Henderson smiled. 'Happy,' he said. 'And friendly. She's a brilliant mum.' And then he seemed to remember where he was, and the smile died on his lips.

* * *

'What did you think?' Mariner asked Glover as they crawled through the Queensway Tunnel on their way back to Granville Lane.

'I'm not sure,' said Glover. 'It's natural that he'd be worried about his partner, but he couldn't sit still, could he?'

'There was a lot of nervous energy there,' Mariner agreed, 'though that may have been because he was desperate for a smoke.'

'If he wanted it that badly why didn't he take up your offer? He didn't seem very relaxed talking about his business either.'

Mariner smiled to himself. Typical of squeaky-clean Charlie to be slow on the uptake. 'Do you think it's possible that at that time of night, with his partner out, Henderson might have been up to something else on the computer?'

'Oh. Yes, I suppose so,' said Charlie.

'But until we can do some more digging we'll have to take him at his word. Meanwhile it does present us with the very real possibility that we now have three women missing. We'll know for sure if we get another parcel of clothes in the next day or two.'

'I can't make up my mind if that will make it better or worse,' said Glover.

Back at Granville Lane, Mariner reported back to Superintendent Sharp before taking this latest development into the incident room. Almost ceremonially, he added the photo given him by Paddy Henderson to that of Grace Clifton alongside the e-fit of Rosa Batista on the ever-growing incident board. At least it felt as if he was doing something positive.

'Do we think this is another one?' Vicky Jesson asked.

'There are enough similarities to treat it as such,' Mariner said. 'But there are some differences too that mean we should be cautious. Dee Henderson is petite and slim, with shorter brown hair. She's significantly older than Grace and Rosa, and is also in a serious, long-term relationship.'

‘Perhaps our washerwoman is becoming less discerning.’

‘We’ll reserve judgement until we know more about Dee Henderson.’

‘So what’s next?’

‘We go and talk to her work colleagues,’ said Mariner.

Chapter Thirteen

The recently opened Queen Elizabeth hospital was as slick and clean as an airport, with easily as much foot traffic. It was white, bright and shiny, with an army of volunteers meeting and greeting, transporting patients from distant car parks and directing visitors.

A woman — whose blue polo shirt asked *Can I help you?* — pointed them in the direction of the first-floor critical care wards. Perversely, the more serious the damage and urgent the care needs, the more controlled everything seemed to be and, from the hustle and bustle of the ground-floor outpatients departments, they rose into an atmosphere of calm. The few staff on duty were quietly getting on with their work. One or two of these seemed to be in military uniform and at one point they were passed by what looked like a couple of MPs. Mariner wasn't sure how welcome he and Glover would be in the clinical environment, but their warrant cards smoothed the way.

Entering the department, they came to a central space, around which were arranged a number of smaller rooms, partitioned off by glass. On most of these the blinds were closed, but in the cubicle directly ahead they could just about make out, amid banks of electronic equipment, a human form. Behind a workstation to their left, a nurse seemed to be hunting around for something, lifting papers and opening and closing drawers. Eventually she glanced up. 'I'm sorry, are you looking for someone?' The photo ID clipped to her jacket said *Doctor Ellen Kingsley*. After identifying himself, Mariner asked to speak to the person in charge.

Her smile was distracted. 'Oh, well, that would be me,' she said. 'If you could give me a couple of minutes?' Without waiting for an answer she resumed her search. Then with an 'Aha, at last,' she disappeared briefly through a door behind her, and returned shortly afterwards, coming out from behind the workstation. Tall and slender, she looked young to carry the responsibility of running this section: forties, at most. There was a row of chairs to the side of the desk and she gestured for them to sit. 'I'd take you through to my office, but I could be paged at any time.' Reminded of this, she checked the device at her hip.

'That's fine,' said Mariner. 'I appreciate you talking to us. We'll try not to keep you too long.'

Her fair hair was tied back but several fine wisps escaped, clinging to her dampened face. Her skin was pale, but her cheeks flushed, a rosy pink. And her concern about Dee Henderson's whereabouts seemed more than simply professional. 'Of course I want to help,' she said. 'We're a tight team here and Dee is an important part of that. Is there any news?'

'Sorry, no,' said Mariner. 'We're trying to build up a picture of her exact movements yesterday evening. When did you last see her?'

'When she left at the end of her shift,' said Kingsley, 'although as always, she was late getting away. It wasn't until Paddy phoned this morning that we knew anything was wrong.'

'What time did she leave?'

'I suppose it was about twenty past ten by the time she'd got her things.'

'And as far as you know she was going straight home.'

'If you can call it that. It's a pig of a journey, especially at that time of night. It's not quite so bad when she's on earlies. Paddy always tries to pick her up when he can, but with the children—' She broke off. 'Oh . . . no. I've just remembered. Dee might not have gone straight to the bus stop yesterday. She said she was going to see if she could book some tickets at the Town Hall. I wasn't sure that the box office would be open at that time but—'

'She was taking a detour?' Mariner checked.

'That's what she said.'

'And how did Dee seem yesterday?'

'Fine, her usual cheery self. I don't know how she does it after an eight-hour shift, but somehow she manages it.'

'Was there anything bothering her, any problems at home, do you know?' Jesson asked.

'I can't imagine so, aside from the usual niggles of everyday life. It wasn't easy for Dee and Paddy to get together in the first place. They had some hurdles to overcome, and I think that's made them strong.'

'What kind of hurdles?'

'Well, Paddy's injuries for one thing.' She stopped abruptly. 'He didn't tell you all this?'

'It wasn't something he mentioned,' Mariner said, 'though he did say they'd both been married before.'

Sensing hesitation, Jesson added: 'If we're to get a clear picture of what has happened to Dee it would be helpful to get as much background information as we can.'

Ellen Kingsley was dubious but continued just the same. 'Paddy was injured in Afghanistan. Dee looked after him when he came back to this country. It's how they met. They got to know each other and one thing led to another.'

'So Paddy was here, at the QE?' asked Mariner.

'No, this was what, about five or six years ago, when the military hospital was based on the old site, the other side of Selly Oak.'

'This is the military hospital?' said Mariner, looking around him. 'I knew it was here, but I suppose I thought it operated separately.' Somehow he had assumed it to be in its own discrete building.

'Oh, it used to be, but here we're integrated with the main hospital,' said Kingsley. 'We treat both civilian patients and military personnel.' As if to underline the point, the door swung open, and a young man in uniform crossed the room in front of them, nodding an acknowledgement to Kingsley before disappearing into a door opposite. 'We have the most up-to-the-minute equipment for managing critical care up here. Some of it is stuff that's so expensive the hospital couldn't afford to duplicate it just for the sake of keeping the departments separate. Also, we have the most highly skilled and qualified staff, so it makes sense to concentrate all the specialist resources and expertise in one department, regardless of who it is we're treating.'

'That sounds like progress,' said Mariner.

'It is. This way, we don't differentiate between patients, which is how it should be.'

'So you're . . .?'

'I'm civilian, but we have a combination of forces and civilian staff. Many of our patients at the moment are soldiers, so we run certain wards along the lines of a military hospital. When the soldiers regain consciousness it's important that they have that structure and familiarity.'

'Aren't the civilian patients intimidated by the uniforms?' asked Jesson.

Kingsley smiled. 'Most of the time they're in our care they're pretty out of it, to be honest.'

'How serious were Paddy Henderson's injuries?' Mariner asked.

'Physically I don't think he was in such bad shape, not like some of the boys we have coming through here, but Paddy did suffer psychologically. I wasn't around then, so I only know what Dee has told me, but I think it was a bit tricky. Even now, from what Dee says, there are times when he's not the easiest to live with. But she understands and knows how to handle him. Theirs is one of the strongest relationships I've come across. Scares the life out of me. Occasionally we have socials that partners get invited to and they seem to have a really close bond. I mean, I know that's never the full story, but there always seems to be genuine warmth and affection between them, you know? Paddy's very protective. And they're devoted to the kids.'

'And being part of the military hospital, does that cause any tensions?'

'You mean between the civilian and non-civilian staff?' Kingsley gave Mariner a withering look and, standing up, walked him and Jesson over to the windows of the one visible cubicle. 'This is what we're dealing with, day in day out, Inspector. If you think we have time for petty rivalries, then you're very much mistaken.'

They looked in on the figure lying in the bed, wired up to the machinery and swathed in bandages. 'What happened to him?' Mariner asked, hesitantly. It was hard to tell whether the person underneath was male or female, young or old.

'Private Craig Lomax,' she said. 'Aged nineteen. An improvised explosive device has blown away his lower legs and part of his body.'

'What are his chances?' asked Jesson.

'It's really hard to say,' said Kingsley. 'They had to keep him at Camp Bastion for two weeks because he was too fragile to move. And since he came in here a couple of weeks ago he's had some nasty episodes, though each time so far we've managed to stabilise him again. There was a glimmer of hope yesterday afternoon when he actually began to regain consciousness, and for an hour or so things were beginning to look promising, but it was too soon.'

'Meaning what?' Jesson couldn't tear her eyes away from him.

'He wasn't ready emotionally to confront what had happened to him. It's a common reaction. When he finally came round he became extremely distressed. It happens. The shock and the pain are too much for them and they get overwhelmed. We got the psychiatrist here straight away to try and see if we could bring Lomax through it, but in the end we were forced to put him back into a medically induced coma. It was touch and go for about an hour. It's why Dee was a bit late leaving.'

'She spends a lot of time with him?' asked Mariner.

'She's Lomax's designated ICU nurse.'

'It all sounds incredibly stressful,' said Jesson.

'For Lomax certainly, and for his visitor. We had to send him away while we sorted things out. But for us?' She shrugged. 'It's what we do, isn't it? I don't imagine your job is a barrel of laughs all the time.'

'How does Dee cope with it?' asked Jesson.

'She's experienced and tough as old boots. You have to develop a bit of a hard shell in this job anyway, and she's pretty resilient. We keep each other going.' She paused. 'I have to ask . . . do you think Dee's disappearance might have anything to do with these other two women you're looking for?'

'It's too early to be certain at this stage, but yes, we will have to consider that possibility,' said Mariner. 'And what about the long-term prospects for Private Lomax?'

'It may yet turn out well. We had a couple more from the same unit come in. The others are making good progress and have transferred to the main ward. We can't be sure how it will go for Lomax, but there are plenty of us willing him to pull through.'

'I saw Military Police hanging around, didn't I?' said Mariner.

'Yes. From what I can make out there seems to be some question over whether the unit should have been on foot patrol in that particular area on that particular day. Lomax caught the brunt of it, so we've got to hope that it wasn't the result of someone else's cock-up.'

'When will you know if Private Lomax will make it?' Jesson's interest seemed compulsive.

'The next few days will be critical, and then he'll have a long road of rehabilitation ahead of him, but he has a chance. Lots of our boys go on to lead full and active lives, even after all this.' She grimaced. 'Not sure how I'd do in their situation.'

'Nor me,' said Mariner.

As they were leaving, Mariner held open the door to admit a group of people, dressed for the outdoors, who came wordlessly into the unit and dispersed around the different rooms. Visiting time. Mariner watched as a man of an age to be Lomax's father went into the room and drew a vinyl hospital-issue chair alongside the bed, pocketing his cigarettes as he sat down. Before he'd even taken off his coat he was leaning in, his lips moving in an unheard greeting to the young soldier.

Alongside Mariner, Vicky Jesson seemed mesmerized. 'That could be me,' she said quietly. 'My lad, Aaron, wants to go into the army when he leaves school.'

Dr Kingsley saw them watching. 'He practically lives here,' she said. 'We have to turn him out every night and make him go home, just to get some rest.'

Mariner didn't have kids, but even as a father, he doubted that he'd be able to imagine how it would feel to see your child in that condition, and he was struck by an overwhelming surge of compassion for the man. He and Jesson walked down the stairs and out of the hospital without another word.

* * *

By six that evening Mariner was sitting alone in his office entering details of the interview with Ellen Kingsley into the policy log. A lot had happened in the last couple of days and he was beginning to lag behind with the admin. Superintendent Sharp appeared in the doorway and made a point of looking at the clock. 'What are you still doing here?'

'Making the most of an opportunity,' said Mariner. 'Jamie's at Manor Park 'til Monday. I can't go home. I wouldn't know what to do with myself.' He sat back from the computer and clasped his hands behind his head. 'Anyway, makes a change for me to be here late. Vicky's usually the first one here in the morning, last one away at night, even though she's the one with the family to think about.'

'I suppose work is important to her at the moment, for obvious reasons,' said Sharp. 'She's a woman who wants to be defined by something more than just her role as a mother.'

'Hm, like anyone else we know?' said Mariner.

Sharp laughed. 'God, yes. How do you think I know? She's exactly like me! But I think she wants to be known as something more than Brian Riddell's partner too.'

'Well, she's doing pretty well with that. Do you know where they're up to with who shot him? I didn't like to ask.'

'I don't know. Tony could probably tell you more about that.'

Mariner's personal mobile chose that moment to ring. It happened so rarely that it took him several seconds to recognise the tinny ring tone.

It was Suzy. 'Hi, where are you? I've been trying your landline.'

'I'm still at work.' Mariner caught Sharp's eye and she waved to indicate that he should carry on before retreating back upstairs to her own office.

'At this time?' Suzy was saying. 'Who's with Jamie?'

'He's at Manor Park for the weekend. I got a call a couple of days ago to say they could have him.'

'So you've got a free weekend.' Her tone was measured. 'It would be good to see you, if you've got time.'

'You could come over,' Mariner suggested.

'Sorry, I can't,' said Suzy. 'We're playing tomorrow and Saturday night. But you could come here. You said you wanted to come and hear us, and there's a champagne reception afterwards.'

'Naturally.' Not content with being a brilliant academic, Suzy was also an accomplished violinist and played in a chamber orchestra for fun. Mariner thought about an evening rubbing shoulders with the Cambridge elite. He briefly considered making up an excuse, but that was hardly fair and she was right: he *had* expressed a wish to go to one of her concerts, even if only out of politeness. 'I might have to see how it goes here,' he hedged.

'Of course,' she said, ever reasonable. 'But it would be lovely if you could make it. Oh, and by the way, it's black tie.'

Not for me it isn't, thought Mariner as he hung up the phone. Sharp was passing, on her way out this time.

'Suzy,' he told her.

'Good,' said Sharp inexplicably. 'How is she?'

'She's fine. Wants me to go over to Cambridge tomorrow, but I don't know . . .'

'How's it going, all this?' Sharp gestured towards the paperwork on his desk.

'Well, I'm not quite ready to gather all the suspects together in one room yet, if that's what you mean.'

'Then you should go,' she said. 'It will do you good to get away from here for a day or two. I doubt that anything actionable is going to happen in the next couple of days. If it does then there are others around who can pick up the slack, and if not, well, we could do with some members of the team coming back to things afresh next week. If this investigation turns out to be a long haul, we're all going to need to pace ourselves. Don't you always say it's a good idea to make some space to mull things over in this situation?'

Did he? 'I'll think about it,' he said, which he did as he drove home and let himself into the empty house. And he thought about Suzy as he got into bed, confident that for once he would have a completely undisturbed night.

Chapter Fourteen

Mary Sutor enjoyed her job as a call-handler on the Granville Lane CAD team. She'd been doing it now for nearly five years and prided herself on being able to efficiently grade calls according to their urgency. Every month the office ran an informal sweepstake to identify the biggest time wasters. Contenders ranged from people calling 999 to say that their car wouldn't start, or that their budgie had escaped, to one woman who asked if they could instruct her on how to change the batteries in her TV remote control. On Friday morning Mary had a call which, while it wouldn't top this month's list, would probably feature on it somewhere.

'My cleaner hasn't turned up,' said the man at the other end of the line.

Mary rolled her eyes at Linda, who sat opposite her. 'Sir, you've rung through to the emergency service,' she said, with exaggerated patience. 'We're not here to help if your cleaner doesn't show.'

'But it's very unlike her,' the man persisted. 'She always lets me know if she's not going to come.'

'Have you tried ringing her?' Mary asked, as Linda answered another call.

'Yes, but her phone seems to be switched off.'

At that moment another incoming call flashed up on Mary's monitor and it was a number she recognised. Angela Beck was one of their regular 'customers,' whose husband routinely lost control of his fists.

'Sir, I'm going to pass you on to another of our operators who will take your details,' said Mary. 'I hope your cleaner turns up. Thank you.' And swiftly transferring the call to one of the less experienced staff members, she moved on to Angie Beck.

'One for the hoax statistics, I think,' she said afterwards to Linda.

Linda grinned. 'Perhaps he thought one of us might pop round and do it for him.'

* * *

Mariner had been half hoping that developments in the case during Friday might provide him with a reason to stay in Birmingham this weekend, but no parcel of clothing belonging to Dee Henderson arrived and, to compound things, Superintendent Sharp, recognising that morale was beginning to flag, stepped in and insisted that they start a rota of forty-eight-hour R&R to clear their heads.

There were, on the other hand, a few loose ends for which Mariner was responsible, so by the time he'd tied them up to his satisfaction it was late afternoon before he joined the Friday surge out of the city. But as he left the M6 to join the A14, cutting a swath through the countryside under the big Northamptonshire skies, he felt the tension in his shoulders begin to ease a little, his concentration now on negotiating the solid convoy of HGVs that were heading for the port of Felixstowe.

On the few occasions when he'd visited before, Mariner had really liked Cambridge, for its quaintness, its gentility and — if he was being brutally honest — the stark contrast with much of Birmingham. Suzy's friends had, on the whole, made him welcome, but he'd found it hard to fully relax with them. Her job as a doctoral research student planted her squarely in the realm of academia, where there seemed to be few people with whom it was possible to have a normal discussion about, say, football or beer. For them, intellectual posturing seemed to take on the intensity of a professional, competitive sport and every exchange felt like open combat, which Mariner usually hadn't the energy or the inclination to sustain for very long. Still, perhaps tonight would be different. All he'd be required to do was listen to some music.

He'd arranged to meet Suzy outside the venue where she was playing, so followed her directions into the city centre and one of the tiny number of legitimate car parks. He texted her to say he'd arrived and she came out to meet him at the entrance of the college. She looked chic in a fitted black cocktail dress, her violin and bow grasped in one hand, and didn't seem to mind that he was wearing his trademark grey lounge suit among a sea of tuxes. After a lingering kiss that made Mariner instantly hard, she said, 'You look tired. Are you sure you'll manage to stay awake?'

'Not completely,' he said. 'But I'll try not to snore too loudly.'

Taking his place in the vaulted college chapel, it felt surreal to be sitting there in a row of such elegantly dressed couples. The chamber orchestra took their places to a rattle of applause and, as the music soared and echoed, Mariner was spellbound by Suzy, the black dress against her olive skin, her face creased with concentration as she thrust the bow back and forth, the light sparkling off the fine silver bracelet on her wrist, a traditional Cantonese talisman that she never removed.

* * *

'And what do you do?' It was never Mariner's favourite question, especially in a situation such as this, and especially at a time like this; asked by the eager young man with the PhD in whatever it was, who no doubt knew as much about policing as Mariner did about splitting the atom. Mariner was caught offside by two things: an enquiry directed at him that went further than the rhetorical, and the banality of the topic. Consequently he was forced to revert to his usual fallback position. 'I'm in security,' he said, vaguely, as he did in these situations, glancing around at the gathering of cocktail dresses and dinner jackets, and taking in the polite and terribly civilised murmur of conversation.

Suzy, beside him, with her hand tucked under his arm, rolled her eyes. 'Oh, don't be such a wimp. He's a detective chief inspector with the West Midlands Police,' she blurted out to the young professor. 'And he's the senior investigator on the Grace Clifton case.' Mariner wished she hadn't.

For a moment though, he thought he might get away with it; that this guy would have his head stuck so far into dusty tomes (or up his own backside) that he'd be unaware of current events. But his eyes had lit up, encouraged by the creeping dawn of recognition. 'Thanks, Suzy,' Mariner said with a look.

'Gosh.' The young prof's exclamation was imbued with implied criticism. 'You're struggling a bit with that one, aren't you?'

'We are,' Mariner admitted.

'Didn't you guys think that Grace Clifton had run away?'

'At the time we had justifiable reason to think that,' said Mariner. 'We took the same approach we would with any missing person and considered all the options.'

'Yeah, but even so.' The young man looked at him askance. 'Aren't the first forty-eight hours the most crucial? You must have lost some serious time there.'

Great, thought Mariner. *Some prick who's read a few criminology books*. He could feel his blood starting to rise. 'And what would you know about it?' he asked calmly.

'Barney's specialism is the deployment of stop-and-search,' cut in Suzy, to diffuse a growing awkwardness, but Barney chose to ignore her.

'Oh, don't mind me,' he said, holding Mariner's gaze. 'I'm just making an *educated* guess.'

'Don't, Barney,' Suzy reprimanded him gently.

'Yes, well, maybe there's a little more to education than reading about someone else's opinion of what goes on in the outside world,' Mariner pointed out. 'Some of us actually have to live it.'

'Must be a challenge, though,' Barney persisted, 'in the absence of someone you can fit up for it.'

By now Mariner was desperate to wipe that faux-innocent expression off the man's face, preferably with a well-timed punch, but before his impulses could overwhelm him, he slammed his glass down on a nearby table, with just enough force to draw the attention of the hundred or so other people present, and stalked out through the neo-Gothic archway, Suzy trailing after him.

'Sorry,' she said, as they emerged into the cold night. 'I thought you might enjoy the opportunity for lively discussion with like-minded people.'

'Like-minded?' Mariner laughed scathingly. 'What the hell made you think we'd be that?'

'Barney was just baiting you.'

'Good old Barney, what fun.'

'OK, introducing you to him might have been a mistake. I'd forgotten. I think he got stopped by the police for speeding a couple of weeks ago, and they gave him a hard time.'

'I can't imagine why,' said Mariner. 'Could it be by any chance that he was telling them how to do their job?' Out on the street Mariner realised that, having made his dramatic exit, he had completely forgotten where he had parked his car, so he had to stop and wait for Suzy to catch up. She was still only wearing the cocktail dress and the wind was getting up, so he automatically took off his jacket and draped it round her shoulders.

'He didn't mean anything by it,' Suzy said, pulling it round her.

'No, he didn't, did he?' he said. Mariner turned to face her. 'That's exactly it. It was meaningless. A nasty, futile snipe at me and all my officers who, despite what Barney Fuck-face might think, are working their bollocks off to try and find out what's happened to two — maybe three — vulnerable young women. It makes me sick, all of you, sitting here in your rarefied little world, passing judgement on those of us who actually get our hands dirty—'

She recoiled, as if he'd physically struck her. 'All of us? Is that what you really think?'

Mariner slumped. 'No, of course not,' he said. Up until now he'd never felt in any way lacking because he hadn't been to university. But here in Cambridge he could feel the beginnings of an unwanted chip developing, and he didn't much like it. 'I should get back,' he said, defeated. They had reached his car. 'This was a bad idea. I'll drop you off on the way.'

'But you're shattered,' Suzy said. 'Why don't you get some sleep and drive back first thing?'

Mariner shook his head. He couldn't bear to stay here any longer. 'Too much to do,' he said, getting into the car. 'As your friend so helpfully pointed out, we lost time. And I need to make the most of Jamie being away. He'll be back again on Monday.' He was using his responsibility as an excuse and Suzy knew it too.

'No more progress with finding him somewhere permanent then?' she said, lightly, as they started off.

'I'm doing what I can,' Mariner said irritably. 'He's on a couple of lists but we have to wait for other residents to "move on."'

She smiled. 'Pop their clogs, in other words.'

'If you like,' he said, grudgingly. 'Anyway, not much I can do about that, short of bumping them off myself.'

'You could give it a try,' she said, mischievously. 'You of all people ought to know how to do that and get away with it. I could help you.'

'That's in very poor taste.'

'I have very poor taste in all sorts of things,' she said, laying a hand on his thigh. 'It's probably why I like you so much, no offence.'

'None taken,' replied Mariner. But his heart wasn't in it. He kissed Suzy goodbye and as he set out back along the A14 towards the Midlands, his car battered by the rising winds, he couldn't help wondering if a watershed had been reached. Even worse, he wouldn't have blamed her if it had.

* * *

Without the early morning wake-up call from Jamie, and exhausted from the late-night drive, Mariner overslept and woke feeling groggy. His ideal occupation for the day would have been a long walk, preferably involving a good pub somewhere in the middle, but driving rain slapped against the window panes, blown horizontal by what had developed overnight into a gale-force wind. It wouldn't be much fun walking anywhere. Tempting as it was to go into work, Superintendent Sharp had effectively banned all of them from the station, so for a while he wandered the house aimlessly, like he had an itch he couldn't scratch. Going into the kitchen he stuck back the picture label that had come off the door, right next to the hole Jamie had created with his head the first couple of days he'd been here.

The wear and tear was far from Jamie's fault. It was Mariner who had imposed yet more disruption on a man for whom change was an anathema. Initially it hadn't been too bad; the first couple of days had gone spookily well until, predictably, almost as if Jamie had suddenly realised that this was for keeps, everything had become a battle. The slightest thing had thrown him into a major meltdown, and now both Mariner and his house bore the scars. Things had stabilised since then as, by trial and error, Mariner had started to work out how to handle Jamie, and the flashpoints were becoming fewer and fewer. So today he would make a start on repairing the damage to his house.

After a visit to the nearest DIY superstore Mariner spent the morning sandpapering, filling and painting over the cracks. It was, in its way, therapeutic, until thoughts about Suzy began to encroach and he was forced to replay their conversation of the night before, which only made him feel bad all over again. Perhaps he'd been hasty in coming straight back here. Suzy was always so forgiving, and he'd behaved like a git. There was only so long that she would put up with it, then that would be another relationship he could kiss goodbye. There were other purely selfish reasons why he should have been kinder to Suzy too. He'd been living like a monk since Jamie had moved in. Last night had been an opportunity squandered in more ways than one.

* * *

While Suli took Haroon to visit his parents, Millie had spent much of Saturday preparing supper and was now adding the final touches. For the first time since having the baby, she had made a deliberate effort to reclaim her old grown-up self, with her hair and make-up, and had even managed to squeeze into one of her pre-baby dresses, though it meant she'd have to go easy on the pakora tonight. All in all she'd made a special effort, so when the doorbell rang on the dot of seven that evening, announcing the arrival of Greg and Louise, she was a little surprised to see that Louise was dressed down in one of her usual, shapeless dungaree outfits.

'Sorry,' Louise said straight away. 'We couldn't get Abigail settled. I'm sure she knew that something was going on. I wanted to bring her with us but Greg insisted we were going to have a proper night out, so for the first time we've got in a babysitter. And now I'm prattling.'

'Don't worry,' said Millie. 'It's great that you could come.'

'Abigail will be absolutely fine,' Greg soothed, ushering her in through the door. 'I've got my phone switched on and we can be home in a couple of minutes if we need to be. Try and relax, darling.' They had brought wine, expensive chocolates and flowers, so, taking them through to the lounge, Millie introduced Suli and left him to organise drinks while she retreated to the kitchen to find a vase and to attend to the cooking. After a while Louise came to ask if she could help.

'I think we're under control,' said Millie. To her immense relief, the steady murmur of conversation she could hear coming from the lounge seemed to indicate that Suli and Greg had hit it off. 'You could give that pot a stir though, since you're here.'

'I love this worktop,' said Louise, running her hand over the polished granite surface. 'Ours is just cheap MDF, and I think it completely spoils the look of the kitchen. But Greg says it's functional and would be much too expensive to replace.'

'I expect he'll come round to the idea eventually,' said Millie, speaking from experience. 'Right, I think we're all set.'

'So who have you got sitting for you tonight?' Suli asked, as they sat down to eat. 'We might be on the lookout for someone soon.'

'She's the daughter of a work colleague,' said Greg. 'Though it's not the most convenient of arrangements. She lives out in Kinver, so I'll either need to drop her back home afterwards, or we'll be shelling out for a taxi.'

'But she's a sweet girl,' said Louise, 'and much more appropriate.'

'Whatever that means,' said Greg. 'Our neighbours have a teenage son who does babysitting,' Greg explained, for Millie and Suli's benefit. 'But Lou wanted a girl to do it, didn't you, darling? Not that Abigail will know the difference at her age.'

'But I've met Jodie and I like her,' said Louise. 'I just feel more comfortable with her.'

'It's true, she is a lovely young woman,' Greg agreed. 'One of those bright young kids who came to us as an intern. She's very capable and I'm sure she'll go far.' He became quite animated while talking about the girl and Millie wondered for a moment if she might be Greg's distraction. Perhaps he was protesting a little too strongly about a late-night drive to Kinver. She tried to look for signs that Greg was anxious about anything else, but if he was, he was one hell of an actor. It was Louise who seemed more edgy, which was nothing new. And it was the first time she'd left her baby daughter so perhaps it was inevitable.

'Millie tells me you're in the gun trade,' said Suli.

'Yes, sports rifles, that sort of thing,' said Greg. 'I didn't have much choice really. It's a family business so it was pretty much expected. Have you ever done any shooting, Suli?'

'Not since I had a spud gun as a kid,' said Suli. 'I wouldn't mind having a go, though.'

'You must join me for some clay pigeon shooting. Uncle has a range out in Shropshire. It's mostly for clients, but you must come out and see what you think.'

'I'd like that, thanks.'

'How about next Saturday then?' Somehow Greg made it sound like a challenge, and Millie had a sudden sense of foreboding.

'Aren't we fairly busy next weekend?' she said.

Suli frowned. 'I don't think so. No. That sounds good, Greg. I'll look forward to it. You and Millie sort of have a common interest then,' he went on.

'Sorry?'

'What with her being a police officer.'

To his credit, Greg didn't quite choke on his wine, but for several seconds he did seem to have difficulty swallowing and there followed an awkward pause. 'I didn't know that,' he said, recovering quickly. 'That's um . . . impressive. Are you based here in Oldbury?' he asked.

'South Birmingham,' said Suli. He placed a hand over Millie's. 'She does a great job. I'm very proud of her.'

'Quite right,' said Greg, slurring a little. The drink seemed to have suddenly caught up with him. 'In that case I'll have to be on my best behaviour, won't I?' It was said in jest, but there was an edge to his voice.

'Oh, yes,' Millie said, playing along and wagging a teasing finger at him. 'I'm going to be keeping a close eye on you. I've already looked you up, in fact. Your company has quite a history. One of the original Birmingham gunmakers, so quite a tradition.'

'Hm.' Greg's head nodded, though his expression had glazed over a little. 'Yes, I suppose so.'

After that the conversation turned to more mundane things, mainly the babies and their sleeping and feeding patterns. Later, when Greg and Louise had gone, Millie and Suliman loaded the dishwasher together.

'I agree with you,' said Suli. 'Louise does seem a bit highly strung. Too much time at home alone, do you think?'

'I don't know,' said Millie. 'Those two are a mass of contradictions. Just about everything Louise has told me about Greg, he seemed intent on disproving tonight. You two seemed to hit it off, though.'

'Yeah, despite everything you've told me, I quite liked the guy,' said Suli. 'Maybe he's good at putting on an act.' He chuckled. 'Your job caught him out, though, didn't it?'

'He probably made assumptions about our culture,' said Millie. 'It wouldn't be the first time, would it? I expect he thought I'd be a "safe" friend for Louise — another subservient, traditional wife. And I learned something about you tonight. I didn't know you were keen on shooting.'

Suli shrugged. 'I don't know that I am. I was just being sociable. I thought it might help if I took an interest.'

'But you'll go with him?'

'If he asks again. Is that OK with you?'

'Why wouldn't it be? You can find out a bit more about him. You will be careful, though?'

'Don't worry, he knows what you do for a living now.' Suli sighed. 'Always on the job, aren't you?' he said, affectionately, putting his arms around her.

'I can't help it. It's who I am.'

'You want to go back.'

'A bit of me does, yes. Is it that obvious?'

And at that moment, with impeccable timing, Haroon decided to remind them of his presence.

Chapter Fifteen

Mariner had resisted for as long as he could but by early Saturday evening, it seemed that all he could think about was Grace Clifton and Rosa Batista, and inevitably he found himself back at Granville Lane. Despite the usual queue down at the main desk, he was the only person up in the incident room at this time of night and he welcomed the opportunity to study the facts of the case and think alone. The display board had now been divided into three distinct sections, one for each woman, though Dee Henderson still had a big question mark above her until they knew for sure that her disappearance was linked to the other two. There were similarities of course, but there were also differences — not least the absence of a follow-up parcel so far. For that reason, Mariner set her slightly apart.

Frustratingly they still didn't know exactly where Rosa Batista had disappeared from, but Mariner scrutinised the maps that had been drawn for Dee Henderson and Grace Clifton. These indicated the last place each woman had been seen, and the routes that they were likely to have taken to get to their respective intended destinations, had they taken the most direct course. Both women came from, and would have ended up in, different parts of the city, but if Dee had stopped off at the Town Hall, as Ellen Kingsley had indicated she might, there was a specific intersection of the two that ran the length of Hill Street. Was there something about that particular stretch of road that was significant? Picking up his jacket again, Mariner headed back out to the car park before realising that he would probably be indulging in a few bevvies while he was out. So, pocketing his car keys, he crossed over the road to catch the bus into town.

Alighting on Bristol Street, Mariner crossed the road and walked through to Hurst Street past the Diskery. He hadn't been in that place for years but its survival seemed proof that there were still enough vinyl enthusiasts around to keep it afloat. On Hurst Street he turned left, making his way up towards the Arcadian theatre and restaurant complex. He had to weave a path through the pavement furniture outside the bars, placed there less to take advantage of the mild British climate than to provide a refuge for smokers. For Mariner, who'd never indulged, apart from the odd packet of Consulate in his youth, the ban was a mixed blessing. Undoubtedly it had vastly improved the atmosphere inside pubs, bars and restaurants, but it also often meant inhaling clouds of cigarette smoke along the pavements outside. It never failed to amaze him, the number of people who were prepared to withstand any kind of cold and rain for the sake of a nicotine fix.

He came to one of the old city corner pubs that had been refurbished beyond recognition and went in for his first pint of the evening. Predictably in this neighbourhood the only beer was extortionately priced foreign lager.

'Don't you have any of the proper stuff?' Mariner asked, but the young barman looked blank.

'He doesn't know what you're talking about.' A man sitting on a bar stool a little further down the bar smiled knowingly at Mariner, his own half-pint glass half empty.

About Mariner's age, he was running to fat, his face scrubbed and clean-shaven, and he gave off a cloud of cologne. 'Quiet in here for a Saturday, isn't it?' the man went on.

'I wouldn't know,' Mariner said. 'I think it's the first time I've been in here.'

Encouraged, the man stood up and slid along the bar towards Mariner. 'Are you new to the city?' he asked.

Glancing back at the tables for the first time, Mariner realised that apart from a group of giggling young women in one corner, the other customers were exclusively male and most of them were in pairs, some sitting very close to each other. His new friend was homing in. With deliberation he shook back his cuff to check his watch. 'No, I'm local,' he said. 'Just killing time before meeting my wife for dinner.' He hoped the excruciating cringe in his gut hadn't made it as far as his face.

'Ah, well, there are some great restaurants around here.'

They continued with some awkward, mainly weather-based small talk while Mariner swallowed his beer and then left, to continue on up past the Back to Backs. This was close to the Chinese quarter of the city and the air was rich with the distinctive aromas of oriental cooking, the restaurants doing a good trade. From there he crossed over the four lanes of the Suffolk Queensway and came into Hill Street, picking up the queue of cars edging forward for the New Street station drop-off and the route that both Grace and Dee would have walked. The traffic flow here was too hectic, surely, for a stranger to be able to snatch a woman from the pavement unnoticed.

At the traffic lights Mariner crossed over again and continued up Hill Street towards the Town Hall and Council House. Here the street was one-way to nowhere and few vehicles passed him. One side of the road was given over to offices, empty at this time of night, and on the other side he walked past an upmarket brasserie, a basement bar he'd never noticed before, and the lobby of the Belvedere Hotel, the predictable smattering of dog-ends on the pavement outside. And then he was in Victoria Square, face to face with, or rather confronted by the arse of, Gormley's Iron Man. It was the point at which Grace and Dee would have parted company again, as it were. Turning through 180 degrees, Mariner stood and looked back down Hill Street. This had to be the most likely place for something to have happened. But how the hell was it managed without arousing attention, and why here?

Walking up the steep incline had made Mariner thirsty again, and this time he wanted a proper drink. His bar of choice would have been the no-frills Post Office Vaults, but the limited space was full to capacity and starting down the stairs he could see right away that trying to get a seat would be hopeless. He hadn't the stomach for Broad Street, so, emerging again and turning right, he walked along New Street to the Burlington Hotel, which he knew would be more civilised and usually had at least one decent beer on tap. Even this was rowdier than expected, and as he was jostled at the bar he inadvertently knocked into the woman standing next to him. As they each turned to apologise, Mariner found himself looking into the face of Dr Ellen Kingsley. He took several seconds to place her, in full make-up and wearing a tight-fitting skirt and a sleeveless top with a plunging neckline that emphasised her toned shoulders and small, firm breasts. Not that he was looking.

'Hello,' she said. 'Or should that be *'ello, 'ello,'ello*?' She was flushed and her smile a little staged, both accounted for by the row of empty glasses on the bar in front of her. 'You're not following me, are you?'

'Not yet,' said Mariner. 'Are you celebrating?'

'Sort of.' She nodded towards the noisy group further along the bar. 'Carrie, one of our anaesthetists, is getting married. It's kind of a hen night. But they've all just decided to go on to a club and I'm not really in the mood, so I thought I'd finish this drink and head home.' Her face clouded suddenly. 'We lost a patient today.'

'Lomax?' Mariner asked, automatically thinking of the boy's father.

'No. He seems to be holding steady. It was one of the other boys, who was actually doing well.' She frowned. 'Just shows you can never really tell. Dee will be gutted.'

'You're sure about going home, or can I get you another drink?' Mariner asked.

She weighed it up for a moment. 'Oh, go on then. I could probably manage another vodka tonic, thanks.'

The bar staff seemed to be on a go-slow, but eventually Mariner got served and they took the drinks to a table at the back of the room.

'You're not working then,' Ellen Kingsley said.

'Not exactly, no.' He wouldn't tell her why he was here. It would have sounded gruesome. 'I'm making the most of my freedom.'

'Intriguing.' Her eyes narrowed. 'Don't tell me. Your decree absolute has just come through.'

Mariner shook his head. 'It's nothing like that, nor is it permanent. I've got caring responsibilities.'

'Elderly parents?'

'You won't guess it,' said Mariner confidently. After she'd fired off several shots into the dark, Mariner felt obliged to explain about Jamie.

'Wow, that's quite something to take on,' she said. 'I'm impressed.'

'Don't be,' said Mariner. 'It's got nothing to do with altruism. I didn't have much choice. My chickens coming home to roost, you might say.'

'Well, I still think it's commendable.'

'Believe me, you wouldn't if you knew how relieved I am that he's away this weekend.'

'But you obviously feel guilty about it.'

'That's true enough. If I'm brutally honest, I never understood why my ex's first priority was to get her brother into residential care. From my high and mighty position, it looked to me like a cop-out. Now I completely get it. At the moment it feels like Jamie's being passed around from one person to another, so that I can have a life.'

'You can't help the demands of your job. It must be a lot like mine: long stressful hours that don't allow much time for anything else.'

'Some people seem to make it work,' Mariner said, thinking of Vicky Jesson.

'Maybe that's a difference in the level of commitment. This woman, Mercy, she's reliable?'

'Very. And she's kind to Jamie. I can't fault that. It's her son I worry about. The more I hear about him, the worse it gets. Mercy openly admits he's never had a proper job, and the only time she sees him is when he wants something — usually money.'

'Does that bother her?'

'If it does, she doesn't mention it to me. She's got one of those indulgent ways of talking about him that parents can have, as if she's blind to all his faults. She's always making excuses for him.'

'She's his mum,' said Ellen. 'That's her job. You must have seen that before.'

'I suppose so. I paid her a bit extra one week. Jamie had been especially difficult, and she'd said she was going to get her hair done. I wasn't sure then if she had and when I asked her about it she admitted she'd given the money to Carlton after all. According to her, "He needed it more."'

'So, I'm guessing from all this that you're not married,' she said. 'Any special reason for that?' She held up her glass. 'Sorry. You'll have noticed I've had a few drinks. It turns me into a nosey cow.'

'I don't know,' said Mariner, in answer to her question. 'I suppose if I was a different generation I'd have a couple of failed marriages under my belt by now, but as it is I've settled for a string of failed relationships instead. How about you?'

'The same.' She sighed. 'It's just never happened, though there have been a couple of long-term situations that didn't quite work out. And now I'm getting increasingly used to living on my own. I like my space.' As if to illustrate the point, she spread out her arms on the banquette. 'It means that I can keep things on my terms. And I've never been particularly desperate for kids. Just for the record, though, I'm not quite a dried-up old spinster just yet. I still get offers.'

'Oh, me too,' said Mariner, and he told her about the approach in the gay bar earlier in the evening. It made her laugh. 'You mean you didn't see that coming?'

'I know. Naive or what? And if I was to make you an offer?' Mariner asked, only half joking.

Her eyes widened. 'You don't hang about, do you?'

'Well, I've had a few drinks too,' said Mariner. 'And I've just realised I haven't really eaten today.'

'Me neither. Actually, I'm starving.'

'Want to go and get something?' said Mariner.

She studied him for a moment, thinking it over. 'OK,' she said eventually.

They ate steak frites at an intimate French restaurant off New Street. In the usual sing-song voice they were informed of the day's specials and told that their waitress this evening would be Sophie. 'That's in case we can't read,' said Ellen, when Sophie duly arrived, the badge on her chest pronouncing her name. In the course of the meal they also consumed the better part of two bottles of house red between them, so they were quite drunk by the time they piled into a taxi. As it lurched around the first corner, Ellen was thrown against Mariner, and when he slipped a protective arm around her waist, there she stayed. He must have briefly nodded off then, because all too soon the taxi drew up outside a row of mews houses that could have been anywhere in the city.

'About that offer,' Ellen said sleepily. 'I'm happy to consider it, pending CV and health screening, of course. Do you want to come in?'

'All right,' said Mariner, taking the fare for the cab from his wallet.

Stumbling into Ellen's house, Mariner couldn't help noticing a series of stunning monochrome photographs on the wall, of mountains against the cloud. He stopped to look more closely. 'These are good,' he said. 'Who took them?'

'I did, most of them,' she called from the lounge.

'This is Tryfan,' he said.

'Yes, Christmas Eve about twenty years ago.'

Mariner did a mental calculation. 'I might have been there on that day too. I've got a similar picture on the wall of my office.'

While he was talking she came up behind him and snaked her arms around him, running one hand down to grope around for his fly.

'Now who's getting ahead of herself?' said Mariner, and when he turned he found that she had taken off the top and skirt.

'Bugger the pictures,' she said, taking his hand. 'My bedroom's much more interesting.'

Kissing her briefly, Mariner picked her up and attempted to carry her up the stairs but her legs, dangling over his arm, blocked their ascent. Instead he finished up heaving her over his shoulder in an undignified fireman's lift. It made her giggle, but towards the top of the stairs the giggling gave way to a gasp. 'Bathroom!' she managed to splutter, waving her arms in the general direction, and Mariner delivered her there just in time.

Chapter Sixteen

Mariner was chasing Jamie up Hill Street, petrified that, at any moment, he was going to dash out into the speeding heavy-goods traffic. Dozens of people, their faces pressed up against the steamed windows of the restaurants, watched as he ran past. A strange yet familiar tune was jangling in his head. Breaking free of the dream, Mariner opened his eyes on a grey dawn. He was cushioned on something soft and giving, still wearing nearly all his clothes, even his shoes. Lifting his head made his brain bounce around inside his skull, sending shooting pains around his eyes and forcing a bitter taste up into his mouth. Gulping it back, he groped around for his jacket, trying to work out if this was still part of the dream, and as his phone started up again, he swore under his breath as he scrabbled around to stifle it as quickly as possible.

The light snapped on with a painful intensity and Ellen Kingsley blinked sleepily at him from her place beside him, under the duvet. 'It's all right,' she said. 'I'm used to this routine too, remember?'

Having finally located his phone, Mariner held it to his ear. It was Vicky Jesson. 'We've got a body,' she said.

'Well, a mummy, to be more precise. I'll stop by and pick you up.'

'Sure.' Mariner was about to terminate the call, when he remembered something. 'Oh . . . er . . . actually, I'm not at home.'

'Where are you?' asked Jesson, her voice entirely neutral.

Mariner covered the mouthpiece. 'Where am I?' He relayed the address to an inscrutable Jesson, before turning to Ellen. 'Sorry, I've got to go. Are you all right?'

She managed a weak smile. 'Thundering headache, and food's off the agenda for the foreseeable future, but it's nothing I don't deserve. Bad news?'

'For someone, yes. I'll call you later.'

'Don't worry,' she said. 'I know you'll be busy. But maybe we can try a re-match sometime?'

'Look forward to it,' said Mariner.

Outside in the semi-darkness Mariner found it was drizzling, the cloud was low and the street slick in the beam cast from the headlights of Jesson's car. 'What the hell were you doing in work at this hour?' he said, ducking into the passenger seat. He saw from the clock, as they navigated through the empty city streets, that it was still only a little after seven.

'Oh, you know,' Jesson said. 'I woke really early and couldn't get back to sleep, everything going round in my head. My mum's staying the weekend anyway, so she just told me to go . . .' She didn't need to say more. Mariner recognised that kind of compulsion. It was what had drawn him back to Granville Lane yesterday afternoon.

'You found a diversion,' said Jesson. It wasn't an accusation, just a slightly amused statement of fact.

'For a couple of hours,' said Mariner. 'Ellen Kingsley.'

'Dee Henderson's boss?' She turned to glance at him. 'Is that a good idea?'

'Probably not, but one of her patients died yesterday, so it passed some time for both of us. Not that it has anything remotely to do with you, but all we did was get rat-arsed. Nothing happened unless you count her throwing up and me passing out.'

'Delightful,' said Jesson. 'You know how to give a girl a good time.'

They were coming out of the city now, picking up speed on the Rubery bypass. Mariner's head was throbbing and he was beginning to feel slightly queasy. Something on the edge of his consciousness was bothering him too, but he couldn't quite pin it down. 'Where are we going anyway? And what's this about a mummy?'

'The surgeon's word, not mine.' Jesson took them out along the main Stourbridge road, before turning left towards the outlying commuter villages of Fairfield and Dodford, and happily breaching the thirty-miles-per-hour limit. The rain had eased, but a low-hanging mist remained, and once on the minor roads she slowed down, but with just enough swing around the corners to unsettle Mariner's stomach further. He opened a window.

'Don't you dare throw up in my car,' warned Jesson. At a T-junction she turned left again, deliberately ignoring the police 'Road Ahead Closed' sign that had been placed there.

'Who found it?' Mariner asked, taking in deep draughts of the sharp air.

'A woman out foraging for mushrooms,' said Jesson.

'People still do that?' Mariner said. 'In this weather?' The mention of mushrooms reminded him of those in a cream and garlic sauce he'd consumed the evening before and he gagged slightly.

'Yeah, who'd have thought?' Jesson eyed him sideways. 'You'll warn me if you're about to puke, won't you?'

Coming over the brow of a hill the road dipped down between high hedges, at which point Jesson braked gently as they picked up a line of marked and unmarked police vehicles parked higgledy-piggledy along the verge. It ended at a more substantial blockade being manned by a uniformed officer, and marked a crossroads with, on one side, a farm track leading off to the left, and almost directly opposite this, the entrance to a public car park that was surrounded on all sides by woodland.

'Pepper Wood,' said Mariner.

'You know it?'

'I've walked through it often enough. One of the Royal Hunters Walks. All this used to be part of the Royal Forest of Feckenham.'

'Well,' said Jesson, 'you learn something new every day.' In an efficient feat of precision parking, she brought the car to rest between a squad car and the Land Rover that Mariner recognised as belonging to one of the West Mercia Divisional Surgeons. As they opened the car doors, the ripe smell of manure hit their nostrils, leaving Mariner fighting back another wave of nausea. Jesson retrieved a couple of zoot suits from the forensic services van nearby and brought one set to Mariner. Zipping it up, and managing to not fall over in the process, his overshoes immediately sank into the mud and leaf mulch underfoot.

Kitted out, Mariner and Jesson entered the public car park as a jagged line of uniformed officers was beginning to seal off an extensive area of the woodland with their magic circle of crime scene tape; a fraction of the sixty miles of the stuff West Midlands Police managed to get through every year. Ducking underneath, they signed into the crime scene log before making their way along the designated entry and exit corridor. The area was carefully waymarked, directing them around the outer edge of the car park, though as Mariner glanced across he could see that any chance of isolating tyre tracks in the quagmire was slim. Another uniformed officer directed them into the trees and after a few yards they picked up the aluminium stepping plates put down to preserve the scene, they were already beginning to sink into the mud.

After a few metres the plates left the main footpath and veered off into the woods through patches of deadened bramble and knots of creeping ivy. Eventually, up ahead they saw a group of half a dozen people standing over something on the ground. A gap opened up to let them through. 'Aha, the cavalry have arrived.' Mariner recognised the surgeon as Evan Gray, his round, boyish face the only visible part of him above his jump suit. 'Lovely day for it.'

'Bit early for me today,' said Mariner.

'Oh, some of us have been up for hours,' said Gray cheerily. 'Nothing like a two-year-old insomniac to put a spring in your step of a morning. You've got here at just the right time.' The facetiousness evaporated as he returned to his gruesome task.

As Mariner stepped forward, Jesson's use of the word 'mummy' began to make a terrible kind of sense. The body, lying in a shallow grave, had been tightly wound in cloth. Probably once white, it was now stained a dirty brown. It was buried in a grave no more than eighteen inches deep and had been discovered because some creature, most likely a fox, had begun to dig it out. In doing so, the animal had exposed at one end, the vivid white toes of what could only be a human foot. Now Gray, working at the opposite end, had dug the soil and leaf matter out from around what should logically have been the head, and he was beginning to carefully unwrap the linen. Over his shoulder the crime scene photographer leaned in, capturing every second on video. As Mariner and Jesson watched, Gray eased back the folds to reveal an alabaster-white face, the flesh taut and smooth and bordered by what were now lank and damp, dark curls.

'Grace Clifton,' said Mariner gulping back a burning reflux. He always did his best to avoid throwing up at crime scenes; it set a poor example to junior officers. At that moment a tiny chink of sunlight penetrated the mist and trees to dapple the carpet of brown leaves beside the makeshift grave. As it did, a spark of light winked back at them. 'What's that around her neck?' asked Mariner.

Gray eased back more of the cloth, and with a spatula he lifted from her throat a fine gold chain. As he raised it, a tiny charm slid down towards his finger. 'The letter P,' said Gray.

'P?' Jesson echoed. 'That doesn't make much sense.'

Stepping back, Mariner turned through 360 degrees, scanning the landscape, looking for any other sites where the ground might have been disturbed. 'How far have we walked? Thirty, forty metres?' he said to Jesson. 'This is well off any kind of path. And there are no tracks, even in the soft mud, so she must have been carried. Whoever brought her here has to be fit and strong.' He was remembering the weight of Ellen Kingsley's slender frame. 'It has to be a man. Try and get hold of Superintendent Sharp for authorisation of the manpower to conduct a thorough search. We've found Grace, but it may well be that this is where Rosa and Dee have been brought too. And have the FLO meet me outside the Cliftons' house in an hour.'

A little way off, Mariner saw an open basket tipped on its side, the contents, a few scrawny-looking fungi, spilling onto the ground. 'Where's the person who found her?' he asked one of the uniforms, a lad so young his complexion hadn't yet settled from adolescence.

'Miss Collins. The old dear who lives up at that farmhouse across the road, sir.' He indicated back beyond where Jesson had parked the car. 'She was in a bit of a state so I thought it was best to let Kelly — PC Shreeve — take her home and make her a cup of tea.' The boy looked suddenly panicked. 'I hope that was all right, sir. I told Kelly to stay with her. She's quite old and I thought—'

'It's fine,' Mariner reassured him. 'I'm sure that was the best thing to do in the circumstances. I can't imagine she's going to be very high on our list of suspects.'

Leaving Jesson at the scene, Mariner retraced his steps through the woods and back to the car park, where in addition to all the police vehicles there was now also the typical group of curious onlookers, accompanied by a dog or two. They watched him with interest as he crossed over the road to Jesson's car to deposit his forensic suit, before walking on up the track from that side of the road.

Mariner was glad of a few minutes alone. In any other circumstances it would have been an idyllic start to the day. Now that the rain had passed, the low autumnal mist was breaking up to reveal patches of a crystal clear blue sky set to emerge from behind the white clouds, the ripples of sunlight lighting up the brilliant reds and oranges of the trees. Today was going to be a beauty. But all Mariner could think of was Grace Clifton's parents. They were about to have the worst day of their lives.

He kept on along the track until he came to a long, low, whitewashed and timbered house with an elaborate trellis around a faded front door. He couldn't see a door bell or knocker, so rapped the letterbox. PC Shreeve appeared and took Mariner through to a kitchen whose wide windows looked out over rolling fields and woodland. A faint smell of boiled cabbage did little to settle Mariner's churning stomach. Irene Collins was seated at a small Formica-topped table, still wearing her heavy woollen coat, belted around a stout middle, with a scarf tied around her neck and some kind of crocheted hat jammed down on her head. Her hands, in fingerless gloves, were clasped around a delicate bone-china tea cup. As Mariner went in, a ginger cat blinked at him from its cushion beside a wood-burning stove.

Mariner introduced himself before taking one of the chairs on the opposite side of the table. 'It's Miss Collins, I understand?' From what little he could see of her face, he put her age at someway north of seventy.

'Mrs,' she corrected him, mildly. 'My husband passed away eight years ago.'

'You've had quite a shock.'

She took a deep breath. 'Yes,' she said 'It was quite awful. I don't think I shall ever get it out of my head.' She took a shaky sip of her tea.

'I understand,' said Mariner. 'But it would be helpful if I could ask you one or two questions. Is that all right?'

'Yes, of course. I'll do whatever I can to help, but I didn't really see very much. When I realised — I just wanted to get away, you see?' She looked up at Mariner. 'Would you like a cup of tea?'

'No, I'm fine, thank you.'

As she herself had predicted, Mrs Collins could add little more to what he already knew. She had gone across to the woodland just as it was starting to get light to gather her mushrooms. 'It's been such a good year for them,' she said. 'All this rain and the mild weather. You have to be very careful, of course, but if you know what you're looking for . . . anyway, I was just walking around looking at the ground. I left the path because that's usually better, and I know the woods very well. But I'd forgotten to wear my glasses, so really I was just looking for anything bright that stood out from all the dead leaves. When I saw that little row of white, rounded stalks sticking up, I just thought . . . well . . . you know. Then I got closer and saw the nails . . . I couldn't make sense of it at first. It seemed incomprehensible . . . I thought I must be imagining it . . . then it dawned on me . . .' A tremor passed through her hands as she took the cup to her lips again and sipped at her tea.

'Did you see anyone else around at that time?' Mariner asked.

'No one at all. I rarely do. I go at first light, so it's too early even for people taking their dogs.'

'What about before today?' Mariner asked. 'Have you seen any people or vehicles there that you wouldn't expect to, at odd times of the day perhaps?'

She shook her head. 'It's hard to say. The woods are very popular with walkers, dog walkers and bird watchers. Then of course there are the forestry people who come and go. Quite a lot of the time there are cars or vans of one kind or another parked there. It's more noticeable when there's no one.'

'And you haven't seen anyone around there behaving in an unusual manner? Perhaps someone unsuitably dressed who hasn't got a dog, or binoculars to watch the birds?'

'I can't think that I have. I'm sorry.'

'There's nothing to apologise for,' Mariner smiled. From his inside jacket pocket, he produced one of the cards with his phone numbers on it. 'If you think of anything after I've gone, you can tell it to Kelly here, or you can reach me on these numbers. You've had quite a shock. Is there anyone you'd like us to contact?'

'Oh no, I'll be all right,' she said. 'Everyone has been very kind.'

Walking back down the track to the woods Mariner saw that from here, thanks to the high beech hedges, the road and car park were all but hidden from Irene Collins' house, so that if anyone had wanted to come to the woods during the night they could very easily have done so in privacy. A little further down the road he could see what looked like a complex of barn conversions and realised they would also need to talk to whoever lived there — but those were the only other properties in sight.

Approaching the lane, the smell of manure became stronger again. In his mind's eye Mariner saw Grace's pale and lifeless features and the fleshy, marbled toes that Irene Collins had come across, and finally the contents of his stomach came bubbling up to the surface. It was while he was vomiting into the hedgerow, the foul taste of soured red wine in his mouth, that it came to him, the thing that had been nagging at his brain. Dropping a couple of tabs of mint chewing gum into his mouth, he went back to find

Jesson at the car. 'We know that Rosa had two jobs,' he said. 'I think in addition to the cleaning, she works in hospitality, as a waitress or something. That's what the badge is about and it's why she would be going out in the evenings and coming home late at night.'

'It beats the other alternative,' said Jesson. 'But wherever she works it must be somewhere that lets her dress casually,' she added. 'The clothes we were sent included jeans.'

'That would be acceptable in some bars,' said Mariner. 'Or it could be that she changes into some kind of uniform when she's at work. We think she's been trying to hide her job, remember? When you get back, contact the foster mother and see if she feels able to ask Dominique the direct question.'

* * *

On the way back to Granville Lane, Mariner had Jesson drop him off outside the house belonging to Councillor and Mrs Clifton. The FLO was waiting outside in her car and Mariner quickly briefed her on the team's grim discovery in Pepper Wood before they walked up the drive and rang the doorbell.

For most of the time Mariner enjoyed his job, but this was the part he hated most, and neither time nor experience made it any easier. Along with Grace's parents, her brother and sister were also present, and he was conscious that his every word and gesture would be remembered and replayed in all of their minds — perhaps not today, but frequently in the future — and that he needed to make this as quick and painless for them as he possibly could. He could have scripted their responses himself. The Clifton women seemed to dissolve, seeking comfort in one another, while Grace's father and brother absorbed the news with quiet stoicism and stunned disbelief. Councillor Clifton asked his daughter to take her mother from the room.

'I want to know everything,' he said to Mariner when they had gone. His tone was meek, all the self-importance leached out of him. While Mariner recounted the details of how Grace had been found, Clifton leaned forward in his seat, his knuckles whitened by the tight clasp of his hands, and Mariner felt a new sympathy for the man.

'Grace had a gold chain around her neck,' he said. 'A necklace with a letter P on it. Do you know anything about that?'

But Clifton didn't, and neither did his son. 'I'll ask my wife and daughter,' he said, his voice hoarse with emotion, 'when the time is right.'

'Of course,' said Mariner.

Showing Mariner out a little later, Clifton said, 'I know you weren't sure at first. You thought, as we hoped, that she'd run away.' There was no trace of bitterness in his tone, only weary resignation. 'I don't blame you.'

'You don't need to,' Mariner told him truthfully. 'I'm perfectly capable of doing that myself. I'm very sorry,' he went on. 'It goes without saying that we'll do everything in our power to find out who is responsible.'

Chapter Seventeen

Mariner had the FLO drop him back at his house, where he was able to get a quick shower and a change of clothes before going into Granville Lane. 'Stay close,' he instructed her as he got out of the car. 'And make sure someone asks Grace's mother and sister about that necklace.'

Despite the shock and the disappointment that this was how the search for Grace Clifton had ended, the incident room was buzzing, a new resolve fuelled by the imperative of finding out what had happened to her, and why. When Mariner arrived, Vicky Jesson was sharing details of the morning's events.

'And there's no doubt that it's her?' asked Superintendent Sharp.

'None whatsoever,' Mariner confirmed, slipping into the back of the crowded room.

'How did her parents take it?' Charlie Glover asked.

'About as you'd expect,' said Mariner. 'They're devastated, of course, but Councillor Clifton was very restrained under the circumstances. It could have been far worse. We've got people out searching the rest of the woods?' he turned to ask Sharp.

'As we speak,' she said, standing up. 'All right with you if Dawson and I handle the press on this?' she asked Mariner. He was only too happy to let her take the lead. 'Right, I'll let you all get on.' The meeting broke up as people went about their assigned tasks.

'How are you feeling?' Jesson asked Mariner.

'I've had better days.'

'Did you ask about the necklace?'

'Clifton didn't know anything about it, but he's agreed to talk to his wife and daughter when he gets the chance,' said Mariner. 'They weren't in any fit state to answer those kinds of questions. I've told the FLO to prompt the conversation if necessary, but we probably won't be hearing from them for a while.'

'I keep wondering, why *P*?' said Jesson. 'We've been all over her laptop, social networks and that. I can check the list again, but I can't think of anyone we've come across with that initial, except for her best friend: P for Pippa.'

'Pippa Talbot?' For some reason Mariner hadn't thought of her. He wasn't so sure. 'Do girls that age still wear trinkets dedicated to their best friend?'

'It would be unusual,' admitted Jesson. 'By eighteen they've normally grown out of all that little-girly stuff.'

'Unless it signals more than just friendship,' said Mariner. 'Everyone's been pretty keen to tell us that Grace doesn't have a *boyfriend* right now, but do we know for certain that she's interested in boys? And do we know anything about Pippa's sexual preferences?'

'Even if it does relate to Pippa, she might not know anything about it,' Glover chimed in. 'Grace could have had a secret crush on her friend.'

'It's possible, I suppose.' Jesson was dubious. 'But if it's not Pippa, it could be a friend or boyfriend that either no one's telling us about—'

'Or who no one knows about,' said Mariner.

'It could be a secret admirer that Grace herself was unaware of,' added Glover.

'All of which are feasible,' Mariner said. 'We'll need to trawl back though everyone she knew, talk to family and friends again to see if they can identify anyone with that initial.'

Jesson's mobile rang and she stepped away to answer it. 'Dominique's foster mum,' she explained, as the call came to an end. 'Dominique has confirmed that her mum works in a hotel. It's called the Bell and something, but that's all she could get.'

'The Bell and something?' Glover frowned. 'There's the Bell in Harborne, or there used to be the old Bell and Pump folk club in Edgbaston, but they're not hotels.'

'Perhaps her mum told her it was a hotel because it sounds . . . I don't know, more respectable?' said Jesson.

'I don't think it's the Bell and anything,' said Mariner, recalling his walk the previous night. 'I think it's the Belvedere Hotel on Hill Street. To get from Symphony Hall to the Arcadian, Grace Clifton would have walked right past it.'

Charlie was still frowning. 'That name seems familiar.'

'You know it?' Jesson asked.

Frustratingly, Charlie shook his head. 'I think so, but I can't think why. It'll come back to me.'

'Vicky, you go and talk to Pippa Talbot about the necklace,' said Mariner. 'If it's not relevant then we need to rule it out as quickly as possible, and it would be useful to see if there's anything she can add to her statement now that we've found Grace. You can gauge her reaction too. Charlie, you can come with me.'

* * *

Although a well-established hotel, in recent years the Belvedere had undergone something of an identity crisis. Lacking the historical credentials of the Burlington or the Plough and Harrow, it had been radically refurbished in various attempts to adapt to the fierce competition of the newly built city centre hotels. What had emerged was an uncomfortable hybrid of traditional and new. The reception area was rooted predominantly in the past, with a mock-Regency theme comprising richly patterned carpets, plush upholstery and crystal chandeliers that gave an illusion of opulence. The adjacent bar, on the other hand, was a vision of glossy black and chrome furnishings built more for style than comfort.

Identifying himself, Mariner asked to speak to the hotel manager, but he and Glover were kept waiting in the lobby for nearly half an hour before a tall, immaculately groomed woman in her mid-thirties — doubtless the product of some kind of graduate training programme — asked them to come through to her office. Miss Karpinski offered refreshments, which they both declined.

'What can you tell us about Rosa Batista?' Mariner asked.

The manager seemed surprised by the question. 'Rosa? She has been with us for a short time only,' she said, her voice lightly accented. 'I can tell you a little, but our housekeeper and bar manager will be able to tell you more about her day-to-day work. I will ask them to join us. Excuse me one moment.' Lifting the receiver on her desk she asked the person at the other end to fetch Gilda and Ricardo.

'How would you describe Rosa?' Mariner asked, while they waited.

'Up until this week I would have said that she was a good worker — very reliable,' said the manager. 'But she didn't come to work last Monday morning and we haven't heard from her since then.'

'We think there might be a very good reason for that,' said Mariner. 'Can you tell me something about the nature of her work here?'

'A few weeks ago, Rosa started working two different jobs for us. She started out as a part-time cleaner doing the ten-'til-two shift on week days. I understand she has a young daughter so she needed a job that would fit into her time at school. Then, in the middle of August, we had a bad virus rip through our bar staff. Rosa happened to be in on a day when we realised we would be really short-staffed. She offered to cover the bar for a couple of nights. I think she was glad of the extra money. The references she brought with her when she first applied to work here were for bar work anyway, and she had much experience. It seemed like the perfect solution for us. To begin with it was just temporary cover, but then we had another of our bar staff resign, so we gave Rosa a proper contract for the bar, Friday and Saturday nights.'

'But she still comes in to clean?'

'On the days when her daughter is at school. She wanted it that way, and I thought, why not? Up until this week, I don't think she has ever had a day off sick. She works very hard and she uses her initiative. She is determined to provide a solid future for her daughter. On one occasion when the bar manager was absent she took over as acting manager and I know that I can trust her.'

'Do you know who cares for Rosa's daughter when she is here at the weekends?' Mariner asked.

The manager shrugged. 'I don't know. I guess the child's father?'

There was a knock on the door and she called out to admit two people. Ricardo, the bar manager, was a short and stocky Mediterranean-looking man of about forty, with thinning, slicked-back hair. Behind his glasses he had the remains of what looked like a nasty black eye. His colleague, Gilda, was a little older than him: a small, undernourished-looking woman, dressed in a domestic's tunic. She took the only spare seat and there was a further delay while Ricardo disappeared to fetch a chair for himself. When he too was sitting down, the manager explained the reason for Mariner's visit. 'The police are asking about Rosa Batista,' she said.

'It appears that her daughter, Dominique, has been at home alone since last Saturday night, and no one else seems to have seen Rosa since then,' Mariner added. 'I wonder if you could tell me if she arrived for work on Saturday night?' He directed the question at Ricardo.

Ricardo's accent was stronger than the manager's, and Mariner had to concentrate hard to pick up everything he said. He confirmed that Rosa had worked her usual shift on Saturday, leaving, as far as he was aware, to go straight home shortly after midnight. He too seemed puzzled by Rosa's disappearance and was adamant that she would not have walked out on her child. 'That girl is the light of her life,' he said.

'And that's the last time any of you saw her?'

Gilda shrugged. 'She didn't come to do her cleaning shift on Monday morning,' she said. 'Sometimes this happens with other workers but this was so strange for Rosa.'

'Has anyone tried to contact her?' Mariner asked.

'We have a number for her mobile phone, but it goes straight to voicemail,' Gilda said. 'I tried maybe four or five times, then I gave up and told Miss Karpinski.' As she spoke, she glanced towards her boss.

'Didn't you think it was odd, when up until then she had been so reliable?'

The manager's tone remained cool. 'I think you don't know much about hotel work, Inspector,' she said. 'It is not well paid. It is a common thing for workers to suddenly not come to work and then you have to find someone else.'

'What time does the bar close?' Mariner asked Ricardo.

'Eleven thirty,' said Ricardo. 'There was a group out for a company social event and they made a real mess, so it took a little while to clear it up. After Rosa had finished cashing up the tills she came to help too, then we went to have a cigarette outside and I left her to lock up at about midnight.'

'How did Rosa seem? Was anything bothering her?'

Ricardo shrugged. 'I think we spoke about what we would do the next day, on Sunday. She was going to buy her little girl a new coat.'

'Was there anything different about Saturday night? Did you notice anyone paying Rosa particular attention during the evening?'

Saturday had been typically busy, Ricardo said. People were letting their hair down, but things hadn't got out of hand the way they sometimes could. Nor had he noticed anything untoward in Rosa's interactions with the customers.

'What do you mean when you say things can get out of hand?' asked Mariner. 'Does this have anything to do with the accident Rosa suffered at work a few weeks ago?'

'Oh, *that* . . . that was not so much an accident,' Ricardo said. 'But it was very unusual. One of the customers, he was making a nuisance of himself.'

'In what way?' asked Mariner.

'He got very drunk and abusive. I asked him to leave, but he refused. I tried to calm him down but there was a scuffle. Rosa came to help and we were both a little hurt. She was OK, apart from just a little bruising, but I went to go to the hospital to get my eye checked out. It seemed like we were there nearly all night. I told Rosa to go home, but she stayed with me.'

'Do you know this customer's name?' asked Mariner.

'I'm sorry, no,' the manager said firmly.

'Was he local, have you seen him again?'

'We asked him not to come back to the hotel and I haven't seen him since,' she said, and Ricardo confirmed this with a nod.

'Did you report this incident to the police?'

The manager spoke up. 'When the man had calmed down he apologised, so there was no need to take it any further.' She and Ricardo exchanged a glance, and Mariner wondered whose decision that had been.

'And neither you nor Rosa did anything to provoke this behaviour?' Mariner asked Ricardo.

'No. I mean, men flirt with her a lot. Rosa's an attractive woman, and she's very . . . warm and sunny, you know. Everybody loves Rosa. But she knows where to draw the line and she's very professional. It's her job to be nice to customers, even the arseholes, so she's polite but she doesn't encourage them.'

'Does she ever meet up with any of them after work?'

'If she does, she's very discreet and I've heard nothing about it. I think it's unlikely, though. She always wants to get home to her little girl.'

'Does Rosa have a boyfriend?' Glover asked.

'She's never mentioned one,' Ricardo said. 'She was married before, though, when she lived in London, to her little girl's father.'

'Does she ever mention seeing him?'

'I think he went back to Torquay.'

'He's from Torquay?'

'No, you know *Torkey,'* said Ricardo. 'He's Torkish.'

'Ah, Turkish, I see,' said Mariner. 'How does Rosa get home at night, after work?'

'She takes the bus,' said Ricardo. 'Sometimes she has to run. The last one is at quarter past twelve.'

'Would she have made it on Saturday?'

'Yeah.'

'What does Rosa wear when she works in the bar?' Mariner asked.

'A white shirt and dark skirt,' said the manager. 'It's the uniform.'

'Does she have a locker, and somewhere she gets changed?'

When Mariner felt they had learned all they could, he asked to be shown to Rosa's locker. There was little in it. Taped to the inside of the door were a couple of snapshots of Dominique and stuffed in the bottom of the locker was a plastic carrier bag. Inside they found a dark skirt and black heeled shoes, the ones she would change into for her shift on the bar. There was no blouse. 'What are the chances our washerwoman has got it?' said Glover.

Before they left, Mariner asked the manager if she had a photograph of Rosa on file. It would be the first one they'd managed to come by. Karpinski went to the filing cabinet and took out a shot that would have been used for the hotel publicity materials. Glover and Mariner exchanged a look. Like Grace Clifton, Rosa Batista was a young woman walking the city centre late at night, and like Grace Clifton she had dark, curly hair. They could have been sisters.

On their way out they saw Gilda standing on the pavement nervously smoking a cigarette. After a moment's hesitation she came over to them. 'I heard you found that other girl who went missing,' she said. 'Do you think Rosa's ended up the same way?'

'We don't know yet,' said Mariner tactfully, but walking back to the car, he checked his phone and found a message from Sergeant Paul Sholter, who was leading the search at Pepper Wood. Sholter was asking for him to call back urgently.

'I've been trying to reach you, sir. We've found another mummy,' he said. 'Dr Gray is out here, and we're about to move her.'

Chapter Eighteen

There was a symmetry to it, Mariner thought, as he and Glover sped out again between the Worcestershire hedgerows. When he'd last been here to view a body, it had been daybreak. Now, in the late afternoon, the light was fading and a shelf of thick cloud rolling in, bringing with it a mist that was beginning to obscure the fields and hedges. This time as they progressed through the trees at the deposition site, they veered off in a southerly direction and a way off through the gloom saw the white protective tent that had been erected over the find, all theatrically lit by arc lamps. The uniformed officer on guard stood back to let them through and they found Gray and his assistant squatting beside the bandaged body. The face had already been exposed, gleaming supernaturally white in the argentine light. Mariner took the newly acquired photo of Rosa Batista from his pocket. There was no doubt that this was her.

'That poor kid,' said Charlie, quietly.

Reaching out with a gloved hand, Gray directed one of the lamps to just below Rosa's face and lifted something from her neck. It was a fine gold chain. He confirmed what they couldn't quite see for themselves. 'Another letter P.'

Before he and Glover left the scene, Mariner sought out Paul Sholter. 'How much ground have you covered so far?' he asked.

Sholter shone a powerful torch onto the large-scale map in its protective cover. 'We've searched all the woodland to the west and north of where Grace was found,' he said, indicating the area on the map, 'including this coppice where Rosa is. All we have left now is the section over here, to the south east. It's about another square mile, mile and a half.'

'OK,' said Mariner. 'Call everyone off for now and start again tomorrow morning when it's light. There might be one more out there.'

'You think they're going to find Dee Henderson?' asked Glover as they made their way back to Granville Lane.

'If she met the same fate as the other two, then we should receive a parcel of clothes very soon,' said Mariner.

* * *

It was late when he got home, but after a restless night's sleep Mariner went into work on Monday morning fully expecting to find a third parcel waiting for him. His apprehension was unfounded. He even went down to harass the clerk in the post room in person, but was told that there was nothing for either him or Superintendent Sharp. Returning to the incident room, Charlie caught his eye. 'Nothing new, boss?'

Mariner had never noticed Glover call him 'boss' before. That was Tony Knox's habit. Sharp came down from her office. She didn't look as if she'd had a very good night either.

'Nothing?'

Mariner shook his head. 'She's been gone since Wednesday night,' he said. 'We might have reasonably expected a delivery by now.'

'Do you think the press coverage might have put him off?'

'It's possible,' Mariner conceded. 'Or it just might mean, as we've considered, that Dee Henderson is nothing to do with our washerwoman. We've already recognised that she's not exactly his type. It could just be someone else taking advantage of the opportunity in the hope that we will make that assumption.'

'Someone like Paddy Henderson you mean?' Sharp said.

'He's got a history of mental health problems,' Mariner reminded her. 'He had PTSD after coming back from Afghanistan. Ellen Kingsley told us that he's "very protective" of Dee. In some circumstances that can be code for jealous and controlling.'

'Would Henderson have reported his wife missing, though, if he's somehow behind her disappearance?' said Sharp.

'He might have done — if he's watertight,' said Mariner. 'Or if he thinks he is. He'd need to do it now if he's to take advantage of our investigation and let's face it, he wouldn't be the first perpetrator to put himself in the spotlight, would he?'

'Go on.' Sharp leaned back on a nearby desk and folded her arms, waiting to be persuaded.

Mariner walked over to the incident board. 'So far Dee Henderson hasn't exactly matched any of the criteria of the other two. She doesn't fit the physical profile. Different hair colour, slightly older.'

'Are two victims enough to create a profile?' said Sharp. 'Any similarities between them could just be pure coincidence.'

'True,' said Mariner. 'But the clothing's a pretty powerful signature. If we had that for Dee, we would know for sure.'

'Grace's clothing didn't come to us directly,' Charlie reminded him. 'So Dee's could just have got lost in the post.'

'But Rosa's was sent to me personally,' said Mariner. 'He corrected his mistake. And there are other differences between Dee and the other two,' he went on. 'Dee isn't routinely in the city centre; she's only ever passing through. And her timing varies. Depending on the train she catches, she doesn't always get the same bus, and sometimes — when Paddy picks her up — she doesn't travel through the city at all. She'd be harder for someone to pin down.'

'Unless hers was a more opportunistic encounter.'

Vicky Jesson came in while they were talking. 'What's going on?' she asked.

'We're testing out Paddy Henderson for Dee,' Sharp told her. 'Henderson's alibi is comfortable, though,' she reminded Mariner. 'He wouldn't be able to rely on the kids to lie for him.'

Jesson scoffed. 'You can say that again.'

'But he's only secure up to about nine thirty,' countered Mariner. 'After that, by his own admission, the kids were all asleep in bed. He could easily have slipped out to go and pick Dee up. We haven't found her phone. What's to say he didn't ring or text her to say that he would collect her?'

'Then what?' said Jesson, dropping her bag and scarf on her desk.

'I don't know,' said Mariner. 'Perhaps they had a row about something.'

'For instance?' Glover asked.

'That's easy,' said Jesson, pragmatically. 'Dee Henderson left her first husband because she had an affair with Paddy. Nothing to stop her doing the same thing to him. Once an adulterer, always an adulterer.'

'You think that might be it?' said Sharp.

'I think it's possible,' said Mariner. 'And even if Dee's not having an affair, does Paddy fully trust her? After all, he's very familiar with her track record, so he knows how that can work. He's been there himself too. It brings us back to that fine line between being protective and being jealous. He might even have imagined something that just wasn't there.'

'But to *kill* her?' Sharp still wasn't convinced. 'Isn't that taking it a bit far?'

'He's an ex-squaddie,' said Mariner. 'The man must be physically fit and if he's handy with his fists it could even have been an accident. Fortunately for him various other women happen to have fallen victim to an unknown killer, and he must be experienced at operating covertly — all he has to do is dispose of the body, report Dee missing and leave us to do the rest.' He scratched the back of his head. 'All pure conjecture, of course,' he conceded.

'Henderson drives a van,' said Charlie Glover, suddenly. They all turned to look at him and he glanced up from the notes he'd been reading. He held up a pocket book. 'A dark blue one. It says so in here from whoever did the background checks. And several people reported seeing a dark-coloured van around after the Grace Clifton reconstruction. I'm just saying, that's all,' he added defensively.

'Let's get hold of the CCTV from the hospital site on the night Dee went missing,' Mariner said to Charlie. 'Paddy might have picked her up in the city centre, but it would make more sense for him to fetch her straight from work.' He thought for a moment. 'And it wouldn't do any harm to check out his alibis for the nights that Grace and Rosa went missing.'

Sharp, on her way out, turned and shot him a questioning look. 'P for Paddy,' he said. 'Just covering the angles.' When Sharp had gone he turned to Jesson. 'How did you get on with Pippa Talbot?'

'Understandably she's in a bit of a state,' said Jesson. 'But she has no memory of seeing Grace wearing that necklace. If anything, I think she was surprised — said it wouldn't be Grace's style to wear that kind of thing. "Cheesy" was the word she used. I asked her if she thought Grace could have had a crush on her, but I think she was quite disturbed by the idea. If that was the case, I don't think Pippa knew anything about it.'

'It's looking less likely,' said Mariner. 'The search team found Rosa Batista in another shallow grave in Pepper Wood last night.'

'Dear God.'

'She was also wearing a gold chain around her neck with a letter P charm on it, but there's nothing to suggest that Pippa knew Rosa.'

Jesson took a moment to absorb that. 'So the necklace is something to do with whoever took them?'

'It would make sense. Aside from what's happened to them since they disappeared, it's the only thing so far that we can be sure they have in common. The big question is whether they knew P before their last fatal encounter with him.'

* * *

Charlie Glover was onto something, or thought he was. As soon as Mariner had mentioned the Belvedere Hotel, he felt sure he'd heard of it before, so now he was going back over past cases to try and find out how that was. It had taken him a while, but he'd found it, eighteen months ago: an attack on a young woman there. The victim, Chelsey Skoyles, aged twenty, had been dragged into the yard behind the hotel and assaulted late at night. There was only one witness to the actual attack — a guest named Mr Hausknecht — and as the assailant had run off when he and the hotel's night porter had gone out to help, there were no clear suspects. The notes also stated explicitly that the girl had been highly intoxicated, making it difficult to get an accurate picture of exactly what had happened. One cryptic note at the bottom of the page said simply 'Sceptre.' Charlie wondered if, at some time, there had been an Operation Sceptre that it was linked to. It sounded like the sort of meaningless title that might be used. But even if it was part of a wider investigation, it appeared that the lines of enquiry had run dry and the case had consequently been shelved. Noting who had attended the incident Glover realised it was unlikely to be re-opened.

But it might explain why Ricardo and Karpinski had been so cagey, thought Charlie. Two separate incidents at the hotel, then a member of staff goes missing. The idea that their washerwoman was not new to preying on women made a certain kind of sense to Charlie. Chelsey Skoyles might have been a practice run — and well worth talking to again. The key witness might prove more difficult. Charlie noted from the case file that his home address was in Philadelphia, USA. But he was getting ahead of himself.

* * *

Early in the afternoon Mariner had a call from the city pathologist, Stuart Croghan. He was ready to commence the preliminary post-mortems for Grace Clifton and Rosa Batista. For a couple of years now forensic PMs for the city had been conducted in Sandwell, but the facility there was temporarily closed, so Mariner and Jesson met Croghan at the brand-new mortuary at Queen Elizabeth hospital. The high-tech suite included a separate viewing room, which meant that they could have chosen to watch the pathologist working through a window and a bank of high resolution colour monitors, communicating with him via a two-way intercom. Mariner, though, preferred to be right there beside Croghan, seeing what he saw at first hand. So, gowned and masked, to minimise any risk of cross-contamination, they joined Croghan in the examination room. The only disadvantage to this arrangement was the exposure to the customary unpleasant smells, which somehow could never quite be subsumed by chemicals.

The two women, unwrapped from their coverings, had been laid out on gurneys side by side, a few feet apart, and Mariner was struck again by the uncanny physical likeness between them. He said as much to Croghan.

'There are lots of similarities in their current condition too, if you take the time difference out of the equation,' said Croghan. 'Grace is in a greater state of deterioration, which would indicate that she was killed and buried several days before Rosa. But they are both very clean,' he went on to observe. 'I'm not sure that we're going to get much in the way of forensic material from either of them. I think they've been bathed, or at the very least submerged in water at some point. Death in both cases was from asphyxiation. We have a number of burst blood vessels behind the eyes that bear this out.'

'They were strangled?' asked Mariner.

'That I'm not so certain about,' said Croghan. 'If you look at their throats, there's no evidence, even at this stage, of any bruising, and the hyoid bones are intact, which would be unusual. Drowning is a possibility, of course, but we won't know for certain until we open up the lungs. What is interesting, though,' Croghan was standing nearest to Grace Clifton's body and drew Mariner and Jesson's attention to her face, 'are these faint bruises on either side of the nostrils.' He pointed to the round, purple marks. 'You can see that Rosa has them too.'

'Caused by what?' Jesson asked.

Croghan looked up at her. 'That's your domain, but I'd say their noses have been pinched or even clamped in some way. Rosa also has some old bruising above and around her left eye. From a few weeks ago, I would think.'

'She was involved in some kind of fracas with a customer,' Mariner said. 'Are they showing any sign of recent sexual activity?'

'Nothing obvious. No bruising around the pelvic area. We've taken the usual swabs, but my guess is that the purpose of the washing was to flush out any bodily fluids. My guess would be that you're looking for someone who is to some extent knowledgeable about forensics.'

'That could be anyone who watches TV crime drama these days,' said Mariner. 'They've been restrained too,' he added, noting the vivid bands around the wrists and ankles of each woman.

'Correct,' said Croghan. 'And the depth and lividity of the chafe marks would suggest that they were tied with something rigid.' He lifted Grace's wrist. 'You can see how deep the marks are, and that the skin is raw and broken in places.'

'So, wire or something?' said Jesson.

'Or nylon cable ties?' Mariner hazarded.

'We haven't recovered any fibres here, so that would make sense,' Croghan agreed. 'We did find this on Rosa's upper lip, though.' Taking them over to one of the side benches, Croghan picked up a glass slide and placed it underneath a microscope, so that an image appeared on the monitor above. It was a tiny fleck of something dark.

'What is it?' Mariner asked.

'It's a plastic adhesive material, like duct tape, though we'll know for sure when it's been analysed.' Croghan picked up another slide and slid it under the viewer. 'And when we did the swabs, we retrieved this from Grace's ear.' Magnified many hundreds of times the image resembled a wiggly piece of string.

'From the cloth she was wrapped in?' Mariner speculated.

'No, it's too coarse for that,' said Croghan. 'It looks to me more like a fibre from sack-cloth. Hessian, or something of that nature.'

‘Something she was gagged with?’

‘Possibly,’ said Croghan. ‘But we salvaged an almost identical fibre from the top of Rosa’s head, caught in her hair, so alternatively something that was used to cover their heads at some point. Toxicology should tell us whether or not they have been drugged, but given the amount of time they’ve been missing, it’s possible that any sedative may have worked itself out of their systems before they were killed.’ Croghan had returned to Grace’s body. ‘Also, as you can see, the pubic hair has been removed, by shaving. It may, of course, have been personal preference, but it’s the same for both women — which would be another coincidence. Do we know if either of them was a fan of the Brazilian?’

‘Strangely enough, that’s not a question we’ve asked, but I would be surprised, given what we know about them so far,’ said Mariner. ‘We haven’t made this generally known yet, but along with the clothing for each woman we were sent a sample of pubic hair.’

‘How charming,’ said Croghan. ‘Then I’m sure you’re right. Whoever shaved them has been meticulous. The skin is smooth. You sent the hair to the lab?’

‘Yes, should get the results any day.’

‘Good, they should be able to tell you what kind of razor or shaver has been used. If it’s any help, overall I’m getting the impression of someone who has taken good care of these women, treating them respectfully, reverentially even.’

‘Any thoughts yet on how long they have been dead?’ asked Mariner.

Croghan sighed. ‘It’s never enough, is it? You always have to end with the hard stuff. Wrapping them in the sheets will have effectively offered some protection from the usual pests and will, of course, have skewed the effects of air temperature and moisture. At a rough guess — and this is going out on a limb — I would say for Grace it’s somewhere between seven and ten days, and Rosa three days to a week.'

'Those are big windows,' said Mariner.

'I'm sorry, it's the best I can do.'

Mariner had already seen the two soiled cloths, spread out on a bench on the far side of the room. 'Anything you can tell us about the cloth?' asked Mariner.

'Ah, our Turin shrouds.' Croghan walked them over to the bench for a closer look at the material. 'They look like your common or garden bed sheets,' he said. 'More or less identical, they're made of heavy-duty pure cotton, the kind that is commonly used in a setting where linen has to be frequently laundered.'

'Like a hotel?' asked Mariner.

'That would be about right,' said Croghan. 'Most domestic stuff these days is much lighter — polycotton or percale. We'll know more when it's had a full analysis.' Reaching over, he lifted the edge of one sheet where there was a clean rectangular step in the fabric. 'You can see here that a chunk has also been cut out of it, which makes me wonder if it was stamped with a laundry mark,' he indicated. 'It's the same for both of them and would be consistent with your idea of a hotel.'

Before they left, Croghan came out to the viewing suite with a small plastic bag containing one of the necklaces. 'Again, identical on both women,' he said. 'You might want to keep this one back for tomorrow morning.'

'What's happening tomorrow morning?' asked Jesson.

'Councillor and Mrs Clifton are coming in to make a formal identification,' said Mariner.

'What about Rosa?'

'If we can't get hold of any of her family down in London we'll have to ask the teacher, Sam McBride, to come in.'

Chapter Nineteen

Chelsey Skoyles herself came to the door of the house on Winchester Drive. She looked sleepy and her hair was tangled, as if she had just got out of bed, although Charlie could hear a TV playing nearby. Pudgy and with dyed blond hair and a number of piercings, Chelsey wore too-tight tracksuit bottoms and a short T-shirt. Squinting at Glover, she absently scratched at the inch or so of white belly visible between the two.

Glover identified himself, presenting his warrant card. 'I'd like to ask you some questions about what happened to you at the Belvedere Hotel last year,' he said.

'What?' She gazed back blankly.

'The assault,' said Glover. 'I want to talk to you about it. Can I come in?'

'I suppose.' Leaving the door open for Glover to follow, she slouched back along the hallway. He found her slumped back in front of the TV in an untidy living room, the air stale from unopened windows, watching what looked like a child's cartoon show. Sitting down, Glover found himself momentarily distracted by the garish colours and sounds. 'Can we turn the TV off for a bit?' he asked.

Without looking at him she picked up the remote and hit the mute button. 'What did you want, then?'

'I just want you to tell me about the night you were attacked,' Glover repeated, suspecting that Chelsey was what Helen would have called a few sandwiches short of a picnic.

'I told that other bloke, ages ago,' Chelsey said, puzzled.

'I know, but it would help if you could tell me too,' said Glover, as if he were addressing a five-year-old. 'In case we missed something, or there's anything new you've remembered in the meantime.'

Chelsey heaved a huge sigh. 'We was out on Broad Street — me and Laura and Stacey — and I'd had a skinful. Stace went off with this bloke and I don't know what happened to Laura but I ended up on my own. I was starving so I went and got a McDonald's from the all-night one by the library, then I couldn't get a taxi, so I went down to the station. There's always loads there.' She seemed to lose her thread.

'Then what happened?' Glover prompted.

'I was taking a shortcut down this alleyway, and I got shoved in the back. This bloke just came out of nowhere. He got hold of my arms really tight and dragged me in by these big bins and pushed me against the fence. I banged my head.' She touched her scalp. 'He had his hands all over me and up my skirt, so I screamed. He told me to shut up, but he was trying to hold me down and get his trousers undone, so he couldn't do much about it. I just kept yelling.' Her lower lip quivered at the memory. 'Then this door opened right by us and these two men came out. He just let me go and legged it. One of the fellas went after him, but he couldn't catch him. I was just sat on the floor, crying. I tried to get away too, because I was scared but the other man said they'd called the police so I'd be all right.'

'That was the American man, and the hotel porter?'

She nodded. 'They took me in the hotel and got me a cup of tea and we waited 'til the police came. They were nice to me.'

'You said this man who attacked you came out of nowhere and pushed you from behind. This is really important, Chelsey. Where do you think he could've come from?'

'Dunno. All of a sudden he was just there.'

'Could he have come from the hotel?'

She thought about that for a while, before shrugging. 'I suppose so.'

While they were talking, a door slammed shut, shaking the whole house, and a middle-aged woman appeared, weighed down with supermarket carrier bags. Seeing Glover, her eyes narrowed. 'Who are you?' she demanded.

He got up to show her his warrant card 'I'm DS Cha—'

'Police? What the fuck are you doing in my house?'

'It's all right, Mrs Skoyles,' Glover said, trying to placate her. 'I just came to ask—'

'Ask her what? What do you want with her?'

'I was asking her about the attack last—'

'It's a bit late for that! You've got no fucking right barging in here like this.'

'I didn't—'

'Chelsey, get up to your room,' she ordered, before rounding on Glover. 'She don't want to talk about it — it upsets her. She's only just getting over it. And your lot weren't fucking interested. Not when it happened.'

'What do you mean?'

'I mean get out of my house now. We don't want you here. You should have done your job before. Go on, get out. Now!'

Glover had no option but to retreat. But the episode left him feeling slightly mystified. Hostility towards the police was common enough, and Charlie had experienced it more times than he could recall, but here it seemed misplaced to say the least. Chelsey hadn't seemed remotely upset to be talking to him, and he would have expected the family to welcome any further investigation into the incident. Perhaps when Mrs Skoyles had calmed down . . . Meanwhile there were other lines of enquiry to be pursued. He started his car and headed back to Granville Lane.

* * *

After the post-mortems, Jesson and Mariner stopped off at one of those ubiquitous American-style coffee shops in the hospital entrance to try and purge the smells still lingering in their nostrils. Sipping her cappuccino, Jesson smacked her lips and grimaced. 'I can still taste those chemicals.'

'Operant conditioning,' said Mariner. He was watching, out of the window, the people coming and going. 'So if P is our killer, the necklaces may have only been put on the women shortly before, or after, their deaths. Both women had contact with him, so he must have picked them up somewhere. The most obvious place is in or around the Belvedere. Rosa worked there and Grace probably walked past it on a regular basis. For all we know she may have been inside too.'

'We should check with her friends,' said Jesson. 'And her colleagues from Symphony Hall.'

'So,' said Mariner, 'our man picks them up and takes them somewhere where they can be undressed and then washed clean. Each body is then wrapped in a sheet and transported out to Pepper Wood, where he carries them some distance before digging a shallow grave for each and burying them. The clothes are laundered and ironed, the shoes are polished — then they're sent to us. This person has access to somewhere private where he can do whatever it is he does with them, strip and bathe them, launder their clothes, then wrap them and move them. Could you do all that in a hotel without being noticed?'

Jesson looked doubtful. 'You might get away with it for a few hours, perhaps even overnight.'

'But this is all pointing to the women being held for some time, possibly days.'

'I suppose that might be possible if you were on the staff,' she conceded. 'You'd have access to everywhere — bathrooms, laundry and linen store. And keys to the rooms. A strategically placed "do not disturb" or "closed for maintenance" sign would help.'

'But only for a limited time and even then, it would be a huge risk,' Mariner pointed out. 'And what about when you're ready to move them?'

'There must be a trade entrance to the hotel round the back. In the dead of night it might just have been possible to make his exit unnoticed and, as we know, the right kind of vehicle can easily blend in.'

'Like a dark-coloured van, you mean?' said Mariner.

They finished their drinks and started making their way back to the car park. 'We should look at the staff and guest lists for the hotel,' Mariner said, as they walked. 'You'd better call Charlie and let him know where we're going. Where is he, anyway?'

But wherever Glover was, he wasn't answering his phone, so Vicky left a message instead.

* * *

Having been ejected from the Skoyles' home, Charlie had returned to Granville Lane. According to the incident report on Chelsey Skoyles' attack, the Belvedere's night porter didn't speak very good English and, as he had called the police first, he only arrived on the scene after the assailant had run off. Charlie was therefore putting through a long-distance call to Larry and Gaynor Hausknecht at their home in Philadelphia. The five-hour time difference meant that, in the US, it was just coming up to 9 a.m. Larry Hausknecht, when he came on the line, was unfazed. 'To be honest, we've been expecting your call. I'd have thought someone would have gotten in touch with us long before now,' he said. 'I told the officer at the time that I'd be happy to help in any way I can — and to call me as soon as the guy was caught. Is that why you're calling? You've got him?'

'We're not quite there yet,' said Glover. 'Mainly as there hasn't been much of a description to go on . . . I mean, I understand that it was dark and you didn't get a good look at him—'

'Sure, it was dark,' Hausknecht interrupted. 'But I got a pretty good look at the bastard. I can picture him right now. And I gave a detailed description to the police officer who came to the hotel that night.'

Frowning, Charlie stared at the notes in front of him: *sole witness unable to provide adequate description due to conditions.* 'Would you mind just running through it again,' he said.

'Sure,' said Hausknecht. 'The guy was about my height — maybe five-nine or five-ten — lean, with short, dark hair and a real short beard, like he hadn't shaved for a couple of days. He was wearing a suit and tie. The tie was shiny, with some sort of metallic effect. He was kind of dishevelled, I guess because of what he'd tried to do to that poor girl, but apart from that he looked like a respectable type of guy. I ran after him, but he was gone pretty fast, so he must have been athletic, you know?'

Hausknecht was right. That was a detailed description. Glover didn't like to contemplate why it hadn't been recorded in the file.

'Mr Hausknecht, if I can arrange a video conference, would you be prepared to help us put together an e-fit of this man?'

'Sure. And how is the girl, Chelsey? My wife and I were worried about her. She was pretty clearly intoxicated, and if I'm honest the officer who came out seemed more concerned with that than what had happened to her.'

'She's fine,' said Charlie. 'I spoke to her today and she's . . .' Charlie hesitated. 'She's being well supported by her family,' he said.

'Well, I'm glad to hear that.'

* * *

Leaving the car parked on double-yellow lines outside the Belvedere, Mariner dispatched Jesson to obtain guest lists for the nights that Grace and Rosa went missing as well as the night of the other alleged attack. This time they would take a more assertive approach.

Meanwhile he walked back down Hill Street and round to the back of the block to investigate the rear entrance of the hotel. A narrow passageway ran along the rear of the buildings and below the hotel's spidery fire escapes was an open trade entrance, with waste skips lined up against one fence. Along the opposite side of the yard, a crude canopy had been erected over a shallow ramp that went up to the double door access. As Mariner stood there, the nearest of the two doors opened and a young man in chef's whites came out to deposit a bulging rubbish bag into one of the bins. When he'd gone back inside, Mariner went up three concrete steps and tried the second door. It opened easily, taking him into a carpeted corridor, which he followed past toilets marked pretentiously 'Dames' and 'Hommes' to find himself at the back of the hotel lobby. As he walked past the lifts, one of them pinged, as if sensing his presence, and the doors slid open. It was empty, so Mariner stepped inside for a second and scanned the control panel to get an idea of the size of the hotel. Six floors to choose from, but here was something else he hadn't thought of . . . he pressed a button, the doors closed and the pressure dropped beneath his feet as the lift began to descend. Seconds later it delivered Mariner into the sodium-lit cavern of the underground car park, with spaces clearly designated for the businesses occupying the surrounding buildings. In the section marked out for the Belvedere Hotel, there was a single vehicle: a green Ford Escort van with a discreet logo on the driver's door.

Back up in the hotel, Mariner found Vicky Jesson in a corner of the bar, sitting in a leather tub chair, and studying a sheet of A4.

'How's it going?' asked Mariner.

'I met no resistance, if that's what you mean,' said Jesson, looking up momentarily. 'Given how things have turned out, I think they've been expecting us to come back. This is the staff list and she's gone to print off the rosters and the guest lists for the dates that we're interested in.'

'Anything?'

'I've found one thing.' As Mariner pulled up a chair beside her she held out the list, the tip of her forefinger pointing to one particular name. 'Our friend, Ricardo,' she said. 'His full name is Ricardo Ponti, with a P.'

'Well, well,' said Mariner. 'Anyone else?'

'A Narinder Patel, but that's about it,' said Jesson.

At that moment the manager appeared. She greeted Mariner with a nod. 'These are the staff and guest lists for the dates that you have requested,' she said, handing him the sheaf of papers.

Mariner thanked her. 'We'd like to speak to Ricardo too,' he said.

'I'm sorry,' the manager said. 'It is Ricardo's day off today.' She leaned over Jesson. 'But here is his address,' she said pointing to the list.

'Thank you,' said Mariner, getting to his feet. 'I'd also like to take one of your sheets with us.'

She arched an eyebrow. 'A sheet?' Although the discovery of the bodies had been made public, details of exactly how they'd been buried had not.

'Yes, a bed sheet. One will do fine.'

She must have been curious, but she kept any questions to herself and several minutes later she returned with a sheet zipped into a protective polythene pouch.

'I'll return it as soon as I can,' said Mariner. Through the transparent plastic covering he'd already noted the red print of a laundry mark along one border. 'Do you have your own laundry here?'

'No, we use a laundry service.'

'There's something we hadn't thought of,' said Mariner, as he and Jesson left the hotel. 'Our washerwoman might actually *be* a washerwoman, or man.' On their way to the car Mariner told Jesson what he'd found below ground level.

'So at the right moment it would be pretty easy to get someone, or something, into a vehicle without being seen,' she said.

'Tailor-made,' said Mariner. 'The bad news is that the hotel's security arrangements at the back of the building are crap, so in practice anyone could get in or out.'

Ricardo lived not far from the city centre — in a terraced house in a seventies development just off Sherlock Street — so it made sense for Mariner and Jesson to go directly there. Inside, the compact house was meticulously clean. They arrived while Ricardo was in the shower and he came to the door wrapped in a thick robe. 'I'd like to get dressed,' he said.

'Agreeing to that might have been a bad move,' said Mariner, as he disappeared upstairs. 'Gives him time to work out a story.'

'He's very keen on cleanliness,' observed Jesson. 'Isn't it meant to be next to godliness?'

'Perhaps we should have brought Charlie,' said Mariner.

Ricardo joined them moments later in a lounge that was an extravaganza of leather and animal print.

'You know that we've found Rosa?' Mariner said.

He looked genuinely upset. 'I do,' he said, crossing himself. 'I keep thinking of that poor little girl without her mamma.'

'So you'll understand that we need to ask a few more questions. When you left work on Saturday night, did you come straight home?' Mariner asked him.

'Not right away,' said Ricardo. 'I was meeting a friend in the Piccolo bar on Hurst Street.'

So definitely not straight *home then*, thought Mariner. 'Will your friend be able to corroborate that?' he asked.

Ricardo flushed. 'I don't know. I think maybe he was going out of town for a few days.'

'Do you have contact details for him?'

His colour deepened further. 'I think I might have mislaid them. The staff in the Piccolo can tell you I was there. I go in there pretty often after work.'

'Tell me a bit more about this incident with the guest a few weeks ago,' said Mariner. 'Can you remember anything at all about this man?'

'He was not a nice man,' said Ricardo. 'That I remember.'

'Can you describe him to me?'

'He was pretty tall and big — yes — with very round face and a little beard.' He brought his thumb and forefinger together under his chin to signify a goatee.

'You said it was a group on a work's night out. Do you know which company they were from?'

'Yeah, was one of those betting shops.'

'Do you remember which one? William Hill? Coral? Sceptre?'

'Yes, that's it,' said Ricardo. 'Sceptre.'

'Do you remember anything else about the man or the incident that you think could be important?' But Ricardo couldn't help.

'Who knew you'd be such a connoisseur of betting shops?' said Jesson as they left Ricardo's house.

'Put it down to a misspent youth,' said Mariner. 'Shit, I've got to get a move on,' he said suddenly. He turned to Jesson. 'I need to go and fetch Jamie. If I drop you off, can you write up the notes for all of this?'

'Of course.'

Chapter Twenty

In every other circumstance a shining example of a law-abiding citizen, Mariner drove out to Manor Park breaking all the rules, though only when he was certain he could get away with it. He'd driven this same route out to North Worcestershire so many times now that the exact positions of the speed cameras were imprinted on his mind, and he knew exactly the short stretches of road where he could exceed the speed limit with impunity. He was going to be late anyway. Skidding through the gates and into the main drive, Mariner saw Jamie wandering around the lawned area to one side, while Izzy, one of the staff, lounged on a bench alongside the entrance, keeping a discreet eye on him. She turned her wrist, pointing at an imaginary watch and shaking her head, as Mariner pulled up a little way off.

'Sorry,' Mariner mouthed back. 'Hello, Jamie,' he called, getting out of the car, and just about caught the 'Spectre Man' greeting that Jamie muttered in response.

'Why does he call you that?' asked Izzy. Like a number of the staff at Manor Park, she was Australian and the twang of her accent was strong. No more than mid-twenties, her blonde hair was cut short and she wore the staff uniform of jeans and polo shirt.

'Because when we first met, his sister called me Inspector Mariner, and that was the best he could make of it,' Mariner explained.

'Inspector? You're a copper? I didn't know that.' She seemed amused by it.

'No reason why you should,' said Mariner. 'How's he been?'

'Good. Jamie's never any trouble — are you, mate? Just had one little incident, but entirely our fault. We took him swimming and he must have got water up his nose. He went completely nuts for about twenty minutes. Next time we're going to try him with goggles and a nose-clip.'

'Well, good luck with that,' said Mariner, knowing how resistant Jamie was to anything new. While they were talking Jamie had loped over to the car, and now Mariner opened the passenger door for him. Izzy started up the steps towards the building before turning back. 'Oh, nearly forgot. Message from Simon: looks like we've got a permanent vacancy coming up soon. He'll let you know.'

Mariner got the distinct impression she'd enjoyed saving that 'til last. 'That's great,' he said. 'Any idea which days?'

Izzy shrugged. 'Full-time, I guess. He didn't say any different. Have a good week, guys.'

Christ. What a difference that would make to Mariner's life. As they drove back to the city, he felt a sudden lightness. 'I know it's only Monday night,' he said. 'But how about a takeaway?'

'Fried rice,' said Jamie.

* * *

When Jesson got up to the incident room she found Charlie Glover hunched over his computer. 'There you are,' she said. 'What have you been up to? The boss was trying to get hold of you.'

'Oh, I was just going back over a set of old statements,' said Charlie. 'Checking nothing has been missed.' He didn't see Jesson roll her eyes. 'How about you? Anything new?'

Jesson told him about the underground car park and about the encounter with Ricardo. 'Looks like the next step is Sceptre Betting. Great.'

'Sceptre?'

'Yes, do you know it?'

'I've heard of it,' said Charlie. 'Do you want me to go?'

Jesson looked at him anew. 'OK, thanks. Never my favourite places to visit.'

* * *

On Tuesday morning Mariner and Jamie were back to Declan and the day-centre routine, but somehow, knowing this might soon be coming to an end, it didn't feel quite so bad. Jamie safely dispatched, Mariner picked up a text from Stuart Croghan, letting him know that Grace Clifton was ready for formal identification by her parents. Jesson was on her way to the Belvedere with a couple of uniforms to lead a more thorough analysis of their staff and guest data. As for Charlie, once again Mariner wasn't sure where he was.

* * *

As promised, first thing on Tuesday morning, Charlie Glover phoned the head office of Sceptre Betting plc and spoke to one of the admin staff. He reminded her of a recent night out at the Belvedere Hotel.

'Oh, yeah,' she said. 'I was there. It was a great night.'

'Not for everyone,' said Charlie. 'I understand one of your colleagues had a bit too much to drink and assaulted one of the bar staff.' The line went quiet. 'It's all right,' said Charlie. 'Unless the hotel or the individuals involved decide to press charges, which they don't wish to do, we can't take any action. But I would like to speak to the man involved. What's his name?'

'It was Mark,' she said. 'Mark Kent. He's the deputy manager of our Corporation Street branch.'

'Will he be at work today?' Charlie asked.

'No reason why he wouldn't be.'

* * *

Mariner went to see Stuart Croghan ahead of the identification to ask about the toxicology report. 'High levels of Rohypnol in the bloodstreams of both women,' said Croghan. 'Essentially they've both been sedated — a lot. And the absence of water in the lungs means that they were dead before being submerged in water.'

'Thanks,' said Mariner. He'd keep those details to himself.

Grace Clifton's parents had aged ten years and seemed to respond to everything he said in slow motion. 'You do understand that we have a positive identification for Grace from DNA and that we are in no doubt that this is her,' Mariner reminded them. It was important to make that absolutely clear. He didn't want the Cliftons, least of all Grace's mother, clinging to any misguided hope that there might still be some element of doubt, that her daughter might still be alive.

'We just want to say goodbye,' said Councillor Clifton.

They steeled themselves, Clifton gripping his wife's hand tightly. Had there been any uncertainty as to the identity of the dead girl, the reactions of her parents put paid to that. There were no histrionics, just a harsh intake of breath, a flicker of anguish in the eyes before the tears began to flow quietly and uninhibited. The FLO had come along for support and afterwards brought hot drinks, allowing the couple a few minutes to begin to process what they had seen. When she felt it appropriate, she fetched Mariner to come and sit with them. They were dazed and disorientated. From his inside pocket, Mariner took the gold chain in its polythene packet. 'You may remember I mentioned to you that Grace was wearing a necklace when we found her. This is it. Do you recognise it at all?' he asked.

Two pairs of eyes stared blankly at it, numbed by grief, and Mariner wondered if they were capable of recognising their own names right now. 'I've never to my knowledge seen that before,' said Mr Clifton, eventually, his voice raw.

'Who is P?' her mother asked.

'We were hoping you might know,' Mariner said. 'As Grace was wearing this necklace when we found her. We thought it might be significant to her.'

'If it is — if it *was*, then I don't know why,' her father said. 'But then, the more I'm asked about my daughter, the more I realise there are plenty of things about her I didn't know.'

'Thank you, anyway,' Mariner said. 'And I'm very sorry.' As he got up to leave Councillor Clifton followed him out.

'We'll try and think about who this P might be,' he said. 'It's just that at the moment . . .'

'I understand,' said Mariner. 'It's difficult enough coming in here today for this.'

'Oh, we would have been here this morning anyway,' said Clifton, absently. 'My wife's father was brought in during the middle of last night again with breathing difficulties. It makes all of this doubly distressing for her.'

'I'm sorry,' said Mariner. 'I didn't know he was unwell.' He wished someone had told him.

'Emphysema,' said Clifton. 'He gets these attacks. Usually he's in here for a couple of days on oxygen, then when he's stable again, they discharge him. But the episodes have been getting more frequent, and this time it doesn't look good. I think the stress of what has happened to Grace . . .'

'I hope things work out,' said Mariner, inadequately.

* * *

Exiting through the back of the mortuary, Mariner walked around to the main hospital entrance to get some fresh air. On the way he put a call through to Jesson at the Belvedere. 'How's it going?'

'As yet, we've got no staff common to all three dates,' she said. 'And there's no one who's been on our radar before, unless you count minor traffic offences and one caution for shoplifting four years ago. We're working back through the guests at the moment, but no one stands out so far. I'll let you know if that changes.'

Before leaving the hospital Mariner climbed the stairs to the first floor to see if Ellen Kingsley was about. While he didn't exactly regret his behaviour on Saturday night, he had left himself vulnerable and Jesson was right. However peripheral Dr Kingsley might be to the case, getting involved with her while it was going on had not been a good idea. And it wasn't what Suzy deserved either. As he walked, again unchallenged, into critical care, he could see Ellen through the window in Lomax's room, supervising a young nurse as she checked the equipment currently keeping him alive. She turned to say something, and at the same time saw Mariner. Breaking into a smile, she gave a final word of instruction to her colleague, before emerging into the central concourse to meet him. 'Can't keep you away,' she observed.

'There was something else I had to attend to here, so thought I'd stop by. Have you got time for a coffee?'

'Sorry, there's no one permanently covering Dee's absence yet, so I can't leave this area. Is there any news?'

Mariner shook his head. 'Nothing yet.'

She hugged her arms protectively around her. 'I heard that you'd found the other two women.'

'They're still searching,' Mariner said. He hesitated a moment, both of them suddenly awkward. 'Look, I suppose I really came to apologise. I wasn't entirely honest with you the other night. There is someone, but it hasn't been going well, mainly because it hasn't had the chance to. I was feeling sorry for myself.'

'Ah, well.' She looked him up and down. 'Disappointing, but no harm done.'

Mariner nodded towards Private Lomax. 'No visitors today?'

'At Buckingham Palace,' Ellen said. 'His unit are being honoured for bravery. They rescued some aid workers a couple of months back, before all this happened.'

'Can't they wait until he's well enough to accept it himself?' She flashed a wry smile and Mariner understood. 'They don't know that he ever will be,' he said.

'It will be collected on his behalf and brought back to him here. Something for him to wake up to. And all the details of the occasion will be recorded.' She held up a scrapbook. 'With luck, someone will have taken photographs too that we can add in.'

'That doesn't look very NHS,' said Mariner.

'It's not, but nonetheless it's an essential part of the recovery process. Dr Hayden introduced them. We keep a kind of log book of exactly what happens to each patient while he's in here. What treatment he's received, but also who's visited and so on. It helps to fill in some of the gaps when they regain consciousness. Most of them read and re-read it to try to make sense of things when they get back into the real world. They tell us it's a lifeline. Dee would normally be keeping Lomax's up to date, but in her absence it still needs to be done, so I've been completing it.'

'Could I have a look?' asked Mariner.

'I don't see why not. There's nothing confidential written in them.' She handed him the book. Like a child's scrapbook, it was decorated on the outer cover with photographs and cuttings. Opening it, Mariner turned the pages until he found the day of Dee's disappearance. The entry for that afternoon read: *3.30 p.m. emerging. Dr Hayden came. Stayed two hours, but not ready.*

'What's all this about?' Mariner asked.

'Well, I was in surgery at the time, but from what Dee has written here, it looks as if Lomax began showing signs of regaining consciousness at about three thirty. That's what this coding means here.' She pointed to the page. 'She will have paged Dr Hayden straight away. According to what Dee told me later, shortly after that Craig came round fully, as expected, but almost immediately went into crisis.'

'Meaning what exactly?'

'He got very agitated and distressed. It's an intense cocktail of fear, disbelief and anger that hits some men very hard and very quickly. There would have been no option but to sedate him again.'

'Is that unusual?' asked Mariner.

'Not at all. If anything, it's commonplace. That's why we're always prepared for it.'

'And Dee would have been there, during all this?'

'Yes. I understand she and Dr Hayden bore the brunt of Lomax's aggression. They had a rough time in there for a while. Then between them they took steps to make him comfortable again.'

'Put him under.'

'Yes.'

'And this Dr Hayden, she's one of your team?'

'He,' Ellen corrected him. 'Yes, very much so. Leo's an essential element.'

'So what exactly does he do?'

'He's a clinical psychiatrist, specialising in post-traumatic stress. When Dee first realised that Craig was regaining consciousness she will have contacted Leo and he would have got here as soon as he could. It's standard procedure. Leo's skilled in rapidly assessing a patient's state of mind, and their capacity to cope with dramatically altered circumstances. We knew that when Lomax came round it was likely to be harrowing for him and Leo has techniques for dealing with that. It was Leo who recognised that it was too soon for Lomax, and it will have been his decision to put him under again.'

'Does Dee often work with Dr Hayden?'

'Well, we all do,' said Ellen. 'But I guess you could say that Dee's quite often Leo's right-hand man when he's here. They get on well. Holistic care, I suppose you'd call it. One treating the physical, the other the emotional.'

Mariner thought again about Paddy Henderson. 'Was there anything between them?' he asked, carefully.

'Well, there's a bit of banter, of course,' she said quickly. 'It's a very necessary part of the job, to relieve tension. You know that. But Dee and Leo are both utterly professional.' Although Mariner couldn't help noticing her failure to meet his eye as she said this.

'Would it be possible to talk to Dr Hayden?'

'Of course, but Leo isn't based here full-time. He's only needed in particular circumstances, so his main job is elsewhere at a private clinic. There are some regular times when he comes in to monitor patients, so I can check the rotas to see when he'll be in next.' She went to look. 'He'll be back in on Friday, unless we have any other emergencies.'

'Paddy Henderson. His treatment has ended, has it?'

'Paddy?' The question surprised her. 'Yes, ages ago. I mean, I know that he still gets flashbacks, nightmares from time to time, but that's par for the course. Often it can go on for years. Why do you ask?'

'On the day after Dee went missing we asked him about her journey home, and he said, "if I'm there I can pick her up." It gave me the impression he was here quite regularly anyway.'

Ellen smiled. 'Dee roped him in. You'll have seen the "Heroes Welcome" collectors in the main foyer? Once a month Paddy comes in to do his stint at rattling the tin. When Dee's on earlies he tries to arrange it around that, so that he can bring her in and take her home.'

Their conversation ended and Mariner watched her go back into Lomax's room to return the scrapbook, talking to the soldier as if he were fully awake. As Mariner was leaving, a porter came into the department carrying a pile of clean linen, which he deposited on a trolley at one end of the ward.

If Dee was right-hand man to Leo Hayden, how would Paddy Henderson feel about that, Mariner wondered. Still no body or parcel of clothing for Dee had turned up. Was this because their washerwoman was feeling the heat, or was it because Dee's disappearance was nothing to do with him or her at all?

Chapter Twenty-One

Charlie had driven into the city centre and parked behind the former law courts on Corporation Street. He'd never had cause to go into betting shops except when he was on the job and he found them dismal places, all the more depressing because he knew they'd been a favourite haunt for his dad. Now that internet gambling had made it all so easy, though, places like this must surely be on their way out. It would be no great loss.

Although imposing, Mark Kent turned out to be a disappointment. Well over six feet tall and heavily built, he had the kind of bulging muscles that Glover associated with steroid use. His brown hair was tied back in a lank ponytail, and his complexion was washed out. From beneath his shirt collar Glover could see the tail end of a tattoo in some kind of Gothic script, creeping up towards a ragged beard. Unless Larry Hausknecht had been very mistaken, or Kent had radically altered his appearance in the last eighteen months, he couldn't possibly be the man who had attacked Chelsey. He was, however, interestingly evasive about what had happened on the night that Ricardo and Rosa got hurt. 'I was very drunk,' he said, as if that excused his behaviour.

Glover showed him the photograph of Rosa. 'Do you remember this woman?'

Kent coloured up. 'She got in the way. I didn't mean to hurt her, and I said I was sorry. It's a dump, that place,' he added belligerently. 'I don't even know why we go there.'

'Do you go there often?' asked Glover.

'I think the boss must get good rates or something.'

'Do you dress up for these nights out?'

'What do you mean?'

'You know — suit, tie?'

Kent laughed. 'Do me a favour. I don't even own a fucking suit.'

'We'd like to take a swab, with your agreement, of course, for elimination purposes.'

'Elimination from what?'

'The enquiry into this woman's murder,' Charlie said, holding up Rosa's picture again.

Kent looked visibly frightened now. 'I don't know anything about that,' he said.

'In that case I'm sure you'll want us to rule you out as soon as possible,' said Glover. He gave Kent a business card with the Granville Lane address on it and on the back he noted down the dates when Grace, Rosa and Dee had gone missing. 'It would help too if you could tell us where you were on these dates. No hurry, it will do when you come in.'

* * *

Stepping outside the hospital, Mariner rang through to Vicky Jesson again. 'Have you found anything?'

'No,' she said, sounding wearied by it all. 'And we're about coming to the end. We'll be packing up soon and coming back.'

She sounded despondent and Glover seemed to have gone completely off the radar. If Mariner wasn't careful, his team would start to fragment. He made a snap decision. 'Do you know the Country Girl on Raddlebarn Road?' he asked Jesson. She did. 'Meet me there in half an hour. I think we might be looking in the wrong place.'

'Now he tells me,' said Jesson.

'Aw, don't be like that,' said Mariner. 'If you're very good I'll buy you a sandwich. And can you do something else for me? Find out from Ricardo the exact date when he and Rosa spent half the night in A&E. And ask him if Rosa went down to the cafeteria at any time.'

'OK.'

Mariner tried then to call Charlie Glover. When there was no reply he left a message telling Charlie the arrangement for meeting up. He could take it or leave it. Ringing off, Mariner went back into the foyer. He realised he had noticed without really seeing the 'Heroes Welcome' volunteers with their collecting tins. Today it was the turn of a woman in her fifties — the mother of a serviceman perhaps, or perhaps even the grandmother. Drawing out a handful of loose change from his trouser pocket, he dropped several coins into the plastic canister. In return he was given a friendly smile and an emblem of crossed rifles.

At the enquiries desk Mariner was directed to the fifth-floor geriatric ward. For a while he thought he might be too late, but then he spied Councillor Clifton off in the distance pacing one of the corridors.

'How is he?' Mariner asked.

'His condition's improving, but they're keeping him in.'

'This may seem a strange question, but when did your father-in-law last have an attack of emphysema?' Mariner asked.

'A couple of weeks ago,' Clifton said. 'That's the problem. They are getting closer together and more severe.'

'Did Grace ever come to visit her grandfather here?'

'Yes, she was very good like that. Better than the other two, in fact. She used to call in on her way to work.'

‘Was your father-in-law in hospital around the time that Grace went missing?’

Clifton considered for a moment. ‘Yes,’ he said eventually. ‘We had to go straight from here to the engagement party, and of course it was disappointing that Donald couldn’t come along to that either.’

Mariner’s next stop was the hospital linen store. It appeared that the laundry services, like so many aspects of the NHS these days, were contracted out to a private company, whose logo was above the door, but the store room, with its shelves of clean linen and tubs of dirty laundry lined up underneath, awaiting collection, was staffed by Sunita, a tiny woman of about fifty. She accepted Mariner’s warrant card and his request as if his visit was the most natural thing in the world.

‘Have you worked here very long?’ Mariner asked, as she went to retrieve a sheet from the cupboard for him.

‘Nearly thirty years,’ she said proudly. ‘I started off at the old site and then came across to set things up here too. It’s all changed, of course. In the old days we used to have our own laundry and wash everything ourselves. Now all I have to do is exchange dirty for clean, and then distribute it around the hospital, so they won’t give me the staff any more.’

‘You must like it, though,’ said Mariner.

‘It’s a wonderful job,’ she beamed. ‘And I know my linens. Any place me and my husband stay, I always judge it by the quality of the sheets.’ She chuckled. ‘It drives him mad.’

Mariner thanked her and took the sheet. Having used up most of his coins donating to ‘Heroes Welcome,’ he was forced to pay over the odds in the car park, practically enough to fund a small principality. He didn’t always bother with claiming expenses, but he would this time. Leaving the hospital, he drove across to the other side of the Bristol Road, to the pub where he’d arranged to meet Jesson.

Although still a popular haunt for university students in the evenings, business at the Country Girl had presumably taken a hit since the closure of the old hospital, which now stood derelict and securely fenced off to keep out vandals. It was astonishing just how fast the new site had become established. Not long ago, it was impossible to move around these streets for parked cars, yet now the traffic flowed freely. Today the lunchtime trade in the pub was steady, and Mariner was pleased to see Charlie already there.

'Got your message,' he said unnecessarily. 'What are you drinking, boss?'

Ten minutes later Vicky Jesson joined them.

'So what have you been up to, Charlie?' Mariner asked.

Charlie described his encounter with Mark Kent. 'He's a thug,' he said. 'But I don't think he's our man. I've asked him to come in and provide a forensic sample along with alibis for the key nights, though, just to be sure we can eliminate him.'

'Good idea,' said Jesson, impressed.

'The staff from Sceptre Betting frequent the Belvedere on a regular basis,' he went on.

'So that might explain why the hotel didn't want to make a fuss about the incident,' said Vicky.

'Something else,' said Charlie, reluctantly. 'I remembered why the Belvedere rang a bell with me.' He told them about the attack on Chelsey Skoyles. 'I didn't know if there might be a link.'

'It's possible,' said Mariner, interested. 'It would make sense that our washerwoman hasn't started with abduction. There may be a history of other offences.'

'Well, I've read the case notes,' said Charlie. 'And reasonably enough, the officers made the assumption that the attacker came from out on the street. They didn't consider the possibility that he could have come from inside the hotel.' He faltered.

‘And?’ said Mariner.

Glover recounted what he’d gleaned from Chelsey and with Hausknecht. ‘The trouble is, I don’t think the case was pursued with much vigour. The implication from the case notes is that she was drunk, incapable and asking for it. Chelsey’s mother was pretty hostile towards me too. But the American’s agreed to help with putting together an e-fit, so we may get something out of it.’

‘It was worth looking at,’ concluded Mariner. He took a couple of swallows of his pint. ‘Out of interest, who was the original officer involved?’ he asked.

Charlie concentrated hard on picking up his beer. ‘I can’t actually remember,’ he said. ‘I’d have to check back with the file.’ It was an uncharacteristic lapse.

Vicky Jesson also had some limited intelligence to report. ‘Aside from one or two guests who stay regularly at the hotel, no one was there on both nights when the women disappeared.’

‘And who are the regulars?’ asked Mariner.

‘Two of them are musicians playing at Symphony Hall, who I suppose could theoretically have known Grace. Of those, one is Peter Sandstrom, a percussionist. But no one has told us that Grace ever mixed with the musicians, and his orchestra is on tour at the moment in South America, so it won’t be easy to get hold of him. Did you get anything new from the hospital?’

Mariner recounted his conversation with Ellen Kingsley. ‘I’d be interested in talking to this Dr Hayden to ascertain if his relationship with Dee is purely professional. It might be that Dee was getting too close to him, or looked as if she was, which would bring us back to Paddy Henderson. It might have upset him.’

‘You really think that would be enough?’ asked Glover.

‘As a motive, it would hardly be unique. And as I’ve said before, Dee’s killing may not even have been deliberate. He still gets episodes from when he was in

Afghanistan.' Mariner paused while the waitress delivered their sandwiches. 'An argument between them could have got out of hand, which might explain why Henderson's so cut up about it. Either way, it would be interesting to invite him in for questioning.'

'Are we talking intelligence or evidential?' asked Jesson.

'Intel for now,' said Mariner. 'But then we'll see.'

'Why did you want to know about Rosa's trip to A&E?'

'I was coming to that,' said Mariner, taking a bite out of his ham and cheese panini. 'We made an assumption that heavy-duty sheets could only come from a hotel, but that's not the case, is it? Hospital sheets are heavy-duty and laundry-marked, too.'

'So what are you saying? That our washerwoman might be someone at the hospital?'

'Or someone who's a regular visitor there. We can place Rosa at the Belvedere. It's also a reasonable assumption that Grace walked past it. But so far we have no link between the hotel and Dee.'

'Unless she walked past too,' said Jesson, reasonably.

'But that's just speculation,' Mariner pressed on. 'I found out earlier today that on the day she went missing, Grace Clifton was at the QE visiting her grandfather before going on to Symphony Hall. We've wondered all along how it was that Grace and Rosa could have been taken off the street without anyone noticing and have even considered the possibility that it's someone they know. But what if it's just someone they've *met* before, someone they've talked to and who's made a deliberate effort to get to know them?'

'That's a hell of a lot of people,' said Charlie. 'Have you got anyone in mind?'

'It brings me back to Paddy Henderson,' said Mariner. 'He told us himself that when he can he tries to get over to the hospital to pick Dee up, to save her that tortuous journey home.'

'But surely if Grace was visiting her grandfather before work it would be too early in the day,' Jesson said.

'Dee works various shifts. I'd have to check, but if she was on an early shift that week, Henderson could easily have been hanging around the hospital then. And he's there on a regular basis anyway.' Mariner brought out the crossed-rifles badge.

'Isn't the idea that you wear it on your lapel,' said Charlie, 'instead of hidden away in your pocket?'

'Yeah, I'm not sure that I fully agree with it,' said Mariner, unable to articulate exactly why that might be.

'Me neither,' said Vicky, unexpectedly. 'Some soldiers might be heroes, but it doesn't mean they all are.'

Charlie looked personally affronted, but they moved on.

'My point is,' said Mariner, 'that once a month Paddy Henderson is in the hospital main foyer shaking a collecting box. The one thing we've been told about Grace and Rosa is that they're friendly — that they would do anything for anyone. The likelihood is that they would also give to what they perceive to be a worthwhile cause, and in doing so they would engage with Paddy Henderson.'

Charlie picked up the badge. 'There was one of these in the drawer at Rosa's house, I'm sure there was.'

'We need to find out if Paddy Henderson was collecting at any of the times when Grace was visiting — or on the evening that Rosa was in A&E,' said Mariner.

'You're thinking of Henderson for Rosa and Grace now too?'

'It's not impossible, is it? We've established that he had the opportunity.'

'What about the motive?'

'Again, I refer you to the PTSD.'

'It's a bit flimsy.' Glover wasn't convinced.

'But he's a regular visitor to the ward, so it would be easy enough for him to get hold of the right kind of sheets. They're just sitting there.'

'And his name fits with the necklaces,' said Glover.

'There's something else,' said Jesson. 'One of the first things they learn in the military is to keep their clothes washed and pressed and their boots highly polished. It would be habitual for him.'

'We need to get all over his alibis and see if there's any chance he could have met Grace or Rosa,' said Mariner.

'I bet the hospital foyer is covered by CCTV,' said Charlie. 'If we look at it for the days that Grace and Rosa were around we might see them talking to Henderson.'

'That's a good idea,' said Mariner. He held Glover's gaze.

Glover eventually twigged. 'Oh, not me,' he complained. 'I didn't mean . . . I thought maybe a uniform . . .'

'But you'd know exactly who and what you're looking for,' argued Mariner. 'And we can't afford any mistakes. Start with Rosa. As far as we know, she's only been there on that single occasion, so he'd have to have met her then. He could have approached either woman in the canteen, or at any time. Both Rosa and Grace would have been wearing their name badges. He could have talked to them, found out where they worked, and met them "by chance" when they knocked off. That's when he could very easily have picked them up. We should get hold of Henderson's service record too and see if he's got any history of violence. We'll bring him in for questioning again. At the moment he thinks we see him as a victim in all this, so we might catch him off guard.'

They finished their drinks and sandwiches and went out to the car park. 'That's quite a structure,' said Jesson, as they approached the cars. 'What is it?'

Turning, Mariner followed her gaze towards the ornate red-brick tower peeping out above the trees. 'Oh, it's part of the old hospital,' he said, getting out his car keys. 'A water tower or some such, I think. You'll have driven right past it.'

* * *

That evening Jamie fell asleep early, giving Mariner a rare opportunity to catch the late news. It featured a brief story about more than thirty soldiers who had been presented with medals by the Queen that day. The focus of the piece was a unit who had defended a vulnerable outpost over several days, sustaining a number of fatalities. The whole item lasted only a couple of minutes, but at the end of the footage Mariner thought he saw a face he'd seen before. Using the digi-box facility, he rewound the short clip, pausing at the relevant moment. At the back of the group was Lomax's father, there to collect his son's award. Soldiering it seemed was a family tradition — he was in uniform too.

Afterwards, on the internet, Mariner looked up what Lomax and his unit had done to deserve the accolades. The story was one of a number concerning foreign aid workers, for whom abduction seemed to be an occupational hazard. Mariner couldn't help but wonder what motivated people to go out there and do that work in such inhospitable environments. The stories that made the headlines were typically rescue missions involving all-out battles with the kidnappers and resulting in casualties. But eventually Mariner found Lomax and three other soldiers named in a mission to recover three French aid workers that had ended peacefully, despite demands for the release of imprisoned extremists in exchange. Alongside pictures of the three women there were links to a further story telling how one of them, Monique Rousse, had subsequently been killed in a later incident.

As Mariner was coming to the end of the article, his landline rang. It was Simon, the manager of Manor Park, apologising for the suddenness of the call, but letting him know that there would be a full-time vacancy for Jamie, starting from next Monday, if he wanted it.

'Your choice, of course, if you want to have Jamie home for weekends, but we can arrange that as a regular thing, or we can do it as we go along. I'll email across the contract and financial agreement for you to sign. How does that sound?'

'Perfect,' said Mariner, with great restraint.

Chapter Twenty-Two

The interview with Paddy Henderson on Wednesday morning turned out to be less than productive. He was distant and lethargic, and they often had to repeat their questions. Here was a man with a lot on his mind, reflected Mariner. But the question was why? Henderson's assumption when they contacted him was that Dee had been found, but he'd been willing enough to come in to answer further questions. His alibi for the night when Grace had vanished remained less than secure, and was being followed up on, but now Mariner put her photograph down on the table.

'Of course I know her,' said Henderson, sitting up straight for the first time since they'd invited him to take a seat. 'She's been all over the news. She's one of the reasons I came to you in the first place about Dee — her and that other girl.'

'Is there any chance you could have seen these two women before that, perhaps in the atrium of the QE?' asked Jesson.

'I might have. I meet a lot of people there,' Paddy said. 'If I did, I don't remember them.'

'How well do you know Dr Leo Hayden?'

'The psychiatrist guy? I don't *know* him. I mean, I've spoken to him, like. Dee's always going on about how wonderful he is. I could have done with someone like him when I came back.'

'How often have the two of you met?'

'I don't know, maybe a couple of times at social dos, Christmas and that.'

'What did you talk about?'

'Bloody hell, I don't remember — nothing really. I think Dee had told him I'm a plumber. He's living at his parents' place and he said the central heating could do with upgrading, like. I offered to give him a quote sometime.'

'And did you?' asked Jesson.

'No, I've never got round to it. Look, what is all this? I want to get home to the kids.'

'How do you feel about Dee working so closely with Dr Hayden?' asked Mariner.

Henderson considered his answer more carefully this time. 'To tell the truth, I weren't that keen. He was a bit too all over her, like.'

'And you've never met Leo Hayden outside of these social occasions.'

'No.'

After about an hour, Mariner suggested they take a break so that Henderson could go outside for a smoke. They were making little progress and so far the searches of his house, premises and van had turned up nothing. In addition, Henderson's alibi for the night of Rosa's disappearance was solid. Nor was there anything in his service record to indicate issues with violence or his relationships with women. To compound all that, after hours poring over footage from the hospital's CCTV system, Charlie had turned up nothing that put Henderson in direct contact with the two other women. He had enough to successfully identify Rosa and to confirm that she'd been at the hospital on a night when Henderson was there. They stood round to watch as she crossed the atrium to join the queue at a vending machine, but she didn't go anywhere near Henderson, who was standing about fifteen metres away. She didn't return to the area again. 'She must have bought her crossed rifles somewhere else,' said Charlie.

'Are we making any progress with finding out where the necklaces might have come from?' Mariner asked Jesson.

'Only the worst kind,' she said. 'They're cheap and mass-produced, sold in hundreds of outlets, online and on market stalls all over the country.'

Mariner went to see Superintendent Sharp.

'Everything we have is purely circumstantial,' he admitted. 'We're going to have to let Paddy Henderson go. I wondered about possible surveillance.'

'We can't afford it,' said Sharp, as Mariner had known she would.

'We could assign him a FLO,' said Mariner. 'It would amount to the same thing.'

'Do you think he'll accept one, after all this?'

'It's worth a try, isn't it?'

'I'll think about it,' said Sharp.

'I'm going to need to get away for a couple of hours,' said Mariner. Sharp arched an eyebrow. 'I've managed to get Jamie back into full-time residential care, but there are some things I need to sort out.'

'That sounds like good news,' said Sharp.

'I haven't told Mercy, the woman who helps me out with him.'

'But surely she must have known that it was a temporary arrangement?'

'I suppose so,' said Mariner. 'But I worry about her.'

'Oh, I'm sure she'll survive, Tom,' said Sharp. 'She has done up until now.'

'I want to give her something, like a parting gift, though, and I know the most useful thing for her would be money. But I can't trust that son of hers won't get his hands all over it instead of her.'

'That's her decision, though, isn't it?' said Sharp and Mariner couldn't disagree.

* * *

Mary Sutor was back at her CAD station on Wednesday morning when a previously seen name popped up on her monitor with an incoming call: William Alder. 'My cleaner hasn't come again this morning,' he grumbled. 'She didn't come last Friday and she hasn't come again today.'

'Perhaps she's unwell?' Mary suggested.

'I told you last week,' he insisted. 'She'd have rung me. This is most unlike her. I'm worried, what with these other young women who have been killed . . .'

Mary rolled her eyes at Linda. 'All right then, sir. Let me take some details and I'll see what we can do.'

Mary was about to contact an area car, when she remembered Charlie Glover. They attended the same church, so she knew him a bit, and also knew that he was part of the Grace Clifton investigation. She'd sound him out first. When Mary's call came, Charlie was just starting on his third hour of CCTV and was consequently desperate for any kind of distraction. 'What can I do for you, Mary?'

'We've had a couple of calls from an old boy whose cleaner hasn't turned up. I've tried telling him that's not what we're here for, but he's a persistent old bugger. I'm sure it's something of nothing, but she is potentially a missing woman, and with what's going on at the moment—'

'Where is he?' asked Glover.

'Not far,' said Mary. 'Just up the road in Bournville.'

It was the excuse Glover was looking for. 'OK,' he said. 'Give me the details and I'll go and talk to him.'

* * *

When Mariner returned to the incident room, Vicky Jesson called him over to her desk. 'Have you seen this?' Under the headline banner *Phantom Surgeon* was a tongue-in-cheek article posted on the internet by a worker at the Salvation Army clothing depot. 'They've been getting matching sets of green surgical scrubs left in clothing banks around the city,' said Jesson.

'And?'

'Well, we're looking at this possible hospital connection, and we know that our man's probably forensically aware, so what better way to cover up than with scrubs? Anyway, I gave them a call. Turns out they've had three lots turn up in the south of the city over the last three weeks, all identical.'

'Identical in what sense?' said Mariner. 'I thought scrubs were all the same anyway.'

'In the sense that they are all freshly laundered and neatly pressed, even down to the hat and face mask. If our guy knows his way around the hospital laundry, perhaps he can help himself to those too.'

Mariner felt the familiar tingle between his shoulder blades that suggested they might be closing in. 'I've got to go out anyway,' he said. 'What's the postcode for the depot?'

* * *

William Alder's bungalow was part of a low-rise sheltered housing complex that consisted of about a dozen dwellings connected by covered walkways and separated by small gardens. Glover parked in a bay beside number sixteen and got out of his car as a woman walked past, carrying a tray. 'Hello,' she said. 'Are you here to see William?'

Glover showed her his identification. 'Apparently he's worried about his cleaner.'

'Well, I hope you haven't had a wasted journey,' she said, cheerfully. 'He can be a bit of a fusspot, our William.'

'Well, it doesn't do any harm to check these things out,' said Glover diplomatically.

Glover had a considerable wait after ringing the doorbell of William Alder's bungalow, but it was explained as Glover followed the older man through to his living room. He lurched to one side as he shuffled along and held his left arm tucked in close to his body. He'd had a stroke. His slacks and a sleeveless sweater hung loosely on his emaciated frame.

'And you haven't seen Coral since last week?' Glover asked, sitting down on the chintz two-seater sofa, opposite Alder's matching armchair.

'That's right,' Alder said. 'She should have been here last Friday and again today.' His speech was slurred and sibilant, so that Glover needed to lean in a little to catch everything he was saying. 'It's very unlike her,' William went on. 'If ever she can't come she always lets me know. Since I've been ill I rely on her to get some shopping in for me. The managers are too busy to do much.' He dabbed at the corner of his mouth with a pristine white handkerchief.

'And Coral cleans for you twice a week?' asked Glover. 'Does she clean for anyone else in the complex?'

'I don't think so. She was already helping me out when I came to live here and it suited us both to carry on the arrangement. She has other people she cleans for, of course: Miss James and Mr Pearson — he lives next door to my old house. And she has a new chap on Thursdays: a medical man.' He said the name but Charlie didn't quite catch it.

'Haine?' he repeated.

'No, *Haydn*,' said Alder, making an effort to enunciate. 'Like the composer.'

* * *

Leaving Granville Lane, Mariner drove across to Harborne High Street to his appointment with Paul Jenner, the Barham family solicitor, and administrator of

Jamie's trust fund. It was he who had first informed Mariner, on the day of Anna's funeral, that he was Jamie's legal guardian and now Mariner needed Jenner's authorisation to set up the standing order with Manor Park. It could all have been arranged via phone or email, but the initial elation at the prospect of getting his life back was beginning to wear off a little now, and it seemed only right that there should be a face-to-face conversation about it.

Jenner saw no issue. 'Financially Jamie has been very well provided for. We've always known that,' he said, as the two men sat facing each other in his cramped and untidy office. The first time Mariner had come here was following a burglary, when the place had been ransacked, and it was hard today to see any discernible difference. Even Jenner himself looked a little neglected, his receding snow-white hair seeming to slide off the back of his head and down over his collar. 'As the sole surviving family member, Jamie has inherited from his siblings and parents and the money has been carefully invested, thanks to mechanisms that Eddie, Anna and now you yourself have put in place. He can very easily afford to live at Manor Park, or somewhere like it, for many years to come. In fact, I would venture, 'til the end of his natural life. So I'm not sure what else I can help you with.'

'It's not just a financial undertaking, though, is it?' said Mariner. 'It's about the quality of Jamie's life too. It's a big decision that I'm making on his behalf.'

Jenner looked surprised. 'You want me to tell you that you're doing the right thing?'

'I suppose I do,' Mariner admitted, suddenly recognising that fact for himself. 'You've known Jamie and his family for much longer than I have.'

Jenner leaned back in his chair, steepling his hands in front of him. 'Are you satisfied that Manor Park will meet Jamie's needs?'

'Absolutely,' said Mariner with confidence.

'Then you're only doing what Anna herself did before you,' Jenner pointed out. 'She intended that Jamie's place at Towyn would be a long-term arrangement. You were concerned about the quality of care he was receiving there, so you removed him. But like Anna, you have a demanding job. What's the one thing Jamie needs above all else?'

'Consistency,' said Mariner.

'Which is exactly what I imagine Manor Park will provide for him. It is — if I may be forgiven the vernacular — what my grandson would call a no-brainer. Now, let's get down to the paperwork, shall we?'

* * *

Charlie Glover got back to Granville Lane ahead of Mariner, so was able to check over the case notes and, when Mariner walked in just minutes later, he called him over. 'I've just been out to see this old chap, William Alder,' Charlie said. 'CAD asked me to go and talk to him because he reported his cleaner missing.' Glover saw Mariner's expression change. 'I know. Pointless visit — I thought the same thing. But then he let slip that this woman, Coral Norman, also cleans for a Dr Hayden.'

'Shit,' said Mariner. 'And she's been missing since when?'

'At least last Friday.'

'Well, that has to be more than just coincidence. Let's see what Leo Hayden has to say for himself.'

* * *

Mariner rang through to the critical care department of the hospital and asked to speak to Ellen Kingsley. 'Is Dr Hayden there today?' he asked.

'He's at the Gannow,' she said. 'The private clinic I told you about.'

'Do you have contact details for him there?' Mariner said. 'We need to get hold of him urgently.'

‘Is everything all right?’ He could hear the curiosity in her voice.

‘We just need to check something out,’ Mariner said neutrally, hoping that she would be content to leave it at that. This was the risk of getting personally involved with someone related to a case. At the time, of course, he’d had no reason to think that she would be anything more than a peripheral player in it all. He hoped that wasn’t about to change. Luckily she seemed, at least for the moment, to sense the need for professionalism.

After going off the line for a couple of minutes she returned and gave him the address of the Gannow Clinic. Mariner had never heard of it and said so.

‘It’s pretty exclusive,’ said Ellen. ‘They handle a range of mental health issues, including addiction. They have one or two quite well-known clients.’

‘It’s a rehab centre?’ said Mariner.

‘Not exactly. It’s much more than that, but just to warn you, they are likely to be cagey with giving out information.’

‘Thanks for the heads up.’

‘I hope you get it sorted,’ she said, leaving a number of unasked questions hanging in the air.

* * *

Instructing Charlie to begin processing the relevant search warrants, Mariner took Jesson with him and drove over to the clinic.

‘Well, this place is tucked away,’ Jesson said, as they drove in between two twelve-foot-high hedges. They had passed the centre twice, once in each direction, before she’d eventually spotted the discreet sign partially concealed by the foliage that had grown around it, and which gave absolutely no indication of the nature of the establishment.

'Same old story,' said Mariner. 'We like to think we're more accepting but the reality is we still prefer to keep mental illness out of sight when we can.'

A sweeping gravel drive widened into a small parking area in front of the Victorian red-brick house that held nothing smaller than a two-litre engine and no vehicle older than last year's registration, though the personalised plates were harder to date. 'Staff or patients, do you think?' said Mariner getting out of the car and eyeing up a top-of-the-range Jaguar SUV.

Automatic doors ushered them into a thickly carpeted reception area. The lighting was low and discreet, soft music played in the background, and a small font-like sculpture held a tinkling eternal fountain. Behind a reception desk that looked like a cast-off from the Starship Enterprise was a row of seven-by-five-inch glossy photographs of the staff. That was something Ellen hadn't mentioned — that Leo Hayden was a good-looking bastard.

Mariner had often thought he must give off a signal that announced exactly what he was and, true to form, the girl behind the polished mahogany desk looked up from her glossy magazine with an expression of wary distaste. Or maybe it was that she'd noticed them draw up outside in a three-year-old Mondeo. They waved warrant cards in front of her. 'We're looking for Dr Leo Hayden,' said Mariner. 'We need to speak to him urgently.'

'Can I ask what it is regarding?' the girl asked, playing to type. Mariner had known highly trained guard dogs who were easier to get past than medical receptionists.

'It's confidential,' he said. 'But it is imperative that we talk to him.'

'Well, I'm sorry, Dr Hayden isn't here, and hasn't been for about a week now,' she admitted. 'He phoned in sick, early on the morning of last Thursday, because he'd been up all night with stomach trouble. He said he was likely to be off for a few days and asked me to cancel all his patients. Sometimes these attacks can last a little while.'

'This has happened before?' said Mariner.

'Yes, he contracted some stomach problem working abroad and gets these flare-ups from time to time. A few days at home and he'll be right as rain.'

Mariner and Jesson exchanged a look. A man could do a lot in a few days. And this time Hayden had already been off the radar for a week. 'In that case I'll need his home address, please,' said Mariner, frustrated by the setback.

'I'm not sure that I can give you—' she began.

'Perhaps you'd be more certain if I charged you with obstructing a murder investigation,' said Mariner, calmly.

'I will just need to check with Mr Bloom,' she said, flustered now.

Mariner waited patiently for her to return. 'What's he like, Dr Hayden?' Mariner asked, when she'd returned and was looking up Hayden on their system.

Her face softened. 'He's nice,' she said, handing him a printout of the address. 'Got lovely manners, and he's very popular, even though he hasn't got much time for some of the clients. It's like cats,' she added, enigmatically.

Jesson saw Mariner's blank face. 'The more you try to get them to like you, the more indifferent they get?' she speculated.

'Yes, that's right.' The receptionist beamed.

'I wonder if that's how Leo Hayden likes his women in general,' said Mariner, as, moments later, they left the building furnished with the man's address.

Chapter Twenty-Three

Leo Hayden had a house on the edge of Solihull, where the streets were wide and tree-lined, and the properties large and sprawling. As they drove around the outer circle to get there, Jesson dialled the phone number but there was no reply. 'Too ill to get out of bed?' she wondered aloud.

'Get some uniformed back-up,' said Mariner, 'just in case Dr Hayden decides to put up a fight. And ask Charlie to meet us there with the search warrants.'

The house was a perfectly symmetrical rectangle, like a child's drawing of a house might be, with a two-car garage attached to the left-hand side. It sat behind high walls, complete with wrought-iron gates and a security pad.

'Not very welcoming,' remarked Mariner as they parked and got out of the car. He pushed the buzzer, but it produced no response. 'Any ideas?' he asked Jesson, studying the rows of numbers to determine which, if any, were faded from use.

'Shame we don't know his date of birth,' she said. 'Is it worth contacting the clinic again?'

On the margins of his line of vision Mariner sensed a movement and looked up to see a middle-aged woman watching him from a ground-floor window of the house next door. He lifted his hand in acknowledgement. Embarrassed at having been caught out, she seemed about to withdraw before thinking better of it and tentatively responding. Her garden was open plan, so Mariner walked up to the front door, which opened the moment he got there. 'Detective Chief Inspector Mariner,' he said, showing his identification.

'Oh.' She hadn't been expecting that. 'I hope you don't think I was being nosey . . .'

'Not at all,' said Mariner, not entirely truthfully. 'No harm in being aware of what's going on around you. We're looking for your neighbour, Dr Leo Hayden.'

'Oh, he'll be at work,' she said confidently.

'Not today,' said Mariner. 'And we can't seem to raise him from the house. I don't suppose you would know his security code?'

'You could try 2-4-7-1,' she said. 'It was the code Mr and Mrs Hayden, senior, used. They gave it to me, just in case something should happen and I needed to get in.'

'Thank you,' said Mariner. 'We'll try that.' A thought occurred to him. 'I don't suppose you hold a spare key to the house too, do you?'

She went off to fetch it. 'I did tell Leo I'd still got it, when he moved back here a little while ago. I offered to give it back to him, but he said I may as well keep it for now.'

'It's a good idea,' said Mariner, pleased and disconcerted at the same time. If Hayden was their washerwoman, would he have been careless enough to leave a spare key with the neighbours? 'When did you last see Dr Hayden?' he asked.

'Oh, not for a few days now.' She thought for a moment. 'Actually, it would have been last week sometime — Thursday, I'm sure of it. One of those tree surgeon people came to the door, ridiculously early, and I saw Leo leaving in his car to go to work. I gave him a little wave, but I'm not sure if he saw me.'

'What time would this have been?'

'Perhaps about half past eight.'

'Where are Mr and Mrs Hayden, senior?' asked Mariner.

'Oh, he passed away some years ago now, and then shortly afterwards she went to live with her sister in South Africa. The house stood empty for a while. We thought it would go on the market, but then Leo came back.'

'Is Leo the only child?'

'Yes, they had him quite late in life, but he's done ever so well for himself.'

'Except that Hayden didn't go to work on Thursday morning,' said Jesson, as she and Mariner let themselves in through the electronic gates.

'But if he is our man,' said Mariner, 'why the necklaces? What's the letter P got to do with anything?'

'Search me,' said Jesson. 'Middle name?'

As a formality Mariner rang the doorbell and when, as expected, no one responded, they let themselves into the house. Though the rooms were spacious and the polished wood floors and Persian rugs spoke of wealth, the place had an air of careless neglect about it. The furniture was dated and the carpets threadbare in places, and Mariner guessed that Leo Hayden wasn't much interested in his surroundings. He seemed to live modestly, the house felt cold and uninhabited. A vaguely unpleasant smell seemed to get stronger as they went further into the building.

They found Coral Norman lying sprawled face down on the floor of the utility room, with what looked at first glance like a pair of tights or stockings still wound around her neck, the ends trailing across the stone tiles as if they'd been artistically arranged that way. A large woman, she wore her grey hair cut short to the nape of her neck so that a dark purple stain of bruising could be seen radiating out from underneath the band of brown nylon. Squatting down, Mariner felt her wrist for a pulse, but her flesh was cold and as he got nearer, the stench became overpowering, forcing him to cover his nose and mouth with his hand. Her head was turned to the side, the eyes glassy, and from the side that rested on the floor, post-mortem lividity, where the blood had pooled, spread up into her face like a port-wine stain birthmark.

Jesson walked through from the hall, holding a beige leather handbag Mariner didn't recognise. 'This was hanging on a coat peg,' she said. Opening it, she took out a purse and checked the contents. 'Bank cards here for a Miss C. Norman,' she confirmed. 'And there's a mobile phone.'

'See if you can track down a next of kin,' said Mariner, stepping away from the body. Taking out his own phone, he summoned scenes of crime and rang through to Superintendent Sharp. 'We need to issue a nationwide alert for a Dr Leo Hayden,' he said, 'including ports and airports, though we may well be too late. He hasn't been seen since around the time Dee Henderson disappeared and we've just found his cleaner strangled at his house. He's dangerous so shouldn't be approached.'

'You think he might be our washerwoman?' asked Sharp.

'I'd say there's a very good chance,' said Mariner. 'We've already identified the hospital as the probable contact point, and he'd have easy access to sheets and scrubs. If nothing else he's got some explaining to do,' said Mariner.

'Hello?' Charlie Glover's voice rang out, hollow through the empty house.

'In here,' Mariner called back, pocketing his phone and pulling on latex gloves.

Glover appeared in the doorway. 'Oh, no,' he groaned. 'This is Coral?' He handed Mariner the all-important signed search warrant. He'd also brought with him a couple of uniforms, so, while they waited for the

SOCOs, Mariner had them conduct a basic search of the rest of the house. 'We're looking for any sign that Grace, Rosa or Dee has been here — and any indication of where Hayden might have gone,' he reminded them.

Through the utility room Mariner took the access door that opened into the garage. It was whitewashed and spotlessly clean, tools arranged on wall brackets according to the outlined shape underneath. There was no car, but a muddy mountain bike hung from brackets on the wall. Taking out a polythene evidence bag, Mariner scraped some of the dried soil into it. 'So where do you like to go mountain biking, Dr Hayden?' he said to himself. 'Pepper Wood, by any chance?'

Calling one of the uniforms over, the two of them set about searching the ground floor and outside the house for any kind of cellar or basement. But, if the house had one, they could find no obvious entry point. Next Mariner went back inside and climbed the stairs to the first floor. Charlie Glover was going through the wardrobes in what looked like the master bedroom, its king-sized bed unmade. Drawers that he'd already searched were still open, clothing spilling out.

'If he's gone away, he's left a lot of stuff behind,' said Charlie. He nodded towards an en suite. 'And there's a toothbrush and razor in there.'

'He's a doctor,' said Mariner. 'And he's on call to the critical care unit. He might have had a bag already packed for that.' Looking out of the window he saw that Stuart Croghan had arrived.

'There's this too.' Leaving what he was doing, Glover took Mariner out onto the landing and pushed open the door to what was obviously a spare bedroom. In the middle of the room was an ironing board. 'Might be worth taking a sample of his detergent,' said Glover.

Vicky Jesson was sitting behind a desk in the study, poring over the computer. 'Password protected, of course,' she said. 'As we might have guessed.'

'Pleasing, though,' said Mariner. 'It might indicate that he's got something to hide. Shut it down and we'll get it back to Granville Lane for Max to have a look at. I'm trying to work out where Dee Henderson fits into all this. She knows the man, works with him.'

'Do you think she could be involved?' Jesson said.

'As an accomplice, you mean?'

'Why not? Think of Fred and Rosemary West.'

'But their whole relationship was founded on shared deviancy that went back years. There's nothing to suggest that Dee is that way inclined,' Mariner pointed out. 'There could be something between them, though. She could have eloped with him.'

'What — and abandon her children without so much as a goodbye? That would be pretty unusual,' said Jesson. 'Hayden and Dee were working together on the Wednesday afternoon before she disappeared. Isn't it more likely that she'd worked out what Hayden was up to, or even just noticed something about his behaviour that caused her to question him, or make some kind of comment? If Hayden *is* our washerwoman and he thought Dee was onto him, then he'd have had to do something about that right away.'

'It would have been easy for him,' Mariner agreed. 'He could just have offered her a lift home.'

'And Coral?'

'Same thing. If we're right about Dee, then Hayden did something with her during the night on Wednesday. He comes back here, having disposed of her or maybe even bringing her with him. Coral turns up first thing Thursday morning to clean his house and she sees or hears something that arouses her suspicion.'

'But why leave Coral here and incriminate himself?'

'He's pushed for time,' said Mariner. 'And he's got a nosey neighbour. On Thursday morning he'll have wanted to keep up the pretence that he was going to work. And by now he might be panicking. Two people have already worked out what he's up to. He needs to get away fast. Let's see what Croghan has to say.'

'What is it with doctors?' said Jesson, as they descended the stairs.

'Power,' said Mariner. 'It's as simple as that.'

After allowing Stuart Croghan what he thought was a reasonable length of time with the body, Mariner could no longer resist returning to the utility room. 'Is this the same person who killed Grace Clifton and Rosa Batista?' was his first question.

Croghan's response was typically measured. 'Couldn't say for sure, of course,' he said. 'Although it's a death by asphyxiation, the MO is very different and she doesn't fit the physical profile of your other victims, does she?'

'We're thinking she wasn't part of the plan,' said Mariner. 'How long has she been here?'

'Several days,' said Croghan. 'That's about as accurate as I can be right now.'

'Could she have been here since last Thursday?'

'It's possible. The ambient temperature is low, and it's dry in here and very clean, but as you can tell, decomposition has already started.'

It was bad news. So far no passport had been found. If Hayden had made his escape days ago, he could be anywhere by now.

'Do you think he brought the others back here?' Glover said.

'We can't be certain until forensics have done their worst,' said Mariner. 'But if he can pick them up and get them into his car, why not? He can drive straight into the garage and from there bring them into the house unseen. Here he has everything at his disposal.'

On their way out, Jesson stopped by the door of the lounge. 'Have you seen this?' She went over to the baby grand piano. 'It's beautiful. Must be worth a fortune, and it's just sitting here.' Lifting the lid, she idly pressed some of the keys in a simple tune. 'That's it,' she said, raising her head.

'What?' Mariner was at a loss.

She played the tune again. 'It might seem a bit obscure,' said Jesson. 'But it's the first thing my girls learned to play when they started piano lessons. It's called *Papa Haydn*.' She looked up at Mariner. 'P for Papa?'

* * *

It was getting late and Mariner had a decision to make. Reluctantly he phoned Mercy. 'There have been some developments at work,' he said. 'Would you be able to meet Jamie from the bus tonight and get him something to eat?'

'No problem.' She was as laid-back as ever. Mariner felt like a traitor.

He returned to the Gannow with a further warrant granting him access to Hayden's personnel record at the clinic and some time to look over it. This time he was shown into the modern, well-appointed office of the clinic's director, Alexander Bloom, which looked out over expansive gardens and a lily pond with benches arranged around it. Two of them were occupied by people who could have been staff or patients — it was hard to tell the difference.

'What can you tell me about Leo Hayden?' Mariner asked, sinking back into one of the very comfortable easy chairs that faced Bloom's desk.

'We're very fortunate to have him working here,' said Bloom. 'He's good at his job and he gets results, although I'm not sure that his heart is always in it.'

'How do you mean?'

'I've always had the impression Leo doesn't like working here much. He makes it clear that he values his work at the military hospital more highly, to the extent that he can occasionally be openly disparaging about some of our patients.'

'So why does he stay?' Mariner asked.

Bloom turned his palms upwards. 'We pay him extremely well. Our patients have a lot of ready cash at their disposal. Leo thinks that's half the problem. They are spoiled and self-indulgent, with too much money and too much time on their hands, and actually that's what makes them so unhappy.'

'Is he right?' asked Mariner.

'About some of them, undoubtedly. They enjoy the luxury of being able to pay someone to listen to them. I think after some of the situations Leo has worked in, he finds that difficult.'

'I understand he's worked in Africa,' said Mariner.

'Primarily in conflict zones, helping traumatised victims,' said Bloom. 'He came here from the Congo, where he was working with women and children who had suffered terribly. They'd been beaten and raped and witnessed their loved ones slaughtered. I can see Leo's point of view. Much of what we do here must seem trivial by comparison. But I think for him it's a means to an end, an easy way of making money that will enable him to continue with what he sees as more worthwhile work. I think he has plans to return to Africa at some point soon.'

'Does he ever make his views known to the patients?' Mariner asked.

'He's a professional,' said Bloom, 'and behaves accordingly. He keeps his personal feelings in check.'

'Does he like that, being in control?'

'It's not unusual in our profession. After all, what we're often trying to do for our patients is create order from chaos.'

'I understand Dr Hayden has some ongoing physical health problems,' Mariner said.

Bloom inclined his head. 'He contracted an intestinal problem when he was on the African continent. I'd never come across it before, but it flares up from time to time and when it does, I understand it's quite debilitating.'

'So he requires regular time off?'

'It strikes perhaps every couple of months.'

'And he's on emergency standby for the QE too,' Mariner said. 'What happens if he gets a call to go there?'

'His list here is cancelled, and if there's anything urgent, I or one of the other staff pick it up. It was a condition Leo insisted upon, but we happily agreed to it.'

'How well do you know Leo personally?' asked Mariner.

'Hardly at all. He's a quiet man — keeps to himself. I have to admit to being shocked by this turn of events. It really doesn't add up that it's Leo you're looking for.'

'Do you have patients staying overnight here?'

'We have a small number of beds, yes,' said Bloom.

'Then I'd like to see one of your sheets, please.' But as Mariner had already guessed, the Gannow Clinic sheets were made from nothing so coarse as pure cotton and bore no laundry marks. He didn't even bother to take one. Mariner's final request before leaving the clinic was for a copy of the photograph from Hayden's personnel record, which could now be circulated nationally.

* * *

When Mariner eventually made it home that evening he found everything quiet. Mercy and Jamie sat watching TV companionably together, Mercy apparently content to watch endless reruns of *Pointless* all over again.

'Thanks for stepping in this afternoon,' said Mariner. 'I really do appreciate it.'

'Oh, it's no problem — you know that.' Mercy waved away his thanks. 'I'm always happy to help.'

'Actually,' said Mariner, seizing the opportunity, 'it shouldn't happen again. Jamie's been offered a full-time place at Manor Park, starting next week.'

'Oh,' said Mercy. Her face fell momentarily before she rearranged it into a smile. 'Well, that's good, isn't it? Jamie likes it there, don't you, Jamie?'

'He does,' said Mariner. 'And it means you won't have to be running around after us anymore.' He was shamelessly putting a spin on it and felt guilty for doing so. 'You'll have more time to take care of Carlton.'

'Oh, he doesn't need me,' said Mercy. 'He's his own man.' She didn't say anything further, but as they waited for her taxi to arrive, she was unusually pensive.

Chapter Twenty-Four

On Thursday morning, Charlie was applying himself once more to the CCTV footage, this time with one eye on the headshot of Leo Hayden pinned above the monitor. He was continuing to review the particular days when Rosa and Grace had been visiting the QE. But so far he'd been unable to identify anyone who resembled the doctor. 'If Hayden goes to the cafeteria a lot, he'd know where the CCTV cameras are and could easily have been making a deliberate effort to avoid them,' he said to Jesson.

'You'd think, given his attitude towards the Gannow patients, that he might have selected one of them as a victim,' she said.

Mariner spoke up from where he was adding Hayden's details to the incident board. 'That job is his main source of income,' he pointed out. 'He wouldn't want to foul his own nest. Besides, he *likes* the women he's taken and respects them. They're specially selected for their physical attributes and after he's finished with them he cleans them and wraps them carefully before burying them, then he launders their clothes and polishes their shoes.'

'That's what I don't understand,' said Jesson, her freckled nose wrinkling. 'There's no sign of sexual activity, so what does he *do* with them? What does he get out of it? And why go to all that trouble afterwards?'

'Maybe it's about protecting them,' Mariner said. 'He's seen women subjected to some atrocious treatment. In his twisted mind, maybe this is his way of trying to make amends.'

'By killing them?' Jesson wasn't buying it. 'And ironing their clothes? I don't know many blokes who even know how to use an iron.'

'But you saw how tidy his house is,' said Mariner. 'He's obsessive. We're hardly talking about Mr Normal here, remember?'

'So where do you think he is?'

'Well, he could have phoned in sick on Thursday morning from anywhere,' said Mariner. 'The neighbour saw him leave the house, but we don't know where he went.'

'And if Dee's with him, is she still alive?'

'The last positive sighting of both of them is in critical care on Wednesday evening. The question is, was Hayden alone when he left, or did Dee leave with him?'

The company responsible for parking security at the hospital monitored vehicles arriving and leaving each car park from a central control room. Mariner went back over to the QE to watch the CCTV footage for himself from a tiny office, whose only view of the outside world was via the extensive bank of monitors. This was not a job for claustrophobics. But Anwar, the younger of the two men on duty this morning, seemed cheerful enough in his work. Hayden's Audi had been recorded arriving in one of the designated multi-storey staff car parks at 3:09 on Wednesday afternoon, soon after Dee had summoned him. He'd helpfully parked close to one of the internal CCTV cameras, which enabled them to watch him get out of his car, retrieve something that looked like a briefcase from the back seat, and walk to the nearest exit with a long, confident stride. A little after eight o'clock the same evening he was seen returning alone and leaving the car park. Cameras on the main hospital site followed the car's progress as he left, turning out onto Metchley Lane. It meant that Hayden must have picked up Dee Henderson sometime after that. 'Thanks,' said Mariner. I'll need to take a copy . . .'

'Sure,' said Anwar. 'But don't you want to see the next day too?'

'He came back?' said Mariner.

'Eight forty-five last Thursday morning. He was here for about half an hour. He parked at the far end, so you can't see him get out of the car this time, but you can see him leaving.' Anwar scrolled to the relevant clip, and they watched as Hayden's car drew up alongside the barrier once again and the window slid down as he reached out to swipe his security card. 'That's the last we've got of him on our system,' said Anwar. 'Nice watch,' he added. 'TAG Heuer, by the look of it.'

Mariner had no idea what that meant, or how Anwar could possibly tell from that distance, but he got the footage downloaded, along with the rest, to a memory stick, which he was able to take away with him.

* * *

It was with some reluctance that Mariner returned to the critical care ward to see Ellen Kingsley — this was all getting a bit too close for comfort. Today she was able to leave the ward and they went to her office to talk.

'You're looking for Leo in connection with this enquiry,' she said straight away. 'I don't understand.'

'We had a tip-off to go to his home,' Mariner told her. 'We found his cleaner there. She had been strangled.'

'What? Oh my God.'

'Ellen, we need to talk to him urgently. If you or any of your staff have the slightest idea about where he could be, you must tell us.'

'But I can't see how that is even possible. He's such a lovely guy. And I haven't a clue where he might be. I've been thinking about him a lot and it's made me realise how little I know about him. He's one of those people who seems quite chatty but manages to give away very little about himself.'

'Did he come here last Thursday morning, first thing?' Mariner asked.

'No. It's not one of his regular times and we didn't call him in for anything. The last time he was here was Wednesday afternoon. I'm sure of that.'

'I have to ask you again,' said Mariner. 'Are you absolutely sure there's been nothing going on between him and Dee?'

'I'm as certain as I can be, working alongside them both,' she said. He could see her trying to make sense of it.

'Is it possible that Hayden could have developed an infatuation with her?'

'Not that I noticed.' She blushed.

'What is it?'

'Oh, God. It's nothing.' She looked away. 'Leo and I, we had a bit of a fling when he first started here. It was very brief. Over before it started really.'

'Why?'

'It was a bad idea — with the two of us working so closely together.'

'Was there anything unusual about his behaviour, did he have any particular tastes?'

'Like what?'

'Was he into tying you up, for example?'

She shot him a look. 'The relationship didn't really last long enough for that.'

* * *

Mariner took the car park footage back to Granville Lane. Following the nationwide alert, there had been a couple of possible sightings of Hayden's car. 'It's hardly a distinctive model,' said Charlie. 'But one of them is on the Wednesday evening, quite close to the hospital.'

'We need to revise our parameters,' said Mariner. 'Hayden was back there again for half an hour on the Thursday morning, leaving at nine fifteen. It's after that he disappears, so that's when we need to get him on CCTV to see which direction he took from there.'

'The postmark on Rosa Batista's parcel was generated by the machine in the main hospital post room,' said Charlie. 'If Hayden is our killer, maybe that's where he went?'

'So why haven't we had a parcel of Dee's clothes?'

'Perhaps it's got lost in the post, or he was thwarted that morning in some way?' said Glover. 'Shame we can't actually see him get out of the car.'

'Where's Vicky?' Mariner asked.

'One of Hayden's ex-girlfriends got in touch. She's gone out to talk to her.'

Jesson returned a couple of hours later. 'Anything useful?' Mariner asked her.

'Not sure,' said Jesson. 'The relationship didn't last long. They met through an internet dating site. They emailed a bit, then spoke on the phone and went out a handful of times. According to her, he was the perfect gent: kind, courteous and attentive. Pretty ordinary, in fact.'

'So why did it end?'

'That's where it gets a bit more interesting,' Jesson said. 'She ended the relationship, partly because he spent a bit too much time going on about his ex — whose name she thinks was Priya, with a P. Hayden took it quite well, she said, but she left him in a city centre bar. It was the same night that Grace went missing.'

* * *

By late Thursday afternoon Charlie Glover, working alongside a couple of bleary-eyed uniforms, had done his best to scour the available CCTV footage from around the QE, but it was of limited use. 'It's fragmented,' Charlie explained. 'We can see Hayden leaving the hospital site and just about piece together his journey to the Five Ways roundabout from GATSO footage, but that's where we lose him. If he's used any motorways in the vicinity, we can hope that he'll be picked up by the cameras along those roads, but if he hasn't, there's no way of knowing where he went from there. It's too late to set up ANPR and we wouldn't have a clue where to target anyway.'

'And on the footage we have, you're certain he has no passengers with him in the car?' asked Mariner.

'Definitely only him driving,' said Glover.

'Not looking very promising, is it?' said Jesson.

'He's had a long time to get away,' Mariner agreed.

* * *

Winter came on suddenly the next day, with an icy front from the Arctic bringing a hard frost and an early morning fog. With it, in the middle of Friday morning, came a call from much closer to home than Mariner was expecting. West Mercia Police at Cleobury Mortimer had been contacted by a farmer. 'He went up to bring his sheep down from the hill, and noticed a car parked behind one of the walls of the old quarry,' the station inspector told Mariner. 'He didn't see it until he drove right up there on a quad bike. We sent a couple of uniforms up to have a look and they've confirmed that it's the Audi you're looking for, belonging to Dr Leo Hayden. From a distance they thought it had been abandoned, but now it looks as if there's definitely at least one person in it, presumably Dr Hayden. The SOCOs are making a start, but I've asked them not to move anything until you can get out here and take a look for yourself. He's not going anywhere.'

Titterstone, the larger of the Shropshire Clee Hills, was, like its neighbour, Brown Clee, visible, now that the fog had cleared, from the Stourbridge Road going out of Birmingham.

'The only hill named on the Mappa Mundi in Hereford Cathedral,' Mariner told Jesson as, an hour later, they arrived at its foot. '*The high reared head of Clee.*'

'Great,' murmured Jesson. 'He's going all Adam Dalgliesh on me.'

'A. E. Housman,' Mariner corrected her. 'And don't get too excited. It's about the only bit of poetry I know.' They'd left the main road now and were winding their way along a narrow lane and up the hill, passing a row of what must once have been miners' cottages.

'Must be lonely up here,' said Jesson.

'Now perhaps, but it didn't used to be,' said Mariner. 'All they quarry now is the dhustone used for road building, but years ago it was a whole mining community, digging for basalt and limestone, and there was a fully operational iron-smelting mill. There was a great little pub up here too, the Dhustone Inn. Good Banks's beer, a roaring fire and a game of dominoes. Nothing like it.'

'I can't imagine why you've never married,' said Jesson in reply. She shivered. 'Too bleak for my liking. And what the hell are they?' she added, as the two enormous white dice came into view. 'There's a Civil Aviation Authority navigational relay station just at the top of the hill,' said Mariner. 'I'm pretty sure this is a favourite spot for army winter manoeuvres too,' he went on. 'So lonely isn't really the word.' Branching off to the left, he steered the car carefully around some lethal potholes and into the gorge of the disused quarry, between scree slopes that banked away from them on either side. He drew to a halt beside the disordered collection of West Mercia response vehicles.

'All right,' Jesson conceded, as they got out of the car to suit up. 'Perhaps there is something in this hill-walking malarkey.' From this height and now that the mists had cleared, the counties of Shropshire and Worcestershire were spread out below them like a chequered quilt, stretching all the way to the Welsh borders and the Black Mountains beyond.

When they were dressed in protective clothing, and after brief introductions, the crime scene co-ordinator led them round to Hayden's car, tucked in the shade behind one of the remaining quarry walls. Random concrete structures rose up from the derelict smelt mill, overshadowed by the giant receivers, and now the white-suited West Mercia SOCOs moving into the area made it look like the set of a low-budget sci-fi film. A couple of uniformed officers were pacing the perimeter of the scene trying to keep warm, their breath condensing in misty puffs in the frigid air.

Up close Jesson and Mariner could see the car's passenger window a half-inch or so open, with a hose pipe trailing from the exhaust and in through the tiny vent. Cloth of some sort, tightly wound, had been wedged in to plug the remaining gap. The driver's door hung open to reveal Leo Hayden, slumped in the reclining driver's seat, his eyes closed. He could have been taking a nap, but for the tell-tale purple hue of his eyelids and lips. Inside the open boot was a woman's body, curled in the foetal position and perfectly preserved in the cold. Dee Henderson still wore her nurse's tunic. The brown nylon scarf, tied tight around her neck, was identical to the one they'd found on Coral Norman. Mariner took out his mobile and rang Sharp to report the find.

'So that confirms it,' said Sharp. 'Leo Hayden was our washerwoman.'

'Looks like it,' said Mariner. 'Either his conscience got to him, or he thought the game was up.'

'It doesn't really matter in the end, does it?' said Sharp. 'The important thing is that we've got him and put a stop to it. Well done, both of you. We'll celebrate when you get back.'

'Well done?' said Mariner to Jesson as he ended the call. 'We didn't *do* anything.'

A bitter wind blew across the hillside, and once a thorough forensic search had been conducted, the bodies were removed and the vehicle transferred to a covered loader to be transported to Birmingham for closer examination. By now it was mid-afternoon and Mariner was cold and hungry. Not far along the road he and Jesson passed another favourite pub of his, the Angel Inn, and he suggested that they stop off for refreshment and to warm up a bit. 'It's not as if we've got anything to rush back for, have we?' he said.

Chapter Twenty-Five

Jesson and Mariner sat in the pub in companionable silence. 'It's funny,' said Jesson. 'We should feel good, but all I've got is this strange sense of anti-climax.'

'Fatigue,' said Mariner, lifting his half pint to his lips. 'It'll hit home soon.' But like Jesson, he too felt peculiarly disengaged.

'There are so many things we'll never know, like why he did it, or even exactly *how* he did it,' she continued. 'Pity he didn't leave a note.'

'We can speculate, though,' said Mariner. 'I think we've figured most of it out. Hayden strikes up a conversation with Grace and Rosa in the hospital cafeteria. He can see their names on their badges — he can even see where Grace works. We know he's outwardly charming and they would no doubt be flattered by the attentions of such an important man. He gets enough information out of them to know where they work and what their shifts are, so that a few days later he can contrive to meet them "accidentally" in the city centre. And he talks them into going with him, at least far enough that it entails getting them into his car.'

'Rosa, I can understand,' said Jesson. 'A lift home would have been helpful. And Dee is obviously different. She'd have no qualms about going with him. But Grace had arranged to meet her friends. Why would she change her mind and go with him?'

'She was a rebel,' Mariner reminded her. 'Who knows what she'd told him about her frustrations with her parents and her life in general. He's an exotic. He's travelled the world, so she took a risk. Maybe she saw Hayden as her way out. Remember, we don't know how many women Hayden actually approached in the first place. He chose Grace and Rosa, presumably because he thought they'd be compliant, and he was right. Once we make this public, I wouldn't be at all surprised if we get other women coming forward to say he tried it on with them too. Dee must have rumbled him, or he thought she had. He had no choice but to get her out of the way — the same way he did with Coral.'

'But I still don't understand why he'd leave Coral behind,' said Jesson. 'As soon as we found her it was obvious that he was our man. If we'd found his house empty, his disappearance would only have been circumstantial.'

'I think by that time he was in over his head,' said Mariner. 'Dee and Coral weren't part of the plan, plus he knew them personally, so killing them brought home to him the enormity of what he'd done. No, what I can't work out is where he took Grace and Rosa. There isn't any firm evidence yet that either of them has even been inside his house.'

'He's a bugger for cleanliness, though,' Jesson pointed out. 'Perhaps he's just very thorough.'

'But to leave no trace of them at all? That would be quite an achievement. Do you think there's anywhere in the hospital or at the clinic he'd have been able to take them?'

'Without anyone else seeing or suspecting? It's hard to see how,' said Jesson. 'I'd love to know *why* he did it too.'

'He's screwed up,' said Mariner. 'His new girlfriend dumped him, and that, combined with the horrors of what he must have seen in the Congo, sent him off the rails.' But even as he said it, he was already thinking that it was too convenient an explanation.

'And what brought out him here, to this hill?' Jesson went on. 'Conscience or cowardice?'

'Conscience, surely,' said Mariner. 'He had every opportunity to run away. He left the hospital last Thursday morning, with Dee in the boot and Coral dead at his home, but at that stage nobody had a clue. We weren't onto him until nearly a week later and we haven't found his passport. He could have quite easily disposed of Dee's body and disappeared completely. So why didn't he do that?'

'Like you said, he suddenly came to his senses,' said Vicky. 'Everybody's been telling us what a nice guy he was. Perhaps what he's done to these women was an aberration, a period of madness.'

'That simple?' said Mariner doubtfully.

By the time Mariner and Jesson got to the appointed city pub later that afternoon, the celebrations seemed to have got underway without them and people were already starting to drift away — some to catch up on work that had been left untouched for days, and others back to their families, intent on starting the weekend early. Here, too, the atmosphere was subdued, and few people seemed inclined to stick around. Jesson and Glover both decided to leave and Mariner couldn't blame them. Soon only he and Sharp remained.

'There's bound to be a certain lack of satisfaction because we didn't catch him,' said Sharp, perceptive to his mood. 'In a weird way Hayden gave himself up, didn't he? And not all cases are neat and tidy, with explicit and rational motives. You know that as well as I do. Anyway

I'm off to brief the ACC, and you should get yourself off home, too.'

'Yeah, I will,' said Mariner. *But just not yet.* Jamie wasn't due back for another hour and he wanted to write some of this up while it was still fresh in his mind, so instead he returned to the incident room. He was still there when the forensic report from Leo Hayden's house came through. It contained nothing very illuminating, except to confirm that Leo Hayden must have been *very* good at clearing up after himself. There was nothing to place Grace, Rosa or Dee there at all. APR had identified most of the fingerprints as naturally belonging to Hayden and to Coral Norman. There were however several prints, and other trace elements from person or persons unknown, mainly in the kitchen and bedroom. For Mariner that simply meant that Hayden had gone on more than one internet date, and that some of those women had made it back to his house.

Mariner called through to Max, the IT technician. 'Nice one, bro,' he said. 'You got him.'

'He got himself really,' said Mariner, without enthusiasm. 'Is there anything interesting on his computer?'

'A bit of porn, but tame stuff,' said Max. 'No special proclivities showing up, but there are a couple of email rants about his clients at the Gannow. Dude was having some trouble reconciling that kind of work with his experiences in Africa. I'll send you the transcripts.'

And Mariner could do no more today. Last one out, he switched off the lights in the incident room and was home in good time for the day-centre bus. The escort today was an older woman who Mariner hadn't seen before. 'Where's Declan?' he asked.

'Called in sick,' the woman said. 'It's meant to be my day off today. Still, I don't mind the extra money.' It made Mariner feel bad about Mercy all over again.

* * *

Millie was ambivalent about Suli's shooting trip with Greg Easton on Saturday morning. 'Are you sure you still want to go?' she asked, over breakfast.

'I'm looking forward to it,' said Suli. 'It's not often that I get the chance to play with boys' toys.'

'Be careful,' she said, as he was leaving. 'I don't want to end up a single-parent family.'

Suli looked at her. 'What's the matter?'

'I don't know. Maybe some of Louise's anxiety is rubbing off on me.'

Suli put his arms around her and hugged her close. 'I really hope not. It's clay pigeon shooting, that's all. I don't think I'll be in mortal danger.'

But after he'd gone, Millie found that she couldn't relax, and even Haroon seemed unsettled. On impulse she texted Tony Knox. *What are you up to today? Could use some company.* Happily, Tony was, as so often seemed to be the case these days, on a mission to avoid domestic chores, so agreed to meet later at a nearby pub.

* * *

On paper Mariner and Jamie had little in common, but what they did share was a liking for the outdoors and the stamina to walk for miles. As it was Jamie's last weekend at home, Mariner had planned a walk over Clent and Walton Hills, but just before they set out, he got a text from Tony Knox asking if they wanted to meet him and Millie for a lunchtime pint. Mariner texted back suggesting the Navigation, a Black Country pub where Jamie had been before and so would be relaxed, and instead of the hills, they set off for a walk along the canals.

Mariner felt a twinge of nostalgia to be sitting in a bar with his old sergeant and constable. If you overlooked the baby sleeping in his car seat, and the autistic man sitting a safe distance away stabbing at his iPad and occasionally muttering under his breath, it was just like old times.

'First things first,' said Knox, raising his pint. 'Congratulations on catching your washerwoman.'

Millie joined in the toast. 'Birmingham women can rest easy again. There's no doubt it's him?'

'It pretty much adds up,' said Mariner, with muted enthusiasm. 'We think he's been hanging around the hospital foyer, talking to these young women and possibly stalking them, before abducting them. Then he tied them up before bathing them and shaving off their pubic hair, and buried them wrapped in a sheet — oh, and at some point he put a necklace on them.'

'A necklace?' said Millie.

'With the letter P,' said Mariner.

'P for pervert, presumably,' said Knox.

'Well, thank God you got him,' said Millie. 'Must be a good feeling.' Haroon stirred in his seat, contorting his face into a sleepy grimace, and they all turned to watch.

'How's your friend?' Mariner asked Millie. 'What was her name — Louise?'

'Hm, I might have been wrong about the domestic abuse,' Millie admitted. 'But there's definitely something odd about them. Suli's gone shooting with Greg, her husband, today on the family estate. They've got a clay pigeon range where customers can go to try out their products. It was partly why I wanted to get out of the house. I've got this feeling about it.'

'Suli will be fine,' said Mariner. 'He can take care of himself.'

'Remind me, who is it this bloke works for?' asked Knox.

'Pincott and Easton,' said Millie. 'You must have come across them on Athena.'

'I've heard of them,' said Knox. 'And they'll be on NABIS's radar, but then so is every gunmaker in the country.' It came as no surprise to either Millie or Mariner to learn that Operation Athena was working closely with the National Ballistics Intelligence Service.

'Even if they only make sports guns?' said Millie.

'That might be what they do officially, but I'm guessing that some of their employees have skills that could be put to less legitimate uses,' Knox pointed out. 'Especially for the right price. We like to keep an eye on things.'

'Are you any nearer to finding out who might have shot Brian Riddell?' asked Mariner.

Knox rubbed a hand down the back of his head. 'It's so frustrating,' he said. 'We're starting to build a case around the main players for illegally importing and re-boring weapons, and it was assumed that once we started reeling them in, intelligence about the Riddell shooting would follow. We're convinced it's tied in with the gang-related stuff going on in the Aston/Newtown areas. That was Riddell's patch after all, and he was involved in some key arrests over there a couple of years ago.'

'You've got DNA from the crime scene?' asked Mariner.

'Yeah, they recovered a fresh lump of chewing gum. But it hasn't matched with anyone known to us. The UCs are well established on the inside, but apart from the odd bit of wild conjecture they haven't picked up a whisper about the shooting. It's weird. It's as if nobody knows.'

'And no chance the UCs have been compromised?' Millie asked.

'If they were, they'd be dead or maimed for life,' said Knox, chillingly. He swallowed the rest of his pint. 'Who's for a top-up?'

'I'll get them,' said Millie. 'Will Jamie have another?' she asked Mariner.

He glanced over to Jamie's half glass of shandy. 'No, he's fine,' he said. 'But he might have another bag of crisps. Jamie — Hula Hoops?'

Jamie's eyes flicked up from the iPad momentarily. 'Loops,' he said.

'It's his last weekend at my place,' Mariner said to Knox, explaining about Manor Park.

'That's brilliant,' said Knox. 'You'll be a free man again. Have you broken it to Mercy yet?'

For a moment Mariner was surprised that Knox had remembered her name, but then he recalled that it was Knox, of course, who had stumbled across Mercy in the first place, in that friend-of-a-friend way of his that could be so useful; through Jean no doubt. 'I think she's quite disappointed,' he said. 'But her help was only ever meant to be a temporary thing. I think she'll be OK, as long as her son doesn't give her any grief. You haven't come across a Carlton Brown in the course of your new job, have you?'

Knox pulled a face. 'Nah, doesn't ring any bells,' he said, as Millie returned with the next round of drinks.

* * *

When Millie got home she was relieved to see Suli's car already parked outside the house, and over dinner he was enthusiastic about his day. 'Greg was right when he talked about the family estate,' he said. 'It looks like half of bloody Shropshire.' He'd taken pictures on his phone and held one out to show her. 'Can you believe that?'

'Louise said they were well off,' Millie said.

'It's a great marketing angle,' said Suli. 'I can see how it would impress clients, especially the Yanks. Greg's uncle is a character, to put it politely. I didn't entirely take to him.'

'What do you mean?'

'He never seemed to miss an opportunity to put Greg down. I went for a pee after lunch, and when I came back, Greg and "Uncle," as he calls him, were having a bit of a ding-dong about some deal that Greg is under pressure to close. The final straw seemed to be that a company vehicle has gone missing and Greg hasn't got round to reporting it yet. When I walked back into the room, you could have cut the air with a knife. Thankfully Uncle didn't come with us onto the range. But it didn't exactly put Greg in a relaxed mood. He was tense and twitchy all afternoon. To be honest, it wasn't much fun after that and I was quite glad to get away.'

'It might explain why Greg is so domineering,' said Millie. 'It doesn't excuse him, but if he's under that kind of pressure at work, I suppose I can understand why he comes home stressed.'

'I wasn't sure at one point if he regretted asking me there.'

'He made the invitation before he found out I'm in the police,' Millie reminded him. 'Perhaps he wouldn't have, if he'd known. Did you say anything to him?'

'I asked if everything was all right. He just told me there's this big contract hanging in the balance.'

'And what about the shooting?'

'It was fun,' Suli grinned, 'though I wasn't much good at it.' Lifting his arm, he rolled his shoulder a couple of times. 'I'm going to ache for days, too. Anyway, what have you two been up to?'

Millie told him about their day. 'Though I half expected Louise to come over this morning. She must have been on her own today too.'

'Oh, she's not. Greg told me,' said Suli. 'She's gone to her mum's for a few days.'

* * *

A strange, two-headed creature gazed back at Tiffany Davey from the mirror.

'You look fabulous, babes!' said the voice in her ear and Lex's face, resting on her shoulder, broke into a wide grin. 'But you've got to lose the splint. It spoils the look.'

As usual, Tiffany didn't argue with her friend. Ripping back the Velcro, she took off the bulky splint even though she'd been told to keep it on constantly for the first two weeks. She tried to flex her wrist. *Ow, it hurt.* She'd have to remember to use her other hand tonight. But Lex was right. She did look pretty good, and a tiny piece of her dared to hope that this would be *the* night. Perhaps the eve of her twenty-second birthday would be when she met her special someone. Around the age of fourteen, Tiffany had been part of a comfortable majority among her friends, which year by year had shrunk, until finally becoming a minority of one.

She was the only one who had never been on a date and had only ever been kissed by a man who wasn't a blood relative on two occasions. The one time when a boy from school had seriously attempted to snog her at the prom, it had made her feel slightly sick. Though she didn't have absolute proof of this, Tiffany was certain too that she must be the only one of them left who was still a virgin. As her friends were starting to get serious with their blokes, Tiffany felt more and more like she was missing out and was getting increasingly tired of her aunties and her mum's friends asking her all the time, 'Got a boyfriend yet, Tiff?' So in the last few months, spurred on by Lex and Sophie, she'd made a big effort to lose some of the puppy fat, had her hair tinted and her eyebrows shaped. She was never going to be the thinnest or the prettiest girl, and her hair was beyond taming with even the most powerful straighteners. But she wanted to believe it — tonight was going to be different. She said as much to Lex while they were getting ready.

'Well, then,' said her friend. 'You've got to put yourself out there and make it happen.'

Chapter Twenty-Six

Shortly after Mariner and Jamie arrived home, ducking in out of a sudden cloud burst, Mariner's phone pinged with a text from Suzy. She'd been at a conference in nearby Coventry and wondered if he was busy. The message was bland, leaving his options open. Mariner called her back straight away. 'Jamie and I just got back home,' said Mariner. 'We've been out all day. But you could come over?'

'Sounds good,' she said. 'It's all winding down here now, so I should get away by about seven. Go ahead and have dinner without me. They've fed us really well here.'

'Great,' said Mariner. 'It will be good to see you.' He meant it. He hadn't been sure after Cambridge if he'd really screwed up, and now the prospect of seeing her made him ridiculously happy. Since squandering that last opportunity, he had quite literally ached for her, so tonight was a very welcome surprise.

Suzy had only been over to Mariner's place a couple of times, and her visits had been far from relaxed for anyone concerned. Jamie had been wary of Suzy, just as she had trodden carefully around him, and Mariner was on edge for both of them. Tonight things seemed remarkably easy. Jamie barely acknowledged Suzy when she arrived, and he allowed them to sit near him in the living room, where he was watching *Pointless*.

'He must be getting used to you,' Mariner said, slipping his arm around Suzy. 'Ironic, now that he's about to go into Manor Park full-time.'

'You've got him a place? That's fantastic,' said Suzy, 'for both of you.'

'Thanks,' said Mariner, 'for making me feel less selfish than I actually am.'

'You've had quite a week,' she said. 'Caught that guy, too.'

'Sort of,' said Mariner. 'But you're right. The worst seems to be over, which is a relief. How was your conference?'

'Oh, boring academic stuff. You know us in our "rarefied little world" . . .'

'I'm sorry,' said Mariner. 'I didn't mean those things I said in Cambridge. Really, I wasn't talking about you.'

'I know, and you're forgiven,' she said. 'It was my fault anyway. Barney's an arsehole. I should have remembered that.'

* * *

After the long walk it seemed logical to Mariner that Jamie should be tired and ready for an early night, leaving Suzy and him to enjoy each other's company. He was in for a disappointment. Initially co-operative, Jamie went up to his second-floor room to brush his teeth the first time Mariner suggested it. But after that he seemed to change his mind and getting him into his pyjamas and then bed took forever, none of which was helped by Mariner's impatience. When he finally got down to his own room, Suzy was dozing and despite all other intentions, the day caught up on him too. He woke a couple of hours later, aroused and hard, but Suzy was sound asleep. A break in the showers had exposed the full moon, and through the thin curtains it cast a pale light over her. She lay on her back, completely open and trusting, one arm thrown across the pillow above her head. Mariner couldn't help himself and slid his hand under her skimpy camisole.

'Hey,' she murmured. 'What do you think you're up to?'

'Sorry, I didn't mean to wake you,' said Mariner.

But under the duvet she'd found his erection. 'Like hell,' she said. 'What were you planning to do with this?'

She guided him in, and as he moved rhythmically over her, she arched towards him, her arms raised, and the moonlight caught the silver strand of the bracelet on her wrist. Mariner stopped abruptly and Suzy tensed. He'd been honest with her from the start about his less-than-reliable functioning, and it was a moment she'd been dreading.

'There's something wrong,' Mariner said.

Suzy wriggled against him. 'Feels all right to me,' she said encouragingly, drawing him in deeper.

'No,' said Mariner, pulling back and rolling off her. 'It isn't. Oh, Christ, we've made a mistake.'

* * *

Tiffany was a couple of hours into her birthday night out and so far it wasn't going well. She was beginning to think she must be giving off bad vibes or something. The others had both been hit on loads of times, but no matter how much she smiled or tried to get into a conversation, the men always ended up either drifting away or chatting to one of her friends instead.

Now she was standing on the sidelines at the bar again, feeling stone-cold sober despite all the shots they'd plied her with, and increasingly despondent. She was annoyed with Lex and Sophie. They had promised they'd stick with her all night, but since a pair of hot guys had come along (one and his wingman, of course; it was never three) she'd been effectively abandoned. Now she was hot, miserable and dying for a fag. Catching Lex's eye, she gestured as much. Her friend shook her head in disapproval. Tiffany was the only smoker among them too, but she couldn't be expected to lose weight and give up smoking at the same time. She made her way out to the front of the club. It was pissing down outside and she hadn't brought an umbrella — too cumbersome on a night out. Stepping out, she saw a man a little way along the street, standing under an awning. He momentarily lit up with a tell-tale glow as he drew on his cigarette. He must have seen her too. 'Room for one more under here,' he called.

Tottering on her too-high heels, Tiffany scurried across to join him under the canopy. She winced from the pain in her wrist as she got out her cigarettes and was fumbling around for her lighter when she heard the strike of flint by her ear.

'Here you go.' His voice was vaguely familiar and as the lighter flared, she sort of recognised his face too. 'You don't remember me, do you?' he said. He must have sensed her confusion and held out his arms. 'I know. I don't look the same without the kit.'

'Oh . . . you're from the hospital,' Tiffany realised. A squall of rain gusted around them and he placed a protective hand on her back, drawing her in a little closer. She found it strangely intimate. He was too old for her, but he was fit in every sense of the word: quite tall, slim and good looking. He smelled nice too, of soap and aftershave. 'How's your wrist?' he asked.

'Actually, it really hurts,' Tiffany confessed. 'I took the splint off.'

She held out her hand for him to see, and he took it between his, rubbing it gently with his thumbs, his cigarette gripped between his knuckles. His touch felt like an electric shock. 'Hm, that might not have been the best idea.' Releasing Tiffany's hand again, he picked up a beer bottle from a ledge beside him and offered it to her.

Tiffany didn't really like beer but she took it anyway, because it was the cool thing to do. She tried not to grimace as she drank.

As she handed it back, he took one last pull on his cigarette before dropping it on the pavement and flattening it with his heel. 'Well, that's me done for the night,' he said.

'Aren't you coming back inside?' said Tiffany, trying not to sound desperate. She wanted to see the look on Lex and Sophie's faces when she went back in with him. He might dance with her, his body pressed up against hers.

'No, I'm heading off,' he said. 'I think I'll find somewhere a bit quieter.'

Tiffany realised suddenly that it was exactly what she wanted to do. 'I've had enough too,' she said truthfully. 'My friends have got off with a couple of blokes.'

'And you're left out? I can't believe that, a lovely girl like you.' He was gazing intently at her face, and quite unexpectedly he reached out and placed a hand on her neck, stroking her jawline. Then he leaned down and kissed her very gently on the lips. Tiffany thought her knees would give way.

He broke the kiss. 'Look, my car is parked just down there and it's a bloody awful night. Can I give you a lift anywhere?' He held up his hands. 'I'm perfectly safe, I promise. Hardly had anything to drink.' He lifted up the beer bottle. 'Especially if you polish this off for me.'

Tiffany hesitated for only a moment. They'd found the creep who was preying on women; she'd heard it on the radio this morning. She gazed up into his handsome face and, for an instant, imagined them in bed together. It would be more than an inexperienced fumble with him; he'd really know what he was doing. Anticipation tingled warmly between her legs. 'All right,' she said. Taking the bottle from him, she drank what was left. There was more than she'd thought and drinking it quickly, she had to stifle a little burp afterwards. 'I'll be back in a minute,' she said. 'I should just go tell my friends.'

'Sure,' he said. 'I'll wait here.'

Terrified that he might change his mind and leave without her, Tiffany hurried back into the club, past the bouncers. But once inside, the prospect of walking into the heaving, throbbing mass on the dance floor to try and explain to her friends defeated her. It was taking her too long. So instead she got out her phone. She felt a thrill of excitement anyway texting Lex to say: *Met a gr8 man! Cu 2moro.* After he'd made love to her, she would take a picture of him and send that. She might be a slow starter, but now they'd see that poor old Tiffany had made it worth the wait.

* * *

Mariner was pacing the living room in his boxers, his phone clamped to his ear. He'd tried West Mercia first, hoping that the crime scene photographer could email him through some of the pictures, but getting hold of him was proving impossible, so in desperation he'd phoned Stuart Croghan.

'Jesus, it's the middle of the night,' Croghan grumbled, as if Mariner hadn't noticed. 'What's the urgency?'

'Have you started processing Dee Henderson and Leo Hayden yet?' asked Mariner.

'Yes, of course we have. I assumed you'd want to confirm everything as soon as possible. I haven't got the report together yet, though. There's a lot more to do.'

'That doesn't matter,' said Mariner impatiently. 'Have you removed their clothing?'

'Yes. What is all this?'

'Can you meet me there, at the mortuary? It's urgent, I promise.'

'It had bloody well better be,' said Croghan.

Suzy had appeared, wearing one of Mariner's sweatshirts that came down to her thighs. 'What's going on?'

His erection, which hadn't altogether subsided, revived a little. God, he was going to regret this. 'I'm sorry, really I am.'

'Go,' she said with a sigh. 'But I'll expect a good seeing-to when you get back.'

'It's a promise,' he said, knowing that it was one he'd struggle to keep.

* * *

Mariner drove to the QE at breakneck speed through empty night-time streets. Arriving ahead of the pathologist, he was then forced to stand around waiting for him under the covered drop-off ramp outside the mortuary entrance, listening to the steady patter of rain on the steel roof. He used the waiting time to contact Superintendent Sharp and Vicky Jesson, asking them to meet him at Granville Lane in an hour. He wouldn't be winning any popularity awards tonight, but that couldn't be helped. Finally he saw Croghan's Volvo estate approaching.

'You need to calm down and stop obsessing,' said Croghan. 'All the hard work is done.'

'That's the problem,' said Mariner. 'I don't think it is.'

The lights blinked dazzlingly on the steel and white surfaces as they went inside, and Mariner followed Croghan past the observation room and on into the mortuary.

'So what is it that's so vitally important it couldn't wait until the morning?' Croghan asked.

'It is morning,' said Mariner, indicating a clock that said twenty past two. 'Leo Hayden was wearing a watch,' he went on. 'You remember removing it?'

'I didn't do it personally but one of my assistants will have taken care of it,' said Croghan.

'Do you remember which wrist it was on?'

Croghan didn't, but turning on a computer he called up a file in which every detail had been recorded, in photographs and in writing, while the body was being processed. 'Hayden's watch,' he said, reading from the screen, 'was on his left wrist.' He clicked on a jpeg close-up of the timepiece. It was an old-fashioned one with a simple analogue face and a black leather strap.

'Shit, shit, shit.' Mariner pushed a hand through his hair in frustration.

'What's all this about?' asked Croghan, studying Mariner's face. 'Fuck — you think we've got the wrong man, don't you?'

'Can you print that off for me?' Mariner asked, waving at the photograph.

'Of course.' He did so, and Mariner was gone.

'No problem,' Croghan called after the closing door.

* * *

When Tiffany re-emerged from the club she thought for one horrible moment that he'd gone without her, but then she saw him a little way off up the street. She trotted to catch up with him, the scraping of her heels echoing around noisily.

'All right?' he said. 'Did they mind you leaving without them?'

'No, they're fine.' As she caught up with him, he took her good hand, lacing his fingers though hers, with a touch so soft and sensual it sent a shiver down the length of her spine. The rain had stopped now, and it felt good to be in the fresh air, but they seemed to walk for ever through the deserted streets to get to his car. Tiffany almost had to run to keep up with his long strides and her shoes were starting to rub painfully, blistering her heels. Just when she thought she'd have to ask him to stop, so she could take them off, they got to where his car was parked. It wasn't a big, expensive one, as Tiffany had expected, but was more like a workman's van.

'It's not mine,' he said. 'I've borrowed it. But it has its advantages.'

Tiffany didn't care. The beer had gone right to her head bringing all those shots along with it. What with that and the sudden burst of exercise, she felt woozy and light-headed — like she would be grateful to sit down anywhere. She practically fell against the van and he moved in, kissing her more fervently this time, his teeth biting down on her lip, and his pelvis grinding into hers. Tiffany had never seen a grown man's cock — it was something else she was keen to add to her education tonight — and now she could feel his, swollen and hard, digging into her belly. Her inhibitions dampened by the alcohol, she reached down to grab it, but he caught hold of her sore wrist, making her yelp.

'Patience,' he said.

Leading her round to the back of the van, he opened the doors and she saw the mattress inside. Drowsy and increasingly dizzy, Tiffany needed no encouragement to climb in. It was such a relief to lie down and kick off her shoes. He slid in alongside her closing the doors behind them, so that they lay on the mattress with the light from a street lamp streaming in through the windows. His hands were all over her then, yanking at her clothes, his breath coming in heavy bursts and a new determination on his face. In one abrupt movement he rolled her roughly onto her stomach, pushing her face into the cold mattress and wrenching her arms up behind her back. *This wasn't right.* A bubble of panic rose in her chest and turning her head she tried to protest, but he slapped a hand over her mouth, and she found her lips were stuck fast. Snorting hard through her nose she began to feel faint. The front seams of her dress ripped with a crack, and cold air shrouded her body. She knew she had to make him stop, but her head was so heavy that she couldn't focus. Through blurred vision she saw him unfastening his trousers, before everything swam and melted to black.

* * *

At Granville Lane, Mariner knew what he wanted, just not exactly where to look for it. He spent a frantic few minutes searching through the box files of evidence being readied for the CPS . . . until at last, he laid his hands on it. He was just loading the thing onto a computer when he heard the door bang behind him and both Sharp and Jesson arrived at the same time.

'This had better bloody be important,' said Jesson, testily. 'You've just interrupted the best night's sleep I've had in ages.' Dropping into her office chair, she rolled it across the floor to where Mariner was sitting.

'Ditto that,' said Sharp, coming to sit on the desk just behind them.

His eyes fixed on the computer monitor, Mariner pointed to the photograph on the desk beside him. 'Take a look at that,' he said.

'It's a watch,' said Jesson, with exaggerated patience, as if she were talking to a child.

'More specifically, it's Leo Hayden's watch,' said Mariner. 'The one that Stuart Croghan's team removed from his wrist yesterday.'

'And?' said Sharp.

Mariner said nothing but continued to study the screen as the film footage of the hospital staff car park ran through fast-forward. They all watched as Hayden's Audi A3 drew up to the barrier, the driver's window slid down and an arm reached out to swipe the pass card. Mariner hit freeze. 'Look at the watch,' he said.

'It's not this one,' said Jesson, looking again at the photograph.

'And it's on the wrong wrist,' said Mariner. 'Croghan took Leo Hayden's watch off his left wrist. He's just told me, from what's recorded in the file. A man might own two watches, but he doesn't wear them on different wrists and he doesn't wear them at the same time.'

'It could just have been an attempt to throw us off the scent,' offered Vicky, but her voice lacked conviction.

'Then why wear a watch at all? Why not just take it off?' said Mariner. 'We all assumed that it was Leo Hayden driving that car, but now I think we got it wrong.'

'But the neighbour saw him leaving his house half an hour before,' Jesson reminded him.

'Did she, though?' said Mariner. 'She said herself that she wasn't sure if Hayden saw her. She made the same assumption we did: it's Hayden's car, therefore the man driving it must be Hayden. Why wouldn't she? But the farmer who found the car had to get up close to see if there was anyone inside, and only then did he see Hayden sitting at the wheel. That's because the windows are tinted.'

'But Hayden was in the driver's seat on Titterstone Clee,' said Sharp, peering over Mariner's shoulder at the frozen image. 'So who is it driving there?'

'It's our washerwoman,' said Mariner. 'Croghan hasn't started on the post-mortem for Hayden yet, but when he does, I think he's going to find that Leo Hayden was already dead when he was placed in the driver's seat of his car. I think Hayden, along with Henderson and Coral Norman, was collateral. They all got in the way.'

Jesson blew out her cheeks. 'Bloody Nora, that's a lot of collateral.'

'But it explains why we've never received any clothing for Dee Henderson.'

'Shit,' said Sharp. 'What you're really saying is that our man is still out there.'

'That's the worst of it,' said Mariner. 'We need to get everybody back in, go over all the evidence again and pursue any outstanding leads. There's something we've missed. And we need to do it straight away. If we don't move fast, our washerwoman will think he's got away with it, which will give him the confidence to kill again.'

Chapter Twenty-Seven

June Davey was up early on Sunday morning and had assembled Tiffany's presents and cards in a little pile in the living room, all ready for when she got up. June was really pleased with what she'd bought and was certain Tiff would be chuffed to bits with her new phone. Ignoring the protests, June had also made Josh, Tiffany's older brother, get up early so that they could wish Tiffany a happy birthday all together, as a family, like they always did. Right now he was out walking the dog.

After the kids' dad walked out on her, it had become extra important to do as much as they could together as a family and birthday celebrations were amongst the last rituals they still held to. Now June sat at the kitchen table leafing through an album of Tiffany's baby photos (another birthday tradition). Looking at the tiny, new-born Tiffany, she welled up, remembering what a happy day it had been. She'd been convinced at the time that a second child would help to cement her marriage to Tiffany's dad — never mind the ever increasing strain on their relationship. Even the labour with Tiffany had been an easy one. She'd popped out in less than two hours and started feeding straight away. June drained her tea cup. She was putting the kettle on for another when Josh got back.

'Isn't she up yet?' he grumbled, leaning down to take off the dog's lead. 'I want to go over to Lee's later.'

'I'll take her a drink,' said June. 'That might encourage her to come down. She was late in last night.' So late that June hadn't actually heard Tiffany come in, though she didn't like to admit it to Josh. She felt guilty that, perhaps for the first time ever, she had fallen asleep before both her babies were safely tucked up in bed. She made a mug of tea and climbed the stairs to Tiffany's room. She knocked gently on the door. 'Tiffany? Tiff? I've brought you up some tea. Happy birthday, sweetheart.'

June thought she heard the faintest murmured response, but when she opened the door, the first thing she saw was the empty bed. Then she realised that the room was exactly as it had been last night when Lex had called her up the stairs to come and appraise them before they went out. The moment popped back into her head.

'What do you think?' Lex had asked, as Tiffany stood admiring herself in the mirror.

'You look lovely,' June had said, trying to ignore the expanses of flesh on display and the rather heavy make-up. She knew Tiff was longing for a boyfriend and the last thing she wanted to do was knock her daughter's confidence. Now the room was empty except for all the detritus from their preparations.

June couldn't make sense of it. She went through to where Josh was setting up a game on his Xbox. 'She's not there,' said June. 'Where can she be?'

Josh just shrugged. 'I dunno. She must have stayed over at Lex or Sophie's.'

'But it's her birthday. Why hasn't she let us know?'

June rang her daughter's mobile, which went straight to voicemail. 'She's got her phone switched off,' she said. 'I don't like this. What if something's happened to her . . .?'

'Like what?' Josh grinned. 'Let's face it, Mum. Who'd want our Tiffany?'

* * *

On Sunday morning Millie had to drive past Louise's house on her way to the supermarket. It was her habit now to look in on the estate, past the main gates to Louise's house. She expected to see the driveway empty, which it was, except for a van parked across the bottom of it. It reminded her suddenly of what Louise had said about being watched. Immediately she recognised the folly of that — had the van driver been up to no good, he would hardly have parked in front of the house so blatantly. It was the type of van a tradesman would use. Perhaps Greg had decided to surprise Louise with that new kitchen counter after all. *Lucky Louise.* The car behind Millie's beeped its horn and she moved off, pondering the significance of what she'd seen.

* * *

All through the weekend almost everyone involved in the washerwoman case had willingly come back in and, once they'd expressed their initial disappointment and disbelief, knuckled straight back down to what needed to be done. As soon as he thought it a reasonable time, Mariner checked with Suzy that all was OK then phoned Mercy to explain that he'd been called back into work. 'My, er . . . friend is with Jamie at the moment, but I don't know how long she can stay before she needs to go back to Cambridge.'

'That's fine,' said Mercy, as he'd known she would. 'I can come and take care of him.'

'I'll be taking Jamie to Manor Park tomorrow,' Mariner said, in case she'd forgotten. 'I'll try and get back for dinner this evening. Maybe you'd like to stay and eat with us?'

'Yes. I'd like that, Tom.'

Now Mariner was back in his office reviewing his notes from the interview with Paddy Henderson. He heard the sound of a throat being cleared and looked up to see today's desk sergeant standing in the doorway. 'Sorry to bother you,' he said. 'We've got a woman downstairs who's worried about her daughter. She didn't come home last night.'

'How old is she?' asked Mariner, a chill developing in his belly.

'Today's her twenty-second birthday. According to the mother she's got dark, curly hair.'

'Shit.'

June Davey was an attractive woman: petite, with dark hair cut in a glossy bob. She'd brought along a surly-looking young man in low-slung jeans and Converse trainers, who was Tiffany's older brother apparently. Mariner led the questioning and quickly established the circumstances of Tiffany's disappearance. 'And you've tried her phone?' he asked.

'It goes straight to voicemail. But she only ever turns the thing off when she's at work.'

'This might seem an odd question,' said Mariner. 'But has Tiffany had to go to hospital at all recently?'

June Davey looked impressed with his insight. 'Yes, a couple of weeks ago she slipped on some wet leaves and sprained her wrist quite badly. She should have been wearing a splint, but I see she left it at home last night.'

'Did you go to A&E with her?' Mariner asked.

'I met her up there,' said Mrs Davey. 'I got this call from her work to tell me where she was, so I jumped on a bus to the hospital. We had to wait ages before she got seen.'

'Who did Tiffany talk to?' Mariner asked. 'This is important.'

June Davey seemed puzzled. 'Only the nurse when we first got there,' she said, 'and the doctor who looked at her wrist.'

'Did she happen to pass through the atrium, the cafeteria area?'

'I don't think—' June broke off. 'Oh, yes, she did! She went to get a bottle of water. It was so warm in the hospital.'

'And the last people to see Tiffany last night would have been her friends, Alexandra and Sophie?' Mariner checked.

'Yes, that's right.'

'OK,' said Mariner. 'If you can give me their details, we'll go and have a chat with them.'

* * *

Mariner and Jesson went to Lex's house where both girls had finished up the night before. Sophie was already downstairs, sitting quietly on the sofa, fiddling with the zip on her hoodie. Although it was the middle of the day, Lex's mum had to get her out of bed. She was sleepy and hung-over but both girls seemed equally mystified to hear their friend hadn't arrived home in time for her birthday. 'She really looks forward to it,' said Lex. 'She's been banging on about it for days.'

'What exactly happened last night?' Jesson asked them.

'We had a few drinks in the Aussie bar, then we went to RedZone,' Lex said. 'We met these lads. They were a laugh. We were having a good time.'

Sophie spoke up. '*We* were having a good time,' she corrected her friend. 'I'm not sure if Tiffany was.'

'Yeah, well. There were two lads,' Lex admitted. 'And they hit it off with us two.'

'So Tiffany was left out,' Jesson observed.

'She didn't have to be.' Lex was defensive. 'I mean, it was only a bit of fun. She could have stuck with us if she'd wanted to.'

'So what happened when you met these boys?' asked Jesson.

'Tiff said she was going outside for a smoke. We keep nagging her to quit, but she won't listen. Anyway she was gone for ages and when I looked at my phone there was this text saying that she'd pulled and that she'd see us tomorrow.'

'Can I see?'

Lex tapped into her phone and scrolled through the messages before passing it across to Mariner. He read the text, noticing that it had been sent at nineteen minutes past eleven. 'When did you pick this up?' he asked Lex.

She turned down the corners of her mouth. 'About twelve, probably.'

'Didn't it worry you that Tiffany might have left with a complete stranger?' asked Jesson.

The girls exchanged a look. 'We didn't think she had. We just thought she'd gone off in a strop, you know, got a taxi and gone home. She just made up this bloke to make it sound better.'

'So you've no idea who he might be? Was she talking to anyone in the club, or is there anyone she's mentioned before?'

'There is no bloke,' Lex insisted. 'If there is, we never saw him and it would be a first for Tiff. She's never had much luck before.'

* * *

As they climbed the stairs to the incident room after speaking to Tiffany's friends, Jesson said, 'Do you think we might be looking at a doctor from A&E? I mean, first Rosa Batista and now Tiffany. The meeting with Grace Clifton could have been a chance one, like we thought with Hayden.' They moved aside as a couple of civilian staff passed them on their way out for a cigarette.

Mariner sighed. 'That opens up a whole new line of enquiry, but yes.' He stopped, his foot hovering over the next step. 'Grace Clifton smoked, didn't she?'

'So did Rosa,' said Jesson. 'Ricardo said the two of them used to finish off their shift with a cigarette before going home.'

'And we've just been told that Tiffany smokes too.'

Up in the incident room, Mariner went straight across to the board and pinned Tiffany Davey's photo alongside the others. 'We have another potential victim,' he announced, eliciting a number of assorted expletives. 'However, we might also have another lead. One factor we've overlooked with these women is that they're all smokers. These days smokers share a common bond — they're often in the minority and outside in adverse weather. I think our man has been making his initial approaches in smoking shelters. What easier way to initiate contact, either by offering a light, or asking for one?'

'It would be conveniently out of range of the CCTV cameras too,' said Glover. 'So do we still think he's hospital staff?'

'A doctor, or someone posing as one, would automatically command a degree of respect,' said Mariner. 'The women would be off their guard and more likely to talk to him.'

'That would open up the possibility of dozens of men who will have been around on all the dates we're looking at,' said Jesson despondently. The phone beside her began ringing and she picked it up.

'So we start with those on duty in A&E and work out from there,' said Mariner. 'A doctor would have easy access to the post room, to scrubs and to sheets,' he added. 'Did we ever get the results from those linen samples? If not, we need to follow that up. We should find out if there's any CCTV outside RedZone too. If we can link anyone to Tiffany Davey last night, it will be a start.'

Jesson replaced the phone. 'That was Stuart Croghan,' she said. 'You were right about Hayden. He was dead before his car filled up with exhaust fumes. He'd been strangled, probably manually.'

'So as we already know, this is someone fit and strong,' Mariner said. 'See if West Mercia can help us out,' he said to Jesson. 'Whoever drove Hayden's car up to Titterstone Clee had to get away afterwards. It's in the middle of nowhere. I can't believe he wasn't seen at some point.'

* * *

With strict instructions that he must be contacted immediately if there were any developments, Mariner left the incident room early on Sunday evening. He needed time to get Jamie ready for the move tomorrow. From Jamie's perspective, the sooner they got this over with, the sooner he could adjust to his new home environment. It had been a tricky few months but somehow they'd gotten through it.

On his way home Mariner picked up a Chinese takeaway. Suzy had texted him to say that she'd gone back to Cambridge earlier in the day, so, sitting round the table in his living room with Jamie and Mercy, Mariner felt as if he were part of some weird dysfunctional family.

'I'm going to miss you, Jamie,' said Mercy.

Jamie continued shovelling fried rice into his mouth.

'We'll miss you too,' said Mariner, on his behalf. 'But he'll be back here some weekends, so I'm sure we'll still be needing your help from time to time.'

Mercy glanced around the rather less-than-tidy living room. 'I could come round and clean up for you, if you wanted me to,' said Mercy. 'It would be no trouble. Do a bit of ironing . . .?'

Mariner realised in that moment that Mercy was probably lonely. 'How's your Carlton?' he asked.

She rolled her eyes. 'Oh, that boy. I hardly seen him now for days.'

After dinner Mercy helped Mariner to pack Jamie's things. There wasn't much, just a couple of suitcases of clothing, his DVDs and iPad. Mercy had bought him a new sweatshirt, identical to those he already had, and she'd even remembered to cut out the labels that he found so irritating. Before settling Jamie down for the night, Mariner and Mercy took him through the photo book of Manor Park, his preparation for going there the following day. Then they said their goodbyes.

When Mercy had gone off in her taxi and Jamie was in bed, Mariner phoned Suzy. 'I'm sorry about last night and today.'

'So am I,' she said, feelingly, then: 'I understand, although I was very glad when Mercy appeared. She's a treasure, isn't she?'

'Yes, she is,' said Mariner, wondering if having a cleaner might be worthwhile after all.

* * *

On Monday morning Mariner drove Jamie over to Manor Park. They were shown up to Jamie's new room, where Mariner unpacked his belongings and put them away in the wardrobe and drawers before setting out the few pictures and personal possessions Jamie owned. He was zipping up the empty suitcases when Izzy appeared. 'Hi, all set then, Jamie?'

'I think so,' said Mariner.

'I'm glad I caught you,' she said. 'A friend of mine gave me this. He didn't know what to do with it, but I thought that you might have an idea.' She handed him a CD in a white paper envelope.

'OK,' said Mariner, curious as to what it might be. But before he could ask, one of the sirens sounded, signalling that morning activities were about to start.

'Come on, Jamie,' she said, holding up the black-and-white drawing. 'Gym time.'

'See you, mate,' Mariner called after them. Jamie just smiled. And it was that easy. Driving back to the city, Mariner felt oddly empty inside.

* * *

It was Monday afternoon and Millie had just returned to the house from her first foray into the mother and baby group at a nearby church. Haroon was tired and fractious, and she hadn't yet decided what she and Suli were having for dinner that night. For all these reasons, Millie was feeling slightly fraught when the doorbell rang.

'Greg,' she said, in surprise. He looked awful. When she'd last seen him, Greg had been clean-shaven, his hair groomed and his clothes immaculate, but today he looked dishevelled — like he had at least a couple of days' growth on his chin. He looked past Millie and into the house, then back along the street, his right foot tapping a regular beat on the ground.

'Did you want to see Suli?' Millie said. 'I'm afraid he's not home yet.' For some reason she felt reluctant to let him inside.

'No, it was you I . . . um . . .' He glanced away down the street. 'Actually, no . . .' he said. 'It's fine, no. Forget it.' Thrusting his hands into his pockets, he turned abruptly on his heel and retreated back down the path.

'Greg, wait. Is everything all right?' Millie called after him. 'Is Louise back yet? I've just been to the baby group, and I'm sure she'd like it too.'

'No!' he called back over his shoulder. 'I mean, no . . . she's not back. Sorry.'

'Perhaps I'll text her,' Millie suggested.

'What? Oh . . . yes, fine,' said Greg, his head down. 'I've got to go.'

The whole exchange was just weird, but it wasn't until Millie was back upstairs that a terrible thought occurred to her. She got out her mobile to text Louise, but then thought better of it. It would be easy enough for Greg to just text back, pretending to be his wife. The developing field of text analysis had made it possible, in many cases, to ascertain who had composed and sent a message, but Millie didn't know enough about Louise's texting style for that to be of any help. No, she would feign ignorance instead. She punched in Louise's number and pressed 'call.' The phone rang and rang, eventually cutting to voicemail and Millie's uneasiness began to blossom into outright fear. She didn't leave a message. *Now what?* She could hardly challenge Greg on the grounds that Louise wasn't answering her phone. So what should she do? As she was working through the options in her head, her mobile rang, making her jump.

'Hi, Millie, it's Louise. Did you just call me?'

Millie felt the relief wash through her, though she doubted Louise would be entirely convinced by her 'just called for a chat' excuse, delivered as it was through a barely controlled adrenalin rush. 'I felt pretty silly,' she told Suli when he came home.

'Maybe we've got Greg all wrong,' said Suli. 'It could just be that he's far more dependent on Louise than we thought. You know, one of those guys who can't look after himself when the wife's away.'

'Like you, you mean?' Millie teased. 'No. There was something on his mind that he wanted to talk about, before he clammed up.'

'Well, if it was important he'll come back again,' said Suli.

Later in the evening they settled down to catch up on a box set on TV, but Millie couldn't keep her eyes open.

'Time for bed,' she said. It was ridiculously early but it couldn't be helped. Only a couple of hours and she'd need to be up to feed Haroon anyway. But she was woken long before that by Suli, there beside her in the bedroom.

'Mil, you asleep?' he held out the phone. 'It's Louise and she's in a bit of a state. I think you need to speak to her.'

Chapter Twenty-Eight

Rousing herself, Millie took the phone from Suli.

'It's Greg,' said Louise without preamble. 'I don't know where he is.'

'Where are you?' said Millie. 'I thought you were at your mum's?'

'We got back a couple of hours ago, but Greg's not here and I can't get hold of him.' Millie could hear the complete panic in her voice. 'I don't know what to do.'

'Calm down,' said Millie. 'I'm sure there's a very simple explanation. Do you want me to come over?'

'I'm sure he's in some kind of trouble,' Louise went on, ignoring the offer. 'He more or less forced me to go to Mum's. He kept saying he was going to have a difficult few days at work and that I had to go. But now he's not here and I don't know what's going on.'

'Leave it with me,' said Millie. 'I'll talk to someone for you.'

Millie rang Mariner's mobile. 'I'm sorry,' she said. 'I didn't know who else to call. Greg's not exactly a MisPer, I just need someone to check up on him. I'd go myself but—'

'But you're not working and if Suli's got any sense he won't hear of it. It's no problem, I'll look into it.'

'I expect you're scratching around for something to keep you occupied now anyway,' Millie said cheekily.

'Not exactly,' said Mariner. 'It turns out that Hayden wasn't our washerwoman after all. And now another young woman has gone missing.'

'Oh, shit,' said Millie. 'Look, if you haven't got time for this—'

'It's fine,' said Mariner. 'It won't take long.' He was about to ring off when a bizarre thought struck him out of nowhere. 'Does Greg smoke?' he asked.

'He has the odd sly one,' said Millie. 'Though Louise doesn't like it. Why?'

'Oh, nothing probably.' Mariner sat back in his seat. 'We think that our washerwoman has been trawling smoking shelters.' The line went silent. 'Millie? You still there?'

'Oh, God,' said Millie. 'This is going to sound seriously weird, but before you got Hayden, I did wonder about Greg.'

'You thought he could be our washerwoman?'

Millie sighed. 'Oh, I don't know. Put it down to baby-brain. But I've had a feeling about him all along.'

'Tell me,' said Mariner.

'All right,' said Millie. 'Louise admitted eventually that she'd actively sought me out because she was convinced that Greg was caught up in something he shouldn't be. He often stays out late at night and he's cagey about where he's been. A couple of times he told her he was out entertaining clients, but she then found out from his colleagues that that wasn't the case. That kind of thing. My first thought was that Greg was having an affair. They've got a new baby and Louise doesn't exactly dress to please her husband — well, you've seen that. Louise told me too that some of Greg's clothes have gone missing. But it's old stuff, not what a man would wear to impress the other woman.'

'So he might have needed to get rid of them?'

Millie's silence spoke volumes. 'When Greg found out I was in the police he was shocked,' she said. 'I mean real colour-change shocked. Even Suli noticed his reaction. Up until that point Greg had been friendly, but after that . . . it was like he regretted it and he tried to put us back at arm's length — well, apart from today.'

'What do you mean?'

'He came here, to our house. He was a total bag of nerves, ticking and twitching all over. When I told him Suli was out, he said it was me he'd come to see. It seemed like he was about to open up, but then he just changed his mind and left.'

'You think he might have been about to turn himself in?' Mariner asked.

'I don't know.'

'What does Suli think?'

'I haven't told him everything.'

'How did the shooting trip go?'

'That's the other thing,' said Millie. 'Greg Easton is a competent handler of a whole range of guns. Although he's in sales, Louise says he knows the manufacturing process inside out and he certainly knows how to use a gun. We've — sorry, *you've* — been wondering how it is that these women just go along willingly with their abductor. Perhaps it's simple. Perhaps he just holds them at gun point.'

'But we think he's been making his initial contact with them at the QE,' said Mariner. 'All these women have been there recently.'

'So have Greg and Louise. They've been up there regularly since Abigail was born,' said Millie. 'She had a suspected heart murmur, so to start with they had to go for weekly check-ups.'

'Christ. There certainly seems to be a lot here that fits,' said Mariner. 'I just can't get my head around the coincidence of it.'

'It has to be someone,' said Millie. 'And like I said, Louise befriending me was no accident. I wonder if she's suspected Greg all along but can't bring herself to admit it.'

'And now he's gone AWOL?'

'Louise is going out of her mind,' said Millie. 'She knows Greg's in trouble, she just doesn't know exactly what kind.'

'Do *you* have any idea where Greg might be?' Mariner asked.

'You could start by checking out where he works. The Pincott and Easton factory is off Vesey Street by St Chad's.'

'You know a lot about the man's professional life,' observed Mariner.

'I looked his company up,' Millie said. 'Call it background research. I have to do something to stop my brain turning completely to mush.'

'OK, we'll go and have a look. What car does he drive?' Millie gave him the make and registration number. 'Good to know you've still got it,' he said, before ending the call.

* * *

The area around St Chad's Roman Catholic Cathedral was, and had been for two hundred years, a light industrial district, whose streets emptied of people at the end of the working day. At this hour, the place was deserted. Pincott and Easton Gunmakers was housed in the original double-fronted Victorian factory, which, according to the date embedded in the archway above, first opened its gates in 1841. Mariner drove a little way past, parked up and walked back to begin reconnoitring the site. He registered a pair of gates in the centre, opening onto an inner courtyard. As he drew nearer, he saw a light shining from a first-floor window on the opposite side. The main gates were padlocked, but a side gate swung open, meaning that Greg Easton must have also parked out on the street, though it wasn't immediately obvious where. Mariner considered his position. What he'd potentially got here was a man backed into a corner, sitting on a pile of guns that he was skilled enough to use. He was not about to take any stupid risks.

Walking back to his car, Mariner contacted CAD and, after a brief explanation, requested support from the nearest area armed response vehicle. He was given an ETA of approximately ten minutes. He strapped on the flak jacket he carried in his boot and sat down to wait, watching all the while to make sure that Greg Easton stayed where he was.

During the time it took for the unit of two armed officers to reach him there was no activity from the factory. Once Mariner had briefed them, they approached with stealth, denying Easton the chance to destroy any evidence. Crossing the courtyard they found the door leading up to the first-floor offices unlocked, and the two armed policemen proceeded up the staircase ahead of Mariner. At the top of the stairs, Mariner heard the lead officer yell out a warning before easing open the door, weapon raised. He steeled himself for the inevitable gunfire, but nothing happened.

'No threat here, sir,' the officer called down. Mariner stepped into the room to see the man he presumed to be Greg Easton sitting behind his desk. He didn't raise his head as Mariner entered the room, and nor would he again. Blood as dark as molasses dripped from his open mouth, and Mariner could see other organic matter spattered over the glass case behind him. His right hand lay in his lap, loosely gripped around a pistol, his forefinger on the trigger. An open drawer to one side of him contained a box of cheap gold necklaces, each one strung with the letter P.

But something in the atmosphere tickled at Mariner's senses. This didn't feel right — it was too staged. 'Suicide,' said one of the armed response officers.

But Mariner shook his head. 'I'm reserving judgement 'til the pathologist's seen him.' As he spoke, a door slammed somewhere in the building. All three men moved to the window in time to see a figure running across the yard towards the gate. Mariner had a flash of recognition and realised with a start it was the same figure he'd seen running away from his house when he returned from fetching Dominique Batista. 'Fuck,' he said. 'There's no one outside.'

The armed response men thundered down the stairs, across the yard and out into the street, but they were too late. Whoever it was had vanished into the night.

* * *

After calling the SOCOs and notifying Sharp, Mariner phoned Millie to tell her what they had found. 'We're going to need to come and talk to Louise. It might help if you're there too.'

'Will that be OK?'

'It shouldn't be a problem. You're not part of the investigation.'

By the next day, the Pincott and Easton premises had been thoroughly searched for evidence that any of the women had been brought there, and for any trace of Tiffany Davey. Though there were a number of empty offices along with bathroom facilities, none of them showed any signs of recent use. Greg Easton's computer was taken for forensic analysis.

Mariner went to Louise Easton's house to talk to her. She was sandwiched on the sofa between Millie and an older woman, who she introduced as her mother, Olwen. Louise's eyes were red and swollen and all the time they were talking she was twisting a handkerchief in her hands. When Mariner broke the news to her — the crimes that Greg was now suspected of — he saw a fresh wave of grief hit her. 'I can't believe that Greg would do something so bad,' she said, her voice a hoarse whisper.

'I wasn't sure if it was what you were trying to tell me,' said Millie.

'No!' Louise was shocked at the suggestion. 'A few years ago the firm was investigated. One of the staff had been illegally importing guns on the side. Filing off serial numbers and selling them on. It was nothing to do with Greg, but the company isn't doing well and I thought . . . I thought he might have got involved in something like that. But not what you're saying — never that.'

'We don't know for certain that we're right,' said Mariner. 'I've got a list of dates here. When you feel ready, it would help if you could confirm Greg's whereabouts on these occasions.'

'I can tell you where he said he'd be, but I can't know if he was telling the truth,' Louise said, bitterly.

'And we'll need to know the dates of your appointments at the hospital with your daughter. Do you know if Greg has had cause to go back to the hospital recently?'

'Not for a couple of weeks, there's been no need.'

But Mariner knew that there didn't have to be a legitimate reason. There was nothing to stop anyone going into those smoking shelters. Who would know? 'If Greg is involved in this,' he said tactfully, 'is there anywhere else he might have taken these women?' But if there was, Louise couldn't think of a place.

* * *

CCTV from RedZone was unhelpful. The one external camera pointed away from where Tiffany might have met her mystery man; they saw her head pass in and out of shot in a matter of seconds. One of the bouncers they interviewed had a vague recollection of seeing her exit the club for a smoke, along with someone who'd been standing beneath an awning a little way down the street, but all he could say for sure was that it had been a man. The dog-ends from that spot were dutifully collected but there were a couple of dozen at least, so the process of elimination and possible identification through DNA could take days.

The post-mortem on Greg Easton was equally inconclusive. 'He undoubtedly died from a close-range gunshot wound, fired by the weapon that you found in his hand,' said Croghan, as he and Mariner stood over Easton's body. 'But whether or not he pulled the trigger will be almost impossible to ascertain.' And Mariner had seen Carlton Brown running away. He was sure of it. He just couldn't work out what it meant.

Along with the post-mortem report, Croghan gave Mariner a detailed forensic report on the cloth used to wrap Grace and Rosa. 'Sorry,' he said. 'It matches neither the sheet from the Belvedere or the one from here at the hospital. You're back to the drawing board with that.'

'Have you got a bit I can take with me?' Mariner asked.

'I can soon get you one.' Croghan returned moments later with a small corner of soiled cloth.

Mariner took the sample to Sunita up in the linen store. 'What can you tell me about this?' he asked.

'It needs a good wash,' she said, taking it from him. She felt it all over, tugging and rubbing it between her fingers. 'Oh, this takes me back,' she said. 'It's pure cotton and good quality. I'd say it's a thread count of about one-sixty or one-eighty. We don't use anything like this anymore. It's all new ones here, cotton and polyester. They're supposed to be more durable and hygienic because they let your skin breathe more, but it was such a waste. Not as if the NHS has got money to burn, is it?'

Before returning to Granville Lane, Mariner went to the atrium cafeteria, bought a coffee and took a vacant table close to the one he and Jesson had occupied before, and where, at a stretch, he could watch the activity in and around the smoking shelters. He'd considered the possibility of trying to trace anyone who had used them on the days when Rosa, Grace and Tiffany would have done, but he could see straight away that it would be a monumental task, given the rate of turnover. And the encounters would have been so casual, most would have gone unnoticed.

'Penny for them,' he heard someone say, and looked up to see Ellen Kingsley. She was holding her own beaker of coffee. 'Can I join you?'

'Of course,' said Mariner. 'Though I might not be very good company. You may have heard — we cocked up.'

'I'm sure it's not that simple,' she said, taking the seat opposite him.

'I'm so sorry about Dee,' said Mariner, 'and Leo Hayden. You must be missing them both.'

'We're still trying to get our heads around it,' she said. 'Though I'm relieved Leo didn't kill all those women. It all seems so unreal. I went to see Paddy yesterday. He's devastated. Do you have any idea who . . .?'

Mariner shook his head slowly. 'Dee and Coral Norman made absolute sense when we thought Leo Hayden was the killer, but now it's hard to see where they might fit in.' He didn't like to tell her that hospital staff were coming under scrutiny again. An army medic in uniform walked past. 'How's Private Lomax?' Mariner asked.

'About the same,' she said. 'Dee hasn't missed much there.'

'I saw the news item about his unit receiving their awards,' he said. It felt like weeks ago. 'I didn't realise his father was a serving soldier too. You'd think it would be enough to put him off letting his son join the army.'

Ellen frowned. 'I don't think Lomax's dad is around,' she said. 'I'm sure on his medical records it says that he was in care before he joined up.'

'So who was the man who came in to sit with him, the first time I talked to you?'

She thought for a moment. 'Oh, you mean Captain Clarke. Lomax and the other two are in his squad. He was here almost every day to begin with. He was hurt in the blast as well, so was on recovery leave. I haven't seen him for a few days, so I think he must have gone back on tour.'

'Isn't that unusual — that he would have spent his recuperation time in here?'

'Not at all. A lot of the commanding officers come in to see their men. They're pretty tight-knit units generally. Although it was a bit different with Clarke.'

'Different how?'

'I think I mentioned to you that we had the MPs here? I understand the area where Lomax's unit were on patrol hadn't been swept for IEDs and there was a question mark over why they were there at all. I suppose Captain Clarke wanted to know what had happened; to get Lomax's side of the story first. I know he was gutted he wasn't here on the day Craig briefly regained consciousness.' Her pager bleeped. 'Sorry, this is urgent, I've got to go.' She got to her feet. 'Nice to see you again, and I hope you reach a resolution soon.'

'Thanks — you too,' said Mariner, watching her walk away.

Chapter Twenty-Nine

In the days following Greg's death, Millie made an extra effort to stay in touch with Louise, for Abigail's sake as much as anything else. The funeral would be delayed because of the post-mortem and then the inquest, and Millie knew from experience that this could be the most difficult time for families. It didn't help that there was a question mark over the nature of Greg's death, and the stigma of a potential suicide. She went around to the house on one such morning. Olwen, as always, was pleased to see her. 'Louise seems to just have retreated completely into herself. I'm worried for her and for Abigail.'

As they went through to the lounge Olwen called out, 'Your friend Millie is here, Louise.'

Louise was curled up in a corner of the sofa, cradling a mug of tea in her hands. Despite the mild day she was wrapped in a thick fleece and the purple smudges under her eyes were the only colour on her face. Seeing Millie and Haroon, she managed a weak smile.

'How are you?' said Millie, not expecting a reply. 'I wondered if you and Abigail might like to come to the mother and baby group down at the church. We went last week and it's lovely — really friendly. Haroon loved it.'

'I'm not really dressed for going out,' said Louise, listlessly. 'Maybe some other time.'

'Nonsense.' Olwen's tone was brisk. 'It won't take you long to get ready, darling. It's only a baby group. And you have to start thinking of Abigail. She needs to get out.'

After a moment's hesitation, Louise reluctantly disappeared upstairs and while she was getting ready, Olwen and Millie between them got Abigail into her coat and pushchair, so that when Louise returned they were all set to go.

'Have a good time,' Olwen called after them.

The two women walked along the pavement in silence for several minutes, until Louise said, 'Thanks. It's kind of you to call for me. I already feel a bit better just for getting out of the house.'

'I can't imagine how awful this is for you,' said Millie. 'But I'm sure it will get easier, little by little.'

The group was underway when they arrived, so parking their pushchairs alongside the others in the lobby, they took the babies into the church hall, where the floor was covered with coloured mats, littered with toys, and echoed with the sound of children's excited chatter and mums' murmured conversations. Millie introduced Louise to a couple of other women she'd met on her previous visit.

Haroon and Abigail were both happy to be placed on one of the mats and lay looking at each other, waving their arms and legs. 'The start of a beautiful friendship,' said Millie. She was delighted to see that Louise had struck up a conversation, so risked leaving her for a few minutes to get them a drink. When she came back, Louise was talking to a woman she'd recognised as one of her near neighbours. 'This was such a good idea,' she said to Millie as the woman moved off. 'It makes me feel almost . . . normal again.'

After about an hour, the woman running the session announced circle time. 'It's a way of closing the sessions,' Millie told Louise. 'We sing a few nursery rhymes and then it's all over. You've done brilliantly.'

While the mats were being arranged in a circle, Louise left Abigail with Millie while she went to the loo. The toddlers sat on the floor in the middle of the circle clutching musical instruments, while the mums with younger babies sat around the outer edges. The group leader led the singing, with the mums joining in, though Millie's contribution was minimal. Not for the first time she realised she was going to have to brush up on her nursery rhymes. Millie wasn't really sure what happened next. She was sitting on the floor trying to follow the words of the song, with Abigail and Haroon tucked in on her lap, side by side, when she heard a piercing scream from right behind her, and Louise bounded over to snatch up Abigail before rushing out of the room. The singing faltered momentarily as the other women all turned to stare, prompting the leader to sing with increased gusto, to get them back on track again. Holding Haroon, Millie got up and went out to the lobby, where she found Louise, sobbing hysterically as she struggled to get a now-howling Abigail into her pushchair.

'Louise, what on earth is the matter?' said Millie. 'What's upset you?' She looked out onto the street through the glass doors but she could see no one and nothing out of the ordinary. Louise was still fumbling unsuccessfully to fasten the pushchair straps and Millie reached over to help, but as she did so Louise gave up and collapsed onto the floor, weeping and hugging Abigail tight to her.

Millie slipped an arm around her shoulders. 'What's going on? Tell me.'

Gradually Louise brought her breathing under control. 'I don't know,' she sniffled. 'I was just overcome by this terrible feeling of panic and a fear that Abigail was in danger. I just had to get her out of there.'

'You're bound to be feeling fragile,' said Millie. 'You've been through such a lot. I'm sorry, this is my fault. I shouldn't have made you come out today. Perhaps it was too soon after all. Come on, let's go home.'

Together they got the children into their pushchairs and as they set off down the road Louise seemed to recover a little. 'Oh God, I made a real fool of myself in there, didn't I?'

'Not at all,' said Millie. 'They hardly noticed — and so what if they did? You've had a horrible time. Losing Greg—'

'Except I don't think this has anything to do with Greg,' Louise insisted. 'I just came into the room and heard the singing and something cold crawled up my spine. It freaked me out. There's something about that song.'

'Which one?' Millie tried to recall what they'd been singing.

'You know, the one about the princess in the tower. I can't bear it.'

Millie shrugged. 'You don't like the whole princess thing. You told me and I get that.'

'But it's so stupid,' said Louise. 'I don't even understand where this aversion has come from. God knows why Greg stuck it out with me. I'm so ridiculously neurotic about everything. No wonder he—'

'No!' Millie was unequivocal. 'That was *not* your fault.'

'But now I'm going to pass all my anxieties and other crap on to Abigail and she hasn't even got her daddy to try and make things right for her,' said Louise, the tears beginning to flow again.

'That's not true,' said Millie. 'You're a great mum.'

'Greg was wrong, you know. I'm not a feminist. Far from it, in fact, but I hate anything to do with princesses. I find them so . . . sinister. It's practically a phobia.'

'Like clowns,' said Millie. 'Coulrophobia. A lot of people are frightened by clowns and there's no logical reason for that either, is there? Clowns are meant to make us laugh, just as we're meant to admire princesses for being beautiful.'

'Yes, I suppose that must be it.' Louise wiped her face. 'I know I can't stand to have anything to do with them in the house. It was fine until Abigail was born and then suddenly we were inundated with all these twee little gifts with princesses all over them, and I hated it. I got so upset that Greg separated out the worst things and stuck them in a cardboard box in the garage. I think he hoped that I might change my mind one day and let Abigail have them. I won't though, I know it.' She stopped and turned to Millie. 'Would you do something for me? Would you find that box and get rid of it? Take it to a charity shop or something? I can't face it, especially now . . .'

'Of course I will,' said Millie.

* * *

The following morning Millie went back to Louise's, taking a homemade casserole in the hope that it might encourage her to eat something. Olwen greeted her at the door again. 'Louise is lying down,' she said. 'She didn't sleep well last night and is exhausted.'

'Of course,' said Millie. 'I just thought that Abigail might like the company.'

'That's very thoughtful of you,' said Olwen. 'She's napping too at the moment but she's due to wake soon. I'm catching up with some correspondence,' she said, of the papers spread out across the dining table. 'It's old-fashioned, I know, but some of my pals and I still like to exchange proper letters.'

Olwen went into the kitchen and put the kettle on, returning with a tea tray, complete with pot — another traditional touch. 'How did the baby group go yesterday?' she asked, pouring a cup for Millie. 'Louise didn't say very much about it when she got back.'

'It was fine,' said Millie. 'She got a bit upset towards the end, but that's hardly surprising. It's been such a difficult time. I think she was very brave to go. I wondered if I pushed too hard.'

'Not at all,' said Olwen. 'I remember when Ted passed away. Sometimes it was people's kindness that was the most upsetting.'

'Oh, I'm not sure if it was that exactly,' said Millie. 'I suppose grief just comes out in funny ways, doesn't it? Actually,' Millie went on, 'Louise mentioned a box of things in the garage that she wants me to dispose of. I think they're too much of a reminder of Greg. Now might be a good time to see if we can find them, while she's resting.'

Olwen let Millie into the garage, which clearly doubled as a storage space. Wall to wall shelving held a number of cardboard boxes of assorted shapes and sizes. 'What is it we're looking for?' she asked.

'Apparently there's a box somewhere containing all the princessy stuff Abigail was given when she was born,' said Millie. 'Louise really isn't into girly things, is she?'

Olwen smiled. 'You can say that again. She was a real tomboy as a child.'

Millie began lifting boxes off the shelves to see what was inside and for the first time realised what a big job this might be. They contained all the sort of stuff that she and Suli kept in their loft: boxes of old china, pictures that were no longer needed, shoe boxes of old black-and-white photographs.

'I didn't know she'd kept all these,' said Olwen.

It took a few minutes before Millie realised that the sensible thing was to identify the newest-looking boxes, and when she did, it took only minutes to find what they were looking for. 'Here we are,' she said, opening the flaps of a cardboard grocery box.

Inside they found an assortment of mainly garish pink items, from soft toys to baby clothes and a 'princess on board' sign for the car, complete with a hideous cartoon drawing of a baby. She could see why Louise wouldn't want to display that. There were also several children's picture books. Millie took them out one by one to see what their particular offence might be. One was titled *Long Ago*.

'That's strange,' she said to Olwen. 'This is the very thing that seemed to upset Louise yesterday.' She flicked through the pages. 'It's a book of illustrations to go with the words of the song. The drawings are beautiful.' She passed the book to Olwen. 'But after what happened yesterday, I can understand why Greg hid it away. Now, do you think a charity shop would be glad of all of this?' Millie looked up for a response, but Olwen was standing stock-still, and the colour had drained from her face.

'What is it?' Millie asked, touching her arm.

'Louise was upset by this song?' she whispered.

'Yes, she had quite a startling reaction to it, but I don't think even she understood why. I know she has this thing about princesses, but . . .' Millie broke off. 'Olwen, are you OK?' She took the older woman's arm, suddenly afraid that she might be about to collapse. 'Let's go back into the house and you can sit down.'

Millie took her back to the lounge and fetched her a glass of water. After a few minutes, Olwen seemed to regain her composure.

'What's this all about?' Millie asked gently.

'I'm not sure that I can tell you,' said Olwen, flustered. 'It was years ago. Oh, God. I thought we'd put it all behind us.'

'All what?' Millie persisted. 'It might help me to support Louise if I know what the problem is.'

Olwen took a sip of water before drawing a deep breath. 'Louise had some unfortunate experiences as a little girl,' she said. 'It's all in the past. I suppose I thought — hoped — she might have been too young to remember.'

'What kind of experiences?' Millie asked, with some trepidation.

'It was her brother.'

Millie had forgotten that Louise had a brother. 'She told me he pulled her hair,' she said.

'Pulling her hair was the least of it,' said Olwen, with a bitter cough. 'Rory's actually Louise's half-brother. Ted's boy. I've hardly seen him since his dad died. The last time would have been at Ted's cremation.' As she spoke, Olwen began compulsively folding and unfolding the hem of her cardigan. 'He was seven when Ted and I got together, and then, of course, soon after, Louise came along so I never knew if he was the way he was because of that, or if it was because of his own mother. She had what we'd now call mental health problems and eventually she took her own life. I mean, Rory was a good-looking boy, and he could be very sweet. But he wasn't an easy child. There was something sly about him and I could never guess what was going on in his head. We made allowances, of course. He was young and at best his mother had been inconsistent in her care. The poor boy often didn't know from one week to the next whether he would be staying with her or with us. To begin with, he was lovely with Louise: caring and protective. It wasn't until later that I realised how unhealthy his feelings for her were.'

'I don't understand,' said Millie.

'When Louise was first born Rory helped with everything: feeding and changing her, bathing her. I didn't want him to feel pushed out or to be jealous of her, so I encouraged it. In the early days when I was still breastfeeding, he liked to sit with me and stroke Louise's head. She had the most beautiful curls almost from the day she was born.

'When Louise was very little we used to put them in the bath together. It made practical sense, and they loved splashing around. But then, of course, Louise began to realise that she and Rory were different. It was all very playful and innocent to begin with, but after a while it appeared to me that Rory was engineering things so that Louise would have to touch him. Ted said I was overreacting, but Rory would have been about nine or ten by now and the bathing together suddenly seemed inappropriate. When I insisted that they have their baths separately Rory got very angry. It was a turning point,' said Olwen. 'And he couldn't get back at me so he began to be spiteful towards Louise. It was obvious then that he was a troubled boy. Of course he was much bigger and stronger than Louise and looking back on it, what he liked was being in control. The final straw was the babysitting. When he was older we trusted Rory to look after Louise when we went out on Friday nights, but she started to become tearful and clingy, and began wetting the bed. I took her to the doctor more than once because I thought she must have a water infection. Then she got these red marks on her arms. She wouldn't, or couldn't, tell me what they were, and when I asked Rory about them he couldn't answer me. I thought he must have held her and shaken her.

'So one evening when Ted was going out to play snooker, I said I was going to see a friend, except I didn't. I walked round the corner to the park, waited a while and then came back and let myself into the house again. I was reassured at first. I could hear the two of them playing, singing nursery songs. I crept up the stairs but couldn't understand why they weren't in any of the bedrooms. Eventually I found them up in the attic room. Rory had made Louise take off her clothes, then he'd tied her to a chair and was skipping around her, singing. Louise was terrified, whereas Rory was very clearly excited. When he turned and saw me I honestly don't know who was more shocked.' The cardigan hem was now tightly wadded in her fist.

'And this was the song,' said Millie, picking up the book and looking at it again.

'It's about a prince rescuing the princess from the tower,' said Olwen. 'That was the point. Louise was the princess and Rory was coming to rescue her. Except that what thrilled him was holding her captive and frightening her. I hate to think how long it had been going on and Louise never told us because she was afraid of him. I think he'd been . . . touching her too. After that of course I made sure that Rory was never left alone with Louise, but his behaviour just got worse. There was an incident at Louise's seventh birthday party when he exposed himself to one of the girls. He claimed that she had walked into his bedroom, but I didn't believe that for a minute, and he knew it. It was a bad time and such a relief when he went away to school.' Olwen turned her face away from Millie. 'Ted had some particular tastes in the bedroom. I went along with it a couple of times to begin with. When I told him I didn't like it, he dropped it, though I could tell that he was disappointed. It did make me wonder if Rory's mother had been more open-minded in that respect, and what Rory might have seen, as a small boy.'

'It explains Louise's reaction yesterday,' said Millie.

'Actually,' said Olwen, looking suddenly panic-stricken. 'I noticed a picture of Rory among those old photographs. Do you think we should get rid of that too?'

'It might not be a bad idea,' said Millie. 'Louise is very emotional at the moment. You could always return it later.'

Olwen went off to the garage, returning a few minutes later with a curled snapshot. 'It's a shame,' she said, showing it to Millie. 'It's a lovely one of Louise. I think it was taken on holiday at Weston. Louise would have been about three or four.'

Millie's heart was thudding so loudly, she couldn't understand how Olwen couldn't hear it. 'What's that round Louise's neck?'

Olwen peered a little more closely. 'Oh, that necklace.' She smiled. 'Ted bought it for her while we were on that holiday. He used to call Louise his little princess. She liked it then, but that was before . . .' She tailed off.

'Does Louise ever hear from Rory?' Millie asked.

'No.' Olwen was quite categorical. 'I think she might have sent him a wedding invitation. I mean, it's what you do, isn't it? But he didn't come. We never expected him to. He was overseas somewhere at that point. I think he might have sent a gift, though.'

'Where is he now?'

'I really don't know. After he finished at boarding school, he joined the army. It's been the making of him.'

'What would Greg's reaction have been if Rory had made contact with him?' Millie asked.

'Oh, he would have discouraged it, I'm sure. Louise never really liked to be reminded of Rory.'

'Well,' said Millie, picking up the box. 'I'll make sure this goes to a charity shop.'

'Oh, I can do that,' said Olwen, taking it from her. 'I'll put it in the boot of my car and pop up to that one on the main road. As a matter of fact, Louise is running low on a few things, so I wondered if you'd mind me going to the supermarket while you're here. I don't really want to leave her on her own.'

'Yes, of course,' said Millie. She was still holding the picture book. 'Do you think it would be OK if I took this for Haroon? He really seems to like this song, and it's an attractive book.'

'Not at all. I'm sure she'd be pleased it's gone to a good home,' said Olwen.

Out in the hall, Millie tucked the book away underneath Haroon's pushchair so that Louise wouldn't see it.

Olwen fetched her coat and, taking the box with her, went off to the shops. As soon as Millie saw the car reverse out of the drive, she put through a call to Mariner's mobile. Haroon had woken up and was grizzling, so resting him on one shoulder she walked through to the conservatory, trying to lull him back to sleep while she waited for Mariner to answer.

'Hello, stranger,' he said. 'I was going to call you.'

'Oh?'

'Yes,' Mariner said. 'The good news for Louise is that the case against Greg is looking shaky. Those dates we asked her to account for check out and mean that Greg couldn't have taken either Grace or Dee. But we've picked up some odd emails. We're still working on them, but it looks as if Greg might have been the victim of blackmail.'

'I think I know who might have been blackmailing him,' said Millie. 'Louise has a brother — a half-brother, that is. He used to get a buzz out of tying her up when she was little. I've just seen a photograph of the two of them as children. Louise is wearing a gold necklace with a letter P for princess on it.'

Mariner's tone hardened. 'What became of this brother?'

'He was sent away to school, then he went into the army.'

'Do you have a name?'

'Rory, that's all I know. No. Wait.' Haroon had dozed off again so, transferring him to the crook of her arm, Millie went through to the living room table where Olwen had left her correspondence. As she'd hoped, there were several envelopes bearing her full name and address. 'It must be Clarke,' said Millie. 'Rory Clarke.'

'Jesus,' Mariner exhaled. 'I've met him.'

'What?'

'Dee Henderson was a nurse at the military hospital. When we went to talk to the staff, Clarke was there, both times.'

As Mariner was speaking, on the edge of her consciousness Millie heard a low clunk that sounded out of place. Keeping the phone to her ear she went out into the hall, though it was much too soon for Olwen to have returned. There was no one there. She must have imagined it. But then she heard a muffled cry from upstairs — perhaps it was Louise having a bad dream. 'Hold on a sec, will you, boss?' Millie started towards the foot of the stairs.

'Louise? Is that you? Is everything OK?' As she passed the front door, Millie noticed a blob of colour through the frosted glass that she was certain hadn't been there earlier, and when she went and looked through the lounge window, she saw that a car like Greg's had been reversed onto the drive. 'Shit, there's something weird going on here,' she said to Mariner, her voice low. 'I'll call you back.'

'No — wait!' said Mariner. But his instruction fell on deaf ears. Millie was already on her way to investigate.

Chapter Thirty

Easing her weight onto each tread, Millie ascended the stairs to the landing. She could see into the nursery as well as the spare bedroom to her left and the bathroom in front of her, but a door further along to the right was partially closed. It must be where Louise was resting. Creeping along the landing Millie gave the door a gentle push. 'Louise, are you alri . . .?'

Louise was very much not alright. As the door swung open, Millie caught sight of her friend cowering at the far end of the bed, her back pressed against the headboard and her eyes wide with terror. Looming over her at the foot of the bed, and standing parallel with Millie, was a man whose left arm was outstretched. In his hand was a gun, the muzzle of which was just inches away from the soft, downy head of Abigail, who lay fast asleep in her cot. Instinctively Millie hugged Haroon tighter. Rory turned slowly towards her. He was tall and well-muscled under the dark T-shirt. Millie noticed too the razor-sharp creases in his combats and the highly polished boots. *Olwen was right,* Millie thought. He was strikingly handsome, but something behind those eyes was cold and flat.

'This is nice,' he said, as if it were a social occasion. 'Abigail's little friend.' A cry escaped Millie's lips but she quashed it immediately. 'Smart move,' he said. 'I can't stand crying babies, so it would be a mistake to wake either of them. Now, as long as everybody does as they're told, no one needs to get hurt. I've just come to collect my two princesses.'

'You can't,' said Millie, struggling to keep her voice even. 'Olwen will be back—'

'I don't think so,' he interrupted. 'When dear old Olwen gets to the supermarket, she'll find she's got a slow puncture. I know Olwen. She'll be too scared to drive with that. And Louise will come with me willingly enough, won't you, Lou? Now that there's no Greg, someone's got to take care of you both.' As he spoke, he moved away from Millie and round to the other side of the bed, to the end of Abigail's cot. He looked up at Millie, his eyes narrowing. 'Put the baby in here and get over there with her,' he said gesturing towards Louise. 'Do it slowly. No sudden movements.' The gun bobbed in his hand, perilously close to Abigail's head. 'We wouldn't want this to go off, would we?'

Millie felt impotent. She could do nothing without endangering her son's life, so, with trembling hands, she placed Haroon carefully in the cot, arranging his blanket around him.

'Move!' said Rory.

Millie hurried to the other end of the bed and made to sit down beside Louise.

'Wait,' Rory stopped her. 'Take off your clothes.'

'What?'

'You heard.'

With an agonised glance towards Louise, Millie began removing her clothes. Soon she was down to her underwear, feeling exposed and humiliated, and fighting back tears.

'That will do,' said Rory, looking her up and down. 'Get face down on the bed,' he commanded. Millie did as she was told. As she did, a bundle of cable ties landed beside her, inches from her head. 'Tie her hands behind her back, then tie her ankles,' he said to Louise.

'Tighter!' Rory barked, as she fumbled with the plastic strips and Millie gasped as the hard nylon cut into her skin.

'I'm so sorry,' Louise whispered.

'Now turn her over so I can get a good look at her.'

Louise rolled Millie over, pinioning her arms beneath her. She keened with pain and shame, aware of Rory's eyes, crawling all over her.

He wiped a hand across his mouth. 'And now my Princess Lou,' he said eventually. 'We're going on a little trip. Greg's car is ready in the drive. Go and get in the passenger's seat. I'll follow you down with Abigail. And remember, much as I love Abigail, if I get even the tiniest hint that you're doing anything to draw unwanted attention to us, I won't hesitate for a second.' To make his point, he released the pistol's safety catch with a crack, right next to Abigail's head. Louise moaned.

'Go!' he snapped.

Casting Millie a final anguished look, Louise left the room. Now they were alone, Rory walked round to where Millie lay. Up until now he had kept the gun rigidly trained on the babies, but now he brought it round to point at her. Now that he was standing over her, Millie could see how aroused he was. With a steadying breath, he reached down to squeeze his crotch, exposing, in that instant, the inner conflict between sating his desire and making his escape. From the recesses of her frightened mind Millie saw a way to delay or even thwart him. Her fear was real enough. All she had to do was let him see it. 'Let me go,' she whimpered. 'Please let me go. My baby needs me.'

Transfixed, he rubbed his hand the length of his erection.

'I could help you with that,' Millie whispered, glancing down. 'Why don't you let . . .?'

But she'd gone too far. Disgust contorted his expression as he thrust his face into hers. 'Does your husband know he's married to a fucking whore?' he spat.

Impatient now and moving quickly, he put down the gun and took a roll of duct tape and a penknife from his thigh pocket. Cutting a long strip, he pressed it down hard across Millie's mouth. She whimpered with pain, tasting salt as a tooth drove through her lower lip.

'Do you know how long it will take you to suffocate?' Rory asked conversationally. 'First of all, the skin of your face and eyelids will start to haemorrhage as all the tiny little blood vessels burst. Then, after a few painful minutes, starved of oxygen, your organs will shut down, one by one, starting with your brain. Hypoxia.' As he spoke, his hand dived into his pocket again. Millie couldn't see what he took out, but when he reached out it pinched her nose, blocking out the air. She felt her eyes begin to bulge and smart.

'It would have been nice to spend more time with you,' he said. He drew out a phone, held it up to Millie and took several photographs. 'But not a complete waste.' Then, through a haze of terror, Millie watched as, with astonishing tenderness, he lifted Abigail from the cot and laid her along his arm, concealing the gun underneath her. Then, without a backward glance, he left the room.

Millie fought to suppress her burgeoning panic. She tried working her mouth to loosen the tape but it was solid. Already the weight on her chest and the tightness in her ears were increasing with each undrawn breath and seeing her baby boy lying asleep, silent tears began to flow. It couldn't end like this. *Please God, don't let it end like this.* The blood pumping in her ears grew louder, then on the edge of her consciousness, she heard the thundering bang of a single gunshot reverberate around the street outside, followed by the prolonged and agonised scream of a woman. *Louise*! What had she done? Then another sound, much closer. Haroon, startled by the noise, woke up and began crying. *No, darling, no*! Her resources dwindling, Millie desperately tried to propel herself across the bed to get to him before Clarke could. Footsteps hammered back up the stairs towards them. *Nooo*!

'Hey, it's all right. You're OK,' and the face that loomed over hers was not Rory Clarke's, but Tom Mariner's. The tape was ripped from her face, stinging her skin and letting her heave in great gulps of air, retching and sobbing at the same time. Mariner was yelling and suddenly her arms were free, and tingling. A strange woman soothed Haroon, lifting him gently from the cot.

'Oh, God,' Millie gasped, when she had enough air to speak. 'Wha– huh- h-happened?'

'It's over,' said Mariner, drawing the duvet around her. 'It was a close-run thing, and Louise's neighbours had the shock of their lives, but we were ready for him.'

'But Abigail — he had Abigail!' Millie wailed. The woman brought Haroon to her, quiet now, and put him in her arms.

'He had to put the baby in her car seat,' said Mariner. 'When he stood up, armed response had one clear chance. Back of the head. It was a clean shot, though not very pretty.'

The woman passed Millie her phone from where it had been, concealed underneath Haroon's blanket. 'That was inspired,' she said, with a smile.

'It wouldn't have been if he'd found it,' said Millie weakly, her heart still pounding against her ribs.

'We couldn't pick up everything, but it was enough to give us an idea of what was going on,' said Mariner.

'What about the missing girl?' Millie asked.

Mariner shook his head. 'We're still looking.'

'I'm sorry. I should have tried to—'

'Don't be ridiculous,' Mariner was adamant. 'Any questions would have made him suspicious. God knows what he'd have done if he'd realised you were a police officer. It would have added to the danger. You had no choice but to play it his way. You're all safe, and that's what matters.'

* * *

A little later Millie was dressed and sitting downstairs in the living room. Louise and Abigail had been taken to hospital as a precaution but Millie had insisted that she was all right. 'I heard you were tough,' said the unknown woman, putting a mug of sweet tea on the table beside her. 'I'm Vicky Jesson.'

'Of course,' said Millie. 'I've heard a lot about you — all good,' she added, before Vicky could interject. 'It's nice to finally meet you.' She sniffed the air over Haroon. 'Oh, I think you need changing, young man,' she said to her son.

Vicky went to retrieve his changing bag from the pushchair. 'You're a pretty hard act to follow, yourself,' she said, passing it to Millie. 'Is this the book that put you onto Clarke?' She was holding the picture book.

Millie nodded. 'Olwen said Rory liked acting out the story, but for all the wrong reasons. Actually, I need to get rid of that before Louise sees it.'

'Pity. It's a nice book.' Jesson was flicking though the pages. She stopped. 'That's funny, it looks a bit like—'

'Like what?' asked Millie, but she was talking to herself. Vicky Jesson had run out to where Mariner was debriefing the armed response squad.

He couldn't understand why Vicky would be running towards him, waving a child's picture book, but she'd certainly got his attention.

'I think I know where Tiffany might be,' she said breathlessly.

Once she'd explained, it was obvious and, as they raced back towards south Birmingham, Mariner called

Superintendent Sharp to get personnel dispatched to the old hospital site.

They arrived to find the security fencing breached and uniformed officers swarming all over the site. Sharp stood waiting beside a dark grey Ford van, a plan of the site spread out over the bonnet. 'There's nothing in the tower itself, so we've started on the other buildings,' she told them.

'Where's the linen store?' asked Mariner. 'We should start with that.' They pored over the map. 'There,' he said. 'There it is. Laundry.' He looked up to get his bearings, then set off at a run towards a building overlooking the water tower, with Jesson following hard on his heels. Bypassing the ground-floor laundry they hurtled up the stairs, checking rooms on every floor as they went. The wards and dispensing rooms were in varying stages of neglect, almost bare of furniture and all smelling dusty and damp. They found Tiffany Davey lying half-naked, her hands and feet trussed, and with a coarse sack over her head, in a room on the second floor of the building whose windows, hung with blackout curtains, would have looked out over the tower. The grubby mattress she lay on had been covered with a pristine white sheet. She was severely dehydrated and unconscious, but she was still breathing. Jesson held her close until the ambulance got there.

The room itself had been scrubbed spotlessly clean and to one side was a Formica-topped table, which had on it a CD player with a disc of children's nursery rhymes, along with duct tape, cable ties and scissors, and several nose clips, of the kind worn by swimmers. On the floor of a nearby bathroom they found two sets of discarded and semen-stained scrubs, which Mariner was certain would be matched with Rory Clarke's DNA. In the linen store on the ground floor, among the sheets and pillowcases and surgical gowns, they also found a freshly laundered blouse belonging to Grace Clifton, and Rosa Batista's T-shirt.

Chapter Thirty-One

When they came, a couple of days later, the forensic reports were thorough. Mariner couldn't share them with Millie directly, but after what she'd been through he thought she deserved to know a bit more about how Rory Clarke had been operating. So a week or so after her ordeal he found himself back ringing the front doorbell at Millie's house. Suli came to the door and Mariner was grateful that he seemed to harbour no hard feelings over what had happened to Millie. While they waited on the doorstep he said as much. 'Hardly your fault, was it?' said Suli, with a wry grin. 'My wife just needs to choose her friends more carefully.'

'Message received. Again,' said Millie, appearing in the hallway and slipping into her coat. She leaned up to give her husband a goodbye kiss.

'So where are you taking me?' she asked Mariner. 'Somewhere classy, I hope.' Leaving Suli to babysit, they went out to Mariner's car.

'I thought we'd try the Holly Bush,' said Mariner, referring to the unpretentious little hostelry on the Stourbridge Road where he, Millie and Knox had conducted 'informal meetings' most regularly in the past. 'That all right with you?'

'Why not?' said Millie.

But when they got there Millie saw that this was more than just a quiet drink. Taking over one corner of the lounge bar were Tony Knox, Charlie Glover and Vicky Jesson. It was the first time she'd seen Charlie since going on maternity leave, and she hadn't seen Vicky Jesson since the day Rory Clarke was shot, so Mariner left them all to get reacquainted while he got in a fresh round. Tony and Vicky seemed to have started getting to know each other, he noticed, too.

'How's Louise doing?' asked Vicky, when they all had drinks in front of them.

'I think she's just about keeping it together for the moment,' Millie told them. 'Her mum's looking after her, and I think when the dust has settled, Louise will move back to be closer to her. Too much history around here. I can't imagine which is worse — having your husband murdered by your brother, or finding out that your brother is a serial killer.'

'Jesus, and the rest,' said Knox.

'I'm sure the last few seconds of Clarke's life will stay with her for a long time to come,' Jesson agreed.

'She's getting professional help?' Picking up his pint, Mariner swallowed a couple of mouthfuls.

'Yes, she's seeing someone every day at the moment,' said Millie. 'What's the news on Tiffany?'

'We haven't been allowed near her yet,' Mariner said. 'She's still in hospital, and we're not in any great hurry. But when we do get to talk to her, hopefully we'll get a clearer picture of how Clarke picked her up — and Rosa and Grace too,' said Mariner.

Jesson shivered. 'Creep.'

'And what about the others?' asked Knox. 'Dee, Coral and Hayden?'

'The forensic reports have helped to answer a lot of questions,' Mariner said. 'They found indications that, at some point, Dee was in the passenger seat and the back of the van Clarke had borrowed from his brother-in-law. I think he must have picked her up when she left work and offered her a lift home. She knew Clarke. He'd been at his comrade's bedside virtually constantly, so she wouldn't have thought twice about going with him. I think he killed her right away and left her in the van, parked up on the old hospital site, until he went back to collect her later in Hayden's car. He must have gone to Hayden's house by public transport. There were no signs of a forced entry, so Hayden must have let him in. Again, Clarke was known to him and could have sold him any kind of sob story, maybe asked for his help as a psychiatrist. Clarke then kills him, but lies low 'til the morning so that he can leave the house in Hayden's car, making it look as if Hayden is just going off to work. But then Coral Norman arrives, so he has to kill her too.'

'But why leave her there?' said Millie.

'Because he was already planning to put Hayden in the frame,' Jesson said. 'Coral Norman conveniently helped to strengthen the deception.'

'And all the time he's manipulating Greg into helping him,' said Millie.

'I know Louise thought Greg wasn't involved in the import scam,' said Mariner. 'But it looks as if Rory knew different. Some of those guns had come in from Serbia so he might even have passed them to Greg himself. Easy then to persuade Greg to lend him the van and God knows what else. By the time Greg came to talk to you, Rory was beginning to feel the heat and must have been putting pressure on him. Killing Greg in those circumstances was intended to implicate him in the women's murders, but Rory hadn't thought it through. He was starting to lose it by then.'

As he was talking, Mariner became aware that he was being watched. A tall, mixed-race man was approaching this corner of the bar, looking right at him. Given the subject matter, they'd deliberately kept their voices low, so as not to arouse curiosity. Knox must have noticed too and got to his feet. But instead of sending the onlooker quietly on his way, as Mariner had hoped, Knox shook hands with the man. 'Hey, mate,' Knox said. 'You found us all right then.'

'Just followed the smell of bacon,' the stranger said, with a grin.

Tony turned back to the group, all of whom were by now watching with interest. 'I'd like you all to meet Carlton Renford-Brown,' he said. Then, with a flourish, and gesturing towards his former boss, he added, 'And this, Carl, is DCI Tom Mariner.'

Renford-Brown reached across to shake Mariner's hand. 'Tom. Good to meet you. I've heard all about you. I want to thank you for being so good to my mum.'

Mariner squinted at them both for a moment, trying to make sense of what he'd just heard, and noting from the faces of everyone else around the table, including Millie, that he seemed to be the only one for whom this was news. He blamed it on exhaustion, because even when it was explained to him it took a while to sink in.

'Carl's one of ours,' Knox told him, drawing up an extra chair for Renford-Brown. 'We've been working together on Athena. He was one of our UCs, except that we've just pulled him out.' Putting a hand on Renford-Brown's shoulder as he sat down, Knox went to get him a drink.

'And yes, you did see me at Pincott and Easton that night,' said Renford-Brown to Mariner, more than a little sheepishly. 'We'd been keeping an eye on Greg Easton. We knew he was in trouble, and that he was meeting someone, but we had no idea it was his brother-in-law. I got there and saw the same thing you did, but once you guys turned up I had to get going. I couldn't risk being arrested.'

'Were you at my house, too?' Mariner asked, frowning.

'Yeah, that was totally unplanned. Mum had a turn and she called me.'

'A turn?'

'She gets angina attacks from time to time.'

'What? She didn't tell me that.' Mariner was horrified.

But Carlton was relaxed about it. 'It's cool,' he said. 'She's on medication, so most of the time she's good, but now and again she forgets to take her tablet.'

'So why have you been pulled?' asked Mariner, backtracking several seconds. 'Is Athena over?' If it was, it might mean getting Tony Knox back, though after this little performance, he wasn't sure if that would be a good thing or not.

'Not all of it,' said Knox, putting a pint of lager down in front of Renford-Brown, before sitting back down. 'But we made an important arrest this afternoon.'

Mariner saw him exchange a look with Vicky, in which she seemed to nod approval. This was becoming more surreal by the minute, making Mariner wonder if it was all a dream.

'Who?' asked Millie impatiently.

'They've got the man who killed Brian.' Vicky said it so softly Mariner thought he must have misheard.

'*Your* Brian?' he said. 'Brian Riddell?'

She responded with a nod.

'We picked him up this afternoon,' said Knox. 'And we've got Charlie to thank for that.'

'Jesus,' said Mariner picking up his pint. 'Now I am confused.'

'Does the name Mark Kent mean anything?' Knox asked.

It did, but it took a couple of seconds to come back to Mariner. Meanwhile Charlie got there first. 'He's the guy I talked to at Sceptre Betting, who kicked off at the Belvedere,' he said. 'It was him?'

'Not exactly,' said Knox. 'But do you remember asking him to voluntarily provide a DNA sample?'

'Of course,' said Charlie, and Mariner took some comfort from his expression of utter incomprehension.

'Well,' said Knox, enjoying the drama of the story, 'amazingly the moron complied, and his swab proved beyond doubt that he was not your washerwoman, or the man who attacked Chelsey Skoyles. In fact, it's pretty unlikely that he would attack Chelsey anyway, since he's actually her cousin. But what it did prove was that he was at the scene of Brian Riddell's shooting. The lump of chewing gum left there was his. And this afternoon we arrested his older brother, Stephen, on suspicion of murder.'

'Shit,' said Mariner. For several seconds it was all he could muster. 'Well done, Charlie.' He looked across at Jesson, who seemed remarkably composed. 'And, Vicky, I'm glad for you.' He raised his glass to her and they all followed suit. Mariner saw Vicky mouth 'thank you' to Charlie and Tony.

'And now,' she said, getting to her feet, 'I'm sorry to break up the party, but I have children at home who are beginning to get used to seeing their mum again.'

Mariner walked her out to her car. 'Are you OK?' he asked. 'It's obvious they'd already told you, but still, it must take some getting used to.'

'Yes,' said Vicky. 'And Tony was very kind in there.' She nodded towards the pub. 'He left out one important aspect.'

'Motive,' said Mariner.

'Motive,' she repeated. 'Do you remember in the Country Girl, when Charlie claimed he couldn't remember who'd led the investigation into the attack on Chelsey Skoyles?' she said.

'Yes,' said Mariner. 'It was unlike him.'

'Charlie hadn't forgotten,' said Vicky. 'He just didn't want to say.'

By now Mariner had guessed. 'The investigating officer was Brian,' he said. He worked through the logic of it. 'So Brian was shot because he didn't take the attack on Chelsey seriously.'

'Brian's line was that she was a slapper who was asking for it,' said Vicky. 'And not surprisingly, her cousins, the Kent brothers, took offence. Quite strongly as it turned out.'

'I'm so sorry, Vicky.' Mariner put a hand on her arm. He didn't know what else to say.

'It's fine,' she said, and from the tone of her voice, he could believe it. 'I knew better than anyone what kind of man Brian was. You must have wondered at the time why I didn't want to go to Lea Green.'

'It was unexpected,' Mariner admitted.

'Brian had been having an on/off affair with a sergeant from there for years and at the time he died, it was very much on.' Her smile was sad. 'It would be nice to think that Brian took a bullet for his partner, but the truth is that Stevie Kent was just a good shot. Some policemen might be heroes; it doesn't mean they all are.' Mariner opened the car door for her and she climbed in. 'I'll see you in the morning, boss.'

Epilogue

On a sunny Spring Saturday, Suzy came to Birmingham and Mariner drove them down to a country hotel in Aylesbury, Buckinghamshire. After checking in, Mariner took their bags up to the room. 'Right,' he said. 'You'll be OK here for a while?'

Suzy held up a weighty academic tome. 'There must be a residents' lounge,' she said. 'I'll be fine.'

Leaving her there, Mariner continued on to the nearby Stoke Mandeville hospital. He was shown into a sun lounge with French windows looking out onto expansive lawns dotted with clumps of daffodils that rippled in the breeze. After a few minutes, the automatic door swung open and a young man wheeled himself into the room, accompanied by a nurse in uniform. The man's legs ended at mid-thigh and across them rested a child's scrapbook. An ill-disguised catheter bag hung from the back of the wheelchair. Mariner walked across to shake his hand. 'Private Lomax?' he said. 'DCI Tom Mariner.'

'It's Craig,' he said, coming to rest beside one of the chairs.

'I'll leave you to it,' the nurse exited the room with a smile.

'I appreciate you agreeing to see me,' Mariner said, sitting down beside Lomax. He was just a kid, Mariner realised, with a jolt. Though pockmarked with scars, his complexion was soft, with a barely established beard line. There were patches of exposed scalp in his short, fair hair and his forearms were bandaged, a thick, waxen swelling peeping out from one, as if his skin had melted.

He caught Mariner's gaze. 'Grafts,' he said, cheerfully. 'Got them all over, but they're taking well.'

Mariner swallowed back the lump that had suddenly constricted his throat. 'Rory Clarke spent a lot of time at your bedside,' he said, before clearing it. 'I'm curious as to why that was.'

'He knew I was on to him,' said Lomax. 'That IED was meant to have killed me because I'd found out about his nasty little secret.'

'So Grace Clifton wasn't his first victim?'

Lomax shook his head. 'I'd say that was Monique Rousse. You may not know this, but our unit was involved in the rescue of three aid workers.'

'I read about it,' said Mariner. 'You were honoured for it.'

'Yeah, well, that all makes it sound more dramatic than it was,' said Lomax. He gazed out of the window, remembering. 'The four of us trekked over thirty miles across hostile territory, into the mountains. We could only move under cover of darkness, so it took more than three days. We'd located where we thought the women were being held but we had no idea about the number of captors or how well armed they would be. After a couple of false alarms, we identified the exact place. It was desolate and we thought we must have missed them, that they'd been moved on somewhere else. It can happen. Clarke went in first, leaving the rest of us under cover. He had to tread carefully, in case the place was booby-trapped, but it seemed like we were waiting to hear from him forever — must have been at least fifteen minutes.

Eventually we got the call. He said: *They're here and they're alive. You can come in.* So in we went.'

'What had taken him so long?'

'The women were in a bad way. They'd been tied up and gagged and were lying in their own waste. One of them, Monique was practically naked. She'd had half her clothes ripped off. Clarke said he'd been trying to make her decent before we all came in — you know, preserve her dignity. Anyway, it didn't matter. We were just over the moon that it had been so easy.'

'And Clarke?'

'He was wired. He'd led a mission that had been successfully executed without anyone getting hurt. We all knew there would be commendations in it. The other lads and me, we were all for getting out of there as fast as we could. We had no idea if the militia would come back, but once we'd recovered the women Clarke made us wait while he gathered photographic evidence.'

'Was that routine?'

'It wasn't part of the brief, and we just wanted out, but he insisted. Said we had to finish the job. He was in there ages and he switched off his comms. But when he came out he was different, calm and more in control. It was like the adrenalin rush had passed.'

'Did anyone else notice this?'

'I don't know. We were all focused on getting out of there as fast as possible.'

'What do you think he was doing when he went back?' asked Mariner.

'Knowing what I know now? I think he was jacking off. Going in there and finding the women in that state, it did something to him.'

'And then?'

'It took three days to get the women back to the jeeps. They were pretty weak, so we had to help them. It got obvious then that Clarke had a thing for Monique. He appointed himself her personal bodyguard and at the slightest hint she needed help he was in there first before anyone else got the chance. We all started taking the piss out of him over it.'

'And those feelings, were they mutual? Was it the start of a proper relationship?' asked Mariner.

'No, it was nothing like that. The women were in shock; they hardly even spoke. But it was like Clarke took charge of her, so that no one else could. We made it back to base and the women were taken to the aid centre. A few days after, they came to thank us and that was that. Then a couple of weeks on, we heard that Monique had disappeared. Her body was eventually found dumped in the river, bound and gagged.'

'The news article I read put it down to revenge killing by the same rebels involved in the original kidnap,' said Mariner.

'At first that made sense,' said Lomax. 'I said as much to Clarke. Knowing how he'd been with her I thought he'd be upset, but it was like he didn't care. It struck me then that I couldn't remember seeing him at all the night she went missing. It got me thinking about how weird he'd been on the rescue mission. I asked him outright where he was, and he couldn't tell me. I let it go. I couldn't prove anything. Then a couple of days after that we were out on foot patrol and I got blown to kingdom come.'

'And when you were brought back to Birmingham he had to come too, to keep an eye on you.'

'He sustained minor injuries, so he got leave.' He picked up the scrapbook. 'Looking in here, he was watching over me nearly all the time, those early days.'

'But he wasn't there on the Wednesday afternoon when you briefly regained consciousness, so he didn't know what you might have said to Dee Henderson or Leo Hayden. They had to be silenced.'

'Christ,' said Lomax, momentarily lost in thought. 'All those people. He might as well have just opened fire in the crowded hospital. What gave him away?' he asked.

'His watch,' said Mariner.

Lomax expelled a laugh of genuine amusement. 'God, he was so proud of that watch,' he said. 'Cost him a couple of grand, so he said.'

'What kind of man was he?' Mariner asked.

'I suppose he was a good soldier,' said Lomax. 'He stuck to the rules, to the point of being obsessive, and you knew where you stood all right. But he was always at a distance; he never joined in with the banter and that. And some of the sights we saw — stuff that floored the rest of us — he just took it all . . . like there was nothing that could touch him.'

'At the start, I thought he was your dad,' said Mariner.

'I sometimes wish I'd known my dad,' said Lomax. 'But I thank Christ it wasn't him.'

'And how's it going, the rehab?' Mariner asked.

'Oh, you know, good days and bad. I suppose I'm one of the lucky ones.' He seemed to really believe it.

* * *

Mariner returned to the hotel in time for dinner with Suzy. 'How did it go?' she asked him as they ate. 'Did it answer your questions?'

'Some of them,' said Mariner. 'And I think I might have met a genuine hero.' Thinking about the damaged young man, Mariner felt his eyes unaccountably filling up and his head dropped as he blinked them clear again. Suzy reached across the table to touch his hand, while the moment passed. 'Thanks for coming with me,' Mariner said, eventually, 'and for sticking with me.'

'Don't know why I do,' she said, pragmatically, taking her napkin from her lap and depositing it on the table. 'You haven't got a lot going for you.'

'There must be something that makes it worthwhile.'

'I'll tell you if I find it. Actually,' she said, 'I have a bit of a confession to make.'

'Oh yes?'

'I wasn't quite truthful with you that last time I saw you. When I said I'd been at a conference in Coventry, in fact I'd been to have a look around Warwick University. I've applied for a job there. I mean, I haven't got it yet, but . . .'

'Oh,' said Mariner.

'It would mean relocating, of course. I wouldn't expect to move in with you, but I would be a bit nearer. What do you think?'

'I could live with that,' said Mariner, trying hard to sound casual.

'Really?' she said. 'Only . . . I really haven't been too sure about us. About you.'

'I know, and I'm sorry,' he said.

'Anyway,' she said, picking up the key to their room and dangling the fob suggestively, 'if we're all finished here, I think you made me a promise not long ago. Now would seem a good time to keep it.'

THE END

Thank you for reading this book. If you enjoyed it please leave feedback on Amazon, and if there is anything we missed or you have a question about then please get in touch. The author and publishing team appreciate your feedback and time reading this book.

Our email is office@joffebooks.com

www.joffebooks.com

DI TOM MARINER SERIES

DEADLY LIES

INNOCENT LIES

KILLER LIES

BABY LIES

MARRIED LIES

BURIED LIES

MISSING LIES

Printed in Great Britain
by Amazon

44996666R00192